Thank you, Joy!!

Appreciate the
Support!!

Ap LaGrand Blount
H/8

Multiples

A FICTIONAL RENDITION OF REALITY

AJA LAGRAND BLOUNT

ISBN-13: 978-1979740562

This is a work of fiction. All characters, organizations, and events portrayed in this novel are either products of the author's imagination or are used fictitiously.

Front Cover Design by Mario Patterson (info@mariodesigns4u.com)
Book design by author

Printed and bound in USA

Published 2017, by Aja LaGrand Presents, INC
www.ajalagrandpresents.com

This is for those who believed in me.

Chapter One

DAYS PRIOR, DP had walked through the area where he expected to carry out the simple task asked of him. Having found a desirable spot to set up, he currently went through the mental transformation needed to become the heartless son of a bitch required to pull off the job. That transformation didn't take long. Maybe ten seconds at most. All in all, there wasn't that much difference between the man he portrayed himself to be, and the man he actually was. He simply allowed himself to believe so.

With the transformation complete, DP briefly revisited his detailed mental blueprint of the job, finding himself beyond ready for the task at hand. *That means it's time to press play.*

Recharging his psyche, he momentarily closed his eyes, fell into a semi-deep meditative state then snapped out of it possessing absolute tunnel vision. *Yeah, I'm most definitely ready to handle this.*

Leaving his stash house, he proceeded to the arranged location to set up his tools. Raising the window of a quiet attic of an abandoned house, he removed his .30-06 sniper rifle from its case, sliding on the long-range scope.

Everything seemed to be in order.

Inhaling the late April morning freshness, DP paid close attention to the quietness of the neighborhood. By it being so early, the movements around the area was to a minimum. That was good in itself considering what he had planned for the person he was meeting in that neighborhood.

Still, something bothered him. The address given appeared to be empty. Actually, so did most of the houses on the block. He'd been

1

unsure of how to calculate that beforehand. His curiosity led him to do some additional research of his own. He liked to be thorough when completing his task.

Upon inspecting the house, he learned that the residence did appear to be somewhat occupied, just not at that moment. Semi-satisfied with that discovery, he let his previous worries fall to the wayside. But that didn't stop him from wondering why that particular address was given.

Checking his watch, it was 7 a.m. In an hour or two, his job would be done and it would be on to the next. *I never used to believe it when they said when they come for you, they'll send someone close so you wouldn't have any reason to suspect a thing.*

For DP, it had been a while since his last encounter with the target. Based on that notion, the target shouldn't have a reason to suspect it would be him snipping his lights. DP guessed that was the beauty of it. To have the element of surprise on his side, it'll make it easier for the target to pay for whatever he'd done.

A part of him wondered about the justification for the target's demise. But who really cared about the justification when a person's number was called. It was merely about handling the business at hand. That was it! Anything else would be uncivilized.

One thing DP did know, he couldn't allow himself to fall too deep into attempting to figure out the reasons beyond what he had to do. He had been sent to do a job and he would complete it like he had so many others. He understood the game and whatever past him and the target shared was just that - THE PAST! He wouldn't allow that past to get in the way of him making his money.

That didn't change the thoughts of the past they shared and how it reminded him of not having his father around. Up to this point, DP had no proof regarding the target having anything to do with his father's murder. It wasn't until he opened the envelope and seen his picture that it became evident of what the answer could be. Not wanting to let those detrimental thoughts cloud his mental, he sought to remain focus on the current situation.

Clearing the fogginess of his mind, he checked his phone again, wishing the target would hurry up and call. Then he had to chuckle. "*I guess it ain't fun when the rabbit has the gun!*"

★ ★ ★ ★ ★   ★ ★ ★ ★ ★

Ramona laid upon the queen-size bed with her hands behind her head as she stared up at the ceiling. She felt depressed and was engulfed by a strong sense of emptiness. This was the same feeling she basically had all her life. And it stemmed from what she lacked.

At twenty-four, what she needed was something she hadn't necessarily been able to get. Wanting what every little girl wanted, she yearned for her father to be there for her. Unlike most girls, he had been there; but, not in the sense of what she would have hoped for. He did what he felt he should do by teaching her things he figured she needed to know. She wasn't an ungrateful person, and the things he bestowed upon her, she was appreciative for. Yet, she yearned for more than life lessons. She yearned for his love.

From a young age, she tried to find some kind of security, father figure or protector in any male she found herself dealing with. For the most part, every male kept her sheltered or just wanted her for one thing - SEX!

At first, she thought that was the way a male showed their love. Then she quickly realized the selfishness being shown. Young and old, the males in her life didn't care about her so she started asking herself, *Why should I give a fuck about them?* Once adopting that attitude, there was no turning back from the path she would travel.

Her cell phone rang. Reaching for it, she answered without uttering a word. She simply gave the caller the time to identify himself and run his spill. At the conclusion of his testimony, she merely agreed to the caller's terms and disconnected the call. Staring at the phone, she wondered if she would ever find what she truly desired. Snapping back to reality, she dismissed any and all thoughts of having a fairytale life or lifestyle. Those sorts of experiences only existed in the movies. She lived her life in reality - logically and reasonably. In living that life, she knew she had to go about life getting it by any means necessary.

Pushing the negative thoughts to the side, she pushed herself out of bed to get ready for her meeting. Doing her mental checklist, she consciously went over her plans and what tools she would need to carry out those plans.

Making it to her Maxima, she closed the door and turned the key at the same time. Checking her rear and seeing it was clear, she cut the wheel to the left and pulled out onto the open road.

No sooner as she righted the wheel, she spotted an attractive-looking young man eyeing her from across the street. She thought of stopping but felt no need to deviate from her current plans. The guy, however, had other ideas when he walked in front of her car forcing her to stop.

Ramona rolled down the window as he walked up. Openly eyeing him, she liked his style. He was willing to go after what he wanted. That thought alone moistened her panties. She unconsciously licked her lips as he approached. His sexiness forced her to clutch her thighs in an attempt to keep her pearl tongue from jumping.

"Boy, you gone get yourself killed walking in front of cars like that," she proclaimed, looking the handsome fellow up and down.

He leaned on the roof of the car. "What's meant to be will be, baby girl. You stopping seem meant to be. Otherwise, I'll be laying in the middle of the street fucked up." He was all smiles.

"I hear ya talking but what's up? I'm kind in a hurry."

"I wouldn't want to hold you up. Let me slide you my number so when you ain't busy, you could shoot me a holla."

She laughed at his choice of words. Still, they exchanged numbers before she pulled off to make the meeting with John.

* * * * *　　* * * * *

DP felt his phone vibrating in his pocket. The small quacking snapped him back to the present. Out of habit, he peeked at the caller ID. It was a blocked call. He normally wouldn't answer unknown calls but knew it had to be the target calling.

"Yeah?"

"What's up, youngblood. You up already?" the target asked, hearing the clearness in DP's voice.

"You know the early bird gets the worm." He wished dude would get to the point. There was no need to drag this out longer than necessary. He had other things to do.

"What time do you think you'll be able to swing by?"

"You seem extremely anxious, don't you think?"

"Time is of the essence, youngblood. I really need a big favor. Like immediately!"

"I don't do favors but I'll hear you out. Give me thirty minutes."

Twenty minutes passed before the target showed up. When he pulled up, he didn't get out of the car. DP figured he would have gone inside of the address given. Instead, the target calmly sat in the car, which made DP wonder what was going on. DP frowned at the situation. Slipping his finger into the trigger housing, he pondered lining up the crosshairs of his scope with the back of the target's head.

A car drove down the street, interrupting that thought. The car pulled over, parking in front of the target's car. Simultaneously, the target exited his car and hopped into the passenger's seat of the Nissan Altima.

DP peered through the long-range scope, observing the movements of the two faint bodies. Due to the car windows being tinted, that slightly hindered a clear shot.

Moments later, the target called DP again. "Youngblood, you in traffic yet?"

DP tried playing it smooth. "I'm right around the corner. WHY?" he asked, seeing the target was full of nonsense.

"I was hoping I didn't miss you."

"Naw, you didn't miss me. Chill out. I'll be there," DP exclaimed, unable to hide the agitation in his voice.

Ending the call, the target exited the car. The car pulled off, headed to the corner, busted U-turn, and then came to a slow stop near the target.

DP memorized the license plate number as he placed the call to the target. The target answered while raising the phone to his ear. Switching the phone from one ear to the other, he waved goodbye to the driver of the Altima. As he said 'hello', the person in the car must have said something. The target signaled for them to hold on.

However, as soon as DP heard the target's voice, he humbly informed him of his time being up.

"I have some bad news, old timer."

The target thought DP wouldn't be able to show up. "What's that?"

"Your time is up!"

"HUH?" was the last response the target could get out.

The .30-06 slammed softly against DP's shoulder, dispelling a sharp whistle as the round departed the rifle. Within a matter of seconds, the bullet entered into the side of the target's head, blowing his sneaky plans out the other.

Through the scope, the evidence of the target's brain matter mixed in good with the traces of the cell phone as the remaining of what was left of his head decorated the concrete beside him.

With the target's brains being separated from his body, the driver of the Altima didn't waste any time speeding off to leave the target's body crumbling lifeless to the ground.

* * * * *   * * * * *

Ramona plopped John's summer sausage in her mouth, doing all she could to increase the hardness of it. He just wasn't working with much. She tried humming, blowing, and nibbling on it. It would not grow longer than the three inches he had been blessed with. Still, she had to do what she came to do.

Taking him deeper into her mouth, she damn near swallowed him whole. At that rate, it wouldn't take much to put an end to this show. She imagined it only taking a few more swallows before he busted a rod. Nevertheless, she still wanted to have some fun with him.

Licking the length of his shaft, she reached his nut sack, taking both into her mouth. Swirling her tongue in a circular motion, she slightly moaned for the effect. Wrapping her hand around his little friend, she stroked him, which relaxed him and produced a few pleasurable moans of delight. Returning to his tip, she slowly deep-throated his member, hoping it stretched out some. Doubting it had, she went about her business as if her dream had come true.

Easing him in and out of her mouth, she wrapped her lips around his erection, slowly spreading her lips apart, allowing his tool to swim towards the back of her throat.

John was unable to control himself. Forcefully grabbing the back of her head, he humped wildly. Ramona, having to catch his pace, fell in line then went into overdrive. While she went to work, John's moans grew louder, causing him to stammer over his words. He desired to tell her to keep sucking. He was on the verge of sounding off. But the words wouldn't come out.

Ramona practically swallowed John whole, massaging his itty-bitty man in the boat with her tongue. Playfully, she slithered her tongue down to his balls. The way she handled her business diminished John's physical stamina. He wouldn't be able to withstand too much more. His end was near, very near.

Just as she thought, a few more licks were all it took. His Dillinger coated the back of her throat with a load of his semen. Like a pro, she downed all he had to offer, refusing to hesitate sucking him dry. She literally devoured him until his miniature friend shook and wiggled to be set free.

Rising to her knees, "John baby, why don't you light some candles and relax while I clean up. I promise my return will be something epic and mind-blowing."

John done as instructed, running some hot water in the Jacuzzi and lighting some vanilla scented candles. Climbing into the Jacuzzi, he sat back and waited on Ramona's return. Falling into a very composed state, his thoughts traveled to the sensational fellatio he'd received.

He screamed out, "Mona, I can't lie! You got that super head a man would kill for."

"I know! Too bad you couldn't get the pussy." She pulled the trigger on the silenced .38 Special, leaving him slumped in the Jacuzzi.

* * * * *   * * * * *

"Well! Well! Well! If it isn't the infamous T-Mac - Travis Malcolm Robertson. It seems he may have finally met his match. What a shame

7

that is," Detective Bryan Chapman exclaimed with a smirk on his face. "YOU definitely reap what you sow."

"I wonder what he was doing over here," Det. Chapman's partner asked.

Chapman looked up and down Carver Street. "This is where it all started for Mr. Robertson and his crew. He and a guy by the name of Darius Price used to run these Eagle Park streets. A confidential informant gave me the rundown about Robertson's return. And as you can see, it wasn't for long." He watched the cars coming into Eagle Park, turning down Booker. "There's a long list of cold cases associated with him and his crew, but as of now, that doesn't matter. We have to solve his case, and we need to solve it quickly, before there are too many dead bodies to count." His eyes canvassed those standing outside of the crime scene.

"Doesn't he have a son who may still be in the area?"

"Yep, and it has been rumored that he has a similar situation occurring on these streets but NO ONE has been able to link him to anyone or anything." Chapman paused to think. "The word back in the day was that Travis off Darius. Nothing could be confirmed but I'm thinking if anyone wanted revenge, it would be Darius Jr."

"And I'm thinking we need to apply some pressure to these streets. What you think?"

Det. Chapman smiled. "I think that's a great idea, partner.

Chapter Two

"BREAKING NEWS! This just in ... I'm Arlene Jackson reporting live from Madison, Illinois, where this morning, a man was found dead in the middle of Carver Street in the Eagle Park section of Madison, with what appears to be a gunshot wound to the head. The lead detective will not release any details to us right now concerning the murder but wait," she listened to a transmission coming in. "I'm being told the name of the victim has been released."

She waited for the name. "The victim is a Travis Malcolm Robertson. He appears to be between the ages of forty to fifty. But wait," she held her finger to her ear. "The police just released some further details surrounding the deceased. Mr. Robertson was believed to be a known hit man and drug dealer. He stood at the helm of a ruthless organization that wrecked havoc on these very streets years ago, leading to an enormous amount of cold cases.

"At this time, that's all they're giving us. But the police have no leads, no suspects, nor any witnesses. They encourage the public to come forth with any pertinent information regarding this death by contacting the Madison County Sheriff Department. I'm Arlene Jackson, reporting live, from Madison, Illinois."

* * * * *   * * * * *

The moment DP walked into the house, the news covering the story of his latest mark resonated loudly throughout the house. It wasn't a surprise that it was breaking news, considering he did leave the man in the middle of the street without a brain. What bothered him was that his girl was watching it herself. She hardly ever watched the news. And for whatever reason, she had the t.v. blasting as the news reporter kicked a mountain of dirt on the mark's body.

DP snatched the remote from Winter's hand, turning the volume down to a sensible level. "What in the hell you doing watching the news?" he questioned.

"For your information, I was watching it because when I was flipping through the channels, I seen a house that looked familiar and wanted to see what happened. Is that alright with you, Mr. Price, or should I say daddy?" she asked sarcastically.

"You getting smart with me?" he asked playfully, letting out a light laugh.

"Naw, boy! I just tripped off that house and you came to mind. I'm not trying to turn on the t.v. to see a picture of you, especially when you don't bring your ass home at night."

"I'm good, shawty! Find something else to worry about," he suggested, not wanting to hear all that.

As he was about to continue, the news was reporting on another body found in a hotel Jacuzzi. She snatched the remote from him, turning the volume back up. DP sat down, kicked his feet up, and listened to the reporter go into her story.

"This is Nikki Preston, coming live from the Motel 6 in Caseyville, Illinois, where a grueling scene has been discovered." She consulted her notes. "At approximately 11:30 a.m., a housekeeper found what appears to be a human caucus. The only thing left to identify the person is a complete set of bones. From what we've gathered, the bones were still intact inside of a Jacuzzi. There were no signs consistent with what you would expect when finding a human body."

She waved her small pad towards the front of the Motel. "The front desk clerk is being questioned by the detectives on the scene about who the remains may belong to, but as of now, there hasn't been any reports of a struggle or anything else for that matter. There are also no leads but we will keep you updated with any further details as they come."

Winter was the first to speak. "That's some crazy ass shit, Darius!" she shouted, turning down the volume. "Who would want to do some psycho shit like that?"

"Apparently, whoever did it!" he countered, making it obvious he was being sarcastic.

"Alright, smart ass!" she fired back, rolling her eyes. "That's why you need to bring your ass home at a decent hour. I need to know your ass is safe."

Getting up, he pulled his signature black t-shirt over his head. "I need to hop in the shower. You trying to wash my back or what?"

Winter heard the house phone ringing and reached for it. "Let me see what my auntie wants." She stuffed one leg under the other. "I'll see what's up then." She pressed talk. "Hello?"

"Hey, Winter. You busy?"

Winter could hear the strain in her auntie's voice. "No, I'm not. What's up?"

"Is there a way we can meet up and talk?" Sara questioned, understanding what she had to tell Winter needed to be said to her face.

"Yeah, we can meet later. What's the matter?" Winter asked, getting worried.

"It's something I'll like to talk to you about in person if I could," Sara replied, thinking about what she had to tell Winter.

"Alright. I'll see you soon," Winter stated, hanging up the phone.

As she put the phone down, she drifted off into a daydream about her life. She couldn't resist thinking about what her auntie had to tell her. The racking of her brain altered her mind state, casting her back to the past for a minute.

Winter's past had been rough growing up. For the better part of her life, she'd felt alone with no real family other than her auntie. She'd lost her mother when she was just a child, and she never knew who her father was. Even the role her mother could have played was null and void. From day one, her auntie, Sara, raised her as her own. Sara's older sister had other things on her plate and raising a child wasn't one of them. When Sara found out her sister didn't want the baby she carried, she stepped up to accept responsibility for that child.

Due to Sara being unable to have children herself, Winter's mother agreed to those terms; but, with one stipulation: name the child she didn't want Winter.

"Why?" Sara asked, wondering why she cared what the baby's name was.

"Because, it will cold winter night when I have her, and it'll be a cold day in hell before I take the time to care of a damn baby."

Notwithstanding being abandoned, as Winter grew older, she found herself yearning for some kind of comfort and love from a father figure, particularly her own. Since a kid, DP had been in her life; whereas, turning a childhood friend into her lover and man couldn't replace the emptiness of not having her own father around.

Reflecting on what she'd been told, Winter didn't understand why her mother had such hate in her heart nor understood the reasons why she felt the way she did. She wished she could have sat her mother down in an attempt to find out; nevertheless, that would never happen.

It had been hard for Winter growing up without a real mother or father. That didn't change the fact that Sara had done all she could to provide for her. She sincerely stepped up to the task when she didn't have to. There wasn't too much more that Winter could ask for. But Sara wasn't as beautiful as her sister so she didn't attract the men of a quality stature. Her choice in men displaced the necessary role model Winter craved. That left her to question why she seen many men come and go, leaving her to wondering why none of them stayed.

Unbeknownst to Winter, Sara sold herself on the side to make ends meet. Sara had a body of a Goddess but the face of a mule. When times had gotten rough, Sara used what she had to get what she needed, wanted and desired. She had the 'get it by any means' genes and she used it accordingly.

That was a quality Winter also had. The 'get it by any means' gene came naturally to Winter so it wasn't a surprise that she too hid a host of secrets of her own.

Winter mulled over her locked-up secrets, unable to deny them. They were a part of her and they made her who she was. Yet, every time she thought of them, thoughts of DP snuck in behind them. As her man, he was the only person who actually knew her better than anyone. They'd grown up together, raised one another, and always had one another's back. Still in all, DP was on the outside looking in when it came to some of the things she kept close to her heart.

She intentionally placed her skeletons so deeply within her subconscious that she would rather not think about them. She believed that her secrets were that devastating, and needed to be left in the dark. *What the light can't see, it can't reveal*, she told herself, knowing that her secrets could bring her life to a screeching halt. She couldn't live with herself if that happen, nor did she want anyone looking at her strangely.

Rising from the couch, she knew it was best to hold onto her secrets as tightly as she could. That way, things could continue as usual, and no one would look at her sideways. *Because I'll hate to have to fuck someone up.*

* * * * *   * * * * *

The look on Sara's face resembled a look of having carried a heavy burden for way too long. The weight of that burden was written so clearly across Sara's face that it scared Winter to ask what was wrong. The more she observed Sara's countenance, the more alarmed it caused. She'd never seen her auntie looking like that. Worried, Winter had no other choice but to come out and ask. That seemed to be the only thing to do.

"What's wrong, Sara?" Winter asked, unable to hide the trembling of her vocal cords.

Without batting an eye, Sara opened her mouth, and blurted out the truth. "When you were conceived, your mother didn't want anything to do with you." She continued to inform Winter about the agreement to accept the responsibility of caring for her and the purpose of her name. Most of what Sara repeated had been explained before.

Hearing it again locked Winter into utter shock as the words flowed from her auntie's mouth. Sara was admitting to things that Winter had been blind to but shouldn't have been. It seemed as if her life was being turned upside down in matter of minutes. However, what Sara would tell her next would surely shatter her own existence and harden her heart and soul.

Sara inhaled deeply, then exhaled slowly. She had no idea how Winter would receive the information so she wanted to lay it on her softly.

Twiddling her thumbs, she looked away from Winter. "Recently, I was contacted by someone whom you have never met," Sara stated, starting out with the obvious. "As a matter of fact, he had no idea about you until he reached out."

"What are you saying, Sara?" Winter questioned, prying for the truth.

"Your father reached out and I filled him in on the overall situation of your life and upbringing."

"What?!?" Winter recited loudly, trying to get a better understanding of what was being conveyed.

"He didn't want me to tell you about him at first. He had some things he had to take care of. Plus, he didn't believe it would be best for him to walk back in your life when he hadn't been there initially and throughout the years." She glanced into Winter's face. "He wanted to get some important issues out of the way first so he could resurface and possibly build a relationship with you," she explained, hoping her niece understood.

Winter listened intently. As she listened, it was becoming too much for her to take in all at once. She could hear Sara talking, could see her lips moving, but the sound didn't register within her ear drums. Her heart cried out for the love of her father, but at the same time have so much hate and disgust for him. In her eyes, he could have stepped up and been a man.

A man to raise his daughter. A man to protect and care for his baby girl. A man to teach and guide his seed in the right direction. Not a coward ass man who stood from afar and have a look in from the outside, when there was so many things to be accomplished inside.

"Where is he now?" Winter questioned, the words coming out before she realized it.

"Winter baby, the man found dead in the middle of Carver this morning was your father," Sara muttered, seeking to gauge Winter's reaction.

Except, she couldn't give one. Winter simply stared at her auntie unable to form a single word. Even if she wanted, she couldn't exude one emotion or thought. She haphazardly gazed at her auntie with a lost stare.

"Winter, your father was Travis Malcolm Robertson, the infamous hitman, pimp, and drug dealer so many have talked about."

Winter heard her auntie talking, which caused a light bulb to go off inside of her head. *That's where I remember that house from.* She remembered as a little girl going over to that house and briefly playing in that yard. She never stayed that long. It was one of those in and out things. But, she did remember seeing some women hanging around, along with a couple of men.

One of those women had to have been my momma, Winter thought. *And one of those men was my daddy!*

Winter gazed into Sara's eyes, looking to verbalize her beliefs.

"Winter, the house your father was murdered in front of was your mother's. Not too long ago, your father started giving me money to remodel and refurnish the place. I was supposed to rent it out or sell it with the money being split 50/50 between you and I. He felt that was the least he could do."

"So, what was his real purpose of coming back?" Winter inquired. "What I'm getting from what you're saying, it wasn't originally for me?"

Sara didn't know how to answer that question without lying so she had to tell the truth. Hating to be the bearer of bad news, she strongly believed this revelation would strike Winter directly in the heart. Yet, she couldn't withhold it. Winter needed to know that her father had turned into a RAT! The lowest of the low. A vermin that fed off the lives of others.

She knew if she didn't tell Winter now, and she found later, the repercussions of keeping that secret would drive a wedge between them. Sara didn't want that, nor did she want to be associated with helping or assisting anyone who ratted out others for their own personal gain.

Sara searched for enough courage to enlighten her niece of the truth. "Winter," she said, looking at her feet. "Your father turned into an informant for the FEDS," she mumbled, raising her head.

Winter's jaw dropped.

"Your father turned into a confidential informant so he could secure a somewhat safe passage for himself. He agreed to work off an undisclosed amount of debt for his past crimes. He told me he was to put himself in certain situations to where those he dealt with would suffer due to his cooperation."

Winter was flabbergasted. Her father had turned into a confidential informant. Instead of paying for his debts as a man, he took the snake route. She didn't know how to feel about that. She was conflicted. As his daughter, a part of her wanted to uphold his good name. It was apparent that nothing came of his deal-making, considering someone made him suffer for his wrong-doings first. Which meant, someone patiently waited for his return to exact their revenge.

Taking that into consideration, she stood, pulled her jeans out of her crouch, and mumbled. "And I'll patiently wait my turn to exact mine as well.

Chapter Three

"DP, I NEED TO TALK to you about something," Winter said, staring at DP. "And it's important."

He sat down on the couch. "What's up?" He seen a weird look in her eyes. "What happened? Is everything alright?"

By the way she looked, something was terribly wrong. What? He had no clue.

She walked over to him, straddled him, and held his head up, placing a wet kiss on his lips. Moving from his lips to his cheek then down his neck, she came up to his ear and stopped momentarily. She lightly nibbled on his earlobe, stopping again to say something. "I know what you did, Darius!" she said in a low growl, then nibbled on his earlobe again.

The words didn't register initially. Not until she tried to take a bite out of his ear. DP snatched his head away from her bared teeth, attempting to make sense of what she spoke of.

"What!! You know that I did what?" he questioned. He was lost. Grabbing ahold of her hands, he looked into her eyes and seen an empty soul. He never seen that kind of darkness coming from her. To see so deeply inside her let him see a totally different person. The presentation of that emptiness presented him with the coldness, loneliness and pain caused by something he done.

Not wanting to expose his hand, he asked, "What do you think I did, Winter?"

"Just know that I know and one day I will make your ass pay for it!" she spat, snatching away from him.

DP tried his best to get her to tell him more. He reached for her but she slipped away. The further she slipped away, the harder he sought to grab ahold of her. Then, like that, she was gone. Whereas, he heard her calling his name. Seeking to comprehend the madness, her calling out his name resonated louder and louder.

There was no doubt it was her calling him. Looking around, she had completely vanished. She was nowhere in sight. Holding out his hands, he grasped at the empty space before him.

From out of nowhere, his body began to violently shake, jolting his eyes open. He awoke in his bedroom, noticing Winter removing her hands from him. She'd been trying to awake him. He glanced around the room. Right then, he realized he had been dreaming. Unconsciously, he looked into Winter's eyes for any sign of her actually knowing the truth about who he was. As he studied her, he saw nothing leaning him that way. All he seen was the signs of his loving and caring woman. But the dream filtered to the forefront of his mind again.

Why would she tell me those things? Could she really know but refuse to say anything until the time was right?

His mind was truly playing games with him. But he didn't feel as if he was in a pressed situation. Not a situation where he would have to make a detrimental decision to handle his business. Because handling his business surrounded one tactic. He knew handling his was fashioned according to customs he'd grown accustomed to. Unknowing of what to make of the dream, he didn't want to jump to conclusions until he had all the facts before him.

Snapping his head to the left, the ringing of his phone snapped him out of his trance. Staring at it, he looked at Winter as she went about her business. Grabbing his phone, he expected the caller to be one of his homies. He'd been waiting on Ralphie to call so they could handle some business. However, the call was from his contact. There was another job on the horizon.

Quickly taking the call, it ended just as quickly as it began. The instructions were delivered, and DP began plotting his next move. He loved when his plans could fall into their respective order. That permitted the operations to run a whole lot smoother.

Jumping up to bounce, Winter stopped him as he dressed. All of a sudden, she had this somber look on her face which she hadn't initially had; therefore, DP figured there must have been something weighing heavily on her mind. Needing to leave, he couldn't help but want to know what her deal was.

DP thought of the dream he had, wondering if there was any truth to it. *I won't find out by just standing there.* He had to approach the situation carefully. He kept it simple.

"Is everything okay, baby? You don't look too good."

She stepped closer, looked him squarely in his eyes, and shook her head.

DP reached out for her. Before he could get his arms around her, she fell into his arms crying like a newborn baby and gripped his shirt tightly as if she would never hold him again. That got his attention. *What is wrong? She never sheds a tear.* Whatever the situation was, it had to be serious. *But what?* he wondered.

His heart was beating out of his chest. He was sure she could feel it thumping against hers. He just hoped she wouldn't drop the bomb of knowing the truth about who he was on him. He'd been able to keep his other life a secret for the longest time, and he planned on keeping it that way. But he needed to know what her issue was.

"Tell me what's wrong, Winter," he insisted, feeling her pull at his shirt.

Wiping the tears from her face, she looked up at DP. He was a few inches taller than her five-foot-five frame, so as she looked up, her tears streamed into the crevices of her eyes.

"Remember the news covering the man being shot on Carver?" she asked, wiping at her face.

"Yeah. By the house you thought looked familiar."

"Yeah, I found out how I remember that house too. That was my mother's house and the man who was killed was my father," she explained, looking away. "I'm having so many mixed emotions right now, Darius. I don't know what to do or how to feel. I have always yearned to have my father in my life and to be loved by him but..."

"But what baby, talk to me."

"But... someone took that away from me. Just like that!" she said, snapping her fingers.

DP wanted to feel sorry for her. He simply couldn't. As her man, he wanted to say something meaningful but no words would come out. So, he merely listened.

"It's just that when all of that could have happened, his past caught up with him and takes all that away," she stated, ramming her head into his chest.

DP wanted to appear as supportive as he could. "What kind of past did he have?" he asked, fully aware of the details. Even though he could have cared less, he had to play his part, especially since he realized she didn't know it was him who brought about her father's demise. Then again, it wasn't that he didn't care about her losing her father. It called into question how he could actually be the real support she needed when he was the reason for her pain.

I can't do this pretending shit. He wasn't that type of guy. *I'm gonna have to keep it 100.* He knew a time would come when he would have to be straight up with her. He just didn't know how she would perceive that truth.

In the midst of him lingering away from the conversation, she explained what her auntie told her.

"My auntie said he was a notorious hitman back in the day but upon some recent changes in his life, he wanted to become a part of my life," she cried, going into an uncontrollable sob.

DP held her as close as he could, amazed at how weird the entire scene felt. He'd never had to console a family member of one of his marks. The feeling was surreal. *Who would have thought it would hit so close to home?* he had to ask.

Winter balled her eyes out, wetting up the front of his shirt.

Having to listen to her crying will make me detach myself from the situation completely. I'm not going be able to do this.

In his position, there was nothing he could do for her. He'd done what he'd been hired to do, and that was it. But her crying brought about the nagging thought of her father possibly having something to do with his father's death. That was something he wasn't too sure of; yet, the emotions he felt when viewing that picture really rubbed him the wrong way. When thinking in those terms, his feelings about what Winter was going through would eventually begin to irritate him. He understood he wouldn't be able to tell her about what he did. That acknowledgement would place a permanent wedge between them.

Opting to tuck that secret among the rest, DP stood there holding her as he continued to be the fake support she needed.

"Baby, I'm sorry to hear about your lost. I'm always here for you and I'll be here now, more than ever," he explained, thinking about what he told it.

That was a bold face lie. The kind of lie he wouldn't be able to live up to. Then he thought about it. As the words *I'm so sorry!* escaped his lips, they felt as if he actually meant them. It felt like he was, in a sneaky kind of way, already seeking her forgiveness.

Naw, that can't be true. What do I have to be sorry for? When he took the job, he had no idea the mark was her father. It wasn't his fault her father ran out. That thought alone took him back to the dream, leaving him to wonder if she knew, and if that was why she was telling him now.

Maybe she's searching for some kind of sign. He couldn't be sure. She could be holding the truth to her chest. Yet, he hoped the time didn't come when he would have to choose between the life he led and the woman he loved. Because for him, the choice would be a no-brainer.

But would it be the right choice? he questioned.

* * * * *   * * * * *

DP maneuvered through the streets towards his destination. Riding without the radio on, he reflected on the man he was, where he came from and where he wanted to go. Realistically, moving forward, his future would be far different from the life he currently lived and the past that shaped his current being. From the beginning, he'd wanted better for himself and that's why he set his goals so high and wasn't afraid to chase them.

Despite his day-to-day hustle, his motivation surrounded becoming the first person in his family to graduate from college. That achievement alone would highlight his academic success at an all-time high. He'd always had a thirst for knowledge since escaping the womb, so, having an academic scholarship and a full ride wasn't a surprise to him. That still didn't separate the two lives he lived.

One of his biggest fears derived from his two worlds colliding. That collision would be detrimental to everything he achieved thus far plus where he wanted to go. At some point, his thirst for a quick thrill would have to fade into the night like so many of his victims had.

He'd come a long way over the years without being able to see the entire road ahead of him. Somehow, the unforeseen path traveled steered him in the right direction, allowing everything to turn out how it should. Except, what he couldn't see now could alter that perception; therefore, revealing something he really didn't want to see.

A product of a crack-head whore and a cold-blooded killer, many believed he would end up like his father. According to those around him, his future was bleak from the start. As a youngster, he set out to defy those odds of failure. Practically raising himself, he strove to make the most out of life.

From the moment he began walking, he ran the streets or behind one of his old man's whores. It didn't take him long to pick up on his charismatic personality, nor did he have a problem using it to his advantage. By the time he was twelve, his old man had been killed and his mother was so far gone on drugs and whoring that his only option was to follow in his old man's footsteps, somewhat.

Once getting his feet wet, DP soared to new heights quickly, looking to make a name for himself. During that time, his old man's right-hand man took a liking to him, and pulled him under his wing to school him to the rules of the game. Under that tutelage, all the tricks of the trade were bestowed upon him and there was no turning back. Absorbing each lesson in stride, he elevated his status, bringing in money, hand over fist.

Taking what he'd seen coming up to heart gave him a different perspective on how he should do certain things. Applying his lessons, both good and bad, he put his own twist on his hustle. Those little tweaks proved to be the deciding factor in how successful he became. It would be those things that would keep him alive and out of sight of the law. Also, it permitted an acknowledgement that there wasn't much longevity to the drug game or being a killer anyway.

From the very beginning, DP always rationalized an exit strategy, knowing he had to be smart about how he moved. And being smart required him to have a back-up plan. Without a viable plan, the end that was sure to come wouldn't be the kind of end he could dictate. As a visionary, he was the kind of man who wanted to dictate everything he had his hands in.

However, with the situation he currently faced, things were sure to change for him. He wasn't sure how but it entailed him considering activating his final exit strategy. He had too much at stake to be playing around, and the last thing he needed was for things to spiral out of control.

That's not what I need on my watch' he said, pulling over in front of his destination. *Not at this time, nor should it happen to me, period. It just can't happen. And I won't let.*

Meaning every word, he clambered from his car, and set in motion his reason for being there.

Chapter Four

"YEAH, BABY GIRL. Suck that dick!" Ralphie muttered. "Handle your business." He loved every minute of the oral service being rendered. The sensational feeling closed his eyes and relaxed his tensed body. The assault on his flag pole felt like something out of heaven. The combination of Ramona's mouth and the showerhead gave off the aura of floating on a cloud.

The fellatio was so good, he had to take his mind off of her services for a moment. Thinking back to how they arrived at this point, the momentary reflection of her bumping into him at the liquor store swelled the tip of his sword. He faintly remembered a drink being wasted on him. The puckered lips wrapped around his member erased the ruined shirt from his mind altogether. None of that mattered at that point.

At first it did, especially when not recognizing her wearing the bright colored wig. It wasn't until she apologized that he recognized the voice.

Damn, baby girl. I see you forgot about cha boy, huh? he asked, forgetting about his wet shirt.

It's not like that, she said, sounding young and innocent. *I just been busy and not had time to holla at you,* she stated, flashing a sly smile. She slid in to swipe at the liquor on his shirt.

He grabbed her hand. *Don't worry about that. It's nothing the trash can't take care of.*

I'm sorry for being so clumsy. Is there anything I can do to show you how sorry I am? Her sultry tone informed him that she would do whatever it took to make it up to him. She licked her lips seductively. For her it wasn't about the drink she wasted on him. Ruining his shirt meant a lot to her. Never did she want him to be upset with her. At all costs, she yearned for them to walk away from the encounter with a clear understanding of how truly sorry she was.

Ralphie hadn't seen it that way. He wasn't tripping; yet, he didn't wish to waste valuable time talking about it when that time could be spent doing other things.

I'm sure there's something we can work out. He smiled, jumping at the opportunity to get what he originally wanted. *What you about to do right now?* He invaded her personal space.

It depends on what you want to do, she replied, letting him know she was down for whatever.

In that instant, they made plans to meet at the nearest motel. Finding a room at the Motel 6 on the edge of town, Ralphie hopped in the shower with Ramona quickly accompanying him. Before the water could warm up, she was stroking his joint, coercing it to grow to its maximum potential. Once fully erect, she slowly traveled from his neck, down to his chest, and settled on his balls.

Slurping them, she tenderly stroked his third leg, quickly getting into it. She couldn't half-ass with him. Her skills were too impeccable for that. She had to make up for her mistake by going all in. Humming her favorite tune, she damn near swallowed him whole. *It's a must I leave a lasting impression on him.*

Ralphie looked down at her, definitely in awe of her skills. He had to give to it to her. She could definitely work her magic with her God given talents.

Ramona slithered her tongue up the length of his erection until she reached the tip. Placing a big, wet kiss on the head, she slowly parted her lips, allowing all of him to disappear down her throat. She literally deep-throated him on the first try.

Lightly rolling her tongue on his tender side, she lathered his meat log with her saliva, downed half of it, came back up and nibbled on the tip again. Surrounding the tip with puckered lips, she swallowed him whole, returned to the tip, and then swallowed him again. Doing it over and over, she placed sloppy kisses around the head, stroked the base of his microphone stand, then saturated the first four inches of his manhood.

Ralphie cuffed the top of her head. *Damn, this some fire ass head!*

Ramona jerked at the base of his member, continuing to show off her superb head game.

He was having a hard time keeping his composure. His knees grew weak, loud pleasurable moans escaped his voice box, and he had to place his hands on the slippery shower walls for leverage. The more she bobbed her head, the less he could take. Then without warning, he released a thick, creamy load on the roof of her mouth.

She didn't seem to mind. Swallowing every drop, she coated the lining of her stomach with the few grams of protein. *Tasty!* she said, rising to her feet. Wiping at her mouth, she tooted her behind in the air, giving Ralphie more than an eye full to gawk at. Her 5-foot-5 curvaceous, petite frame was a man's personal theme park. Her wide hips and more than a hand full of titties had him in awe.

Ralphie's eyes were glued to Ramona's wet box. *That's the juiciest piece of meat I've ever seen in my life.* Just staring at the sweet piece of nectar shook his dummy awake for round two. Gripping it, he wasted no time sliding inside of her inviting opening from the back.

As he entered her, he secretly verbalized that the interior of her loveliness was fire. SUPER FIRE! Each stroke brought him a more pleasurable moment than the last ever could. He shivered uncontrollably. *I would have loved to suck on this pussy for hours. But maybe next time!* He grunted, shoving everything he had into her bottomless pit.

Ramona braced herself against the shower wall, opening up a clear path to the depth of her ocean. Rotating her hips, it didn't take long before she found the match to his rhythm. She threw it back at him. In return, he attempted to give it to her as hard as he could. Gripping her hips, his intent included touching every wall and crevice hidden within her creamy dungeon.

Creamy might not be the right word for this blessing! he exclaimed, sliding in and out of her.

Slowing his stroke, "This shit is the bomb!" he expressed, digging a little deeper. "This right here," he said, tightening his grip on her hips, "is the perfect example of *'she got that killa pussy!'*"

Ramona simply smiled in-between moans.

Ralphie, on the other hand, was on the verge of busting another nut. Increasing his speed, he sailed into overdrive. Humping hard, his thighs smacked against the back of hers, making an extremely loud noise. That accelerated his excitement.

Lowering his head, he watched her ass slam into his groin, and momentarily stick to his skin. It was like a tidal wave of sorts and the intensity of it caused him to release inside of her. Ramona ground her wetness on him, tightened her internal muscles, and made sure she drained him of whatever energy he had left. She was a murderer on his dick.

Leaning against the wall, he was stuck. There was no hiding it. Left speechless and unable to move, he simply stood frozen in a whirlwind of lust and nut. His mind was beyond mesmerized by the talents of the chick he remained hidden within. Glancing at his semi-hard tool, he felt Ramona clamp on his muscle with her vice-grip.

That crushed the remaining life out of him. Adding insult to injury, she twirled her hips and kilt every ounce of his energy, turning him into her spent slave. He fell into the shower wall. Achieving her goal, she pushed him out of her, grabbed a towel, a bar of soap, and washed up. Rinsing off, she climbed out, and grabbed a towel. Walking away, she left him to wash up himself. He didn't seem to mind. However, Ramona's mind was elsewhere as she eased out of the bathroom and over to her bag. Unzipping it, she retrieved a little something special for her lover. With it in hand, she quietly returned to the bathroom and leaned on the counter humming under her breath.

Ralphie couldn't hear her humming her favorite tune over the showerhead. All he could think about her sensational oral skills. Chuckling, *The pussy was good as hell too.* He would be lying if he didn't admit that as well.

"Man, baby girl!" he shouted over the noise of the showerhead, thinking she was in the other room. "Has anyone ever told you got that killa pussy, for real?"

"I've been told that a few times. I know it's all talk," she replied, thinking if she received a dollar for every time she was told that, she would be rich.

Ralphie was shocked to find her that close. He needed her to know that he was dead serious. He wasn't trying to gas her up with some lame ass game. That wasn't his style.

Aja LaGrand Blount

"Baby, you don't have to downplay it with me." He figured she didn't want to come off conceited.

"I'm not," she voiced.

He rinsed the soap off of him, needing her to know what she had, and what he wanted more of. He pulled the shower curtain back, and what he longed to say came to him as she came into view.

Whereas, Ramona put two slugs in his head, leaving him unable to make his point. As his head jerked back, he was Dead on Arrival. The force from the silenced HK P30 .40-caliber handgun slammed his body into the side of the shower wall.

With a smile on her face, she mocked him, watching his body slide down the shower wall. *Has anyone ever told you got that killa pussy?* She shook her head. "Dudes will say anything to make a bitch feel good, won't they?" she rhetorically asked herself.

Getting serious, she glanced down at Ralphie and asked in a devilish tone. "It is some killa pussy, ain't it?" She cocked her head to the side. "You don't have to answer. I already know the answer. But let me introduce you to some of my little friends." She unscrewed the top of the jar, tapping the side of the tub. Her little friends, eager to get to the fresh flesh, scrambled along the side of the tub and attacked the warm skin and fresh blood.

Ramona, feeling Ralphie's nut ooze out of her, copped a seat on the toilet to watch the show. And as Ralphie's flesh disappeared, she wondered, *What will I do with the rest of my day?*

* * * * *   * * * * *

Detective Bryan Chapman examined the identification of Ralph Pearson. The Illinois ID identified Mr. Pearson as a 25 years old male, standing at 5'7", weighing 175 pounds, and residing on 4th Street in Madison, Illinois.

The detective knew the name from somewhere. But looking at the fleshless corpse made it extremely hard to put a name to the face when there was NO face to compare it to. Actually, there wasn't anything visible for a comparison of anything. What remained was what used to be Ralph Pearson.

Chapman stared at the ID; yet, the picture on the ID wasn't jogging his memory. He figured he should know the face when recalling the name. The photo only provided a tiny glimpse into who the victim could be. That was if the ID actually belonged to the victim.

Who does this kind of shit? he asked himself. *This is some gruesome shit to do to somebody.* He continued to stare at the caucus positioned against shower wall, stripped of everything. Shaking his head, he was unable to understand it, finding it hard to get pass the fact that the body was completely naked of its ligaments.

Overwhelmed, he threw his hands in the air. Looking again, he still couldn't get over the intact bones stripped of everything. There was nothing left. No skin. No blood. Nothing that could assist in making a crime scene to be processed.

How can I start solving this mystery if I have no idea of what happened?

"Who would do this to someone?" another detective asked, as if reading Chapman's mind. "How could anyone do this to another human being?"

"That's what we have to figure out. This makes for victim #2, at least, as far as we know of." He headed towards the door. "Let's see what we can get from the front desk," Chapman stated, tired of looking at the cleaned bones.

At the front desk, the two detectives viewed the security feed. A familiar strut ambling across the screen caught Chapman's attention. "That's Ralphie. I can spot that walk from anywhere." His mind quickly associated Ralphie to Ralph Pearson. He looked to the other detective. "Ralphie has an association with or is tied with Darius Price Jr."

The other detective shook his head. "It would have been nice to speak with him before he died."

"Tell me about it. Up to this point, I haven't been able to make a solid connection between the two. But it wouldn't deter me from waiting for my big break."

"If there's a connection," the other detective said, "the circles they run in may open up with Ralphie's death."

Chapman couldn't be too sure. The circles they ran in were very tight-knit and hard to penetrate. So tight, there wasn't even a picture of Darius Price Jr. on file. The guy was like a ghost. A myth. A GOD.

Still, Chapman hoped it would bring Darius out of hiding to aid in the investigation. His gut told him it was highly unlikely.

His eyes scoured the lobby, spotting the Medical Examiner in the process of leaving. Catching her, "You have anything new to tell me?"

"I've been on the job for years and I'm clueless. I'm pretty much stuck with inaccurate theories and hunches. It does appear to be the same perp from the other murder though," she explained, giving the detective a relieved look.

"That's good," he responded. "I definitely don't need a team of *strip to the bone* killers running around wrecking havoc on these streets."

"I know that's right!" she recited, agreeing with him.

"If you find anything, please let me know," he insisted, letting her go.

"Let's pray for a big break," she remarked, walking off.

"I definitely need one to close this case for good." He glanced around the motel lobby, scratching his head. *And I hope it comes FAST before I'm called to another crime scene.*

Chapter Five

BAM! BAM! BAM!

The hard knocks startled Winter. There was no doubt in her mind that the person knocking on her door was the police. *But why?* she wondered. Her first thought surrounded DP. *What if something happened to him?* She hated thinking that way; but, that was how it had become with him. The late nights, or the fact of him not coming home at all, left her in a place of uncertainty. Anything could happen to him in the streets and she would probably be the last person to find out.

She wished he would see it her way. However, he couldn't. Or he just didn't seem to care about the woman he had at home worrying about him and his well-being. *He'll change his mind if I leave his ass.*

She slid into her slippers, and made her way to the front door. Peeking through the peephole, a very attractive dark-skinned young man in a suit stood on the other side of the door. The sight of the stranger etched a smile across her face for some reason.

What has come over me? she asked herself, rubbing at the nape of her neck.

She peeked through the peephole. "Who is it?" she questioned, loud enough for the man to hear her.

"Detective Bryan Chapman. I'm looking for a Winter James."

"Damn!" she mumbled under her breath. "You looking for who?" The words came off as if she hadn't heard him initially.

"Winter James, ma'am. Do you think you could open the door so we can talk?" the detective asked, trying to get the door opened.

Winter didn't see any reason why she couldn't. She hadn't done anything wrong. She opened the door, removing the barrier between

31

her and the detective. Instantly, a series of highlighted sparks flickered in the detective's eyes as he checked her out from head to toe.

If I didn't know better, I would say he's undressing me with his eyes. She chewed on the corner of her lip. *That wouldn't be a bad thing.* She didn't hesitate checking him out as well.

Winter's eyes explored the detective's tall and sleek frame. At 5'5", the detective had to be close to 5'10". She couldn't tell what kind of physique he had underneath his clothes but that didn't stop her from using her imagination.

The more they eyed one another, the clearer the body language gave away to their thoughts. Chapman unconsciously licked his lips and hoped that whoever this fine young lady was would allow him to possibly get to know her better. Her erect nipples looked very inviting poking through her t-shirt and had his full attention. He found it hard to take his eyes off of them. A spiraling yearning built within his loin. If his nature rose to full staff, he would be like a dog in heat. There would be no turning back. He would strike with the ferociousness of a hungry pit bull, devouring the young lady's petite frame, one inch at a time.

Chapman had to get his mind together. His purpose of being there was to talk to a Winter James. He never expected to be turned on by possibly being in her presence. This young lady's aura was electrifying. So electrifying, he honestly forgot what he came for.

Winter snapped Chapman out of his trance, intentionally breaking the non-verbal communication. There was too much going on. She couldn't speak for the detective; but, the energy between them almost convinced her to go inside and touch herself. She wouldn't be silly enough to invite him in so he could take care of her needs. That wouldn't be a good idea, considering DP could come home at any moment.

I wouldn't mind taking that chance though, she surmised, contemplating the rush of it all.

Deciding against it, it was imperative to get to the real reason for the detective's presence. "Excuse me, SIR! Are you gonna stand there staring at me all day or are you gonna tell me what it is that you want?" she questioned, forcing the detective back to the task at hand.

32

Chapman sought to play it off, finding it to be harder than he expected.

Winter crossed her arms over her chest, covering her erect nipples. Smiling, she knew she'd been in just as much of a trance as he was so it was only right to put something extra on it. Looking into his face, a bright twinkle resonated, displaying his feelings for her. She knew he liked her but what man didn't. When standing at the average female height and being built like a stacked petite stallion, his longing for her was warranted.

"I'm assuming you're Winter James, is that correct?" he asked, licking his lips.

"That would be correct. What can do for you, detective?"

Chapman had a few things in mind but stuck to the script. "I'm investigating the homicide of a Travis Robertson and during the search of his vehicle, I found this photo." He pulled out a folded picture of Winter from his suit pocket. "On the back of the picture is your name and address."

Winter stared at the picture, knowing exactly when it was taken and how her father got it. Her mind flashed out thoughts of how close she was to meeting and perhaps establishing a relationship with her father. Those thoughts alone almost caused her to get emotional.

I'll be damn if I let this officer see me shed a tear over a man I didn't know.

"Do you think you were or could have been in any kind of danger, Miss James? Mr. Robertson WAS a known hit man?" Chapman asked, wondering what else he may have to deal with.

Winter glanced off, pondering the question. *Damn!* was all she could think. *What was his real intentions?* was the first question she asked herself. *Was it to really build a father-daughter relationship or was he coming to eliminate all loose ends from his past?*

Winter blinked out thought after thought but the feeling in her heart spoke volumes. Her heart insisted he wanted to build that relationship she so truly desired to have. Nevertheless, she wouldn't be that naive to merely think narrow-minded thoughts.

"Detective..." She began, unable to remember his name.

Chapman filled in the blanks for her.

"Yeah, Det. Chapman. Do YOU think I was ever in any kind of danger? At least, from what you know or from your perspective?" she asked, looking him in the eyes.

"I'm not sure, Miss James. Right now, I'm still trying to gather all the facts. To say with certainty, based on the totality of the circumstances, I'm not sure. I wish I could tell you more. I just can't," he explained.

"Well, Detective. I wouldn't say I was ever in any kind of danger. I didn't know the man personally. I only recently found out the man was my father."

That threw Chapman for a loop. Out of habit, he extended his condolences. Never did he suspect the visit would be to the daughter of the man so many wanted to pay for his past crimes and sins.

"I'm sorry to hear about the untimely death of your father. I'm not here to exploit the past. I'm only here to collect any information pertinent to the facts surrounding his case. I'm doing all I can to find the person responsible, and, I will catch whomever responsible. I can promise you that," he explained.

Getting that feeling within herself again, Winter felt that it would be her duty to find whomever responsible. She didn't want to be given a host of false promises. She was well aware of how the police operated. They would appear to be working diligently at first; then, something else would come up and their attention would go elsewhere. Nonetheless, all of Winter's thoughts would surround finding the killer first. And she would take care of her business. Her attention wouldn't sway. At least, not until she was standing over the person who killed her father. Only then would she feel complete in restoring her father's good name.

Chapman continued. "If you have any questions or any further information to share, please don't hesitate to give me a call." He handed her his card.

With her mind focused on who could have killed her father, Winter slipped the card in her pajama pants. *That'll be hard for me to figure out. I have no idea who he was or who his friends were.*

"Is there anything you can think of before I go," Chapman asked, acknowledging the fact that she hadn't given him any useful information. Then it appeared as if she was drifting in and out of a deep thought or two. There had to be something she wasn't telling him. He yearned to know what it was.

Winter glanced away, not knowing where to start if she did have anything to say. "I'm coming up with nothing, detective. If something comes to me later, I promise to give you a call," she replied, finding herself drifting off to a far place again.

Chapman verbalized something that didn't register. Winter's mind had traveled many miles away that quickly. It wasn't until the detective turned to leave that she snapped out of her thoughts.

"Make sure you give me a call if something of value comes up," she stated.

He stopped, and looked at her.

There goes that look again, she said. His feelings for her was evident. He had a sweet tooth for her, and that craving for her sweetness would make him sweet for the taking. She merely had to say the word, and whenever she longed to play his games, he would eagerly hand over any and all kinds of information to her. *I'll resort to reeling him in when the time was right,* she recited, mindful of her advantage.

"Thanks for your time, Miss James. I'll be in touch." He turned to leave. "One last thing though." He slipped his hands in his pocket, half-turning back towards her. "This may be hard to take but the word on the street is that Mr. Robertson may have turned into a confidential informant. I don't know how true it is but that's what I've heard." He watched her reaction.

Her response was fluid. "You shouldn't believe everything you hear, detective. You may start to believe anything." She stepped closer. "What makes you think that would make a difference to me?" she questioned, searching for the detective's angle.

"I just wanted you to know," he replied, fumbling with the keys in his pocket. *She may have already known.*

"Well thanks!" she voiced, curious to the detective's real reason for bringing that up.

The detective walked away, heading to his car. Winter, fuming inside, turned and walked inside her house, slamming the door behind her. Picking up her cellphone, she called her auntie; but, before Sara could say *'hello',* Winter went in on her.

"How could you hide so much from me?" she questioned. "How could you?" she asked before Sara could answer the first question. "WHY, Sara?" she screamed, needing to know. "What other things are you keeping from me?"

"Winter baby, it was the best thing to do at the time," Sara contended, actually believing that.

"How can you tell me what was good for me at that time? We're not at that time anymore. We're in the present so you didn't think I needed to know all this shit? Was it good for me when you gave him a picture of me along with my address?" she asked, getting even more agitated as she thought of the picture the detective had.

Sara sat on the phone speechless unable to figure out how she knew of the picture. She figured it would be best if she said as less as possible. Winter was extremely upset so there was no need to add any more fuel to the fire.

"So, what?! Cat got your tongue now?" Winter inquired.

Her tone scared Sara. "I'm sorry, Winter! I truly am. How did you find out about the picture?"

"The police just left my door asking me about if I was in any kind of danger or some shit. So, can you tell me if I was in any kind of danger, Sara?"

"Fuck naw!! Are you fucking crazy?" Sara questioned, not realizing what kind of mental state Winter was in. She lowered her voice. "Winter, you weren't in any kind of danger. He didn't come for any other reason but to step up as your father."

"Yeah, aight! That's what it better have been. But if I find out different, I'll be that see that ass," Winter spat, letting it be known what it was before hanging up.

Sara glared at the phone, knowing that the inner demon inside of Winter was getting closer and closer to the surface. And if she was anything like her father, or her mother for that matter, there was be hell for someone to pay. She just hoped it wouldn't be her.

Chapter Six

"DAMN IT MAN! Are you serious?" DP asked, listening to the caller on the phone. "I'm a call you back."

The call was from Ralphie's mother concerning his death. This was too much for DP to absorb at the moment. He needed some time to think. He had to get his mind right.

To hear how Ralphie had been found was crushing his soul. Ralphie was his dude going back to grade school. Ralphie's peoples were like his peoples. When DP didn't have anyone to turn to, he could always turn to Ralphie and his family.

Reflecting back, DP remembered when they first started getting money together. They were young and thought they were ready for the world when they weren't. That didn't stop them for acting as if they were. As street comrades, everything DP knew or was taught, he passed it along to the homie.

Who would want to do that kind of shit to my homie? he questioned, facing the reality of the matter. That was the question he would surely have to find an answer for. Someone would pay for Ralphie's death.

If DP didn't know anything else, he would make that happen.

Doing some reflecting, there hadn't been any beefs he knew of. *I can't look there for answers.* There wasn't anyone attempting to move in on Ralphie's territory so that couldn't be it either. What DP did know was that money was flowing in for Ralphie like running water. He made sure of that.

After officially getting out of the drug game, he made sure Ralphie stayed with the best work available. DP's supplier hadn't wanted to meet anyone else outside of DP. Honoring that, he played the middle man for Ralphie, and only Ralphie.

DP found his thoughts swaying back to the present, unaware of what was going on. He felt out of the loop. That was a position he didn't like. His first mind propelled him to focus on the beginning. And starting there zeroed in on what kind of person Ralphie was.

Overall, Ralphie was a good dude. He was known to keep some side shit going on with a chick or two. DP couldn't see a chick doing that kind of devious shit. This was the work of a sick and deranged individual.

"What would make anyone strip a man down to his bones?" he questioned. "Where they do that at?"

That's what he wanted to know most of all. He'd done some terrible things to people in his day; whereas, he never thought of stripping everything from their bones. That was even beyond him.

Talking to himself, he recalled the story on the news about the body found in a similar fashion. He checked the Internet, and came up empty. The police didn't have any leads and there wasn't much chatter on the net about it period. It was like everyone was being extremely hush hush about the whole topic.

DP found that strange. Sparking a cigarillo, he laid back allowing his mind to drift to the old days of him and Ralphie running the streets. They had been two peas in a pod. When you seen one, you seen the other. Puffing the weed, his high increased, which brought deeper thoughts of the times he shared with Ralphie.

The sounds of Winter walking in the house cut into his reminisce, converting his thoughts to the facts surrounding Ralphie's death. He was coming up with nothing. He was stuck. While the police would always need more information than him, having nothing to go on would make his job that much harder.

I have to hit the streets to find the answers I'm looking for.

Sitting up, DP grabbed the pages consisting of Ralphie's cellphone records. Flipping through them, he paid close attention to Ralphie's last known locations. Rubbing his temples, he slightly glanced up at the clock on the wall. It was time to make a move. *Before they put the homie in the ground, I want whomever responsible to be laid to rest as well.*

A sweet, alluring scent penetrated his nose. Catching a whiff of Winter's perfume switched DP's mental gears. And her maneuvering towards him cemented those thoughts,

"Hey bay! What's up with you?" she inquired, placing her bag on the table.

"I'm fucked up right now. Just found out that one of the homies was found dead," he explained, leaving out he was found out.

"WHO?" she asked with a lot of concern in her voice. She wanted to be there for her man.

"Ralphie!"

"Did I know him?" she asked, not knowing anyone by that name.

"I doubt it. You know I don't mix business with my personal life. Maybe when we were younger. I even doubt it then," he stated.

"Baby, I'm sorry to hear about your friend. Are you gonna be okay?" She stepped in closer as she spoke.

DP seen how good she was looking. Her appearance was surely a well-deserved distraction. One he would have to take advantage of.

Winter could see the look in his eyes and it made her smile.

He smiled back at her. "I'll be alright. What about you? How you doing with your lost?" he questioned, not wanting to make it all about him.

"I'm making it. There's not too much I can do about it nor do I know how to feel about it since he was ... never ... there for me." Before she could finish her sentence, she drifted off into a deep thought.

DP could see it was weighing heavily on her mind. He pinched her ass to bring her back to the present, and gave her a look that suggested they do something to get their minds on something else.

Without uttering a word, Winter slid on his lap, instantly feeling his erection. Rocking back and forth, she performed a quick lap dance, then slid to her knees. Stationed in-between his legs, she unzipped his pants, pulling out his harden tool. Her right hand stroke him to full capacity. She planted one wet kiss after another upon the tip of his rod. Each kiss seemed to get warmer and warmer, then wetter and wetter.

She covered the entire tip with her glossy lips causing DP's joint to jump with excitement. She didn't miss a beat. She eagerly caught it and slowly slid as much as she could down her throat. Almost gagging, she slowly removed his long demonstration from the depth of her esophagus, lathering every inch of him until it was completely soaked with her saliva. She licked, kissed, and sucked on him with the most dedicated attention.

Keeping his third leg nice and hard, she slobbered him down like a seasoned pro. Her precision was immaculate, causing DP to palm the back of her head. She placed her hand at the base of his joint, stretched him out, then deep-throated him. Coming up briefly for air, she rolled her tongue as she softly sucked the skin off his dick.

Throwing his head back, DP was speechless. This was exactly the kind of release he needed. Ecstasy knocked on his front door, and had the best intentions to alleviate his pain. What more could he ask for?

The tip of his sword swelled, his sack drew closer to his body, and a tingling shot across his lower stomach. It was explosion time.

Winter understood the dynamic of the situation, and picked up her pace. Like a trained head assassin, she got down on DP's sword like it would be the last dick she would ever suck.

Trying to match her rhythm, DP raised his hips in order to slide more of himself in her mouth. Almost choking her, she slowed to a slow creep but still made love to his third leg. She sensually massaged his sword, getting a taste of his pre-cum. *It won't be long now.* Waiting patiently, she openly invited the eruption, therefore pushing the envelope when she tightly gripped the head, twirled her tongue, added some much deserved pressure, and forcing his tool to give her what she wanted.

DP erupted like Mount Rushmore. SPLASH!

Plunging his back into the couch, he raised his hips some to give Winter the opportunity to suck him dry. Unable to move, it wasn't like he wanted to. His body submerged itself into the couch. She had drained him of everything he had within him. Sinking deeper into the couch, he closed his eyes.

And the last thing he remembered was Winter wiping him off and him drifting off to sleep.

* * * * *   * * * * *

DP woke up an hour later.

It was time to take that ride to see what he could find. Winter was sound asleep. There was no need to disturb her. She had her own issues to deal with. Plus, she couldn't give him the answers he needed. The answers he needed didn't hide within the confinement of their home. They rested in the streets. And he was destined to find them. One way or another.

He pulled up in front of the liquor store in Venice, Illinois. It was a storefront type of spot with a big picture window which gave way to the makeshift lobby. Like most times, the front of the spot was bumping. Everyone was lined up out front, setting up meetings, copping drinks and preparing to head somewhere to do them.

DP surveyed the area and noticed someone unfamiliar parked across the street. Making a mental note, he would have to find out who the cat was. For the moment, he studied the face of the guy who attracted a small group of local slut buckets. Giving him a once over, the guy's gear and the car sitting on 6's brought the guy what came with putting himself out there as a big shot.

DP dismissed what the cat had going on, returning back to the task at hand when Bruce, the liquor store owner, stepped out for a quick breather.

Bruce had been at that same location for years. He'd seen many come and go. His salt and pepper beard served him well for his age and the drama he'd had to put up with. He was also aware of Ralphie's untimely demise.

Without hesitation, he walked up extending his condolences. "Man, DP, I'm sorry to hear about your boy. I know that was like your best friend, if not like your brother. If there's anything I can do, don't hesitate to reach out," Bruce insisted.

DP pulled Bruce to the side. He did have something he needed to know. He wasn't known for his subtle approach so he dug right into Bruce. The questions DP had on his mind was weighing heavily on him.

"When was the last time you seen him?"

Bruce thought back. "It had to be the day he died. He was parked right there." He pointed to a currently occupied parking spot. "He was talking to some chick with a colorful ass wig on," he explained, lowering his arm.

"What did she look like?"

"I couldn't tell you, DP. It was getting dark, but, just as soon as they started talking, it was over. They left! I don't know if it was together or if it was separately."

"Can you remember what kind of car she drove?" DP questioned, needing to get some tangible information out of him.

"If it was hers, I seen a Black Maxima, or something similar, with tinted windows pulling off around the same time Ralphie pulled off."

DP automatically thought that the chick was the one who set up his boy to be slaughtered. Some punk ass coward would burn for that. First, DP knew he had to find the chick Bruce talked about.

"Bruce, if there's anything else you can remember, don't hesitate to call me. If you see that chick again, please give me a call as soon as possible. I need to have a real in-depth conversation with her." DP, extending his hand to Bruce, was assertive with his tone.

The two shook hands then went their respective ways.

DP pulled away from the liquor store, noticing the unfamiliar guy from before gone. *I'll see him again.* Stopping at a stop sign, he made a left and rode passed the police station into Newport. Hitting a few corners, he kept his eyes open for what or who he could see. He didn't see anyone who could help him.

After cruising the entire area once, he ended up back in Venice on Mobile's lot. As if on cue, the unfamiliar guy pulled up with a few hood rats riding with him. DP quickly tried raising his window to hide behind the dark tint. Before the window could be completely raised, he made eye contact with the chick in the back seat of dude's car.

DP knew who she was, knew what she was all about; yet, he wouldn't have imagined the move she would make.

She hopped out of the guy's car, boldly stepped to his car and knocked on his window.

DP was hesitant to roll it down. His gut told him not to because it was about to be some bullshit. Figuring it would be rude to ignore her, he could care less about being rude. He didn't have anything to say to the chick, and the stupid shit she did put him in a messed up mood.

To minimize the stupidity, he rolled down his window, giving her a *what the fuck you want?* look.

She definitely picked up on it. Instead of backing down, she went into her spill. She was on a mission and nothing would stop her, not even the deadly look DP gave her. "DP, my guy over here trying to cop some work. It must be a coincidence we ran into you, especially with you being the man around here and all."

"Spell coincidence," he requested, giving her a *you dumb bitch!* look.

"Boy, I know how to spell. Don't be trying to be funny. You gone do something for my boy, or what?"

DP simply stared at the chick sideways. He surmised she had to be one of the craziest bitches on earth to come at him like that. He wondered if this was the chick who had something to do with Ralphie's death. Then he looked over at the guy to see if he was the one to do the rest.

DP's eyes returned to the chick. He couldn't determine if they were trying to run the same game on him. One thing he knew was that his index finger had started to itch. When his index finger itched, someone usually didn't like the reaction they received. He scoured the area as he prepared to put a plan together.

A Venice Police squad car pulled onto the lot, persuading DP to leave the scene immediately.

He looked up at the chick standing at his window. "You need not believe everything you hear, momma. I ain't on shit, and ain't got shit," he explained, eyeing the guy in the car and what the police was doing.

"Boy please! I know what it is. I'm telling you he's good," she said, staying with her attempt to make something happen for the guy.

"Are you prepared to die for him, Dee Dee?" he mumbled, then proceeded to roll up his window.

Dee Dee glared at DP with utter shock in her eyes. Unable to form one word, her throat dried up. She'd heard about him putting in that work. She didn't want to believe it until he said what he just said.

Licking her lips, she attempted to regain her composure as Tasha came out of the store.

With his window half-raised and Tasha eyeing him, his first reaction was to pull off. Tasha was shiesty as hell, and he wanted no parts of anything she had going on.

"If it ain't, Mr. Darius Price. What it do, big timer?" she asked, stepping to DP's half-raised window.

"It don't do shit!" he spat, making eye contact with her.

"You know I'm at the Slip now. You need to swing by and shower a bitch with some of that money you got."

The Pink Slip, commonly known as the Slip, was a strip club in Brooklyn, Illinois.

"You'll love that, wouldn't you? I wouldn't pull my dick out and give you a golden shower if you paid me," he proclaimed, putting his car in drive. "What you need to do is picture me rolling with your dusty ass." He removed his foot from the brake. The 1996 Impala coasted off as he rolled up his window.

Applying his foot to the gas, he glanced back at the license plate number on the guy's car. He memorized it within a second. And with it locked in his mind, he exited the parking lot, and headed back towards Madison.

Chapter Seven

DP HAD BEEN TRYING to reach Winter all day. For some reason he hadn't been able to catch her. That was odd. Normally, she would answer when he called or call him right back if she missed the call. Lately, he noticed she'd been a bit stand offish since finding out about her father. That didn't seem to be the case when she sucked the skin off his dick. That was one for all times.

He presumed the way she acted had to do with something else. Unfortunately, he couldn't really trip off of her distant behavior considering he had his own issues to deal with. For now, he would give her enough space to get herself together. The alone time may be necessary for the both of them. That's why he made his way to his honeycomb hideout in the Bissells apartment complex. He needed to relax and catch up on some sleep.

Whereas, no sooner as he pulled into the parking lot, he spotted the clown from the night before cruising his way with another bust-down in the car with him.

DP could see the dude wasn't on shit. If he was trying to use a thirsty ass chick to find what he was looking for, he would be better off chasing his own tail. *I can't see this dude having anything to do with Ralphie's death. Dude is too stupid to pull something off like that.* He slowly maneuvered through the parking lot, seeking to get a good peek at the chick in the car. It was hard to get a good look at her since she kept her head down. She seemed destined to remain unseen.

Regardless of who the chick was, that didn't stop dude from spotting DP. The moment dude seen DP's car, he rolled down his window, attempting to flag him down.

DP stopped, hoping dude wasn't intent on doing what he thought. That would piss him off if dude came at him with some *I'm trying to get on!* type shit, and put him in the mind-frame of dumping on dude and his freak right then and there. And that's exactly what the idiot did.

Dude held his arm out the window, signaling he wanted to holler at DP.

This guy gots to be the police, DP thought. *Dude don't know me from a can of paint but here he is with the nerve to flag me down.*

DP wanted to air dude out. He would hate to expose his hand but it could be done. Mulling over the outcome, he decided against going that route, and opted to hear the clown out. As he rolled down his window, dude was all smiles. *Here this lame ass dude smiling at me. I bet he's one of them people.*

DP hit dude with a *what's up?* nod, getting straight to the point. "What's up? Do I know you?"

"I don't mean no disrespect, bro, but I'm up here visiting my peoples, trying to make a move or two." The dude let his eyes roam inside of DP's car.

"What that have to do with me?" DP asked, sitting his Sig Sauer P320 .40-caliber handgun on his lap.

"I just figured you could point me in the right direction," the dude replied, leaning his arm out of the window. "I ..."

DP cut him off. "Listen nigga. I ain't who you think I am so miss me with the frivolous bullshit. I don't have time to play with you. The kind of pointing I do you ain't looking for. Ya feel me?" DP inquired, locking eyes with dude.

Birdie felt every word.

DP rolled his window up and made a mental note to get rid of that car. He couldn't help but shake his head in disbelief. Replaying the altercation, the entire scene was strange. The chick never raised her head, not once. He was willing to bet she was a FED. He could sense dude wasn't right. It wouldn't be too far off for the chick to be his partner. For future reference, DP stored that information inside of his mental vault.

Unsure of the two clowns, DP second guessed going to his hideout for fear of being caught slipping. He surely didn't want to be a sitting duck when the FEDS kicked in his door. He couldn't allow them to get him like that.

Navigating around the parking lot, he double checked the area several times to make sure the coast was clear. Finding it deserted, DP felt comfortable enough to park his ride. Pocketing the .40, he hurried inside, eager to get to a blunt and his bed so he could relax.

★ ★ ★ ★ ★　　★ ★ ★ ★ ★

"Well baby doll. It's just you and me now. I'm feeling everything about you. That feeling got me knowing you and I could go places. Let me take you some place so I can get to know you a little better," the dude told the chick.

"Boy, I don't even know your name. You want to sit here talking about feeling me and shit. Who you think you talking to? Some lame ass bitch from wherever you from. "YOU," the chick said, pointing at him, "gots to come better than that!"

"First off, let me introduce myself. They call me Birdie and yes, I'm playing with them birds. I ain't trying to waste too much of your time because I know what I want and I'm sure you do too. So what's its gone be. You rocking with me or what?" he asked, trying to get straight to the point.

"So you think you laying it down like that, huh? Ramona definitely needs a piece of that pie, boo-boo. But I have some bad news. Aunt Flow is visiting real tough. I do have somewhere else you can hide that piece, if you're up for it," she explained, giving him a *let's get it!* look. "But let's get a room first."

Birdie's joint jumped for joy at the sound of the request. He pulled out his sword, subliminally letting her know there would be no need for a room. Whatever they needed to do could be done where they were.

Without hesitation, Ramona clearly acknowledged the invitation, wasting no time climbing over the arm rest to grab ahold of his harden tool. In an instant, she went to work. He could only smile as she pleasured him with her warm mouth and slithering tongue. Doing what she does best, she put in that work. Within the first minute, she literally blew his mind. He instantly concluded this was the best head he'd ever had in his life. Her slobbering him up and down forced him to recline the seat. That gave Ramona easier access to do her.

The spit sliding down the side of his shaft awoken his voice box. "Damn, baby doll! You got that fire ass head," he hissed.

Unfazed by the comment, she stayed on course with what she was doing. It was one of those comments she'd heard plenty of times before. Like the other times, she knew to take it with a grain of salt. She took his member into her mouth just the same, allowing the tip of him to tickle her tonsils. The more she got into it, the more it dawned on her that she might have to leave him alive.

That wasn't something she longed to do. He couldn't leave that scene, alive and well. That he couldn't do. She didn't need anyone alive and able to identify her. This was not the time to start getting sloppy. She had remained low-key and out of sight for the longest time, particularly due to her extermination skills. She had to come up with something fast.

She reclined Birdie's seat a little more. She wanted him to be as comfortable as possible as she thoroughly assaulted his sword. But she felt something cold when she reached for the lever. The first thing to come to her mind was a burner. And if it was, she would be using it to her advantage at the conclusion of her business.

Meanwhile, while Ramona tongue kissed Birdie's joint, he slid his hand up her tennis skirt to find she didn't have any panties on. That excited him. He eagerly drove his fingers towards her third hole, attempting to loosen her up. Anal sex was his thing. When she offered, that was right up his alley. It was an offer he couldn't refuse.

Probing the realm of her circumference, she moaned softly as he inserted his finger inside of her. The more he played with her anus, the juicier it became and the more she wanted him to fill her up.

Ramona sensed Birdie's excitement when his fingers kept widening her dark hole. With every finger inserted, his member increased in hardness. She wouldn't have assumed it could get any harder. But it did.

The farther Birdie jammed his fingers in, the deeper Ramona deep-throated his sword. But playtime was over! It was time for Birdie to spread Ramona out as far as she could go.

With Ramona climbing over the arm rest, Birdie appeared with a bottle of K-Y Jelly and squirted it on his sword. Ramona knew this cat was the truth with that move. Grabbing his joint, she guided him to her entry. Inserting an inch at a time, she easily loosened up for him to fully feel the tightness and its warmth.

She engulfed all of him as she grabbed the steering wheel. Using it for leverage, she slid up and down with extreme precision. Putting on a show, Ramona eased most of him out of her before allowing all of him to disappear once again. The mere sight of her tricks almost insisted that Birdie coat the inside of her intestines with his seed.

Leaning back, Ramona set out to bring herself to climax. Fingering her clit, she used her right hand to massage her budding flower, while her left hand slid down to grab the gun. Riding Birdie like a trained barrel racer, she rubbed her clit, bucked as hard as she could, while reaching for the gun. Yet, what she picked up wasn't a gun.

It was a badge.

When the words *what the fuck?* escaped her mouth, Birdie was blasting off inside of her. He had no clue to what was going on. His head was in the clouds. Licking his lips, his pea-brain had zeroed in on how good Ramona put her lick down, and his face exhibited a shit-eating grin. Sucking his bottom lip, he was about to say something when Ramona dropped the badge to the floor.

Hands free, she reached for what she knew was a gun. Birdie heard the badge drop but didn't pay it any mind. He was submerged in the pleasure of Ramona's backside, gyrating his hips. On the flip side, Ramona had murder on her brain. She swiftly slid off his dick, destined to put in that work.

Mad as hell, she needed to get into a better position so she could get off a couple of shots. *I have to let this punk ass cop have it.* But the safety was on. Pulling the trigger with no luck, she quickly assessed the situation, clicking the safety off as fast as she could.

Birdie heard the click, finally noticing what was transpiring. He reached for his piece, not knowing it was his. All he knew, he needed to regain his composure so he sprang into action. As he gained control of the weapon that left Ramona with no more time to think.

Her survival instincts kicked in. She dropped two stiff blows to his face. Landing a sharp blow to his nose, she slipped her left leg over the arm rest. Slugging him in the gut, she came up and gave him one more shot to the jaw. Her playing for keeps put him in a position to cover up his face.

Aja LaGrand Blount

With that done, she opened the passenger's side door, climbing out. In a hurry, she scrambled away from the scene without any further hassle.

Birdie, on the other hand, tried to focus and assess the altercation. He looked in the rearview mirror to see Ramona darting up the street and out of sight. He looked down at his banger. It was his indeed. That meant what he heard hit the floor had been his badge.

Ain't this about a bitch?

As a detective, he wrapped his mind around the most important lesson of the day. He had almost become the victim of being caught with his pants down. Even still, the valuable lessons had deeper implication. While he loved getting his rocks off, the encounter itself clearly expounded on what just occurred. If he was a betting man, he would bet everything on the notion that Ramona was the perp who left two people dead without an inch of skin or meat on their bones.

And that's why she longed to get a room so she could leave me in the same predicament.

* * * * *　　* * * * *

Winter accidently bumped her leg on the edge of her coffee table, running to get to her phone. When reaching it, she automatically answered it without looking to see who it was.

An unfamiliar voice filtered through the line. "May I speak with Miss Winter James, please?"

"May I ask whose calling?" she questioned, curious to who the caller was. The formal tone made her nervous.

"This is Detective Chapman. I'm the lead detective investigating your father's murder. I'm calling to check up on you."

"Check up on me?" she asked. "When does the boys in blue start checking up on people." She believed the call pertained to something greater than that.

The detective simply laughed. "The purpose of this rare occasion is to follow up on any developments in the case-"

She interrupted him, thinking there had been a new development. "You found out who killed my father?" she asked with too much excitement in her voice.

"Actually, we've hit a dead end. I was really wondering if you ran across something useful that you could share," he stated, reaching for the moon by calling in the first place.

"Share?!?!" she questioned; her irritation oozing out of her. "Now I'm supposed to do your job for you?"

"I'm not saying that, Miss James," he replied. "It was something I thought could be possible."

"I wish I had something to share. I thought you were the one supposed to be doing the sharing." She sought to calm herself.

"I wish I had something to share as well."

"Basically, you called to tell me nothing about my father's death?" she asked, sarcastically.

Chapman hesitated to answer. He didn't want to give away his real reason for the call. In all essence, he wanted to inform her of what he really wanted to share with her. Then again, he didn't want to appear too unprofessional. At that point, he could care less about her father's case. At the end of the day, he wanted to find out what Travis Robertson's little girl had going on. From what he seen, she had more than enough to share with him if she applied herself.

On the other hand, Winter had a similar thought. By knowing the detective liked her, she had to use that to rope him in. She truly believed she could manipulate him for whatever information he had. It would simply take her slightly opening the door for him to possibly kick it in.

"Detective, why don't we meet up for coffee and maybe put everything we have on the table. You know, just for the sake of obtaining a clearer understanding."

"I'll love to do that," he quickly responded, letting his enthusiasm shine through.

Winter heard that enthusiasm and knew she had him. Whereas, she hoped it wouldn't be a waste of her time. She knew the basics and if that's all he could still provide; the meeting would be fruitless.

"Where would you like to meet?" she asked.

"Um," he said, thinking of a place. "Let's meet at the Waffle House in Collinsville."

"That'll be great. I can be there in an hour. Will that work for you?"

He couldn't hide his eagerness. "That'll work for me."

Aja LaGrand Blount

"See you in an hour then!"

Chapter Eight

DP CRUISED DOWN THE STREET in a triple black Camaro, fitted with 22-inch black-and-chrome accent rims, behind tint. The recently waxed paint glistened brightly as the sun shun upon its darken glare. As he drove, he bobbed his head to Lyfe Jennings "Must be Nice" when he seen Winter's Audi Q3 pull into the Waffle House parking lot. "What the hell she doing over here?" he asked, knowing he didn't frequent this part of town that often. Despite having to today, he only made the trip to Collinsville to follow up on a few leads associated with Ralphie.

Turning around, he slowly turned into the Waffle House's parking lot to get a better look at Winter. She parked next to what could have been a detective's car. He could have cared less about where she parked. It was the hair rising on the back of his neck when seeing the person she sat across from.

He slammed his hand on the steering wheel. "I knew that muthafucka was the police!" He was furious. A red tint of blood glazed his eyes. He seen death. Dude had to go immediately. There was no way for the detective to freely walk the earth after this revelation. Days prior, he attempted to set him with a drug sale.

DP's displeasure seeped through his pores. Scanning the parking lot, the traffic was to a minimum with maybe four cars occupying the asphalt. Checking out the detective's unmarked Dodge Charger parked in front of the restaurant, DP felt a sense of urgency. Wanting to place a tracking device on the car, he couldn't risk being seen. Instead of making the wrong move, he jotted the detective's license plate number down, and sped off to the nearest coffee shop.

Inside the Waffle House, Winter wasn't feeling any closer to acquiring any new information from Detective Chapman. He recited the same theories and speculations he had from before. What she needed was hardcore facts, not pipe dreams. This was a waste of time, and was beginning to annoy her. With every passing second sitting there, her mind drifted.

Looking out of the window, a black Camaro pulled off rather quickly. She'd noticed it sitting there but hadn't paid it no mind. She didn't know where it came from or whether it had been there when she pulled up. Unable to remember, that thought alone worried her.

A debatable feeling overcame her. It felt as if she'd been spotted talking to the detective. She tried to dismiss the notion considering the meeting surrounded the death of her father; however, there was no shaking it.

Anyone could run back and tell DP anything they wanted if they saw her with the detective. That definitely wouldn't be a good thing. He would jump to conclusions. It didn't matter that they hadn't talked in a few days. The feeling she had was telling her something. What, she didn't know. She hoped she was wrong about it all.

"Miss James," Chapman said, touching her arm.

Winter faced him, noticing the bruises on his face. She hadn't noticed them when he initially had his glasses on. It wasn't until he took them off that the bruises became visible.

"What happened to your face, if you don't mind me asking?"

"Just part of the job," he replied, embarrassed to think of what happen, let alone tell her.

The detective looked into Winter's eyes. The look he found gazing back at him caused him to take a pause. He thought he seen a glimpse of something familiar. Something very familiar. *Naw, that couldn't be her,* he convinced himself, seeing something in her that he'd seen in someone else.

Winter eased back and gave Chapman a funny look when peeping how he stared at her. "You like what you see or something?" she asked, trying to make light of the situation.

The detective hadn't been prepared for that kind of question. It left him stuttering over his words but her smile gave him the courage to say what he wanted to say. "As a matter of fact, I do!" he exclaimed, searching for the right words. "I'm glad you asked. I've been thinking of a way to approach the subject of me and you becoming a little bit more acquainted."

"I doubt that would be a good idea, detective. Your only priority should be finding out who killed my father, not sticking it to his baby girl," she insisted, flashing her big smile.

Chapman smiled in return, and shook his head. Enjoying her smile and gazing into her eyes, he received that feeling again. His gut advised him that something wasn't right. His gut was rarely wrong.

"Plus, I have a man and if he knew I was even here talking to you, he would probably kill the both of us," she explained.

"Oh really!" he yelled. "Who might your man be?"

"That's not important but I have to go. Have a nice day, Detective Chapman," she said, sticking her hand out.

Chapman grasped her soft hand with a firm handshake. Winter stepped out of the booth, and proceeded to leave. As she attempted to walk off, her leg locked, causing her to limp.

Chapman took notice, reaching out to lend a hand. Yet, he continued to get a nagging feeling that Winter could be the girl from the other night. Everything about her seemed so familiar, even down to the limp. He was sure Ramona injured herself when making her escape. And with Winter showing signs of an injury, he didn't know what to believe.

"One last thing, Winter. Would you happen to know anyone by the name of Ramona?" he inquired, wanting to see what kind of reaction he would get.

Winter lowered her head, pondering the question. The name didn't ring a bell. As she mulled over the name, she finally denied any knowledge of knowing anyone by that name. "I can't say that I do, detective. Why you ask?" she wondered, thinking Ramona had something to do with her father's murder.

"I was just wondering. I see a slight resemblance between you and her."

She shrugged, leaving it at that.

Chapman, a good reader of character, inferred that she was telling the truth. He hated to believe that but he had to. He had no other proof.

Winter turned to leave, slinging her 40" hips and round backside from side-to-side. She had a walk that could hypnotize any man. And it surely mesmerized Chapman.

The detective's attention was easily diverted from his previous thoughts to watching Winter's strut. He was momentarily stuck. Snapping his finger, he savored the moment, knowing there was something familiar about her.

I just can't put my finger on it.

Even with the similarities, he wasn't definite that his feelings were accurate. Pressing the issue wouldn't do him any good because if Winter was Ramona, he believed one of them wouldn't have made it out of that restaurant alive. There would have been a lot of smoke in the city.

Regardless, he couldn't dwell on it. It was best to push it to the side. He ultimately had more pressing matters to deal with and this one would have to wait.

* * * * *　　* * * * *

Switching cars, DP rode through the newly developed neighborhood looking for the address he obtained from the coffee shop. Time was of the essence when dealing with a threat of this particular magnitude. Him and threats didn't gel well. It was either let the threat overcome him or take matters into his own hands by eliminating the threat. He would rather be the one to eliminate it. That way he could have full control over the situation.

Driving slowly, he surveyed the atmosphere. The neighborhood came off as a good environment to raise kids, have a good married life, and be a productive member of society. The lawns were neatly trimmed, and most drive-ways had nice cars and trucks parked out front. The exterior of each home appeared to be in the upward costs of over $300,000. They definitely had curb appeal. He could only imagine how the interiors drew you in.

I can see myself living in this kind of neighborhood once I stop playing this killing game. He came upon the address he scribbled down. An average looking brown-skinned woman retrieved the mail from the mailbox. He assumed by the ring on her finger that she was married and a resident of said house.

He pulled to a stop, rolled down his window, and engaged her in small talk. "Excuse me, miss. I seem to be lost. I'm looking for the Taylor's residence. I have a delivery for them but the address isn't so clear," he explained.

The woman looked up at him. "I'm not sure who the Taylor's are. We've only lived here for a short while and people around here tend to keep to themselves. What's the address?"

"It's..." he started before being cut off by a school bus pulling up.

The woman looked away. "I'm sorry! I have to get my kids. I hope you find whomever you're looking for," the woman exclaimed, stepping away from the mailbox.

The name CHAPMAN was engraved on the side of the mailbox.

DP slowly pulled off as if he was still looking for the address. In his rearview mirror, he could see the woman and her two kids heading towards the house. He navigated through the neighborhood, turned around to exit the area, giving the woman one last wave. She waved back as he made his way out of the subdivision.

Satisfied with his findings, it was time to think about his next move.

＊＊＊＊＊　　＊＊＊＊＊

Detective Chapman had been on the edge ever since his encounter with Ramona. Then to have that kind of reaction with Winter really had him on pins and needles. Aside from his relentless tries, he had not been able to connect the dots between Winter and Ramona. Nor had he been able to find Ramona or anyone who would have a clue to who she was or where she could be found. His uncertain future led him to believe his cover was blown; except, nothing was adding up for him.

Could Ramona actually be Winter?

No one seem to know anything about Ramona or DP, and he found that sort of odd.

Over a year ago, Chapman accepted the lead detective's job so he could tackle the big dogs like DP, and those who ran with him. He was finding it wasn't as easy as he would have hoped. He wanted to associate it to him being new to the area. But it had to be more than that. He knew it wouldn't be a smooth transition transferring in from another department. Even still, he expected more cooperation than he received.

From what he knew, DP had been doing whatever he wanted for years without police interference. As a hard-nose detective, he felt it was his calling to put an end to Darius Price Jr's reign, along with everyone associated with him and his kind.

It was imperative that all of his homework paid off. Obtaining the knowledge of Darius Price legacy led Chapman to believe DP's current existence derived from that of his father. Be that as it may, something was missing. Something didn't quite add up. DP didn't seem be involved with dealing drugs or even hanging around those who did.

On paper, DP was college student enrolled at SIUE taking computer programming classes. There wasn't a known address from him other than a post office box, and he never showed up to take a picture for his school ID. Outside of what certain documents said, he was a ghost.

Chapman wouldn't be fooled. He'd seen DP personally and the word on the streets was that he was the man. The brief encounter between them left him certain that DP could possibly be what everyone said he was. Still, something was amiss.

Feeling the need to re-evaluate the situation, the detective figured it had to be his approach. Needing to go back to the drawing board, he returned to the station to pick up some things before heading home.

But not once did the detective peep the car following him home to his wife and kids.

* * * * *   * * * * *

"Yeah baby, I'm liking how you're using your head!" the burly man exclaimed, sitting up on his forearms.

Ramona removed the Popsicle from her mouth, and stared the overweight man in his eyes. "You really mean that, daddy?" she asked, sounding like a child.

"Of course, baby! You're making daddy feel really good right now," he answered, wishing she got back to the oral sex. He grabbed the back of her head, guiding her to his throbbing member.

Ramona deep-throated him, bestowing her good head on him. The man grabbed a hand full of her hair in order to get her to ease up, yanking off her wig.

"Damn baby, you really know how to blow my mind, don't you?" he groaned.

"That's not all I know how to blow, daddy," she mumbled, running her tongue up his chocolate pudding pop.

"Don't talk, baby. Just suck! I'm about to bust one for ya," he confessed, grabbing the back of her head.

That sent her into overdrive, convincing her to swirl her tongue all over him until he was on the verge of eruption. Stroking him roughly, she clamped down on the tip of his fruit stick. The tip of his snack expanded in her mouth. She recognized the action, knowing the time was nearing for his release. Not the one to shy from a good shot of protein, she worked her magic up to the point of no return. Then, right before his volcano was set to erupt, she eased off the pedal.

The man's eyes shot open, wondering why she stopped. A silenced HK VP40 stared him in the face, daring him to question her. He chuckled, wanting to believe this was some sick joke. He was unable to hide the alarm behind his eyes. Notwithstanding, the locked and loaded semi-automatic handgun provided him with a change of heart. No matter how he wanted to blow off the situation, he seen he didn't have too many options.

"What do you want?"

Ramona cocked her head, pulled the trigger, and left the man's brain splattered across the wall behind him. As his lifeless body flopped backwards, she thoroughly searched his pants pockets, looking for his wallet. Finding it, she searched for clues for what his password could be. Dumping the contents of the fat wallet, she came across a few words scribbled on the back of a business card.

Powering her laptop, Ramona punched in the man's name, ID number and one of the words on the card then pressed enter. An invalid password message popped up. She tried another name. Same

Aja LaGrand Blount

message appeared. Trying the last name, she eventually gained access.

Once in, she scrolled through the directory and came across what she was looking for. Getting up to leave, she glanced back at Lieutenant Leroy Fletcher and thanked him for his cooperation. "I hate to leave you like this. You know, with nut oozing out of your dick and all; but, I have to. I need to display what happens when the police get caught with their pants down."

She laughed at her own demonic thoughts as she dressed, packed up her things and silently walked out of the hotel room.

"Have a good night, Lt. Fletcher. I have another special trip to make," she said under her breath. "If Detective Chapman thinks he can fuck me in the ass and get away with it, he has another thing coming."

Chapter Nine

"HEY BABY, I'M GLAD you're home. How was your day at work?"

Chapman exhaled his frustration. "Stressful! What I thought was something really isn't what it appeared to be. I really need to re-access the situation," he informed his wife, intent on making his way to his study.

"Before you do all that, let me help you relax. I'm a run you a hot bath, light those special candles you like and when you get out, I'm gonna lotion and massage that body of yours until you're thoroughly relaxed and at ease."

"That sounds great-" His response was cut short when his phone rang.

Bryan answered and listened extensively to what the caller had to say. He shook his head at the details being conveyed to him.

Just not too long ago, he had found himself in a similar predicament. His mind flashed back to the day he was almost caught with his pants down, automatically realized who committed the heinous deed, and knew exactly what it meant.

Ramona hadn't forgotten about that day and now a fellow officer paid the price for my sins.

The detective surmised that in the near future he would have to meet the mysterious woman again, hoping it would be sooner rather than later. Enough damage had been done, and he surely didn't need another officer's body found in an embarrassing manner because of him.

Chapman ended the call; yet, couldn't shake the scene described so vividly. Ramona had intentionally left the lieutenant exposed as a way to a send a message. Aside from wanting to hear it, the message was being read loud and clear. Outraged, he wanted to hit the streets to look for her; but, that would be a waste of time. When she wanted to be found, she would present herself and when that time came, he would be there to make his move.

In the interim, a big smile crossed his face as his wife placed her hands on his shoulders. "Baby, you ready for your bath?" she cooed.

Bryan grabbed his wife's hands and placed a kiss on them. Tugging at her wrists, he pulled her onto his lap. His eyes swollen to the size of saucers, surprised at the sight of what she had on.

Mrs. Brenda Chapman was decked out in one of Victoria's latest secrets, which revealed all the things he had been missing.

Staring into his eyes, she aggressively went in for a kiss. It seemed as if they were kissing for the very first time. With Bryan's job taking up most of his time, they hadn't been able to spend a lot of time together. That's why she was excited to have him home. She had to take advantage of him being there.

She truly missed him, and that showed in the intensity of her kisses. The heighten energy of their love caused their hands to roam. Brenda's hand went for his growing loin, massaging it through his pants.

Shifting her position, their kisses became a bit more passionate, causing the heat to rise to the next level. Breaking their embrace, Brenda mounted her husband, resumed kissing him, and unbuttoned his shirt. He palmed her ass, feeling the warmth of her creamy center as if he touched it at that exact moment.

Brenda finished unbuttoning his shirt and started on his pants, yearning to touch his hardness. That yearning prepped her soak and wet love below for a deep penetration. The simple thought of him entering her made her juice box pulsate. Throb. Jump for joy. Bud like a rose in bloom.

She reached into his boxers and retrieved his golden prize. Then, as she intended to go down on him, she was rudely interrupted by her son coming into the living room. "Mom, I'm thirsty," the child cried out, wiping at his eyes.

Brenda covered herself as best as she could, while Bryan sought to collect himself. She clambered off of her husband to tend to her child; however, when their son got a glimpse of his father, he went nuts.

Bryan Jr. ran and jumped into his father's arms.

Bryan hugged his son, sitting him on his lap. "You're not supposed to be up at this time of night."

"I was thirsty, daddy."

"You're gonna have to wait until morning to get something to drink. It's bedtime, little man!"

Bryan Jr sighed.

"I'll make sure you get something to drink as soon as you wake up, ok?"

"Okay!" Bryan Jr said, sounding a little disappointed.

Bryan scooped his son in his arms, bounced him back to sleep, and walked him back to his room. Laying him down, he kissed his son on the forehead, and expressed his love for him. But he had his wife's secrets on his mind. Walking out of his son's room, he left the door slightly cracked, rushing to get back to the situation at hand.

With those thoughts consuming him, Bryan jetted through the house looking for his queen. Busting into the bedroom, she wasn't there. He thought she be laid across the bed half-naked and waiting on him. He could vividly see that scene painted in his mind. But she wasn't.

She must be in the bathroom. His assumption was correct. Opening the bathroom door, she casually laid in the tub. Seeing the top of her head, his excitement got the best of him when visualizing her naked body submerged under water.

As he pushed the door open, his temperature rose along with his third leg. He stepped into the bathroom sending his excitement further into a state of overwhelm. He slung the door close, and called out his wife's name.

The butt of a gun crashed into the back of his head. Dazed but still conscious, Bryan stumbled to the floor. He'd absorbed the blow in stride. The intruder whacked him again, noticing the detective was barely fazed by the initial tap to his dome. That time, the blow turned Bryan's lights out, laying him face down with his arms sprawled to his side.

The intruder pulled Chapman by his legs into the bedroom, where he was blindfolded, gagged, and bound to a chair sitting in the middle of the bedroom.

The intruder returned to the bathroom for the detective's wife, already bound and gagged. The wife was scooped out of the tub and carried to the bedroom. It didn't take much to scoop her up and transport her to the bedroom.

Entering the bedroom, the intruder slammed the wife on the bed. The soft of the mattress bounced her slightly up and down. The startling altercation caused the wife to whimper out in pain. That small bleat brought Bryan out of his unconsciousness.

The intruder strolled over to the detective, removing his blindfold.

Frantically, Chapman's eyes surveyed the entire scene before him. Seeing his wife balled up on the bed resulted in his heart crumbling. He longed to help her; but, at that point, he was just as helpless as her. *What is going on here?* he asked himself. *Who is this guy?* The black mask covering his face made it impossible to see his features. What was evident was that the intruder was male. Chapman tried sizing the intruder up.

Who are you? he asked, letting his emotions get the best of him. *Did Ramona send you to take care of her dirty work? Or, is this a random home invasion?* he continued to ask himself.

The detective didn't have a clue. He could only watch in horror as the intruder snatched his wife off the bed like a rag-doll. When he put the gun to her head, he tried his damnest to scream *'NO!'* in an effort to persuade the intruder not to kill her.

Brenda could feel the gun against her head. Its coldness tensed her body and she almost urinated on herself. Even though her husband was a police officer, she had no experience with guns, especially one being put to her head.

The intruder whispered softly in her ear, informed her to remain calm, do as he said and nothing would happen to her.

Brenda's heart pounded out of her chest with fear. The drift of the intruder's breath on her neck cemented her in place. Her brain froze from the shock of the whole situation. Next, her legs stiffened and urine flowed down her inner thighs. The warmth of the release didn't register in Brenda's mind until she stood in a puddle of her own piss.

Bryan shook his head in disbelief. His heart shattered into a bunch of tiny, little pieces having to witness that. To see his wife break down in such a manner was devastating. He was hurt. His desire to battle the bad guys for a living shouldn't have made it to his doorstep. It definitely shouldn't have been the cause of his wife to be standing in her own urine. Wasn't the silenced weapon to the side of her head bad enough?

Please take the gun from her head, he pleaded behind the gag. That silenced weapon caused the detective great alarm. An alarm that couldn't be denied. It was written all over his face. He couldn't hide it if he wanted to.

The intruder allowed the detective to soak up the details around him for a moment. When he assumed the detective had everything acknowledged, he nonchalantly pulled the trigger on the silenced Sig Sauer .40.

The pulling of that trigger literally blew Brenda's brains out. The act itself was to show Bryan that the intruder didn't have time to play games. He needed the detective to know he meant business.

Bryan jumped back in utter shock at the extraction of his wife's brains. Traumatized, he rocked back and forth in the chair, apprehending that this was a personal visit. Up to this point, the intruder hadn't said anything. The detective didn't know where to begin with his thought process. But, he would have to figure it out.

Brenda's body hit the ground with a loud thump.

Bryan slumped his head, seeking to do all he could to remain strong. That's all he had enough energy for. He tried to keep the tears from flowing; whereas, he couldn't stop the inevitable. The intruder had come into his home and murdered the woman he'd loved all his life. That really made him want to know who this bastard was; except, he could only guess. Since he wasn't a guessing man, he had to come to terms of not knowing.

The intruder, on the other hand, acted as if he could read the detective's mind when he revealed himself, and voiced his first words. "Hold you head high for me, playa."

With his chin pressed tightly against his chest, the detective listened to the familiar voice, not wanting to believe it. He held his chin tighter to his chest. The certainty of knowing who caused him so much pain in only a matter of minutes sealed his fate. There was no coming back from this. Knowing that, he had no desire to look the intruder in the face. It would do him no good. The good he planned to do in the community would have to be carried on by someone else. His work had come full circle.

"Let me see your eyes," the intruder requested.

The detective tried to muster all the strength he could to raise his head. It just wouldn't move. Feeling the intruder's presence, he listened to every sound he could possible hear. Then the sound of his daughter's voice snapped his head up automatically.

"Daddy!?!?!" She was wiping at her eyes, unaware of what was going on. She could see her mother lying on the floor and her first instinct was to run to her.

DP sensed the little girl's movement through his peripheral. He unconsciously flung his gun in her direction and pulled the trigger twice. The first bullet pierced the little girl's chest, standing her upright. The second shot penetrated her head, finishing her off completely.

The detective snapped out. He'd seen enough. DP had gunned down his little girl in cold blood. He couldn't take anymore. He tried his damndest to get loose. He had to get his hands on DP. *He better hope I don't get loose,* he kept stating over and over.

Chapman used every ounce of his energy attempting to break free from his restraints. However, it was all for nothing. He couldn't successfully break free.

DP watched the detective waste his time and energy. Raising his gun, he nodded at the detective with his famous *what's up* nod. "I see you have no rap now, Birdie?"

The mere mention of that name sent shivers up and down Chapman's spine. That name was the cause of all the mayhem and the stench of murder in his bedroom. Bryan apologetically looked at his wife and daughter laid out on the floor. Tears streamed down his face. It couldn't be helped. The river of eye water had to be set free. Whereas, where it could have washed away the current situation for some, it didn't scratch the surface for the detective. His stream of tears could not hide the truth.

The detective tilted his head back, and stared into the light. Saying a silent prayer for the forgiveness of his sins, he smelled his end nearing. Sticking his chin out, he could see the light getting brighter coming towards him. There was hues of blues and reds, sprinkled in with some yellow and what was possibly some greens. The colors seemed to also have a thermos-imaging effect surrounding them, and an unusual heat source.

The detective was unable to identify the heat source off-hand. His delirium surely mistaken the current illusion with the reality of the situation. Because what the detective refused to understand, the different hues of color derived from the sparks coming from the barrel of DP's Sig Sauer. And the heat he felt was the hot slugs ripping into his face at an alarming rate.

Notwithstanding, the light the detective saw did consist of that bright, white light so many spoke of when stumbling towards the heaven gates. But the image Detective Bryan Chapman saw wasn't the image of God. It was Darius Price Jr a.k.a DP, the last person he would see through human eyes.

* * * * *   * * * * *

Ramona patiently sat in her car outside of Det. Chapman's house, waiting for the rest of the lights to go out so she could make her move. Peering into the rearview mirror, she knew she couldn't sit out there much longer. This wasn't the kind of neighborhoods that normally seen people sitting outside in their cars in the middle of the night.

Nonetheless, her patience had run out, and she decided it was time to make her move. Exiting her car, she turned her nose up, sniffing the air. The smell of smoke permeated from somewhere nearby. She scanned the area seeking to locate the source.

Gazing towards the detective's house, a cloud of smoke escaped the back, and filled the sky with black smoke.

With her left foot outside the car, the sounds of a car coming pulled her leg back inside. Closing the door, she peered through the side-view mirror, spotting a car driving down the street.

Slouching in the driver's seat, she watched a Chevy Impala with tinted windows cruise by. Ramona glared as hard as she could through

Aja LaGrand Blount

the tinted windows trying to identify the driver but couldn't. Sitting up, she turned the engine over, and pulled off after the Impala was out of sight.

By that time, the flames were visibly roaring throughout the Chapmans' house, lighting up the night's sky.

Ramona was upset about that. She watched the flames spread in the rearview mirror. *I would have loved to get my hands on you Birdie, but someone beat me to the punch.* She hurried down the street. *I guess better luck next time. Tootles!*

Chapter Ten

WINTER STARED AT HERSELF in the bathroom mirror. The person she seen wasn't the person she normally saw. What stared back at her was a tired and worn out young lady who desperately needed to get her life in order. The unexpected death of a man she never knew weighed heavily on her mind, body and soul. She couldn't understand how that could be but it was.

Throughout her life she'd yearned for the fatherly love she seen so many others getting. Whenever she seen it, her soul cried out for that kind of love. Day in, day out, her heart bleed itself dry seeking an ounce of what she lacked. Yet, it was a love she would never get the opportunity to experience. All she had in the form of a protector was DP. Even still, she lacked the overall love and protection associated with what a little girl should get from a loving and devoted father.

Seriously thinking about it, the reality of the situation hit her hard. Who was she fooling? Travis Malcolm Robertson, her biological father, was a cold-blooded killer/drug dealer/pimp, and the woman who birthed her was his bottom bitch. He wasn't a good man. He was a monster who kept her mother strung up and strung out so he had absolute control over her. Being on that kind of chained leash kept her mother under his foot and compliant to his desires.

That truth was so clearly for her to see as easily as she could see the stressful lines on her face.

Her father was a beast. With him around, she wouldn't have obtained anything she would have hoped for. She would have had a bitter childhood; a crazy and unpredictable adolescent upbringing, and she possibly could have grown up to be an angry young lady. That's not what she wanted.

Nevertheless, there was that burning desire in her gut to avenge her father's death if possible. Deep down, she felt obligated to do that. For whatever reason, she assumed that would bridge the gap between them, forever bonding them as one. She wasn't sure if that would be true but it would have to be. She needed to solidify that bond, making it tangible even if it only provided her with a semi-completeness.

She leaned forward to wash her face, caressing the soap upon her skin. Splashing the warm water on her skin, she rinsed off the soap. Drenching her face again, she made it a point to cleanse her skin of all the soap. Reaching for a towel, she raised up to dry her face.

Opening her eyes, she looked in the mirror and what appeared startled her. The unfamiliar face staring back at her trembled her nerves. It was a face she hadn't seen before; yet, she figured she should have. There was a striking resemblance to herself and if she wouldn't have known, she would have thought it was her. However, the person staring back at her wasn't her. It couldn't be. She wouldn't believe it was her. In fact, if anyone who knew her could see what she saw and look directly into the person's eyes as she did, they would mistake the person for her themselves.

After looking at the image for so long, Winter began to assume it was her herself as well. The sight truly scared her more than it should. She couldn't understand the meaning behind this disclosure. Looking off, she wasn't sure if she wanted to understand it. Then something Det. Chapman said sprouted from the dirt of her mind. The name Ramona and a resemblance to her stood out. Looking in the mirror, Winter wasn't sure if he saw that much resemblance. But it could possible.

I have to reach out to him to find out who he saw, she said, hoping he could give her some insight about who he referred to.

She rolled the towel down her face, wanting to hurry up. At the same time, she was afraid to open her eyes. Who knew what she would see. She simply wanted to wipe away the previous image and everything associated with it. Her life had already begun to spiral out of control. She didn't need any additional burdens added to her shoulders. The stress of her everyday life was becoming too heavy as it was. Everything seemed to be overwhelming her. She couldn't discern if she could handle it all by herself. Trying to cope with the sudden changes was making them hard to deal with alone.

Recently, Winter's support system had faltered to the point of no participation from her loved ones and that bothered her. DP was acting very strange and had become quite distant. That was a first. It had become extremely noticeable over the past couple of weeks, immediately following her father's death. She wouldn't have realistically expected Sara to step up to the plate and be much help, considering she was the one who had kept so many from her in the first place. As the truth neared the light, Sara opted to stay as far away from the exposure as she could. She played the revelations as if it was a plague, and due to her fear of the repercussions, she stayed a fairly good distance away.

That brought her back to DP and how she noticed him running the streets more heavily lately.

Technically, he was out of the game. That didn't stop the kickbacks he received from those he put on. That's not what consumed her mind. It was his new attitude that displayed a different side of him. She wanted to contribute it to the recent death of his friend. Nonetheless, she felt as if she didn't know him anymore.

The person she thought would be there for her hadn't been anywhere in sight. She distinctively remembered him insisting he would be there for her during her time of need. Hence, in reality, she seen that had been a lie.

She made a mental note to sit him down soon to find out what his deal was. With him in the streets so much, maybe he had some pertinent information about her father's death. With how the streets talked, she suspected he knew something. Something had to have been said that could be useless to her plight. The only other question was if he would tell her what he knew.

Winter felt a dying need to hurry up. Drying her face and opening her eyes, she was met with another startling image. One she never seen before.

Blinking twice, she sought to eliminate the image. Instead, it felt like she was floating among the clouds. She could see her bathroom growing smaller and smaller as she traveled into what mimicked another galaxy. It was as if she was having an out of body experience.

Floating upward, Winter glided towards the woman in the mirror. The slow advance to the woman brought Winter a stored away knowledge of who the person was. Within a split second, she was face-to-face with her mother for the very first time in her adult life. The interaction was everything she had craved as a kid. To stand before her mother now gave her the love she needed to fill her love cup for another ten years. Overall, the experience provided both with an opportunity to exchange their truths. In the end, her mother handed Winter some valuable jewels to soak up. And upon taking them in, she apprehended that those life lessons could point her in the right direction if she paid attention to the signs.

Winter's soul burned from the time spent with her mother. *Seek and you shall find,* her mother recited, while placing her hand on her shoulder. That brief contact hardened Winter's heart. Inhaling deeply, an internal truth was placed within her. It would be a truth that could only be unlocked with time and the asking of the right questions.

Winter haphazardly snapped out of the trance-like state just as quickly as she was swept into it. Scratching her head, she attempted to make sense of it. Checking her surroundings, she found herself standing in her bathroom with the drying towel in her hand. She glanced around the room, spint in a 360-degree circle, and questioned her lack of understanding. That was unlike anything she'd ever experience. The remnants of it was hard to shake off. It was mind-boggling; therefore, providing her with a headache.

I can't let this get me down, she said, wrapping up her morning ritual. Wiping at her face again, she peeked over the towel to see what would appear. Luckily, nothing out of the ordinary revealed itself.

Glad about that, she folded the towel and placed it on the counter. She quickly glancing at herself one last time. Unsure of how to perceive the experience, she elected to let it go, at least, until she had time to sit down and think about it later. Because in that moment, it would be hard to level out the known with the unknown.

* * * * *   * * * * *

"Breaking NEWS! I'm Arlene Jackson coming live from the scene of a still smoldering blaze that may have possibly involve one of

Madison Police Department finest head detectives and his family." She gripped the microphone tighter. "At this point, the firefighters are seeking to figure out what happened here. As you can see behind me, the firefighters are battling the remaining flare-ups and seem to have everything under control."

A team of firefighters rushed behind Arlene towards to the house.

"Momentarily, the firefighters will be entering the rubble to see what can be found but based on the structural damage, it may be hard to tell what transpired here. Based on how the house appeared to be burned, the fire could have started upstairs in one of the back bedrooms. This is mere speculation at this point but this is always a possibility. We'll know more soon."

"Arlene, this is Paul in the studio. Is the fire chief on the scene right now?"

She looked around. "Yes, Paul. He is on the scene and I will be looking to speak with him here soon. The info floating around is that the decorated Madison police detective and his family may have been home when the fire started. At this time, that is also mere speculation. Once all the details are known, I'll gladly inform you of what I have. I'm Arlene Jackson reporting live for Channel 2 News."

Ramona knew they'll never find anything pointing one way or another when seeing how the house was destroyed. Unbeknownst to the public, Detective Chapman had been in the house as the flames consumed it. According to her Intel, he had gone home for the night. When she arrived, she suspected the silhouette she seen walking through the house was his.

Or could that have been the person who burned the house down? she asked herself. She seriously doubted that; but she couldn't be too sure. Anything was possible. Be that as it may, no one had heard from the outstanding detective all day. Meaning, it was more than a possibility that him and his family had been burned to a crisp in the fire. That was a sad but true revelation. One that didn't retain a lot of substance for Ramona to dwell on. What was there to dwell on? She missed her opportunity to get her hands on him so with his death, it was on to the next thing. With that, she clicked to the Adam and Eve adult channel, catching a girl-on-girl scene in full swing.

Turning up the volume, the moans permeating from the tube instantly aroused her. The women going at each other's wetness systematically heightened her arousal to the next level, and she didn't hesitate to pull her panties to the side.

Fishing out her rabbit, she clamped it down on her pearl tongue, acting as if she was participating in the pornographic scene herself. Pleasing herself as if one of the white stars was clamped down on her love button, she chewed her bottom lip and gaped her legs open even further.

The brunette inserted two fingers inside of the blonde, then added a third.

Ramona turned her vibrator on low so she could make the most of her session. As a tingle eased up her side, she let out a few moans of delight, and felt an orgasm surging through her body. Suddenly, the feeling struck her like a thunderbolt, thus producing a happy serum. Her thighs quivered from the multiple orgasms; she sucked air for oxygen, and heaved heavily from her heart stopping. Closing her eyes, she thoroughly enjoyed the way the orgasm made her body feel. The sensation caused her to run her fingertips around her areolas and down her stomach.

Shaking uncontrollably, she praised her little rabbit for the pleasure it brought her. If she could, she would clamp the toy on her clit all the time and just leave it there. It was surely a toy that left her breathless like she'd left most of her lovers.

A violent quake circulated through her love below, and a gush of juices flushed her system. She unclasped the rabbit, letting it fall to the floor. Rolling her neck, she watched the blonde ramming wildly into the brunette from the back.

I don't see the purpose for using a dildo when there's so many willing males to let a woman bounce up and down on their dicks.

Closing her legs, Ramona changed the channel, finding no further use for the adult channel. Turning back to the news, the meteorologist was running down the week's forecast. Uninterested in the weather, Ramona let her heavy eyelids close. Thoughts of another orgasm slouched her deeper into the couch.

Getting comfortable, she hugged a couch pillow, then slightly faded in and out consciousness. And before she knew it, she was fast asleep, unable to think about anything but sweet things.

Chapter Eleven

"I'M ARLENE JACKSON, coming live from the residence of Madison Police Detective Bryan Chapman in Edwardsville, and I'm here with Fire Chief Stanley Nelson." She turned to face the Chief. "Chief Nelson, what is it, if anything, can you tell us about this blaze?"

The Chief glared down at the shorter reporter. "It appears to be an act of arson. We initially thought it could have been an accident but after further investigation, it has been ruled a fire intentionally set to destroy any potential evidence of a crime. At this time, I can tell you that there were some bodies found. Once the medical examiner conducts her investigation, we will be able to determine whether or not it was the detective and his family," the Chief explained.

"Thank you, Chief Nelson. Please keep us informed." Arlene faced the camera. "I'm Arlene Jackson. Back to you in the studio, Paul."

DP muted the t.v., knowing there wouldn't be any evidence for them to find. If there was, it couldn't be traced back to him, or anyone else for that matter. The detective's case would simply remain another unsolved homicide for the cold case files. That still wouldn't stop the police from hitting the streets hard to bring a heightened level of heat to the streets. That would be unfortunate when comprehending someone most likely getting the short end of the stick because of him.

In a way, he felt bad; however, life goes on and people did to. He couldn't concern himself with that. His goal revolved around continuing doing what he done best, and that was living his life outside the sight of law enforcement and the haters. And due to the good detective meeting his maker, he figured a nice vacation sounded nice.

That'll be right on time. I need to make that happen.

A thought of Winter accompanying him crossed his mind. He couldn't apprehend where it came from. With how things were between them, it would take some serious encouragement on his part to get her to go. An eerie tension had been introduced, and it was pushing them further apart.

A stickler for details, DP had the luxury of noticing, and he wondered if she'd noticed as well. From his standpoint, he hadn't intentionally pushed her away. It had to be unconsciously considering the nature of the kill. *Never in a million years would I have imagined my hustle to affect her.* But it did, and that connotation made it impossible for him to be there how she needed him to be.

No matter how hard he tried, he couldn't see that working when he was the cause of her pain. Besides, he had his own pain to deal with, and with his selfishness, his priorities came first. In the dog-eat-dog world they lived in, certain things weren't meant to go everyone's way. Unfortunately, everyone had to play with the cards they had been dealt.

A master manipulator, DP was smart enough to take his hand and turn it into a winning one. It was either that or succumb to the pitfalls of life. In any event, it was still hard to see her fret over a man she never knew, even to the point of wanting to avenge his death. That was a shocker in itself.

Revenge, he uttered, faking a chuckle. *That's funny,* he voiced.

His laughter subsided as he faced the reality of how he truly felt about her. It was obvious he didn't care too much about her, definitely when it came down to what he'd done. On the flip side, as a normal, blood-bearing human being, he loved her with all his heart. They'd shared a lifetime of memories and no matter how cold-hearted he wanted to be, he couldn't forget what they've had or been through.

Whereas, Winter's ambitious approach towards finding her father's killer would eventually put him in a position to toss that love out the window. *But she won't find out it was me any time soon,* he surmised. *And if she does, she wouldn't believe it, if I was the one to tell her,* he figured, hoping he was right.

Shaking his head, his thinking of her finding out about his other life would completely sever everything they had, and be her quickest route to the graveyard. He couldn't discern her reaction but he knew coming after him wouldn't be in her best interest. Regardless of her being the love of his life, he wouldn't play with her.

As long as she stays out my way, I'm destined to go to my grave with all my secrets intact. Then something inside of him brought a startling revelation with it. *Even in death, there wouldn't be enough dirt to cover up all I've done.* That worried DP momentarily.

Subsequently moving on, he seen a need to do something constructive with his time. He thought of his future. School was over and his relationship with Winter was looking bleak. He couldn't deny how he felt about her; however, his future with her may become unbearable to withstand. There would never be a sigh of regret on his part. Yet, a strain could easily arise if the situation didn't blow over fast.

But he knew her, and in knowing her, he knew how persistent she could be when seeking any and everything she wanted. With her mind made up, she wouldn't stop short of her objective. That would push her to obtain the answers she desired; while, at the same time, push him farther away from her.

He rubbed his temples as the new lead detective handling the Detective Chapman's case spoke with Arlene Jackson. He turned up the volume to listen in.

Detective Alonzo Smith informed the public of the three homicide victims, along with the suffocation and burning of a fourth. The detective never specified who suffered from what. He only identified the bodies found as Det. Bryan Chapman and his family.

"This was truly a sad day in the police community," Arlene voiced.

But, who could have cared less was DP. He simply smiled, busted down a cigarillo, and filled it with weed. It was time to relax his tense mental state, and what better way to do that than to blow some good blueberry dro.

＊＊＊＊＊　　＊＊＊＊＊

"Hey Cutie Pie! Let me holla at you for a minute. Where might you be going and can I come?" the attractive female asked Ramona as she winked, blew a kiss and licked her lips. Her enticing look said, *let me taste that sweet plum between your legs.*

Ramona stared at the chick shooting her shot. *This bitch is bold as fuck! What makes her think she can come at me like I'm some pussy eating ass bitch or something'* Ramona thought. *What is this world coming to?*

Instead of spazzing out, Ramona chose to entertain the attention. She'd always been strictly dicky; but, heard a woman could get down on a kitty-kat better than any man. The way Ramona heard it, the feeling was like none other. *What's the problem with seeing it was true, especially since the opportunity presented itself?* she questioned.

"Baby doll, I'm going wherever you're going. What you have in mind?" Ramona asked, trying to gauge the chick's mind state.

"Honey, I have so much in mind and when I'm done, I'm gonna make you mines. Just wait and see!" A stupid grin covered the lesbian's face.

Ramona chuckled at the lesbian's confidence, seriously doubting any chick who sucked pussy as a sexual preference could turn her out. That thought alone sent Ramona back to the scene of the white girl slamming the dildo into the other girl. She couldn't see herself going out like that. *I love the real thing too much to be confined to a plastic strap-on and a female tongue.* However, she had to let the lesbian tell her story. *If she knew what's really gonna happen to her, she wouldn't be so fucking jolly.*

Ramona ran her tongue inside her lower lip. "Please let me see what you're working with, boo. If you lead, I shall follow," she stated, willing to give the experience a try.

The lesbian was extremely excited. Jumping in her ride, she put it in drive before starting it. Signaling for Ramona to follow, she turned the engine over then pulled off once Ramona got in her car.

After a few lefts and rights, Ramona pulled in next to the chick at a Holiday Inn. Ramona grabbed her bag from her trunk, and proceeded to the room the chick obviously already had. A thought floated through Ramona's head. *'This bitch gots to be on some real freak time. There bet not be any hidden cameras or any of her homies jumping out of the closet and shit.*

The lesbian eyed Ramona, sensing her vibe once they were inside the room.

"I know you're tripping off the set-up but it was originally for my longtime girlfriend. Her birthday is today but we broke up this morning. Actually, I caught her cheating on me so I had to end it. I wanted to give her something nice for her birthday but she was already taking it up her ass and down her throat when I came home from work," she explained, looking at the rose petals, the bucket of champagne, and listening to the slow jams softly escaping the speakers. "So now, here it is, I'm taking MY talents on the road."

Ramona wasn't fazed a bit. Her interests merely surrounded getting licked so she could move on with the rest of her day. The lesbian, seeing Ramona's lack of interest, strolled over to take off her shirt. As Ramona watched the lesbian saunter over, she casually admired the woman's beauty.

The lesbian stood at approximately 5'5" and maybe weighed 130 pounds. With the shirt off, her perky titties stood upright in the tight sports bra, and her pointy nipples poked through the fabric pointing at Ramona. When dropping her pants, a fatten mound protruded outwardly, grabbing a piece of the boy shorts. The camel toe itself provided a mouthwatering appearance that would break down the barrier of anyone eyeing it.

The lesbian twirled around to show off all her assets.

Her deep evenly tone chestnut brown complexion caught Ramona's attention. After examining her from head to toe, it was the long, dark black hair that fell to the cusp of her behind that accentuated the lesbian's beauty.

Ramona chewed her top lip, taking a peek at the chick's rear. It was one of those round, plump behinds that required a person to use both hands to hold onto. She licked her lips, and craved for the lesbian to come towards her.

A mere foot away from one another, they locked eyes. The energy between them rose significantly. It radiated off the both of them.

The lesbian ran her tongue over her full set of glossy lips, making Ramona's love below jump with anticipation. She couldn't recall a time when she reacted that way when looking at a woman. But in this moment, the lesbian had her wide open and she hadn't even touched her yet.

The chick laid her hands on Ramona's waist, stepped into her personal space, and reached for her shirt. Pulling it over her head, the shirt flew across the room. When Ramona's arms fell to her sides, the chick stepped closer so she could plant soft, wet kisses on her shoulder. She strategically went from one location to another.

The lesbian made her way down to Ramona's breasts, unclasped her bra, and used her fingertips to lightly touch both arms as she removed the bra. The touch had an erotic feel it, causing Ramona to shut her eyes.

The lesbian dropped Ramona's bra and found herself staring at her firm 36C's. The gawking vividly displayed the hunger in her eyes. Cradling them, she nibbled on them both, and left a trail of kisses down Ramona's stomach.

Stopping to unbutton Ramona's pants, she inhaled the aroma of Ramona's warm juices before uncovering a cleanly shaven plum ripe and ready for action. The removal of Ramona's panties was such a delight. An increased state of anxiety overflowed the lesbian's love next by her being so anxious to taste Ramona's creamy filling.

As Ramona stepped out of her pants and panties, the lesbian pushed her on the bed where Ramona submissively spread her legs. To the lesbian's surprise, Ramona revealed a dripping-wet juice box in need of a good licking. She wasted no time crawling in-between Ramona's legs, kissing her way up Ramona's inner thigh. Continuing that route, she clamped onto Ramona's meaty vaginal lips with her glossy lips, spreading them apart with her tongue. Letting her tongue dance at the opening, she moved up and lightly sucked on the little pea in a boat. The light sucking and nibbling sent Ramona into a heavenly whirlwind.

Ramona firmly grabbed the side of the girl's head, smearing her sea of love around the girl's face. She had to admit, *No man on earth had ever touched my soul in such manner.*

The wet face didn't deter the lesbian from remaining diligent. She went full speed ahead when attacking Ramona's love button. Inserting one finger after another, Ramona's juiciness left her lover's fingers soaked, sticky and flaming hot.

The look of ecstasy written across Ramona's face motivated the chick to turn it up a notch. Inserting her middle finger, she motioned for Ramona to *come here*. Happily obliging, Ramona arched her back and feeding the lesbian more than she could handle. The lesbian flicked her middle finger once again. The tip of her nail nicked Ramona's G-spot, thus driving her insane. Another light rubbing of that spot propelled Ramona to release a floodgate of juices inside the chick's mouth.

Erupting steadily, Ramona gripped the sheets, unable to utter one word. Her syrupy moans cried out to the pleasure Gods, and her body convulsed. Her hands locked up, and her toes curled. Taking a deep breath, she squirted out the remainder of her orgasm.

The lesbian maintained her position, and remained focused on doing her job. Aware of Ramona's multiple orgasms, that wouldn't stop her from pulling out all stops. Sliding off the bed to retrieve her bag of toys, she exhibited a devilish glare in her eyes. She unzipped the bag, wondering what would do the trick.

Ramona sensed the lesbian's plans. She slid off the bed to stop her. "Baby, you've done so much for me already. Let me do something special for you." She cocked her head to the side. "It'll be my pleasure." She spotted a strap-on dildo in the bag and she grabbed it. She examined the chick's toys. *This bitch means business.*

Ramona's knees got weak, reflecting on how the lesbian had her feeling. Fighting the pleasure, she needed to get eliminate the feeling altogether. Her willingness to think lightly of what the lesbian said had changed. If she hadn't stopped the chick while she was ahead, she would have ended up loving the way the experience made her feel. She had to turn the tables.

"I'm a need you to assume the position, bitch!" Ramona snapped, taking control of the situation.

The lesbian loved being talked to like that. That kind of talk elevated her excitement to a whole new level and she happily climbed atop of the bed, assuming the doggy-style position. Overwhelmed with joy, she was clueless to Ramona sliding across the room to retrieve her silenced Sig Sauer .22 LR handgun.

Returning to the bed, Ramona positioned herself behind the lesbian, and observed the freak playing in her own wet box. The lesbian moved her fingers in, out and around her wetness. Ramona enjoyed how the lesbian glossed the piercing stud hanging from her pearl tongue. *I have to admit this is truly an inviting sight.* Nevertheless, she had seen enough. She smacked the lesbian on the backside with the dildo, instructing her to roll over.

The lesbian eagerly complied. Once on her back, her enthusiasm rose from ten to fifty as she thought of how good it would feel to have Ramona's tongue slithering in, out and around her juice box. Yet, she reluctantly failed to recognize the burner pointed at her face.

Ramona went across the chick's face with the gun, literally smacking the spark of excitement across the room.

The lesbian was in utter shock, finding it had to identify with the steel connecting to her cheek. She lacked the understanding of why Ramona would be striking her in the first place. She'd done all she could to make her fall in-love. Why her efforts would be repaid so violently. The incident left her flabbergasted.

The lesbian sought to wrap her head around the circumstance. By the time she finally realized what had occurred, Ramona was pulling the trigger. *This one dumb bitch!* she exclaimed, climbing off the bed. *But one that was good at what she did.*

Putting the Sig up, Ramona dressed, and gathered her things. Taking a good look at the lesbian sprawled on the bed, she couldn't leave without cleaning up her mess. Retrieving a clear glass jar from her bag, she unscrewed the top, and let a few of her little friends out to clean up her dirty work.

Screwing the top on the jar, she nodded as the flesh quickly disappeared. *Now, that's how you clean up after yourself.*

Chapter Twelve

THE TENSION IN THE room was thick as Detective Alonzo Smith, a ten-year veteran, stood at the podium sharing his thoughts and feelings with those before him.

"The death of our fellow policeman will not go unnoticed, fellas. I can promise you that! We're gonna turn up the heat in the streets until we find out who is responsible for this heinous act." He pointed towards the window. "Those bastards need to know that we need answers and they'll be handing them over. Every last one of them!" His voice echoed loudly around the room before he continued.

"Moving forward, there will be many late nights and maybe some overtime for those who want it. But it has to be worth it. We have to make those responsible pay, if it's the last thing we do. But before I wrap this up, does anyone know what Chapman was working on?" he asked, wanting to get back on track to carry on the good work Chapman had his hand in.

"I'm not sure, sir," Detective Rico Hawkins said, raising his hand to be acknowledged. "I believe his focus surrounded the Travis Malcolm Robertson's case. With the murder of Mr. Robertson, he pulled his file and went to work on all available parties associated with him. He really wanted to be the one to solve that murder."

Smith hung his head. "I just hope that investigation wasn't what got him killed." He eyed Hawkins. "If you don't mind, meet me after this. I would like to speak with you about some things. If there isn't anything else, that'll be all for now," he declared, dismissing everyone except Hawkins.

With that, everyone went their respective ways, glad to end the depressing meeting. Hawkins, clambering from his seat, listened to the grumbling as he approached Smith.

Smith stepped around the podium, dismissing the whispers. "First thing I need to know is: who is Travis Malcolm Robertson? I've heard the name but can't say I'm abreast of his case."

Hawkins half-sat on the table next to the podium. "Mr. Robertson was a known hit man/drug dealer. He ran with a vicious crew of guys, who were just as dangerous as he was. They ran these very streets with an iron fist. From what I understand, things supposedly went bad between Mr. Robertson and a Darius Price Sr some years back. Chapman did a little digging and found that Darius has a son who still lives in the area. Chapman began focusing on him to see what he could come up with." He lowered his voice. "Didn't too many know this except me, but he tried making an undercover buy from Darius Jr without any luck. On the day of his death, he made a comment before heading home that it was back to the drawing board."

"Back to the drawing board for what?" Smith asked.

"He initially believed Darius Jr may have inherited his father's drug dealing operation because that had been the word on the street. Upon further investigation, that didn't seem to be the case, especially after he tried making the sale with no luck. I don't know what other angles he had on the table but my gut tells me that Darius could have been the trigger man for Robertson," Hawkins stated, inserting some of his own personal beliefs.

"Why would you think that?"

"Because of the situation between Robertson and Price was supposedly over Robertson killing Price. From what I understand, Price's body was never found. And it was speculated that Robertson killed his girl too - for reasons unknown to us - but for reasons that surrounded Price," Hawkins elaborated.

Smith pondered his next question. "Are you thinking Darius Jr could have killed Chapman as well?"

Hawkins bobbed his head. "That's always a possibility! It's one that we have to focus on," he said, believing it before he said it. "I believe Darius Jr took Robertson out then took Chapman out because he figured if the detective wasn't in the picture, he wouldn't have to worry about the investigation."

"Is all this in a file somewhere?" Smith asked, interesting in seeing the Intel firsthand.

Hawkins rose from the table. "Sir, there's so much in those files, this is nowhere near the half of it. But mostly everything in them is mere speculation. Nothing was or is solid evidence. There was just a lot of people coming forth with information but nothing was sticking."

Smith waved Hawkins with him. "Then let's go see what we can make stick!"

* * * * *   * * * * *

Winter had a strange feeling that she may have been the cause of Detective Chapman and his family's demise. That would be a heavy burden to shoulder. She knew that. But as she thought about it, the nagging feeling regarding her meeting with him being the deciding factor unnerved her. She sincerely hoped that wasn't true; whereas, she couldn't be sure. Still, that's how she felt.

Sitting on the edge of the bed, she replayed the entire scene from that day in her mind. There had to be something there that could help her. Slowing her mind, she viewed the entire situation over again, frame by frame. All that stood out was the black Camaro that quickly sped off.

She scrunched her face, wondering if DP had followed her or had someone following her. She couldn't understand why he would do that. But she also couldn't rule it out. Anything was possible according to how she felt. And his actions hadn't made her feel any better. He had been acting stranger than ever recently.

But what reason would he have to follow me?

Whatever the reason could be, she knew something wasn't right. Something weird was going on and it concerned her. She could feel it. As the feeling intensified, she thought back to her out of body experience.

Seek and you shall find!

Those were her mother's words. The same words she repeated over and over again in an attempt to drill them into her psyche. That hadn't been for nothing. They were given as the first lesson ripped out of the brand-new text book and personally handed to her.

Winter looked around for a place to start, choosing the closet closest to her. Throwing the contents on the bedroom floor, she searched and searched for anything that would jar an answer. She came up empty. Everything appeared to be in order as it usually was. Even still, that gnawing feeling had embedded itself within her heart, resisting to remove itself.

I'm missing something, she recited, looking around for anything out of the ordinary.

Not wanting to rack her brain too much, she decided to let it go when unable to find anything. She didn't have the valuable time to waste looking for something that would come to her sooner or later. Worrying about it would ultimately keep what should come to her away. Thinking in those terms, the best thing to do would be to allow whatever she should attract to come as it may.

In the meantime, she ran herself a hot bubble bath, undressed and slid in. The hot water quickly consumed her and before she knew it, she drifted off to sleep. Seconds later, flashes of colorful images played on her mental screen. The images felt so real, they could be felt traveling throughout her entire body as if the events were taking place at that very moment.

In front of her, dead bodies were laid out on the ground. At least, based on her position, they appeared to be dead. The closest one to her laid faced down, while another sat slumped against a wall. She couldn't get a glimpse of the faces; yet, she felt a familiarity to the both of them.

Images of a third body presented itself, and unraveled the binding of her mind. She knew who the person was but wouldn't be afforded the chance to actually see the person's face.

She awoke from the dream, startled, forgetting she'd been in the bathtub. After splashing water everywhere, she regained her composure, hoping to replay the images she'd seen. Focusing, she continuously attempted to recapture the images. However, they wouldn't return to her. Closing her eyes, she sought to recreate the atmosphere that originally brought the images to her. She refused to give up, suspecting the answers to her questions resided within what she hadn't seen. Nothing she tried seemed to work.

Giving up, she opened her eyes, figuring she was trying too hard. Pulling the bathtub plug, she stood and reached for a towel.

Drying her face, she couldn't shake the flashes of the images. Standing there with the towel over her face, she tightened her eyelids, hoping to see a glimpse of what she saw. That attempt failed her. Unable to get the desired results, she dried her feet then stepped out of the tub.

Toweling off, she proceeded to slide her panties on. Her phone started to ring in the bedroom. Hopping on one foot, she tried to hurry with her underwear. The phone rang faster and faster. The more it rang, the louder it appeared to get. If she didn't hurry up, it would stop ringing and go to the voicemail. She could always call whomever back, but, it could be extremely important and she didn't want to miss the call.

Getting her panties on, she held her breast and raced to the phone. Beads of water dripped down her neck towards the middle of her back. Snatching the phone off the dresser, she simply answered it before it went to voicemail.

Breathing hard, she said, "Hello!"

"Why you breathing so hard?" Sara asked.

Winter rolled her eyes when hearing her auntie's voice. "I just got out the tub when the phone rang. I thought it was the detective calling with a new development. What's UP?" she asked, upset it was her auntie and not someone who wanted something.

"I'm just calling to check up on you. You know, make sure you alright," Sara informed, knowing she had another reason for calling.

"Thanks, but I'm cool." She put her free hand on her hip. "The hard part is over. Where were you when I really needed you?" she asked, remembering she was nowhere to be found. She looked at herself in the dresser mirror.

"I thought it would have been best to give you your space," Sara replied, actually believing that had been the best thing to do.

Winter found that funny. "You surely gave me my space alright." Then she switched topics. "Well, I have things to do. I'm standing here naked so let me get dressed and on with my day," she insisted, eager to get off the phone.

"I know you may be mad at me but I really need you to come by sometime today. I have something you need to see."

Winter bounced her leg. "I'm not too eager to see anything else you have for me. I'm all surprised out. Don't you think you've surprised me with enough?" she asked, curious to what else Sara had to show her.

"Don't be like that, Winter. You're sure to like this one. I promise!" She put some excitement in her voice.

"Yeah, right!" Winter exclaimed. "But I'll try to get over there sometime today. That's, if I can."

Sara smiled faintly. "Let me know before you come so I can make sure to be home, ok?"

"Alright. Bye!"

* * * * *   * * * * *

Ending the call, Sara looked into the face of the surprise she had for Winter. She knew springing this person on her could cause more issues. Many more. Then again, it couldn't be any worse than what had already happened.

"So, what did she say?"

"She said she'll try to get over here sometime today. If, she can," Sara answered, thinking of what Winter would do if she did come over that day or any other day. The person she wanted to introduce her to would truly blow her mind. She wasn't certain if Winter was ready for all that.

"How do you think she'll react to me?"

"She's probably gonna flip the fuck out," Sara replied, convinced she would do exactly that when she showed up and seen the person.

"You think so? I know I would be ecstatic to meet my twin sister after all these years," Ramona said, curious to how she would handle the situation if the tables were reversed.

"Well, she's not you. She's liable to snap, crackle, and pop."

"Let's hope all goes well then," Ramona said, figuring Sara was overreacting.

When thinking about it, she assumed Winter would be more upset with Sara than with her. That wouldn't have anything to do with her. It hadn't been their fault no one brought them together prior to now. Plus, that was neither here nor there.

What mattered was that they would finally meeting one another after all that time. Sadly, things could have remained the same, and they could still be living their lives separately, without having any knowledge of the other. That's not how she wanted it moving forward. It was time for them to see what the future would hold for the both of them, together as sisters. Twin sisters at that!

Chapter Thirteen

"LONG TIME SINCE I heard from you. What's really good, old man?" DP asked the contact, wondering why he hadn't called and given him a job lately.

The contact got straight to the point. "We need to talk!" he said, with a firm and demanding tone. There was no need to waste time. DP needed to know what was on his mind.

DP sensed the tone, realizing something was seriously wrong. It had to be. "Where?" he asked, getting straight to it.

"I'm coming to you. "Where you at?"

That was an odd request. One that triggered a thought. *What's on his mind that he wants to come to me?* Contemplating the request put him on edge. A thousand different thoughts ran through his head.

The contact insisted upon an answer.

DP caved in, reluctantly agreed to the meeting, and gave the contact his location. Sitting back, he didn't know how to feel about the contact's aggressive tone. That was a first. And the contact wanting to meet him like that concerned him.

For safety precautions, DP locked and loaded all available pieces just in case the contact had other plans. In this business, there could always be other plans, especially the ones that involved an elimination for whatever reason. He refused go out like that. He would stay on his guard and properly prepare himself for this unusual meeting. Surveying the immediate area, he utilized the surveillance cameras located in the front and back of the house.

The contact pulled into the driveway, parking a Hyundai Genesis behind DP's Tahoe. The contact appeared to be alone.

A chameleon himself, DP knew how appearances could be deceiving. Real killers moved in silence and was invisible to the naked eye. That's how the unaware targets became easy prey because they hadn't observed any outright or immediate threats. DP was too smart to fall prey to that ploy.

The contact rang the doorbell, then tried the door knob.

What is he trying to door for? DP questioned, instantly thinking the meeting was a set-up. He weighed his options. With the contact's actions raising one red flag after another, it seemed as if he was manning some sort of sneak attack. He figured he needed to get better control of the situation by directing the contact to the back door.

He called the contact. "The back door is open, old man. I rarely use the front with the nosy neighbors around here," he explained, taking a seat at the kitchen table by the back door. "And the back door is unlocked so you can come right in," he said as a way of being funny.

Now with the element of surprise, DP sat with his Sig .40 trained on the back door. He wasn't taking any chances. Any unnecessary movements and he would start shooting. NO questions asked. And that surrounded putting holes in nothing but the forehead. He was well aware of how this worked. Any good relationship, whether business or personal, could end just as quickly as it began when the rabbit had the gun. He understood as long as he had the gun, he would be the first to end the relationship, not allowing it to be the other way around.

DP was aware of what and who the contact was. As a negotiator for murder, he outsourced jobs to killers to eliminate the trash. It was prudent to automatically assume he was capable of pulling a trigger or two himself. Yet, the one thing he wouldn't permit was letting the contact bust his guns at him.

The contact remained outside the door, fearing an ambush. Playing it smart, he wouldn't be foolish enough to step into a set-up. He knew better than that. Instead, he kicked the door open with his foot, remained still, and held his arms in the air. Not intent on making any sudden movements, his body language gave off the impression that he came in peace. He was well aware of the game and knew DP was very much aware of it himself. He'd been living the life for way too long not to.

DP was a natural at putting in work. It ran through his veins. He'd been born to end the lives of others. Many would say it was his calling. The contact simply didn't want DP to be the one to call his number.

"Youngblood, I come in peace. Please put your guns down," he requested, eyeing the .40, and aware of others being nearby.

"YOU have to understand, old man. This is an unusual occurrence," DP recited, still not sure what the contact wanted. "What's good?" he asked, aiming the gun at the contact's leg. "What calls for us to meet like this?"

The contact crossed the threshold, closed the door behind him, and then pointed in DP's direction. "YOU!" he exclaimed.

"ME!?!" DP yelled, unable to believe what he was hearing.

"Yeah, you and your extracurricular activities," the contact pointed out.

DP frowned. "What extracurricular activities?" he asked, not comprehending where the contact was going.

"The slaying of Detective Bryan Chapman a.k.a 'Birdie' and his family," the contact recounted, verbalizing exactly what he meant by what he said.

DP clenched his teeth, flashing a *You can't be serious!* look. "I don't know what you're talking about," he asserted nonchalantly, setting the gun on the table.

The contact pulled out the chair across from DP. "Youngblood, you're very much aware of what I'm talking about. I'm quite familiar with your work. You have to remember our work history," the contact countered, directly eyeing DP.

DP chuckled, displaying a look of disbelief.

"This is no laughing matter. I have friends in high places who want answers. They're beginning to worry about your mindset."

"MY mindset!" DP screamed, snatching the Sig off the table. "YOU can't be fucking serious. NO ONE needs to be worried about my mindset. I'm GOOD!" he explained, aiming the gun at the contact.

The contact read DP's body language, and seen he was getting agitated. He need to diffuse the situation immediately. An angry DP wielding a gun was never a good combination.

"Youngblood, no one I personally deal with have any idea of who you are. I'm very discrete with the way I handle them and the info I feed them. However, when you go and eliminate someone's family, a police officer's family at that, you bring a lot of unwanted attention and questions are being asked. They have no idea it was you but I'm being questioned about whether or not it's someone I use," the contact explained.

DP laid the gun on the table, angling it at the contact. "You don't know shit so it's best to keep it that way. To assume is to make an ass of yourself. You can continue to do that for all I care, just don't come at me with this bullshit," he instructed with absolute sincerity.

"Youngblood, that wasn't the way to eliminate that kind of threat," the contact spat, getting irritated when playing DP's little mind game.

"Damn if it wasn't!" DP snapped, unable to catch the words before they escaped his mouth. "Who you think you're fooling?"

"It could have been handled differently. That's all I'm saying. There's an open investigation against you."

"Don't you think I know that?" DP asked, hoping to give the contact a reason to see why he did what he did.

"Didn't you think that'll bring too much unnecessary heat on you?" the contact asked, looking to get his point through DP's head.

"They have to know something to do something, right?" DP questioned, looking in the contact's eyes asking, "What have you told your friends in those high places?"

The contact reluctantly broke down what he knew about the investigation. "It was known by those pulling the strings that Chapman was on a wild good chase with his theories and assumptions. Everyone, but him, knows you're not a drug dealer anymore. The detective was grasping for anything to build a case. Everything he had was old news. It was all set up by those behind the scenes to give off that impression for that particular reason. You knew and we know that the drug game is washed up. The rules had changed. Everyone is telling and there's no loyalty or honor among thieves." The contact examined DP's countenance. "What Chapman didn't know was that crossing that line, and getting on your radar, would end his life and his family's too."

"I bet he didn't draft that in his notes but let me ask you a question: where you fit in with all of this?" DP asked, intent on finding out what the contact knew and what he would let slip.

"I'm trying to stay afloat, youngblood. It's all about getting in and out like you did."

"Apparently, I haven't gotten out just yet with the game still wanting a piece of me."

The contact had to agree with that. The game did *still* want a piece of DP. It didn't like when someone could get so deeply involved in the life then find a way to escape the pitfalls by getting out. DP was one of the few to pull it off by excommunicating himself from the drug game intact and with his life.

By getting out clean, DP's extraction revolved around integrating himself into the irrational sense of a normal society. Whereas, his father's weathered past continued to put the spotlight on him. It didn't matter that it was a dimly lit light. At the end of the day, it was a light that still shun upon him.

For the longest time, DP's low-key nature kept him under the radar. A person could look, searching with a magnifying glass and a flashlight, and still come up empty. That's how he liked it. But for those simple things to change frustrated him. Since a child, he had a good head on his shoulder which opened many doors for him. Refusing to short-stop, he jumped at each opportunity, taking advantaging of what life threw at him, even if it brought out another side of him.

Mulling over the contact's explanation, DP noticed a few issues with it. His story had too many holes to count. As DP sat there, his fingertips tingled and his neck stiffened. When falling into that deep absence of self, it was hard for him to come back without someone losing their life.

Committing murder was easy for DP. It was something he was good at. Something he enjoyed. Every kill brought about a different thrill that produced its own euphoria. When that close to the edge, his adrenaline strengthened his desire to expound on his thirst for action. Unfortunately, the cause associated with that intense feeling catapulted an effect that would have devastating effects.

Glaring sideways at the contact, DP rationalized a perfect reason for doing what he did. The detective would have put a monkey wrench in his plans had he not taken matters into his own hands. Even so, upon rethinking the content of this unusual meeting, he declared the dude in front of him had slipped and fell into the same category, and would have to join his other victims.

The contact watched DP as he talked and could plainly see the mental state he metamorphosed into. Needing to interrupt DP's thoughts, he pulled out an envelope, setting it on the table. "This is why I'm really here, youngblood," the contact claimed, pointing to the Manilla envelope. "The contents of this envelope will blow your mind. Are you aware of the recent murders where the bodies were found stripped down to the bone?"

Hearing about the manner of which the bodies were found grabbed DP's attention. "Yeah, I heard about it somewhat. I know someone who personally fell victim to whomever done it," DP answered, thinking of Ralphie.

"The contents of this envelope may lead you to that killer," the contact expressed.

DP promptly stood in an attempt to reach for the envelope.

The contact snatched it back. "What you're about to see will change your life forever," he said, doing his best to forewarn DP.

DP didn't want to hear that. He merely wanted to see the contents for himself. Gripping the envelope, he yanked it away from the contact. Ripping it open, the first picture showed a woman in a red wig and what looked to be a hooker's dress. There was a familiarity about her, as if he personally knew her or had met her somewhere. The info on the back of the picture revealed that the photo was taken off of a Motel 6 parking lot camera in Caseyville.

The contact informed DP that the man found dead arrived alone ten minutes before the woman did. Except, no camera seemed to catch her arrival. It wasn't until she left that a camera caught a glimpse of her movements.

DP flipped to the next photo, and immediately remembered where and with whom he had seen the woman with. He tried to keep his remembrance to himself but the contact spotted it unfolding through his mien.

"I know you remember the chick in that car, don't you?" he asked.

DP's look said it all as he replayed everything he could remember about the brief encounter. Within seconds, his mind went into overdrive. *Did this muthafucka send dude at me on some set-up type shit?* he wondered, attempting to make sense of it all. *What is dude's angle?* he asked himself, finalizing his decision. *Regardless, he knows entirely TOO MUCH! He has to go!!*

The decision had been made. All threats were to be eliminated, and that meant the contact would be the first to go.

"Youngblood!' the contact screamed.

DP was so far into his daze it kept him deaf to those around him. Anything short of the contact physically touching him, he wouldn't have heard anything with how his mind zeroed in on his plans.

"YOUNGBLOOD!!" the contact screamed at the top of his lungs. Getting no response, he looked into DP's eyes. What he saw made his heart skip a beat. Never would he have imagined seeing what he saw. There had been plenty of times he'd looked into DP's eyes before. Only then, what he seen there pertained to the death of another. At this moment, he received a different kind of look of death. He seen his own in the making.

Trying to play it cool, he sought to refocus DP on the pictures. If he could get him talking, that would give him a greater chance of getting out of there alive.

"Damn youngblood, you zoned out. You cool?"

The contact received no response. DP had transcended to a totally different state of mind. And the contact was well aware of what kind of state that was. It was the state of the unknown. The state of anything could happen. Being in the presence of a man with those capabilities was scary, even for the contact.

The contact, shifting in the chair, prepared for his exit. He had occupied DP's time for far too long. He'd said what needed to be said. Now, it was time for him to let DP sort through the rest on his own.

DP flipped to the next photo, then let his right hand fall to his leg. Scratching his knee cap, he slightly raised his hand to grip the tranquilizer gun mounted underneath the table. With his finger on the trigger, he pulled it and looked up at the contact as the dart struck him in the gut.

The contact, unsure of what hit him, looked down to see the colorful feather sticking out of his stomach. The mixture rapidly intermingled with his blood, and its navigation made his skin itch. The reaction was instant and seconds later, the contact's body began to numb, one section at a time.

As the deadly paralyzing mixture kicked in, the contact felt his consciousness slipping away. Blinking twice, the mixture hit the switch, slamming his face into the wooden table. The collision opened his eyes, and he stared aimlessly into space.

DP, putting the pictures down, slowly rounded the table. Looking down at the contact, he scooped up the dead weight, slung it over his shoulder and transported it downstairs to the basement. Slamming it into the old insane asylum chair, he strapped the contact down.

DP walked away, turning off the light. "I'll deal with your bum ass later."

Chapter Fourteen

DP FELT HIS PHONE vibrating. Pulling it out, he answered it, not caring who it was. His mind was somewhere else. He put the phone to his ear, and said hello.

Winter, surprised to get an answer, expected to get the voicemail as she had many times before. Hearing his voice caught her off-guard. That didn't deter her from going in.

"Darius, we need to talk!"

"Talk about what? I'm in the middle of something."

"That's exactly what we need to talk about. Your distant behavior! This is not like you, and I'm starting to have negative thoughts. We seem to be drifting apart but for reasons unknown," she confessed.

DP knew exactly why they'd begun drifting apart. She was the only one who didn't. Not really knowing what to say, he tried brushing the whole conversation to the side. "Some things are best left unsaid, Winter," he expressed, finding himself fading in and out of reality.

"What are you saying?" she inquired. "Can you just come home so we can talk?"

"I can't!" he shouted.

"What have I done?" she asked. "Why won't you talk to me?"

"Because... I'm in too deep!" he admitted, and hung up on her.

Ascending the steps, she continued to blow up his phone. He sent each call to voicemail. As soon as he had the opportunity to turn the phone off, that's what he did. He was upset with himself for answering in the first place. He didn't need the nagging thought of her being concerned with his behavior on his mind.

He stepped into the kitchen, picking up the photos off the table. *I have other things to worry about and Winter's not one of them.* He glanced at the third photo again. There was something about the chick's features that was familiar to him. It was like he knew her but based on a time he couldn't put his finger on. He had a subconscious memory of her. Memories that once had a life. A life that now faced an undetermined fate.

Could it be her? He doubted it. *But was it?* He didn't want to believe it. She couldn't be capable of concocting those kind of vicious schemes and meticulous plots. Those kinds of schemes and plots derived from a thoroughbred frame of mind. She didn't seem to have that type of schooling.

Murder? She wasn't a murderer. *Or was she?* He knew he was. *Could she be that good?* He knew he was so why couldn't she. That called into question the things done to Ralphie. That was the work of a pro. A chick with that kind of background was rare and the only known killers he knew of was...

DP flipped to the last picture. His jaw dropped to the floor, and the pictures did too. He couldn't believe his eyes. It couldn't be true. He wouldn't believe it. Flabbergasted, he couldn't believe it.

He needed answers. Answers that would explain everything down to the minute detail. This was unbelievable, and despite him might not liking the answers he received, he needed them as if his life depended on it.

Not today, but yesterday.

★ ★ ★ ★ ★   ★ ★ ★ ★ ★

Winter was in disbelief with DP hanging up on her. He never done that before. She didn't know who he was anymore. She couldn't understand what happened so fast. They had been doing so well. He'd always been the type to like his space but he never played her sideways.

Attempting to figure it out, the reality of it swiveled on the notion that she'd been left to fend for herself. That was a heart-wrenching blow. Everything they appeared to have seemed to be over and done with just like that. *This is so out of the blue.* She found it hard to rationalize it.

Because... I'm in too deep! That statement looped on repeat. *I'm in too deep!*

100

She couldn't get the phrase out of her head. What did that mean? Her womanly instincts convinced her to worry and feel concerned for him. Then her gut coerced her to let him be. He was a big boy and big boys would do what big boys do. Still, she wondered what had him so occupied. The more she questioned herself about him, the more she thought of her father.

For some strange reason, that always happened. She hadn't paid it that much attention before. It seemed as if one was synonymous with the other. She couldn't keep dismissing it.

DP's statement of being *in too deep* was leaving a nasty taste in her mouth. *Maybe he knew what happened to my father,* she reasoned. Then a thought crossed her mind that maybe DP had something to do with her father's death. She placed her hand over her chest. *I sincerely hope not.*

She frantically wanted to shake the thought. However, it simply remained at the forefront of her brain, unwilling to go anywhere. No matter how hard she tried to erase the thought, it remained - visibly clear - for her to focus on.

Oh my God. Please tell me I'm tripping.

* * * * *   * * * * *

DP thumped the contact's arm, searching for a good vein. He injected a few milligrams of a reverse paralyzing serum.

It's time to wake up.

Cocking his arm back, he slapped the dog shit out of the contact. He busted out laughing. Smacking him didn't matter. The contact's paralyzed state numbed him completely. The smack was purely for DP's sick pleasure. He got a kick out of doing things like that for the fun of it.

He yanked the needle out of the contact's arm, giving the serum time to travel throughout the contact's bloodstream. The small amount would be enough to make him alert to his current condition. He would also have most of the thoughts he wanted. He would even be able to think of moving and may even attempt to move. Except, nothing would happen. With each thought, his mind would shift through its foggy state and settle upon a path of his destiny. And if he was smart, he would accept that destiny like a real man. It would disappoint DP if he went out like a little bitch.

Regardless, the contact would see his present as his past. He wouldn't understand how it would end; nonetheless, he would have an idea.

The contact slowly came to realize what had happened and what was transpiring. He spotted two small bottles and two syringes laid on a serving tray across from him. Blinking several times, he assumed one of the bottles held something that would kill him. While he acknowledged one bottle would bring him death, he clearly understood the other would give him life. That's exactly what he wanted. Life. However, that might not be an option for him.

The contact felt DP standing to his right, and was able to feel him removing the syringe from his arm. Beyond that, he was unable to feel anything else; but he wanted to. Suddenly, his left ear drum opened up. Where he once couldn't hear any outside noises, he could now hear faint sounds of his immediate surroundings. A slight tingle resonated in his face and neck. Not wanting to believe it, he twisted his neck to the left, feeling his bottom lip drop. Picking it up, he fixed his mouth to say something.

DP punched him dead in his shit. "You talk when I tell you to talk. In ten minutes, you'll have fifty percent of your functions. You'll be in so much pain from what I'm about to do that you'll beg me to take you out of your feeble misery," DP explained, counting off the seconds.

The contact yearned to taste the blood pooling in his mouth and dripping down his chin. But that desire didn't last too long.

DP dropped a large-head sledge hammer on his right hand.

The contact's eyes bulged out of his head as he watched the hammer connect. Out of reaction, he screamed as loud as he could in his head. It had been so loud, he assumed DP, along with those up and down the street outside, heard it. Then again, it wasn't like he felt the hammer smashing his hand. It was the mere thought of watching the hammer connect that sent chills up his spine.

It was in that moment the contact knew this was real. DP wasn't playing games. He'd made up his mind to dump him in the sewer with all the others he killed. That made the contact want to cry. In his predicament, that would do him no good. He had to stand strong. Even then, standing strong would become harder and harder once his feelings and senses returned.

The mere thought of the pain made him long for DP to do him in right then and there. His eyes went from his flatten hand to DP. Looking into his eyes, he saw nothing consistent with that of a human being. What stood before him was the dealer of death. A shell of a man scarred from years of loneliness, abandonment, and misdirection. A man who could have been a good man with the right morals and values had he taken a different path. Yet, that hadn't been what happened.

Upon catching his first body, DP realized his purpose in life. Taking the gift bestowed upon him, he continued to collect souls without a thought. He merely required a picture, a stack of money and a time frame to complete the task and he would handle that business.

Nonetheless, every dog had its day and obviously, the sun had found time to shine on the contact's ass. It beamed upon the contact's head as if it sat directly in front of him. Its rays created an illusion for the contact to drift in and out of. But under the surface of his reality, the slowly but painful throbbing in his smashed hand began to surface. The intensified pain fought tooth and nail to get his attention. The contact knew, sooner rather than later, he would welcome a gun to the side of his head. The pain would be that unbearable.

He gave DP a look of *Why?*

DP looked down on the contact and wanted to spit in his face. Instead, he moved in to whisper in his left ear. "Because the price of going against me is DEATH!" He rose to take in the contact's reaction.

The contact's lips moved. The words escaped weakly. "Things are never ... what they seem to be son ... She's NOT ... who you think ... she is ... I'm not ... who you think ... I am ... Remember! ... Nothing is what ... it's ... suppose to be!"

DP listened as the contact slowly spit the words out. Pondering what was said, he looked up as if a light bulb came on. Shaking his head, he wouldn't worry too much about what the contact had to say. What he needed to worry about was getting his head around a few things. He rose to leave, then stopped to peer over his shoulder at the contact.

The contact, with his head leaning to one side, fought as hard as he could to slow the pain creeping upon him. He purposely sat motionless as if playing dead. Even that would only work for so long.

Still, a nagging thought kept DP from taking the contact out of his misery. There was a feeling of uncertainty intermingled with a strong feeling of belief looming. *Could it be that I actually have a heart after all I've done?* he wondered.

Naw! he surmised, walking up the steps looking to set up his next maneuver. *He'll get his when the time is right.*

* * * * *   * * * * *

The music was blaring in the Pink Slip, rattling the drinks on the table. Ramona, sitting at the bar, nursed a triple-shot of Hennessey on the rocks. Recently, she needed some new type of entertainment to occupy her time so she took up stripping. It wasn't all she thought it would be; nevertheless, it did allow her to stay in-tune with her deadly passion. That was all she cared about.

In a way, she compared herself to the Black Widow spider. Once she found them and fucked them, it was only right to kill them. She laughed at herself. *The things I allow my mind to come up with.*

She scanned the strip club, seeing it was a slow night. All of the potential tricks were pre-occupied or unattractive. She did see one sitting in the corner that looked familiar. She couldn't recall where she remembered him from. There weren't too many occasions where she seen somebody and had the chance to see them alive again.

His presence intrigued her but she wouldn't get too close or seem too obvious. Plus, she wasn't trying to be there anyway. Downing her drink, she simply paid her fees and decided to grab her things to leave.

* * * * *   * * * * *

DP rarely frequented strip clubs unless he needed a well-offered distraction. With all he had going on, he wasn't in the mood to deal with Winter and her bullshit. He knew he had been distant and he understood where she was coming from. But, it was something she wouldn't be able to understand.

104

How could he tell her it was him who killed her father? That would crush her. Nor would she be too understanding to find out he was a hit man in his spare time. She would look at him as if he was crazy, or as if she didn't know him. Truthfully, that would be exactly what it was.

At the bar, he ordered a Remy Martin, with no ice, and a Corona. Taking his drinks, he found an empty table in the back corner where he could be secluded. He had a lot to decipher and despite being in a strip club, some kind of plan had to form. But just as he sat down a thick red-bone quickly eased her way over to offer her services.

She was beautiful with long wavy hair pulled back into a ponytail. Leaning over the table, she pushed her titties together, and pinched her pierced nipples. He gazed into her face, and found her playing with her tongue ring. That aroused him.

He invited her to join him.

Sliding around the table, she sat next to him and felt for his little man. To her surprise, it was stretching out the fabric of his underwear trying to get out of his pants. Gripping it, she stroked him roughly.

DP's excitement was getting the best of him so he wanted a more private setting. "Is there somewhere more private we can go?"

"Baby boy, we have all the privacy we need right here." She climbed on top of the table, raising her leg over his head. Pulling her see-through thong to the side, she laid out one of the prettiest piece of dessert he'd seen all day. To add insult to injury, two peaches on the inside of each thigh described the juicy loveliness between her legs.

He was amazed at the depiction of her platter and how well described it was. When he first laid his eyes on it, it brought to mind a juicy peach. And that's how she illustrated it when she tattooed those words above each peach.

She seductively watched DP admire her fruit stand as she slipped her hands down and spread her folds apart. The revealing of her creamy center compelled him to dive in like Trey Songz.

Whereas, just as he could second guess himself, a darting figure racing by caught his eye. He couldn't see the chick's face but there was something about the color of her hair that caught his attention. It was the same color he seen the girl in the photograph wearing. He pushed the stripper to the side, and hurried to catch up to the chick. As he exited the club, he looked to his right then left. To the left, the chick hesitated at the corner as she peered back at him. She hit the corner, moving briskly to get out of sight.

DP sprinted after her, spotting her running into the parking lot across the street. He entered the parking lot, moving rather quickly, and searched for her location. Stopping, he noticed he'd lost her. A click echoed from the far corner of the lot. Eyes glued in that direction, he couldn't see any movement. He did, however, see the fire exiting the barrel of a silenced assault rifle coming at him.

Bullets hit almost every car in front of him, causing him to duck. Seconds later, the barrage of bullets eased up, a car engine turned over, and a car door slammed shut.

DP, still crouching behind the car, peered through the window, and watched the car sped off. Jogging into the street, he barely got a good look at the car. Unable to get the make and model, he headed back to the strip club. He needed to question the stripper with the tats and piercings.

Chapter Fifteen

"YOU OWE ME, MUTHAFUCKA!" The stripper was angry at DP for bouncing on her like that.

He didn't care. He had to do what he had to do. Pulling out a knot of big face hundreds, he peeled off $200 and was in the motion of handing it to her when she stopped him.

She moved in, reaching for his crotch. "This is what I want."

He didn't have the time to indulge in that kind of activity but didn't see any reason why not. "Let's go then!"

While she gathered her things, paid the DJ and her exit fee, DP ordered another shot of Remy. Taking it to the head, he slammed the shot glass down as the stripper returned ready to go. As they left, he watched her hips sway from side to side. Each cheek had a heavy drop in it with each step she took. *I'm gonna have so much fun with this one. I certainly need to relieve this pent-up stress.*

They arrived at the Motel 6 in Caseyville, and the stripper didn't waste any time dropping to her knees. The door hadn't even clicked close before she was pulling his sword from his pants. She wanted to feel the skin of his mighty soldier in her mouth.

Downing him, she twirled her tongue-ring around edge of his tool, showing off her head game. Grabbing her ponytail, she bobbed up and down on his manhood with ease. She'd done a good job when learning all she could about giving head. If she sucked for grades, she would definitely receive superb accolades for her performance.

The genius-like performance heightened DP's yearning to play in her juice box. Waiting a few minutes as she brainstormed, he jerked himself from her mouth. Thirsty for it, she chased it. He grabbed her hand, pulling her to her knees, led her to the bed, then bent her over.

Sliding inside of her, he went straight into his onslaught. He wasn't playing. He had every intention of punishing her kitty kat as he thought about the chick who shot at him. Mining for the seed in the center of the peach, his pounding was sure to make the stripper sore as hell in the morning.

Unbeknownst to him, the beating actually drove her crazy. The rearrangement of her walls overflowed her well and filled her with joy. Throwing it back, she actually welcomed his shovel to dig a little deeper if he could.

DP grabbed the stripper's long hair, flashing back to the flashes of the chick's gun. Humping wildly, he was on the verge of yanking her hair out if he pulled any harder. Squeezing a hand full of her hair, he pile-drove into her well like a mad-man.

Not to be outdone, she caught his rhythm, bucked with him, loving every moment of the assault. Her joining in increased the intensity of the feeling he felt. So just as quickly as it began, it ended with him busting inside of her.

The stripper yearned for more. She needed more. A whole lot more. That hadn't been enough for her. For her, that was a teaser, and the real show was about to begin.

DP had other plans. He needed information on the stripper from the club more than he needed another nut. Wiping sweat from his brow, he pushed her on the bed.

"What can you tell me about a chick at the club who wears a colorful wig?"

Rolling over, she sat up, reaching for his limb sausage. "What you worrying about another bitch for when you were just up in this juicy peach?" she questioned, pointing at her juice box. "And my name is Peaches, if you care to know."

"Nice to meet you, Peaches, but I need to know what's up with the chick. It's personal and could line your pockets if you're talking about something useful," he explained, getting the stripper's attention with the mention of money.

"I'm not hip about who she is. She maybe started about a week ago. She normally comes in for a few hours then leave. I think her name is Ramona." She grabbed his dick.

"Ramona!" she exclaimed, swatting at her hand.

"Yeah, Ramona!" she yelped. "You know her or something?"

"Get dressed!" he ordered, putting on his clothes. "It's time to roll."

"Let me hop in the shower right quick," she requested.

"Hurry up!" he replied, watching her switch hard as hell towards the bathroom.

As she walked into the bathroom and turned on the shower, he dropped $500 on the bed and left. He didn't have time to wait.

★ ★ ★ ★   ★ ★ ★ ★

DP arrived back at his spot, scooping the photos off the floor. He flipped to the last photo, turning it over to read the brief information on the back. There was bunch of names and possible addresses but nothing stood out until he reached the end.

The name stood out like sore thumb.

Looking back at the picture, his eyes only seen one person. *How could this be?* All this time, she had been living a lie to his face. That was true deception at its finest. *How is that possible?* he wondered. *How could she be that good at hiding the real her when living with such a horrific secret?*

Thinking heavily, he walked passed a mirror, unable to look at himself. How could he look? To do so would force him to acknowledge the answers to his questions. It would be hypercritical to look at himself and not acknowledge the truth. He was no better than her. He'd been living his lie for so long he actually believed the lie himself.

The things a person allow themselves to believe.

An unfamiliar beeping noise resonated from the kitchen. Upping his banger, he stopped dead in his tracks, attempting to pinpoint its location. He peeked around the kitchen corner. Hearing it again, he turned the corner to find no one there. Looking around, he presumed the beeping was from the contact's phone.

As it beeped again, he identified that it was. Retrieving it from the coat pocket on the chair, there was two new messages. The phone wasn't password protected so he accessed the voicemail without a fuss.

Listening to the first one, he recognized the voice but was unable to put a face or name to it. He racked his brain wondering who she was. Replaying the message again, he listened to intensively and memorized it.

Hey baby, give me a call when you get this. I have something special for you tonight.

DP skipped to the second message. His heart skipped a beat as a shiver ran up and down his spine. The sound of the voice was one he was very familiar with. *Why would she be calling the contact?* he questioned. *DUH!* he thought. She was a hired hand like him. But listening to the message and hearing the words coming out of her mouth told an entirely different story.

A story that had to be a lie.

Hey daddy, I need to talk to you about something. It's IMPORTANT so call me right back. AND I mean RIGHT BACK!!!

DP kept repeating *Daddy* over and over again in his head. *What the fuck did she mean* daddy? That couldn't be possible. *Her father is dead!*

Storming downstairs, DP flicked on the light. The contact, in excruciating pain, glared over at DP extremely glad to see him. Not excited as a father would be when seeing his son but excited as in finally *he can put me out of my misery.* The contact was ready to die.

However, DP wasn't ready to kill him just yet. He needed answers more than anything else.

The contact attempted to focus through the pain when identifying the fiery beast within DP set to snap. He tried saying something but he felt tongue-tied as if he would swallow it. He was helpless, and figured DP was there to help him since he walked over with another syringe. He prayed that this was his final call. DP had broken him down to the simplest compound and he was in dire need to be rid of his pain and suffering.

Rather, DP momentarily numbed the pain. The morphine ran through his bloodstream, taking him on a high-flying roller coaster. Closing his eyes as the drug resumed control over him, he opened his eyes feeling renewed.

DP held up a picture. "Who is she?" he asked, direct and to the point.

The contact rode the wave of the morphine. "You wouldn't believe me if I told you." He looked away; his droopy eyes showing concern. He dropped his head and licked his lips.

DP seen the contact thought it was game. Snatching a zig-saw off the table, he lined it up with the contact's wrist, and dug into the flesh of his arm.

The contact jerked his head back, screaming out in pain and agony until DP stopped digging.

"Let's start over," he said, holding the picture up again. "Who is this?" he asked. "Is this your daughter?"

How does he know that? he wondered. *He shouldn't know that.* DP knowing that bothered him. But what could he do about it. It was out of his hands. The fate of them had come to pass. Those in power had made their decisions. The rest was up to DP.

He slowly raised his head. "Darius, the truth will set me free," he whispered.

DP stepped back. The mention of his name in that manner mimicked a different tone. It had more of a fatherly appeal to it. DP's anger pushed that thought to the side.

"Spit it out, old man!" he commanded. "Please don't waste my time."

"My daughter is the woman in those pictures," the contact confessed.

"Get the fuck out of here!" DP exclaimed. "I know who this chick is and she is NOT your daughter," he remarked, seeing the contact still wanted to play games.

Shaking his head from side-to-side, the contact wished DP would hear him out. "Things aren't what you think they are, son. She is my daughter and she has been bred to be your equal. Your equivalent!" he explained, hesitating to continue. "I have some disturbing news but in the state you're in, I'm not sure if you can handle it."

"Cut the bullshit and get to the point."

"You won't find her, DP ... But she'll find you. She knew I would be coming here so if I don't return, she will hunt you down. And you know she has a mean clean up game too."

DP thought of Ralphie. Everything was starting to make sense. Unfortunately, that would be one death that would contribute to Winter's downfall.

He thought of everything the contact said. "If she," he held up the picture, "is your daughter, why would you want her eliminated?" he asked, not completely understanding the situation.

"That wasn't my call, son. In my life, I've had to make some tough decisions. Some I didn't totally agree with. Others were absolutely necessary. My daughter's desire to disrupt the natural cause of things brought about her demise."

DP grabbed the saw again, digging deep into the contact's flesh, quickly reaching the bone. The contact roared from the gut. With slobber running down his chin, he made a startling accusation.

"Ramona is also Winter's twin sister, DARIUS!" he bellowed in an attempt to stop DP from severing his arm.

DP unconsciously smacked the contact with the bloody saw. He couldn't believe that if he wanted to. Yet, a part of him had to believe it. *How weird is that?*

"I'll assume you're going into shock which is allowing you to think these unbelievable thoughts and speak blasphemy. There's no way possible for me to believe that," DP said, convincing himself that he didn't believe it.

"Believe it, son! It's true," the contact stated, knowing it was the truth. "It's the honest to GOD truth, Darius!"

"But you hired me to kill Winter's father. How do you explain that?"

"That would be correct, son, and you did. But you're looking at Ramona's father right here. Me and Travis were both hitting their mother. Our affair was something that shouldn't have resulted into what it did. Travis had no idea their mother had gotten pregnant. I was the only man she confided in. That's why it was set up for Sara to take one while the other went up for adoption," he expounded, then proceeded to deliver the rest of the story.

"All hell broke loose when Travis found out we were screwing." He took a breather. "Travis ended up shooting her several times thinking he was leaving her for dead. Not even at that time was he aware of her being pregnant. Because he didn't know, he believed he was wiping his hands clean of her."

He inhaled his past. "Youngblood, she didn't know if I was the father of them babies or if Travis was. She would eventually die from her injuries but the babies were already separated and living their lives as those who had them saw fit."

DP shook his head. "You gots to be kidding me, right?"

"No, son. I'm not. As planned, Sara took Winter but didn't want to let Ramona go to the state so she called me. She always knew of the affair but didn't know who the father was."

"Wait a minute!" DP interrupted.

"Hold on, youngblood. Let me finish." A bout of pain shot through his arm. "Because she was unaware of who the father was, I took a DNA test for both babies. It turned out I am Ramona's father, but not Winter's."

"Yeah RIGHT! You can get the fuck out of here with that. I'm not about to sit here and believe that," DP declared, getting upset for letting it go on this long.

"This is real talk, son. But it gets better. In the meantime, me and Travis fell out and he ended up shooting me up real bad. His inability to finish the job correctly is why I'm sitting here telling you this story," he explained, hoping DP would catch on to what he was saying.

"So, if Travis shot you, I suspect you're telling me that you're my father as well?" he asked, picking up on the subliminal message.

The contact smile brightly from the inside out. Struggling to physically smile, he liked how DP figured it out so quickly.

"If you're my daddy, Ramona is my sister and you want me to kill her," DP added, continuing to put it together.

"That decision wasn't made by me. But it's one you have to make on your own now that you know the truth, son."

DP had made his decision alright. He reached for the pistol on the table, failing to blink in the process. Pointing it at Darius Price Sr's head, he pulled the trigger, snapping the old man's head back. The contact's brain matter oozed down the wall behind him. Chuckling slightly, DP put the gun down then came to grips to what just happened. Shrugging at the account, he sniffed the gunpowder in the air as he headed up the basement steps.

Aja LaGrand Blount

"I ain't got no damn daddy!"

Chapter Sixteen

"IT APPEARS WE HAVE hit a dead end, Hawk. I'm pretty sure it was the same dead-end Chapman hit when he went through the entire file himself," Detective Smith pointed out, staring up at the ceiling. "You would think with all this information, something would assist us in getting this guy. It's like he's untouchable."

He folded his hands behind his head, leaning back. Unsure of what to do, his mind concentrated on what he couldn't find. There had to be something there. He'd looked through so many pieces of paper, and none of them provided him with a good direction to go in. That remanded him stuck at square one.

Detective Hawkins, sitting on the other side of the table, stared at the same pages they'd been flipping through for days now. They thought the merging of their two minds would yield better results. How sadly mistaken they had been. There had been days of scouring the boxes of files, and they hadn't come up with anything useful.

How could someone so visibly have such a minimized track record? Smith asked himself. It didn't seem right for anyone to be able to stay that far under the radar but have an outlandish reputation that stood atop of mountains and pillars.

Both Smith and Hawkins knew they had to come up with something. What? They simply didn't know. But they would have to figure that out.

"What's our next move, Smithie?" Hawkins asked, tired of thinking and ready for some action.

"I'll be damn if I know. It seems as if we're back to the drawing board. Whatever the purpose for that is. It doesn't look as if we actually need a freakin' drawing board. We need something solid. I'm a see if I can track down Winter James to see if she has something that she'll like to share." He was clutching at straws, and dehydrated for answers.

"Let me know how that turns out. I'm gonna head out to lunch. I'm hungry! You want something?"

Smith had no appetite. "Naw, I'm good!" He was actually considering taking a bite out of the paperwork before him. Maybe that way he could digest it and shit out a logical answer.

With Hawkins exiting, Smith fell into a deeper thought. *What am I missing?* he asked himself. *What is the key to it all?* There seemed to be many variables but no common denominator.

Unable to come up with a reliable answer, he was tired of overworking his brain. Closing the files, he put them back in the box. Patting the top, "I have a big enough headache. If I think about this any longer, I'm sure my head will explode." He walked away, embarrassed but relieved at the same time.

* * * * *   * * * * *

"Ain't this about a bitch!" Winter recited. "Now that I'm calling her, she doesn't want to answer the phone." She figured she should have gone over when Sara had originally called. Thus, she hadn't been in the mood for any more surprises.

Now, she was eager to know what her auntie had to show her. She hoped it had nothing to do with her father. In her current state, she couldn't handle anything else dealing with him. Her wounds were still fresh, and were actually healing. Any awkward shock could easily bust them open. The reopening of those wounds wasn't what she welcomed anytime soon.

Aside from that, she had a lot of other things on her plate. Mostly the trash she wished to dump in the trash, and incinerate. That way she could clean her plate, and flex her shoulders some. The weight holding her down was becoming extremely burdensome. It was literally crushing her.

Simultaneously, her thoughts drifted to DP. Thoughts of him always seemed to pop up in some shape, size or form when she thought of her troubles. It wasn't like he hadn't been an important part of her life over the years. It was recently that things suddenly changed for the worse between them.

She understood people changed and eventually grew apart. That was a part of life. Yet, she wouldn't have thought he would turn his back on her when she needed him the most. Maybe he didn't know how to deal with the situation because of him not having his father around.

Maybe my ass! she thought. "That lousy muthafucka should be here for me, standing right by my side!" she venomously said aloud.

She picked up the phone, feeling the need to call him. Scrolling to his number, her fingers dangled over the buttons. She couldn't bring herself to make the call. There was something keeping her from taking that step. She couldn't shake her hesitation. Nevertheless, she had to get her frustration off her mind.

Putting the phone down, she opened her laptop to send him an e-mail. Through an e-mail everything she wanted to say would pour out, and she could expound on what matter most without being cut off.

As she typed, an aura of comfort came through her words. Every emotion she had or felt gushed onto the screen through the stroke of her fingers.

> *Darius,*
>
> *I love you so much it's ridiculous but I'm extremely hurt by your actions as of late. We have always had one another's back but when I really need you, I'm unable to get one minute of your time. I don't know why you would cowardly turn your back on me when you said you'll be here for me. I have always been the friend, the woman and the lover you wanted, needed and desired. But for you to play me like you have is some fuck shit. I can't openly express the pain stinging my heart right now.*
>
> *But it's there because of your actions. Your inability to reach out to even seem a little bit concerned leads me to believe you may have something to hide.*
>
> *At least, that's what my inner self keeps telling me. If my gut is right, I'll be coming for your dog ass and I won't be playfully wagging my tail, nor will I be wanting to play games.*
>
> *I'll be coming to make sure you feel what I feel ....*

Stopping there, she understood what she had been feeling all along. Her downplaying it had assisted in blinding herself to the truth. Now that she had a better sense of what had happened, she sought to formulate a plan.

Calling her auntie, she received no answer. *Fuck it! I'll catch up with her later. I gots things to do,* she declared.

Grabbing her purse, she rushed to her car, and proceeded to a place where she could obtain exactly what she needed.

★★★★★   ★★★★★

DP stared at his computer screen, anxiously awaiting the information from his search. He figured it shouldn't take too much longer since the phone used to call the contact was powered on. While that was good for him, that would be one mistake hard for the owner of the phone to come back from. Once the software triangulated the phone's position, it would give him an exact address. With that location in hand, he would be equipped with a direction and would know where he was headed.

Parched, he thought of running to the refrigerator for something to drink when the computer chimed, alerting him to locking down the phone's location. "What the fuck?" he mumbled, staring at the screen.

The location was a familiar one. It was a place he wouldn't have thought of. Frowning, he re-read the information to make sure he hadn't misread it. It seemed odd for the person to be there.

The girl did say she was the contact's daughter- Stopping in mid-thought, he reckoned the contact had been telling the truth. If Ramona was his daughter, her being at that location seconded that truth.

Seeking to find out, he forwarded the information to his smartphone, and headed out to cruise the area around the address. Arriving down the street, nothing out of the ordinary stuck out. He did see an Altima parked in front of the address. That let him know that the person who lived there was home. The car reminded him of the car that sped off the morning he killed Travis.

Riding passed the house, he spotted a car that resembled the one that sped off after he'd been shot at. The car also fitted the same description Bruce once gave him. This couldn't be a coincidence. The contact did say she knew who he was. *But she hadn't act like she knew in that parking lot or did she?* he asked. That didn't matter. He had to move those thoughts to the side, and make sure he wasn't the one being shot at again.

Not wanting to seem rushed, he pulled in front of the Maxima, got out, and quickly slashed the left front and back tires. Without a care in the world, he nonchalantly walked up to Sara's front door, and rang the doorbell. Someone made their way to the door. Playing it safe, he gripped the gun stationed in his jacket pocket.

The door opened with Sara's Kool-Aid smile lighting the doorway. "Boy, come in here!" she exclaimed. "It's been a mighty long time since I last seen you. What brings you over here?"

Sara's voice matched the voice on the voicemail. *She's the woman from the first message.* He wanted to pull out his gun and shoot her in the face; except, that's not what he came for. He would have time to deal with her. She wasn't innocent in this. Her hands were just as filthy as the rest, and she deserved to die for the lies and secrets she held onto.

"I'm looking for Winter," he stated, faking a smile. "Have you seen her?"

"I talked to her earlier but haven't seen her. Is everything alright?" She faked concern. "Want me to call her?"

DP glanced around the house. "That won't be necessary," he replied, knowing his real intention had nothing to do with Winter.

Sara hadn't heard a word he said. She trotted off, looking for her phone, wondering why he would pop up at her house unannounced. His appearance made her quite nervous since her niece was hiding in the other room. This was not the time to bring unnecessary attention to her presence when he had no idea of Winter having a twin. She hurried towards the kitchen, faking like she really had something to say. Projecting her voice, she loudly gave Ramona a signal to pay attention to.

For DP, her words hadn't registered, nor did he process what had been said. He did, however, pick up on the technique. Quickly sliding behind her, he slipped his hand over her mouth, and put his gun to her head.

"Just be cool and everything will be alright," he whispered, telling her to be still and quiet.

The tip of his index finger tingled. Understanding exactly what that meant, he surmised his inability to leave that house until everyone inside was dead. That meant he wouldn't have the time to retrieve the answers he came for. Where he wanted to ask certain questions, he longed to end things as quickly as he could, feeling no need to stretch it out if he didn't have to.

"Where's Ramona?" he asked, his lips touching her ear.

The mentioning of that name produced a great alarm within Sara. *How does he know of her?* she asked herself. *What in the hell is going on?* The answers to his questions failed to register fast enough.

"Don't bullshit me!" he spat. "I already dealt with your boo. I heard the voicemails and I know the truth. Make this easy on yourself and point to which bedroom she's in," he demanded, ramming the Sig into her head.

Hating to do it, she raised her arm towards the back room. She seen no other choice. She also had another thought. If she could gain some kind of momentum, she could land a solid blow to his stomach. If she could separate from his grasp, she could join forces with Ramona and overpower him.

Moving her arm in a downward motion, she made direct contact with his gut. Like a champ, DP absorbed the sharp elbow but slightly loosened his grip on her neck. Sensing the loose tension, that gave Sara the courage to make her move.

Throwing another elbow, that blow provided her with additional leeway. Breaking free, she raced towards the bedroom, screaming Ramona's name. She had to warn her of the danger they were in.

Without thinking, DP raised his piece, pulled the trigger, and hit Sara twice in the middle of her back. Before she could hit the floor, he was moving in for the kill; his finger still on the trigger.

Sara's body hit the floor with a loud thump. Blood spurted from the gunshot wounds.

DP hurried down the short hallway, eager to get this over with. Aiming the .40 at the back of her head, he caressed the trigger, applying the slightest amount of pressure to the curve. Then suddenly, the bedroom door jerked open, and the person wielding a semi-automatic weapon handgun rudely interrupted his plans to finish what he started.

$$\star\,\star\,\star\,\star\qquad\star\,\star\,\star\,\star$$

"How may I help you, ma'am?"

Winter stepped to the counter glancing down at the contents on display. "I'm looking to purchase a firearm," she explained.

"Is everything alright, ma'am?" asked, noticing her constantly looking over her shoulder. "You can go to the police if it's something immediate."

"It's nothing you should concern yourself with. I want to obtain something small for security reasons. Would I be able to get it today?" she questioned seeking to move the process along.

"I'm sorry, ma'am, but you will have to wait 2 - 3 days so the process can run its course. If everything pans out, you'll be able to get your weapon then. Would you like to begin the paperwork?"

She figured two or three days wouldn't be too long of a wait. "Um, yeah! I'll go ahead and do that."

"What kind of firearm do you have in mind?" he inquired, unlocking the cabinet.

Winter eyed the variety of handguns before her. "I like that one," she said, pointing to an all-black Glock 27 .40-caliber handgun, approximately 3 ½" long. "I like how small and powerful it looks."

The salesman pulled it out of the case for her. "That's an excellent choice."

Winter reached out to touch it. Having full access to it was entirely different than seeing it in the glass case. The whole experience was new to her. This would be the first time she touched, let along seen a gun before. However, once she placed one finger on the gun, there was a feeling of familiarity.

Picking it up, she felt the weight of the gun, and had to admit, it was an amazing feeling. In that instant, she fell in-love with it. It was something like love at first sight. And, as she looked up at the salesman, she would surely capitalize on that love to the fullest.

Chapter Seventeen

RAMONA SLUNG THE BEDROOM door open. The first thing she seen was her auntie lying face down on the floor. A ton of blood stained the carpet. Acknowledging the obvious, her eyes moved upward to DP standing a few feet away. She locked eyes with him. Through her peripheral, she peeped the gun in his hand swinging upward towards her. Quicker on the draw, her instincts kicked in, and she let off a few shots at him compared to the one he got off. Neither of their shots hit the intended targets but a gunfight was in full effect.

Backpedaling, DP felt the spiraling wind of the two rounds whipping by his head as he ducked into the kitchen.

Ramona, knowing to play it smart, dipped back into the bedroom. The image of her auntie penetrated her mind. Fighting the images, the stills clouded her mental making it hard to proceed. She couldn't be successful this way. What she was up against required a clear and unrestricted mindset.

The siblings, located in different parts of the house, accessed the situation. Both of them knew that only one of them could walk out of that house alive. With them both being good at what they did, neither of them would simply give up. They'll rather die before submitting to the other.

Ramona, in her comfort zone, acknowledged she had the upper hand. DP had ignorantly entered into her lioness' den to stir up trouble without being fully aware of what he was up against.

In the kitchen, DP accepted the notion that he'd overstepped his grounds as he contemplated his position. Weighing the odds, he didn't feel comfortable with the numbers tallied. Equipped with a lonely Sig .40, minus two in the clip, he had no real knowledge of what Ramona worked with. She'd came out of thin air with a HK P30 but he wouldn't be a damn fool to return to that bedroom trying to find out what else she had.

I'll be playing the fool to stick around period. I'll catch up with her later. He made his way to the back door.

In the back bedroom, Ramona listened for the slightest noise or movements. Her guns were locked and loaded. She'd strapped her Kevlar bulletproof vest on, readjusted her mind for the task ahead of her, and had her finger on the trigger of the silenced HK 1911 assault rifle.

A few seconds passed without anything happening. She found that odd so she decided to break the silence. In a taunting manner, she yelled out DP's government name to see if she could get under his skin.

"Darius!!.... Darius! Darius! Come out, come out, wherever you are. It's time to play. Don't you want to play with me, Darius?" Repeating it over and over again, she cracked open the bedroom door, peeking around the corner. Sneaking a peek twice, there wasn't a sign of him in the hallway. She recalled his journey into the kitchen, thinking a man of his caliber wouldn't stop coming for her. She assumed he would be more of the aggressor.

Sticking her head around the door frame, no one was there but her aunt. Refusing to step into an ambush, she sought to be the one controlling the situation. Gripping the HK securely, she let off a series of rounds towards the kitchen. Coming out of the bedroom, she sprayed the wall just in case he used it for cover. She received no return fire, heard no grunts, nor had a dead body dropped to the floor.

That didn't mean she was out of the woods yet. She inched up the wall and slung the HK around the corner into the kitchen. It was empty. She hadn't expected that. The space that DP once occupied had been vacated. That surprised her.

Got damn! she said, snapping her fingers. *I let him get away.*

Lowering her weapon, she exhaled heavily. DP's getting away was a good thing for her. She hated he made his escape but that came with a bit of relief, which gave her time to check on her auntie. Had DP stuck around, there was a possibility that her aunt could die, if she wasn't already dead.

Stepping over to check Sara's vitals, there was a faint pulse. Swiftly rising to her feet, she ran to gather her things. Believing someone may have heard the shots and called the police, she had to get out of there. It wouldn't be smart for her to stick around for questioning.

Instead, she made a complimentary 911 call with the house phone, setting it on the counter, and hurried out of the back door, hoping and praying her aunt would make it.

* * * * *　　* * * * *

After getting the required paperwork filled out for her gun, Winter decided to stop by her aunt's house to see what she had to show her. However, what she seen as she turned onto her street made her heart drop.

Up and down the street, a host of police cars and the paramedics were everywhere.

Winter, unaware of what happened, parked, hopped out, and sprinted down the street. As she made it to her auntie's house, the paramedics wheeled Sara out on a gurney. She seemed to still be alive but the appearance of her being alive wasn't enough for Winter. She had to make sure. She busted through the yellow tape, and two cops grabbed her.

"Let me GO!" she yelled, attempting to break free from their grasps. "That's my auntie right there!!" Her outbursts grew louder and louder. She'd gotten so loud, Detective Hawkins heard the commotion and strolled over to the assist the officers holding her back.

"Ma'am, what's your name?" he asked, holding his hands up to calm her.

She stopped struggling. "Winter James." She pointed at the gurney. "That's my auntie right there. Is she alright?"

Hawkins signaled for the officer to let her go. Pulling her to the side, "We need to talk, Miss James."

"What happened to my auntie?" she questioned, only concerned about that.

"Miss James, I'm Detective Hawkins and this is Detective Smith walking up. Your auntie sustained two gunshots to the back. We have no leads at this time but someone was kind enough to dial 911 so she could be discovered. Do you have any idea who that may have been? Was anyone staying here with her that you know of?" he asked, hoping to get some answers.

Winter thought about it. She came up with nothing. Shaking her head, she came down hard on herself for not coming when she first had the chance to. Now she may never find out what her aunt had for her.

Winter replayed the detective's words. She couldn't believe someone had the nerve to shoot her aunt. The recent events since her father's death had to be one of the reasons. She didn't know what to believe but she gathered that if her father hadn't come back, none of this would be happening.

Hawkins jarred Winter from her thoughts. She could see his lips moving; but, she couldn't make out the words. Her ears felt closed off from the world. She tried to shake the feeling by shaking her head from side to side. That assisted in the pressure easing up.

"Can you say that again?" she insisted. "I didn't catch what you said."

"We are doing all we can to find out what occurred here. We can only recommend that you go be with your aunt as she needs your love and support now more than ever," Hawkins explained.

Winter knew he was right. But she was stuck with the image of her aunt lying upon that gurney.

"Miss James, would you like to ride to the hospital with her or not?" Hawkins asked, seeing she wasn't in a hurry to move. "The ambulance needs to leave."

Gathering strength in her legs, she raced over to the ambulance. As she climbed in, the detectives tried making sense of it all.

"This is becoming a very weird ass case, Hawk," Smith said, watching the ambulance pull off.

"Tell me about it! I'm thinking that none of this would have happened if Robertson hadn't come back."

Smith didn't reply as he pondered that thought. He allowed the notion to skate around his brain. Once one lap was complete, he could only shrug. "Hopefully we can get some prints off of something and have something to go on. There was definitely someone staying with her or had been here today," he said, speaking up.

Hawkins thought about the holes in the walls. "Whomever it was had some heavy heat too. The shells are from a semi-automatic rifle, possibly a Heckler and Koch or something similar."

"Well, let's get this evidence back to the lab for processing and hope we can catch a break," Smith mentioned, walking off.

★ ★ ★ ★ ★   ★ ★ ★ ★ ★

DP hated leaving Sara's house without putting a bullet in Ramona's head. Aside from his departure, the incident was far from over. There was only one thing on his mind, and that was getting at her. His thirst to finish her expeditiously was all he could think about. He was like a hound dog after catching a scent. He tasted Ramona's blood and had the look of the devil in his eyes.

He couldn't calm down for anything in the world. Ramona's face was etched into his memory. That made it even worse. But he only seen Winter. That pissed him off because he wouldn't have fathomed that she had a twin. However, it was the truth. Ramona looked identical to his childhood love, but with a few distance differences.

The most distinctive feature was her eyes. The glare Ramona possessed was totally different than anything he'd seen from Winter's. Ramona's looks and demeanor even had a slightly different swag to it. They looked the same but move differently.

When he thought he could pull up and put in that work, he quickly found out different. Ramona showed him she wouldn't go down that easy. Nonetheless, he would have to show her that it would be that easy when it was all said and done.

Sitting down at his computer, he went back to work to find her using the same process he previously used. Conducting the search for the same phone used to call the contact, he found she was dumb enough to still have it powered on. That amateur mistake would prove fatal once he triangulated her position again. Feeling closer to his goal, his heart rate increased dramatically as he thought of putting a hole in her head. Playing with her wasn't an option. If he did, that would give her the upper hand. That couldn't happen. He had to do her in out the gate.

Pondering further, he knew this road wouldn't end with her. It would encompass any and everything that decided to get in his way. His bottom line surrounded the fact that he couldn't put himself in a predicament that could cost him his life. With the kind of mindset, he understood the purpose of coming out on top.

In the midst of getting his mental on point, his computer alerted him to Ramona's location. When the address popped up, he scratched his head. If the address was correct, she was right down the street from him. He leaned back in his chair as he wondered how long she'd been that close without him knowing it. Rubbing his temples, he speculated about what else she knew. He now had to think about everything the contact said.

Were tabs being kept on me? he asked himself. *Who else knows of me and where I could be found?*

DP figured the answers he sought wouldn't come as he sat there. He leaned forward to read the address one last time. With the element of surprise in his favor, he plotted his next move.

Currently, Ramona appeared to be stationary but he surmised she would be making a move soon. Grabbing his Winchester .30-06, he made his way to the roof. Peering out over the neighborhood, he surveyed the area. His vision was blocked by some trees and a few apartment buildings. That wasn't too much of a big deal. What he had planned would go through any and everything in his way.

Scanning the area, he searched for a car that fitted Ramona's profile. Nothing stuck out. He checked the location of the address again. Everything was quiet. He could only imagine Ramona sitting in one of the apartment's six buildings down with no idea of what he had up his sleeve. Then again, he didn't know what was up hers. For all he *knew,* she was setting up a trap of her own that he didn't know of.

He wasn't having that. He would patiently sit back and wait for his time to strike. He wouldn't be stupid enough to run into another situation where he would be outgunned and outmanned. There was no telling what she had in that apartment, let alone, who she had on her team.

What he did know, she would have to reveal herself before he grew tired of waiting.

***** *****

Ramona lounged around her apartment messed up in the head. It bothered her that the person responsible for shooting her aunt was still alive. Truly sadden by the situation, what sadden her the most was that it was her brother who had shot her aunt. That's what really touched her deeply.

She tried her best to get the thoughts out of her head. That was extremely hard to do because she knew her relation to DP held no weight. Given the opportunity to kill him, she would murder him without second thought.

What honestly plagued her sincerely dwelled upon how DP was her big brother and the distant relationship they had. Despite wanting to kill him, it was difficult to shake the look she seen when looking into his eyes. When she looked at him, she didn't necessary see him but she seen her father. From head to toe, she stood directly in front of the man whom she wanted so much love from. No matter how she looked at it, she seen her father. And she felt like when she killed her brother, she would be killing her father as well.

Oh well, he should have given me the love I needed as his little girl! she stated. *He should have done more then we wouldn't be in this situation.*

Getting passed the hurt and pain of the past, she fast-forwarded to the person she knew she had to be to take DP out. Over the years, she'd heard so much about him from their father. During those times, she'd never wanted to meet him. When thinking of meeting her siblings, she yearned for it to be outside the realm of the lives they lived. Whereas, with DP, there wasn't a reason to meet him with how their father lived.

Her primary goal always revolved around meeting her twin sister, Winter. She truly believed they could be the perfect team. Smiling as she thought about her, Ramona's heart skipped a beat when thinking of her brother.

When her father talked about DP, he failed to mention the coldness his presence brought with it. To be that close to that kind of force gave off the eeriest of feelings. One where a person would have to go all out to get the upper hand on him or become a victim of circumstance.

As she thought of death, her mind drifted to her aunt. She felt so bad for Sara and regardless of her outcome, she would step up and handle her business. Brother or not, DP had to go.

Be that as it may, she could only prepare so much when she knew so little about his whereabouts or how to find him. The info her father had given her was a dead end. That had been the first place she checked and it was an empty and unoccupied residence.

A thought came to her. There was a way she could get a line on his whereabouts. It was not a way she had hoped to use; except, she had no other choice. Pulling out Winter's phone number, she stared at it. Having previously memorized it, she hadn't been courageous enough to make the call. Now the time may have arrived where she wouldn't have a choice.

Overall, she hoped their auntie could have brought them together. Thinking about that, in a way, she had. Still, she didn't want to meet her twin on these terms. To pop up on her like this would be unfair. She longed for their meeting to be a joyful and memorable occasion, not according to her need for information on DP. Whereas, she saw no choice so she pulled out her phone to make the call.

Chapter Eighteen

RAMONA FLIPPED OVER THE picture of Winter, and stared at it like she had many times before. Her heart was telling her what she had to do. She needed to make that call. Knowing that was the right thing to do, she flipped to the back of the picture and stared at the number Sara had given her months ago.

She dialed in the number, then paused. She couldn't bring herself to connecting the call. This wasn't how she wanted to call her twin. These weren't the natural conditions that should bring them together. She yearned for a more intimate and personal encounter.

Believing she could get what she longed for, she grabbed her things as she prepared herself for the possible encounter with Winter. Instead of calling, she figured it would be best to go to where she was. She was sure Winter had heard of Sara being shot so she most likely rushed to the hospital. Understanding that, she would go there so they could stand side-by-side for their aunt like two good nieces should.

As she exited her apartment, she changed her mind, disliking the idea of popping up on Winter like that. She had to think about how she would feel if Winter popped up on her out of the blue.

I wouldn't know how to feel. That made her think about it from that perspective.

Pulling out her phone, she placed the call and listened to the phone ringing. It rang a good five times before a worn-down voice came through the line. She was speechless as she heard her twin's voice for the first time. They sounded almost identical.

"Hello?" Winter said again when she received no reply.

Ramona could clearly hear the pain in her voice. *Damn!* She wanted to be the supportive sister and give her sibling a shoulder to cry on. She couldn't sit on the phone without saying anything. It wouldn't have made any sense to call if she remained mute. Womaning up, she overcame the weird feelings stirring within her, and finally spoke.

"May I speak to Winter?"

"This is she," Winter responded, sounding winded.

Ramona noticed how out of it Winter was. She hadn't even inquired into who called, or maybe she already knew.

"Is this a bad time because we really need to talk?" Ramona inquired, waiting for a response.

"Talk?" Winter asked. "Who is this?" she asked, confused to who the caller was or what she wanted to talk about.

"It's complicated and I'm not sure of how to tell you but I'm..."

But I'm ... was last words Winter heard before the line went dead. Looking at the phone, she wondered what the hell happened. *Who the hell was that?* she asked herself, putting the phone down. She couldn't recall hearing that voice before but the whole conversation unnerved her. It felt like she'd been talking to herself.

Looking around, she didn't think she'd been dreaming. She knew where she was and despite her emotional state, she was coherent to everything transpiring around her. As she glanced around, her eyes landed on her aunt laying in the hospital bed with a ton of tubes hanging out of her.

As she glared at Sara, she pushed the phone call from her mind. Closing her eyes, she said a silent prayer, and asked God to spare her aunt's life. Opening her eyes, she grabbed ahold of Sara's hand. Upon first contact, she felt the warmth of her skin. Then, the warmth of her skin turned cold. It was as if she was sucking the life out of her aunt just with her touch alone. She didn't understand what was happening.

The machines went haywire and the nurses and doctors rushed in, forcing her out.

She collapsed onto the seats in the waiting area, mentally drained, and feeling the heaviness of her eyelids. The pressure on them made them shut automatically, and within seconds, she drifted off into dream-like state. At first glance, it seemed like an outer body experience, one viewed on a much bigger screen. The portrayal was so clear. Naturally, her subconscious tried to change it to her liking but to no avail.

She could see herself talking on the phone. She appeared to be talking to herself. Paying closer attention, the area she stood within looked unfamiliar. Even the car she stood next to wasn't hers. She believed the person was her but something about her wasn't her. The coloring of her hair made her wonder. Her personal style didn't consist of wearing colorful wigs. Aside from the hair color, everything else was on point. Her body language and her voice were on point. But it felt as if she'd had this conversation before.

As she continued to watch herself, a faint sound resonated from a nice distance away. The sound came out of nowhere and the direction of its origin was unknown. It was an unusual sound. One of those sounds that the normal ear wouldn't hear.

Looking to identify the sound, she turned away from herself. She then sensed the need to pay attention to her own actions. Her eyes returned at about the same time a bullet shattered her cellphone and knocked her brains out the other side of her head.

The last words she muttered was *But I'm...*

Winter instantly snapped out of that dream-like state, jumping up. Her thoughts spun about a mile a minute. She wasn't sure if what she had witnessed was true or not. Wanting to believe it was a dream, she thought back to the call. The phone call's abrupt end led her to think the person who called may have been the person Sara wanted her to meet.

Raising to her feet, she needed to speak with her aunt. Unfortunately, the doctor stepped out of the hospital room, simultaneous to Winter heading that way. He exhibited a look on his face which informed her that the news he brought with him wasn't good. He informed her that her aunt didn't make it. Hearing him, she couldn't comprehend what she was being told. She simply gave the doctor a blank stare. She had no desire to cry another tear. She merely sucked it up, nodded at the doctor, and exited the hospital with murder on her mind.

★ ★ ★ ★ ★   ★ ★ ★ ★ ★

Detective Alonzo Smith and Rico Hawkins looked dumbfounded at one another after arriving at the scene of the latest gunshot victim. Standing there, they shook their heads, unable to believe what they saw despite it appearing to be very much true. *What was Winter James doing on this side of town when she was thought to have been at the hospital with her aunt?* was the question they both had on their minds.

As they both contemplated the answer, neither could come up with a definite answer. One thing they did know, it was apparent that Winter had done something she shouldn't have done to get her brains blown out, and that meant she possibly messed with the wrong crowd.

From the looks of the crime scene, this wasn't a random act of violence. Winter's gunning down had been premeditated. It was put into play by those who knew way more than they did, and that bothered them. With all the streets had to talk about, there was no one coming forth with any concrete tips pertaining to the case. But there appeared to be bodies being left in the wake of it all.

Hawkins broke the silence. "Where do we go from here, Smithie?"

"Hell if I know, Hawk! As soon as we finish one crime scene, a fresh one is laid out. This guy is good, whomever he is, and he is most definitely covering his tracks. I'm starting to think that this is the same guy. First, you have Robertson, then Sara, and now Winter."

"It seems we'll have to wait and see what the medical examiner tells us before we make another move. We can't move forward until we have some answers," Hawkins explained, turning away.

"That's about right," Smith replied, walking off with him. "And all the answers we need doesn't appear to be trying to find us either."

"That'll be too much like right."

* * * * *　　* * * * *

"Excuse me, miss. I'm trying to find my twin sister and I think she may be in your care," Winter said, stepping to the counter at the morgue.

Speechless, the medical examiner gawked at Winter. She assumed she knew exactly who she was looking for. She just couldn't believe what stood before her.

"What's your sister's name?" the M.E. asked, not even knowing Ramona's name herself.

It dawned on Winter in the moment of what she'd gotten herself into. She wasn't sure if she even had a sister. She'd taken the dream she had and the brief phone call and surmised that the person who called her was her sister. Using those two things to make a decision, she stood before the medical examiner unsure of if any of it was true.

"This is gonna sound weird but I don't know her name. I got this call from someone, who I'm assuming was her trying to introduce herself but we were cut off," she smiled, hoping to make up for how weird she looked and sounded. She intentionally omitted the part about the dream, and went with seeing the death on the news. "I'm assuming based on the way the call ended, it's possible that she was my sister."

The M.E. gave Winter a strange look. She knew Winter wasn't disclosing the whole story. She did, in fact, know that the girl laying on her examination table was her twin sister.

"What I'll like for you to do, ma'am, is come with me so you can identify a possibility of who your sister may be."

Winter nodded in agreement, following the medical examiner into the examination room. Proceeding through the morgue doors, the feeling was cold. Not because of the cold air hitting Winter as the doors opened but because of the stiff bodies laid out on the tables. She looked around, and seen the job of a medical examiner was a busy one.

The M.E. rounded the examination table against the far wall. "I think this is the one you're looking for." She pulled the sheet back, giving Winter a full view of Ramona's upper body.

Winter couldn't believe her eyes as she stared down at half a face. Ramona's brains had been literally blown out. Momentarily stuck, she couldn't raise her eyes from the destruction done. The reality of the situation wouldn't register. She found it hard to apprehend that she stood over her twin sister with half of her head missing. The sight made her temperature boil as she identified with0 the latest events.

Coming back to the point where she stood before Ramona, she was at her breaking point. This was the last straw. She couldn't take any more. She'd been stripped of everything. She had no more to give, which left her wanting someone to pay for what had occurred.

Someone had to be held accountable. Someone had to feel her pain, even if it meant losing her life as well.

She bowed her head, and whispered a silent prayer for her loved ones who passed and for those who would soon depart due to the wrath she would administer.

Standing there, her soul transformed into a dark and cold hole of emptiness, very similar to the morgue itself. The feeling had a strange connotation to it. Thoughts she never imagined came to her, and she welcomed them. Acknowledging that reality, she sought to transform her pain into a desirable forum of pleasure. And all in all, that pleasure would consist of inflicting her pain onto whomever responsible ten times over.

A devilish smirk crossed her face. She had to smile at the thought circling her mind. *If the medical examiner thought she was busy now, she hasn't seen anything yet...*

The medical examiner interrupted her thoughts. "Ma'am, is this your sister or not?"

Winter scrutinized the corpse's one eye, nodded, and acknowledged that the half-headed woman was her twin.

"Well miss…. what is your name then?"

"Winter James," she snapped, balling up her fists.

"Miss James, since you're unaware of your sister's name, nor have any documentation revealing your relationship to the victim, I can only do a DNA test in order to identify you as a family member and controller of her affairs. Is that something you'll like to do?"

"Sure!" Winter exclaimed, answering without giving it any thought.

"Let's go back to my desk so we can begin that process. I'll put a rush on getting the results so you won't have to wait too long, ok?"

"OK!" Winter stated, not really caring about the results. She already knew the truth but realized she had to go through the formalities. No amount of time waiting could change the fact of her knowing who Ramona was to her. The only thing having to wait would do was give her more time to plot and plan someone's demise.

★ ★ ★ ★ ★   ★ ★ ★ ★ ★

DP pulled up in front of one of his spots; the latest course of events stopping him in his tracks. As he sat in his Tahoe, he mulled over all of the things he'd done. Winter came to mind. When thinking of her, he understood there was no turning back now so one more body wouldn't hurt.

The pondering associated with killing his childhood love posed a similar deliberation when dealing with anyone on the street who had to go. At that point, what they once shared no longer existed. The special place in his heart she once held had been filled with cement. It didn't even exist any longer. The only thing that did was the crosshairs etched across her forehead.

He felt betrayed by her actions. Blinded by that theory, that drove him down a one-lane road. During his life, when faced with a loose end, it was mandatory to quickly tie up those loose ends, and burn the tips. He had to do what he was good at. Being forced to live that way, there was no other way to see it, which returned him to the task at hand when disposing of another loose end.

Lately, DP had been disturbed about what he had to do. Clambering from the truck, he entered the back of his stash house, and descending the basement steps. Flicking on the basement light, he never imagined being that close to his father without knowing it. Reflecting on the contact's death, he swatted at the flies swarming around the decaying body. He shook his head. No matter what he did, there was no other way to look at the contact. Darius Price Sr had been his contact, plain and simple. For as long as he could remember, that's the role he played. As that contact, he solely called with a job or an envelope of money. That was it! Nevertheless, the contact's death was relentlessly weighing on him.

What bothered him the most was the actual comments made surrounding the contact possibly being his father. That negatively brought him front and center with the fact that his potential father had been that close to him but unwilling to step up to let him know.

That simple idea kept DP in a tangled state of mind. He repeatedly sought to shake the horrifying idea of being that close to his old man without knowing it. But he couldn't. In his eyes, killing the man who could have been his father was the only thing he could have done. The man, regardless of his label, had played a vicious game. At least, at this point, it was definite that his father was dead, instead of him parading before him on a regular basis and him thinking he was dead.

However, that gnawing, overbearing muse caused DP to feel human. To feel was beyond DP. He'd groomed himself earlier on to never let his emotions cloud his judgment. Just the same, he was overwhelmed with an emotion he never thought he would feel.

GUILT!

It was evident he had a lot of things to be guilty for. None of those things scratched the surface for the one reason why he felt the way he did. His guilt pertained to one particular thing, and no matter what, he wouldn't dwell on it. He couldn't. Dwelling on it wouldn't change a thing.

To let it would in turn eat him alive. He couldn't have that. So rather than let the guilt of killing his father eat away at him, he chopped his father up into small pieces and would let the pigs eat scarf down all he couldn't.

Chapter Nineteen

THE MEDICAL EXAMINER STEPPED off of the elevator, and walked up to Winter with the DNA results in her hand. "Miss James, our Jane Doe is, in fact, your twin sister."

For the first time in a long time, Winter smiled. She was on the verge of obtaining all the closure she needed. Now all she needed to know was her sister's name. "Were you able to find out her name?"

"There appears to be no record, whatsoever, for her in the computer database. I'm widening the search to see what we can come up with but right now, we're unable to come up with anything."

"What about her property?" Winter questioned. "Did she have any?"

"There were some keys retrieved. That's all I have. You are more than welcome to those if you like."

"I'll gladly take them. Thanks!"

The M.E. nodded. "No problem. Just leave your number so when I have more information, I can get ahold of you," she insisted, taking off to get the keys. She returned with them in her hand, extending her condolences first, then handed her the keys while Winter handed over her phone number.

"Thanks again for your help," Winter stated, almost set to leave. "Oh!" She had one more question. "Do you know the address where my sister's body was found?"

The M.E. nodded, and pulled the address from her lab coat. She knew Winter would be interested in having it.

* * * * *   * * * * *

"I'm hoping this medical examiner can give us some insight that can point us in the right direction," Detective Hawkins said, pushing the down button on the elevator.

"It's a shame how that Winter girl went and got her brains blew out. I had thought of blowing her brains out but just not like that," Detective Smith said with a chuckle.

"I just bet your butt, playa. I just bet you did!" Hawkins replied, causing them both to laugh. "But you can still get some of that though. You're a patient man so don't be surprised if it takes her a minute or two to warm up to you," he said, jokingly.

While both detectives laughed at the joke, the elevator dinged with the elevator doors opening. Instantly, the laughter stopped when the detectives laid eyes on Winter. *What the hell!* was what they thought. What else could they think? They stared at her as if she was a ghost. She had to be one. They'd personally seen the side of her head blown off and smeared across the parking lot.

Winter sensed the questionable glares and it made her uncomfortable. "Excuse me, DETECTIVES!" she yelped, putting emphasis on detectives. "HELLO!?!?!?" she yelled, waving her hands in front of the detectives' face. "You two act like you've seen a ghost or something?" She stepped off the elevator, moving to her left to move around the mesmerized detectives. She couldn't stand there tripping out with them. She had better things to do. They would have to get it together by themselves.

The detectives followed her movements, unable to take their eyes off of her. They watched her walking away, without a word to say. Then, Hawkins found his tongue to be the first to speak.

"You're dead!" he boldly said.

Winter was thrown off by the detective's statement. Frowning, she didn't know how to take the accusation. The detective's words were damaging. "Excuse me?" she asked, with plenty of attitude in her tone. "How could you say some shit like that to me?"

Hawkins snapped out of his state of shock, finally realizing the severity of his words. He quickly apologized. "You are Winter James, right?" he asked, suspecting the woman before them could be her.

"Yes, I am!" she exclaimed, putting her hand on her hip. "Who else would I be?" she asked, rolling her neck.

Smith cut in. "You have to forgive us but we thought you were involved in an accident last night." He attempted to make sense of what was going on.

"You have me confused with my sister."

"Your SISTER!" they both screamed in unison.

"Yeah, my twin sister," she confessed, proudly.

"WE didn't know you had a twin sister," Hawkins mumbled, feeling stupid for what he initially said.

"I didn't either until yesterday. Is there anything you can tell me about her?" she asked, hurting for information.

"We thought she was you so we're here to see what the M.E. can provide," Smith answered.

"Can you please keep me informed then?" she requested.

"I'll be more than happy to give you a call when I have something?" Smith replied, thinking of her aunt. "How is your aunt?"

Winter's eyes glossed a little. "She didn't make it," she muttered, hating to think about her auntie's death.

"I'm sorry to hear that," he replied.

"Me too! I have to get going." She had to get out of there. "But please let me know something when you get the chance, alright?"

"Will do," Smith asserted.

And with that, Winter walked off leaving the detectives stunned. They looked at each other, shaking their head.

Hawkins pushed the down button on the elevator again, and the doors slid open. "Smithie, with how crazy this case is, I think I'm ready for a vacation."

★ ★ ★ ★ ★   ★ ★ ★ ★ ★

As Winter walked into the apartment manager's office, the secretary sitting at the front desk openly stared into her. She was aware of what happened the night before so seeing Winter left her awfully confused. *How could she survive that kind of head wound?*

Winter, inhaling the stares, wouldn't let the secretary's rubbernecking bother her. She had to push forward with her intentions of being there. "Hi, my name is Winter James and I believe my sister lived in one of your apartments. I'm here to get her stuff."

The secretary gawked at Winter as if she hadn't heard anything.

Winter snapped her fingers and waved her hands in the lady's face trying to snap her out of her trance. "Hello! Hello! Is anyone there?" she shouted.

The secretary jolted back to reality. "I'm sorry!" she admitted, regaining her bearings. "What did you say?"

"I said I'm here to get my sister's stuff out of her apartment."

"I would have never guessed Ramona had a twin sister with how private she was." She got up to grab the master set of keys.

Winter took notice to the name Ramona, locking it in her mental vault.

"Here's the keys you'll need to get into the building and Ramona's apartment," the secretary explained, extending her condolences.

Winter accepted the condolences on her way out of the office. As she walked up the sidewalk, she noticed a black Ford Mustang out the corner of her eye. She recalled seeing it somewhere before. Seeing it now made her feel some type of way. She wondered if the car was her sister's.

She pulled out her sister's set of keys, hitting the alarm button. The lights blinked activating the alarm. Deactivating it, she popped the trunk. There was a black duffel bag sitting in the middle of the trunk. Curious to its contents, she halfway unzipped it. It was filled with colorful wigs, clothes, and some other miscellaneous items. Zipping it back up, she picked it up to find out how heavy it was. Sitting it down, she opened it again to find a miniature arsenal underneath the clothes. Quickly zipping it up, she glanced around before pulling it out.

Slipping the bag over her shoulder, she made her way to Ramona's apartment. Speed walking, she couldn't get there fast enough. She checked over her shoulder with every step taken. Her mind was racing a mile a minute as she attempted to figure out who her sister was.

Making it to Ramona's apartment, she didn't know what to expect as she stood outside the door. Sliding the key into the lock, she slowly turned the key, unlocking the door. Twisting the knob, she hesitated before making entry. Her hesitation disclosed that she could be faced with anything. Except, she hadn't expected to see what she saw once she pushed the door open.

Ramona's apartment was relatively similar to her own. The decor was the exact same. The only difference was the color scheme. The moment she stepped inside she felt at home.

Setting the bag down by the front door, she wandered through the apartment. With each step, she felt a piece of her sister walking with her. It almost felt as if Ramona was giving her a personal tour. Coming upon the master bedroom, she found the door locked. Using Ramona's keys, she opened the door to unveil something unbelievable.

"What the fuck is all this shit?" she asked, stepping into the bedroom. The set-up looked like something out of a movie. "Who keeps this kind of equipment in their apartment?"

Soaking it all in, she went to retrieve the bag by the front door, needing to figure out what sort of stuff her sister was into. From everything she saw, she was lost to anything that would expound on that knowledge. Thoroughly searching the duffel bag, she was unable to find anything to get her closer to who Ramona was.

What she gathered was that her sister had a whole lot going on. With the colorful wigs and firepower, her guess was that Ramona had maybe too much going on. Even the finding of different kinds of identifications worried her. Flipping through them, the evidence continued to prove that Ramona would be hard to figure out any time soon.

Regardless, Winter's infatuation with her sister guided her to the elaborate computer set-up for answers. Turning it on, it instructed her to provide a retina scan. That was a technique she'd seen people use as a form of entry in the movies. *This is some real Mission Impossible type shit.* Whereas, she couldn't find anything that remotely appeared to be a scanner. She peered into the webcam to see what would happen. Her closeness activated the sensors and the webcam scanned her eyes.

With access to the computer, she embarked on her search for Ramona's true identity. The apartment manager's secretary had called her Ramona; but, that was probably the name she wanted them to know. She wanted to find out who she truly was.

Initially, she found nothing. *What is the purpose of having all this high-tech stuff if it isn't gonna tell me anything?* she questioned, figuring she could really use DP's computer knowledge right now. He could have easily shown her how everything worked. In that same instance, the thought of him produced a bitter taste in her mouth, almost making her gag. She had to eliminate the thought of him and the taste in her mouth.

Forging ahead, she clicked on certain files, learning that most of them were encrypted. Doubling clicking the files, she found they required a different kind of authority. She assumed if she could gain access to those files, she would obtain a few answers to her questions.

Trying her hand, she double-clicked another file. Thinking she'd gained access, a picture of some kids playing in the park filled the screen. Clicking another, a picture similar to the first one popped up.

This must mean something, she concluded. *With all this equipment, it would have been a complete waste if she didn't use it for its full potential'* She leaned back in the chair to gather her thoughts. With no idea how to work the computer, she apprehended there was something she wasn't able to find. As she thought, she crossed her right leg over the left, tapping a button unknowingly.

She rubbed her eyes then sat up to focus. Readjusting her sight, she glanced down to see a hand scanner peeking out. She placed her hand on it. The computer read her palm and instructed her to close the files previously opened before seeking authorized approval. She followed those instructions, then scanned her hand again. The computer went through its motions, turning all of the files that were once red to green. She'd gained access. Smiling, her smile spread even wider when the computer acknowledged her entry into the system by its greeting.

"Good morning, Ramona!"

Ramona? Her name really is Ramona. But Ramona what?

The computer software opened all the files she'd previously tried to open simultaneously. She watched the files pile on top of one another. The last file contained a list of names.

At the top of the list was the name Ramona James - her sister's true identity.

She became dizzy with emotions, going from being upset to happy to sad. The surprising fact of having a twin sister, and not knowing, overwhelmed her. She hated finding out so late in life about the secrets that had been kept from her. The revealing of those secrets made her question what was really real and what was truly fake.

Who is who? she longed to know. No one seemed to be who they said they were. She was tired of having these types of questions with no one to give her the appropriate answers. That pushed her to search for the answers she needed to know. If she didn't, everyone taken from her would have died in vain.

In any event, she couldn't function effectively with being so tired. Her body was beat down. Looking at the full-sized bed to her left, she eased over to it, and collapsed on top of it. But before she could firmly press her face into the pillow, it was lights out for her. She was literally out for the count.

* * * *   * * * *

Detective Smith and Hawkins arrived at the local Dunkin' Donuts, and ordered a box of donuts and some coffee.

Coffee in hand, Smith slid into the booth. "I'm thinking we should put a tail on Winter."

"Why, so you can know where she is just in case you find the guts to holler?" Hawkins snapped, laughing at his own humor.

Smith had a good come back but he received a text message from the fingerprint analysis. "I think we got action, Hawk. That's from fingerprint. They have a partial hit on a shell from the James' residence."

"Does it say for who?"

Smith read the text again. "Not yet! Let's go and find out."

The detective arrived at the station, and marched into the fingerprint analysis headquarters, eager to find out who the fingerprint belonged to.

"Tell me something good, Mr. Fingerprint Guy," Smith voiced.

The nerdy looking guy spun around in his seat. "Well, I have two good things to tell you today, Mr. Smithie and Mr. Hawk. I have come across a startling discovery."

Hawkins interrupted the analysis' speech before it got too long. "Come on with the punch-line, Mr. Techie Guy," he suggested.

"Since you're in such a rush." He shut up, and handed both of them a piece of paper. "Here! One for you, Smithie. And one for you, Hawk."

Smith looked at the paper, shaking his head. "Oh my!" was his only words.

Hawkins was more interested in what Smith saw. "What does it say, Smithie?"

Smith smiled at him. "Hawk, my buddy! We have us a winner." He handed his partner the paper.

Reading it, Hawkins' face almost hit the floor. "Ain't this about a bitch?" He looked at Smith. "All this time, huh?"

"What does yours say?" Smith asked.

"Holy shit, I was too worried about yours." He quickly skimmed over the words, looking to make sense of it. "Smithie, it appears the person we thought was Winter James is actually Ramona James."

Chapter Twenty

WINTER WOKE UP FEELING refreshed from getting a good night's rest. She rolled over clutching the pillow in her arms, not wanting to let it go. She regretted having to get up but there was so much she had to do. Laying there, she began to prioritize her day.

First on the agenda was the preparation of a private funeral ceremony for her aunt and sister. That was a must. She wanted to send them off in style. That's what they deserved and that's what she intended on doing. That was the most important thing for her to do.

Sitting up, she swung her legs off the side of the bed, placing her feet on the floor. Placing some pressure to her soles, she stood and briefly felt queasy. The uneasiness striking her stomach made her light-headed, and her mouth watered. There was no time to give it a second thought as she felt herself about to throw up.

Jetting to the bathroom, she could taste the vomit in the back of her throat. As she made it to the toilet, she couldn't hold it any longer. She called Earl. His first, middle, and last name.

Throwing up and heaving loudly, she thought about what she ate. She couldn't recall haven't eaten anything in the last couple of days. She'd been running on pure adrenaline, and hadn't found the time to eat.

When was the last time I ate? she asked herself, heaving over the toilet. She couldn't pinpoint the actual time or the meal itself. As of late, eating hadn't been a priority for her. In the end, she figured it would be best if she did put something in her stomach, despite not having an appetite.

Getting off her knees, she rinsed her mouth out, coming to the conclusion she would need to shove something down her throat. She couldn't continue through the day without putting something in her stomach. That wouldn't be a good idea. Sooner or later her adrenaline would run out and she would run out with it. There was no need in chancing that.

First, she needed to hit her grille. Loading a new toothbrush with toothpaste, she went to work. Scrapping the roof of her mouth, and her tongue, it dawned on her that she couldn't recall the last time something more important showed up.

Pondering about the time of the month, she realized, not only had she not been eating, her period hadn't come either.

* * * * *   * * * * *

The light had turned red moments before DP pulled up to it. Gripping the steering wheel, he waited on the light to change. As he waited, an Audi Q3 drove through the cross intersection, and to his utter shock, Ramona was behind the steering wheel.

He had to be tripping. This couldn't be possible. Ramona was dead. That he knew for sure. How did he know? He'd been the one who killed her. That's how. But, how in the hell was she driving down the street then?

DUH! he said, smacking himself on the forehead. *That's not Ramona. That's Winter, the final loose end.* He watched the Audi speed down the road. *Who would have thought she would drive into my line of sight like that?*

Thinking it had to be a God-given blessing, he wondered if taking her out was necessary. It was something he knew he could do but it would also cause a slight pain in his side. Shrugging it off, it wouldn't be an everlasting pain.

Years ago, he should have figured that one day decisions would have to be made, and in that moment, it would always be kill or be killed. Being killed was never an option for him. At no time could he allow his love for another to dictate his downfall. To let that happen would mean that person have ultimate control over him. The only person he could have total faith in, when holding him down, was himself. With him, he knew everything he'd done and all of his secrets would be safe. That was one thing he knew for certain and didn't have to question.

147

Horns blared behind him snapping him back to the present.

Catching the light, he sped through the intersection and into the right lane. Based on the direction she went, she was headed back to the home they once shared together. Eager to get there, he hit the back streets racing to catch her or beat her there. He turned onto the street and could see the Audi parked in the driveway.

Damn it, she made it before me! His sitting at the light holding up traffic put too much time and space between them. However, that wouldn't stop anything. What was done was done. The things he desired to do would still manifest. Then something else grabbed his attention - the car slowly driving towards him.

From a distance, the car approaching resembled a detective's car. As a native of the streets, he'd seen so many different kinds of police cars that he could spot one a mile way. They stood out that much.

The detective's car crept down the streets, scoping out the duplex apartment buildings on the right side of the street. That was a sure giveaway that they were looking for something or someone. The detectives abruptly pulled over to the curb, parked in front of Winter's building, and got out to walk to the door.

Upon seeing that, DP whipped into the nearest parking spot on his right to see how it would play out. Pulling out his binoculars, he glared into the grilles of the two detectives looking to move up in rank. Unfortunately, it wouldn't be on his time. They had to go. Never did he need to be constantly looking over his shoulder so it'll be best to kill two birds with one stone.

He just hoped she would let them in.

* * * * *   * * * * *

No sooner as Winter moved about her apartment, there was a knock on the door. Finding that peculiar, she opted to play it safe. She cocked the hammer of the snub-nose .38 she took from Ramona's duffel bag. The weight of the revolver felt different than the Glock she held at the store. Shaking off the difference, a gun was a gun and it would protect her in her time of need.

Proceeding to the window, she slightly pulled back the blinds to see her visitors were Detective Smith and Hawkins. Shaking her head, this wasn't the best time to deal with them. They weren't coming with anything special that could help her so they were coming to waste her time.

She tucked the banger under the couch, returned to the door to slide the door chain on, then pulled it ajar. Playing nice, she flashed a fake smile, and eyed them both.

"Miss James, we need to talk about something very important," Smith said, peering through the small opening. "Do you mind if we come in?"

Thinking it over, she looked over her shoulder to make sure the detectives couldn't see the banger she tucked under the couch. "Is this gonna take long?" she asked, not wanting to waste precious time. "I have things to do."

"We'll try to make this as quick as possible," Smith retorted, not really knowing how long it would take.

"Well," she hesitated, "come in so we can get this over with." She unclasped the chain.

Once inside, Hawkins nudged Smith, and nodded towards the pictures sitting on the table pushed against the wall. "Miss James, is there anyone else in the apartment that we should know of?" he asked, seeking to protect themselves from danger.

Winter twirled around to face the detectives, noticing them nervous and on high alert. That caused her to focus more on everything around her. Scanning the immediate area, she found no reason for them to conduct themselves in that manner.

"Is there a problem, detectives?" she asked. "You seem on edge?"

"For our safety, would you mind if we search the premises?" Smith asked.

"That won't be necessary. I don't even know why you're here so that's what needs to be established first. I was kind enough to let you in and now you want to search my apartment. How about I put your asses out. Yeah, that's what I'm about to do," she explained, taking a step towards the front door.

The detectives recognized the agitation in her voice. It was evident. They'd overstepped their boundaries when insisting they search. That fact had to be rectified.

Smith, quick on his feet, stepped up to quickly calm her nerves. "Miss James, you told me to inform you of what I knew so we stopped by to speak with you about your sister," he voiced, holding his hands up to stop her.

"My sister. What about her?" she asked, folding her arms over her chest.

"We have become aware of her identity and it's our duty to forward that info directly to you."

She eyed Smith. "You could have called?" She broke the eye contact. "I'm extremely busy and have a lot on my plate. Can you simply give me what you have so I can get on with my day?" she insisted, holding out her hand.

Hawkins handed her a copy of the paper pointing out Ramona's identity.

Winter grabbed the single page, not even looking at it. The detectives paid close attention to that, observing how she set it down then stared at them with a *now you can go* look.

Smith dismissed the look, proceeding with the real reason for them being there. "Miss James, we also need to talk about something else. It's a very serious matter so you may want to sit down for this one," he suggested.

Exhaling heavily, she motioned them towards the sofa across from the couch. "Would you guys like some coffee since you won't leave?" Her attitude was evident.

"Some coffee will be fine, thanks!" Hawkins said, speaking for the both of them.

Scurrying off, she returned from the kitchen, and handed the detectives their cups one at a time.

Smith, taking a sip from his cup, swallowed the semi-warm liquid, trying to prepare himself for the bomb he came to drop. "Miss James, we're actually here to talk to you about your boyfriend."

"My boyfriend?" she asked. "That's odd considering I don't have one of those."

"You were in a relationship with Darius Price Jr at one point, correct?" Hawkins asked.

"That would be correct," she answered, glancing at Hawkins. "What do you think you want to tell me about him?" Her countenance was serious.

Just as he fixed his mouth to answer, his head snapped back from a bullet to the forehead. There were no sounds, no heads up, or any reason to expect that kind of reaction. Before Hawkins could grasp what occurred, he also took a bullet to the forehead. The blood was starting to ooze out of Smith's head wound as his eyes became still.

Across from them, Winter watched the scene unfold, taking to the floor to make her great escape. The stench of gun powder heightened her awareness that whomever shooting hadn't come for coffee. They'd come to kill.

She removed the .38 from underneath the couch cushion, holding it with both hands. Shaken up a little, she shoved the revolver over the edge of the sofa, and pulled the trigger until it clicked. She wasn't sure if she hit anyone or if anyone was still there. She merely sought to defend herself.

In the midst of her shooting, she did get lucky with one of her shots. Once the shooting started, DP took a slug to the left arm. It was a flesh wound but it forced him out of sight to access the damage. Squeezing the entry wound, a pint of blood streamed down his arm. That defined how real shit was.

During his recovery, Winter reloaded her weapon.

I must get in a better position, he reasoned.

Wincing in pain, he stepped from around the wall prepared to riddle Winter with hot lead. However, she moved quicker than he did, and was able to get the upper hand. Popping up from behind the couch, she let loose another six rounds at him.

With his piece almost cleared to fire, his reaction time had been slowed; therefore, he couldn't get off a good shot. She had put him in a precarious position. Instead of aiming at her, he let off a few shots at the floor as he attempted to get out of there. During that hasty retreat, the first few shots honing in on him grazed his right arm. When the following slugs zeroed in on him, he found himself in more trouble than he could have hoped for. He was almost out of Winter's lines of sight when he was struck with another shot to his left shoulder.

He absorbed the need to separate himself from her. There hadn't been any indication she would put up that kind of fight. But she had. The slugs burning his flesh was a testament to that. He let off another set of random shots to buy himself some time to escape, hating that he put himself in this kind of predicament.

What he figured would have been an easy thrill turned into a similar situation he previously encountered with Ramona. Winter had unexpectedly turned into Ramona's evil twin. And that meant he would use the time it took to recover to re-evaluate his next move. He figured he should have learned a valuable lesson when dealing with Ramona. But he hadn't. He had to stop making mistakes, and take heed to his lessons.

Exiting as he came, he was losing a lot of blood, and was in dire need to be patched up. If he didn't get medical attention soon, he could lose the battle for his life. He couldn't see himself going out like that.

Making it to his car, he called his private nurse, hoping she was home. Catching her as she was about to leave, she agreed to meet him nearby to take care of his wounds.

On the other hand, Winter was ready for war. She'd reloaded the .38 and held it tightly in her sweaty palms. Her adrenaline was over the top and sweat flowed down the center of her back. The current circumstance had her on ten.

Easing around the couch, she followed the blood trail leading her to the spare bedroom. The blood came to a sudden stop at the window sill. Stomping her foot, a car started up down the street. She raced to the front, and peered through the window in the nick of time to see a black-on-black Camaro speeding by.

"Muthafucka!" she spat. "It had been him the whole time," she mumbled, smacking her leg.

The truth of the matter came full circle. Stunned, it hurt her to the core. But it couldn't set in. The faint sounds of the sirens approaching softened the pain. She had to get out of there. With the police approaching, she put her tail in gear, grabbed all she could, and headed out the door. In her whip, she left a long tire burn on the pavement as she fled the scene.

Her freedom depended on it.

Chapter Twenty-One

"WE'RE COMING LIVE FROM the scene of a horrific double homicide," Arlene tightly gripped the microphone, "at the residence of a Winter James, a 24-year old female, where two of Madison's finest investigative detectives were found dead with gunshot wounds to each of their head."

She moved a loose string of hair from her face. "An all-point bulletins have been put out for Winter James for questioning purposes. There is no evidence or probable cause to suspect she had any involvement but the police are looking for her to rule out her involvement. At this point, that's all I have. Things are being kept under wraps here on the scene. What I can say is that this leaves the city and the police department in a sadden state. If anyone has any valuable information considering this matter, please contact the local authorities. I'm Arlene Jackson reporting live from the scene of the double homicide of two Madison police detectives. Back to you in the studio, Shaun."

As the news coverage ended, four all-black Suburbans pulled up, with the FBI and ATF jumped out. They promptly walked up to the apartment building where other officers congregated. The agents' arrival was met by the local police handling the case. The heads of the two federal agency branches flashed their badges, and introduced themselves and stated their reason for being there.

"I'm Special Agent Mark Blair, with the FBI. And this here is ATF Special Agent Samuel Pointer. Who's in charge here?"

"That'll be me!" Sergeant Jack Watson, a burly looking man, screamed, moving through his men.

S.A. Blair, a tall man with strikingly strong facial features, waited for the Sergeant to finish his approach before he spoke. "We're here to claim jurisdiction. We understand you have lost a few good men. We're not trying to downplay that. We're here to assist in the best way we can and your cooperation will be greatly appreciated." He glanced around at those listening. "We can work hand-in-hand in this continued investigation and resolve it quickly or we can bump heads. Bumping heads is not what we're here to do. We're here to solve this case and put whomever responsible behind bars. At this time, I'll like our team to come in and process the scene." He looked to the Sergeant for his approval.

The Sergeant nodded.

"Later, we'll be making our way down to your station to go over everything your team may have so we can go from there. Does anyone have any questions?"

NO ONE said anything. Everyone was pretty much in compliance with the plan. When Blair seen no objections, he went to work, and sent his FBI forensic team to fall in line. He stepped to the side, giving them the room they needed to enter the crime scene and collect the available evidence and samples.

Working diligently, they tagged and bagged everything of value, taped off the apartment, and left everyone to go their respective ways. Back at the station, there was a bit of frenzy as certain officers attempted to locate the pertinent files the slain detectives had been working on.

Off hand, Blair sat back while waiting on the results from the blood samples recovered from the walls. Sitting down at a computer, he had to do something. He couldn't sit there doing nothing. Pulling up everything he could find pertaining to Winter James, he devoured the information on the screen.

The details specified that some recent encounters in her life had taken a very bad turn for the worse. First, her father was brutally murdered in cold blood, followed by her aunt, then her twin sister. Now, two slain police detectives were found dead in her apartment. Things weren't looking too good for her at that point; but, as a veteran agent, he wouldn't automatically jump to conclusion. Nevertheless, it was extremely hard to rule out her involvement, considering she was missing and hadn't come forward for questioning. That fact alone didn't slip the agent's mental note.

Looking up from the screen, Blair snapped his fingers at one of the local cops. "Do we have an all-points bulletin out for Winter James?" he asked.

"Yes, sir. We do!"

"Widen it, please. And include that she may be armed and dangerous."

"Will do, sir!"

"Blair!" Pointer shouted, coming around the corner. "We have two different kinds of bullets here. None of them are from the officer's gun. The bullets lodged in the wall coming from the direction of the blood are from a Sig Sauer .40. Those bullets are consistent with those pulled from the decease."

Blair contemplated what went down. "So, we had a shootout between whomever shot the detectives and who was trying to shoot someone else, along with the one who wasn't trying to get shot. The question is could any one of these people be Winter James?"

Before anyone could answer, the forensic analysis came forward with a match for the blood samples found at the scene. The analysis handed it to Blair, who cleared his throat so he could read it aloud.

"The blood sample came back for a Darius Price." Reading it to himself, his mind twirled around thoughts of who Darius was and what kind of Intel they had on him. "What do you have on a Darius Price?" he asked, glancing at the Sergeant.

A local detective stepped up with a file in his hand.

"Where have I heard that name before?" Blair asked, more to himself than to anyone else.

"It's either because of Darius Price Sr of the old or of Darius Price Jr of the new. Here's his file."

The Sergeant sat up. "The other day we got a hit on a partial but have nothing to go on when finding him."

Blair walked around the small computer desk looking for his communications tech. Finding him, he pointed and said, "We need Darius Price Jr on the FBI MOST WANTED LIST. NOW!!" He turned back to the detective, motioning him to sit down. Turning to him, he said, "Please fill me in on everything you know." He gave him a serious look. "It's imperative that I know everything."

* * * *   * * * *

After dumping the car, Winter hopped in Ramona's Mustang. Unaware of who may know of that car, she couldn't ride around in anything she could be easily identified in. Taking no chances, she dolled herself up in a wig and a few facial pieces she'd found, and slid on a pair of sunglasses. At first glance, she didn't resemble anything close to the Winter James she knew.

Yet, due to the recent activities, most of her plans had been changed or pushed up. The memorial service she wanted to have would have to wait and it was possible that it might not happen at all. That was something she truly felt bad about, since she wanted to send her loved one off nicely. But time was of the essence and she had more immediate plans to tend to.

She pulled up to her auntie's house, and the feeling was eerie. This wasn't how it was supposed to be. But it was the way it was. Looking at the house, she could feel it in her bones that what she truly needed was somewhere in that house. With all of the secrets coming out, the rest had to lay within the confinement of Sara's house.

Breaking the tape blocking the front door, she entered the unlocked door, not wanting to waste time. She barged in as if someone was refusing her entry. She was on a mission; but she stopped just inside of the door. It felt as if someone was watching her. Figuring she was tripping, she had to shake that feeling. She needed to relax and focus on finding her answers.

Stepping into the house, she shut the door, closed her eyes, and said a silent prayer for herself and her aunt. Ending the prayer with AMEN, she opened her eyes and headed straight to her aunt's bedroom. Most of Sara's personal belongings had been moved around. To the naked eye, there seemed to be no physical evidence left to retrieve. She wouldn't be fooled that easily. There was a host of shoe boxes on the floor; but, there appeared to be no shoes in them. That seemed like valuable clues to her.

Pushing the boxes on the floor, she began checking the remaining boxes at the bottom of the closet. There were maybe three or four rows of boxes left. The top rows were empty like the rest. The next row had a few boxes that contained what seemed to be letters. They were addressed to her aunt so she tossed them to the side. She continued to find boxes full of letters and pictures. Slowing to examine the pictures, she found one of her aunt and the woman she seen in her bathroom mirror that one day. If she didn't know for sure then, she knew now that the woman was her mother.

She soberly stared at the picture as a tear escaped her eyes. Looking at the old photo, she saw how gorgeous her mother was. Holding onto the picture for dear life, she didn't want to let it go, knowing she had to if she wanted to find what she was looking for. Setting it down, her search eventually paid off when she came across a diary. Opening it, she read the words, and instantly surmised it once belonged to her mother. As she read, she was hooked by her mother's words.

The words scribbled on those pages spoke volumes to her soul. They penetrated her deeply, awakening an internal spirit that released a fulfillment of completeness. Rapidly absorbing page after page, she searched for the truth. She felt so close to finding it that she couldn't stop reading. Sure enough, the more she read, the clearer reality became to her. When she arrived at the part about her mother's pregnancy, she was all in.

The words on those stained pages voiced the concern of living in harm's way if the father of her babies wasn't the man it should have been. The dilemma her mother faced kept her fearful for her life. There was undoubtedly a hold held over her that wouldn't allow her to let go and do as she saw fit.

Winter realized that it would be her mother's refusal to let go that would ultimately be her downfall. Her mother was scared of the possibility of being killed or severely beaten because of the decisions she elected to make. That understanding compelled her to arrange a safe passage of sorts for her unborn children. Never did she actually want them separated, but she knew it would be the best thing to do. Her deep-rooted fear was that leaving them together would be disastrous especially when only a few knew she was carrying twins. That's when the plan for Sara to take Winter was made. Initially, the other twin was to go to the state; however, Darius Sr. stepped up to take her.

Winter had to stop reading when getting to the part of her mother's affair with DP's father. She pinched the bridge of her nose in an attempt to hold back the tears. It was heart-wrenching. Thoughts of DP being her brother and the life they lived together fractured her heart. As much as she wanted to, she wasn't able to read any further. She closed the diary, unable to process her thoughts.

Looking off, she cried. *This was supposed to be given to me whenever I was ready for it.* She wiped at her face, comprehending that the truth of the matter would have been revealed to her upon receiving it. She assumed that's what Sara wanted to give her.

If she had only came when Sara originally called, things could have been different. Even if that was correct, everything happened in its own time and for its own reasons. Had she come when originally called, there was a good chance she wouldn't have made it out alive herself. Not to downplay the death of her loved ones, she was glad to be alive. Where she formerly looked at the situation as being left alone, she viewed it differently now.

She may be alone but she wasn't defenseless. Surviving was in her blood and she would have no problem making it on her own. For the life of her, she kept something up her sleeves and this occasion would be no different. Certain things were naturally in her and when she needed them most, they would naturally come out. As long as she believed that, she had faith in herself that she would come out on top.

Shaking the remainder of the boxes, the floor board underneath her rattled. Tossing the rest of the boxes out of the way, she found a latched door. Unlatching and lifting it, she faced a set of stairs leading down into what appeared to be a cellar.

The cellar was pitch black so she ran to the kitchen to fetch a flashlight, then returned to head down the steps.

Stepping off the last step, the space was bigger than she thought. It was some kind of storage space. Along the walls, there was brown boxes neatly stacked from the floor upward to the ceiling. In front of the boxes were smaller-sized green crates.

Curious about it all, she opened a crate first, and couldn't believe her discovery. It was comparable to hitting the jackpot. The crates contained enough firepower and ammunition to arm a small army. There were hand grenades, assault rifles, handguns, and much more.

159

Crate after crate, that's all she found, along with silencers, scopes, and stands. This was a stockpile of weapon truly put together in the preparation of war.

But whose arsenal, is it? she wondered. *Could it have been my father's, DP's father or someone else's?*

The questions kept popping up in her head. Instead of continuing to ask, she moved along to the brown boxes, ripping open the flap of the one closest to her. Her jaw dropped when she saw what was in the box. This moment had to be a dream come true.

In the box was stacks upon stacks of heavily wrapped $100 bills. She moved quickly from box to box, dying to know if she would find what she had in the original box. And she did. Spinning in circles, she figured there had to be millions of dollars hidden down there. And now it was all hers.

Excited about that, she grabbed a few handguns, a slew of clips, several stacks of cash, and the diary upstairs. Packing those things in a box of their own, she put everything else back how she'd found it. She certainly didn't want anyone becoming aware of this glorious discovery. This was hers, and she wasn't willing to share it with anyone.

Chapter Twenty-Two

DP FOUND HIMSELF OUT cruising around the neighborhood when he spotted a black Mustang parked in Sara's driveway. He automatically assumed it was Winter. Not sure if it was her, but if it was her, he hadn't planned to run into her that soon. Mulling it over, he couldn't see it being anyone else bold enough to be in that house after what happened. Nevertheless, if it wasn't her, he would sit and wait to see who it was.

In spite of his pain, he wanted it to be her. He longed to put a bullet in her face. She'd shot him. That's something no one had been able to do. That was a tall accomplishment in itself but he didn't want that to be the driving force behind his ambitions. He had to play it cool. His pain would make it difficult to tackle the task as he normally would.

The Winter he was dealing with was far unlike the person he previously known. Times had changed. Where he once had the upper hand on her, he now hoped to get a solid location on her whereabouts by laying on her. That way, when he fully healed, he could move in swiftly to handle his business.

As he sat and waited, Sara's front door opened slowly. Seeing that, his heart rate thumped with excitement. The adrenaline from that excitement consumed him. Sitting his .40 on his lap, he was ready to kill.

Winter peeked her head out, checking to see if the coast was clear.

DP smacked the center console, aware that if he was 100% he would have easily taken her out. She had no clue to his lurking, and that ignorance would have provided him the blanket to move in and finish the job. However, he had to sit there and watch her coming out of the house with caution. The mere sight of her sent tingles up and down his trigger finger. He grabbed the .40, and slipped his finger within the trigger housing. He wanted to kill her; but, he battled to suppress those temptations. There would be plenty of time for that. He needed to employ some patience. That would be hard. The cold sweats flooding his pores increased the level of energy surging throughout his body.

Winter placed a box in the trunk, then raced back to the house. He wondered what she had in the box, figuring whatever it was had some grave importance considering she risked her life to get it.

She returned with a second box, placing it next to the other. Slamming the trunk close, she clambered in behind the wheel, and backed out.

A true gentleman, he gave her time to get ahead of him before pulling out himself. Driving slow, he tried to keep as much distance between them as he could. That was a hard feat when no one else occupied the street but them. It seemed bizarre to be behind her, even for him. He figured, if she was on her p's and q's, she'll pick up on him tailing her.

Being the analyzer, he assessed how it looked. To him, it would look fishy for a truck to slowly cruise down the street behind him all of a sudden. That would raise a red flag if he was ever in her situation. Maybe it's only because *I'm behind her that I'm thinking of these factors?*

The Mustang's brake lights illuminated.

He stepped on his brakes once peeping her stepping on hers. Riding the brake, he wasn't sure if he should stop or keep going. Unsure of what to do, he eased off the brake to keep going. But she had picked up on something. He wasn't sure what. But, she continued to slow down.

Not wanting to appear too obvious, he proceeded down the street as if she wasn't there. He wasn't worried about being seen. He rode behind limo tint. If that hadn't worked, he was decked out in a ball cap and sunglasses. At first glance, she wouldn't recognize him anyway.

Nonetheless, Winter felt strange and that feeling informed her of a danger lurking. The feeling struck her bone deep, her nerves twitched, and her senses perked up. Checking her rearview, a black Chevy Tahoe filled the small mirror. Adjusting it, she wanted to get a good look at the truck. Getting that, she pulled over recklessly, hopped out, and raised a brand-new Glock 22s at the truck. She aimed directly at the driver, and opened fire relentlessly.

The shots traveled fast and with an accurate precision; except, they ricocheted off the windshield.

DP slammed on the brakes as the bulletproof windshield absorbed the shots. Hearing the bullets tinging off the windshield forced him melt into the driver's seat. *I'm glad I paid that extra money, or else I might have been in trouble.* Breathing deeply, he collected himself, inhaling his anger.

Winter emptied the entire clip at DP.

Taking advantage, DP smashed the gas, attempting to mow her down. If he couldn't put a bullet in her head, his next best thing would be to carve the treads of his Goodyear tires across her forehead.

Winter reacted quickly, threw the gun at him, then dove in-between two cars parked at the curb.

Zooming by, he knew had he been his old self he wouldn't have to wrestle with her. He would have knocked her off, and gone about the rest of his day. But he had to leave her to live another day. That was a blessing he wouldn't normally extend so she better thank the Lord for that gift. Because the next he saw her, God Almighty wouldn't be able to save her.

He turned the approaching corner sharply, stunned by the brief interaction with his childhood love. She'd turned into a cold-blooded psychopathic killer as if the light switch had been flipped. He found that amusing. It wouldn't make a difference. She was dead meat.

Glancing over his shoulder as he completed his turn, he caught a glance of her getting up in pain. *Don't worry, Winter baby! It'll only be a matter of time before it's over for you.*

★ ★ ★ ★ ★   ★ ★ ★ ★ ★

Minutes prior to the lover's quarrel, S.A. Blair and Pointer received an anonymous tip regarding a Winter James sighting at her aunt's house. When moving out, they wanted to proceed with caution. They strapped on their bulletproof vests, checked their weapons, and devised a plan. They wanted to go into the situation well-prepared and under one mindset.

163

Pulling out of the station's parking lot, a deep baritone voice blared through the radio. "Shots FIRED! Shots FIRED! We have reports of shots fired at..."

Blair looked at Pointer, believing it to be Winter or Darius doing the shooting. "I have no choice but to believe she did it, Pointer," he proclaimed, referring to the death of the two detectives.

The driver whipped the big Suburban to the scene, leaving the agents holding on for dear life. When they pulled up, there was nothing to see. The street was deserted. And there wasn't any sign of DP or Winter. The agents immediately blocked off the entire block to give the FBI's forensic team time to work the area. While the team combed for evidence, Blair and Pointer entered the house for the very first time.

Looking around, Blair examined the dried up blood in front of the bedroom door. A shiver flustered him. The setting inside of the house held a different feel to it. He wandered around wondering what brought Winter there. There must have been something important there she needed and was willing to take a chance of being seen to get it.

"Pointer!" he yelled. "Holler for the forensic team to conduct a full search of the house once they're done outside."

"Copy!" Pointer replied, exiting to pass along the instructions. Quickly returning, he held up an evidence bag containing shells. "Blair, this is all they've found so far. A total of 15 shells possibly from a Glock."

"There seem to be a variety of guns being used around here. Maybe it's not her. What you think, Pointer?" he asked, looking at his partner.

Pointer was cut off by another agent walking in with Winter's gun.

Blair's eyes lit up. "Today must be our lucky day, Pointer. Now let's see what we can find in this house."

★ ★ ★ ★ ★   ★ ★ ★ ★ ★

Wincing in pain, Winter wiped down every surface of the car she thought she may have touched. She worked frantically while thinking about what else she could have done. With everything happening so fast, she had a decision to make and she made it. If she wouldn't have been on point, he wouldn't have hesitated to do her in. Whereas, that didn't eliminate the excruciating pain in her abdominal area.

She pushed the transforming pain to the back of her mind. DP had seen what she'd been driving so that meant she would need another form of transportation. She needed to stay mobile. Resuming one of Ramona's identities, she hopped in the Mustang and found the closest car dealership to see about trading in the Ford.

During the ride, she was extra careful to minimize any further touching of the interior, and whatever she touched, she planned to wipe down before getting out. Pulling onto the lot, her objective was to complete a quick trade transaction and get as far away from the car as she could.

Getting a good deal, she traded the Mustang in for a 1999 Chevy Lumina with tinted windows. Feeling good about the trade, she mentally prepared herself for full offensive directive. DP had to get what he had coming. She couldn't forgive him for his transgressions. She wouldn't be that silly to think she could. He wasn't the kind of guy that would allow her to forgive and forget. He wouldn't stop coming after her until she was dead so she would take the same approach.

Unaware of where to start, she cruised through Madison, making sure to keep her eyes open for any car she thought she may have seen him in. She was out for blood and he would feel her wrath before it was all said and done.

Coming to a stop sign, she spotted a black-on-black 1996 Chevy Impala parked down the street to her right. That was a car she'd seen him in before. Making the turn, she recalled something about a nurse named Natalie who patched up one of his buddies when he couldn't get to the hospital. He'd said something about her being the one they went to when they needed medical attention to minimize the hospital bills.

Driving pass, she scoured each house, seeking to remember which one was Natalie's. She came up short. Going around the corner, she came back just as Natalie was coming out of the house. *This must be my lucky day.* She slowed to give her enough time to hop in the Impala and pull off.

Natalie took the bait and pulled out in front of her.

165

This will be like taking candy from a baby, she thought.

Pulling onto the main road, she allowed several cars to separate them as she followed Natalie to the local Walgreens. Natalie pulled into the pharmacy drive-thru, apparently to pick up a prescription. Winter, aware of Natalie's position, quickly pulled into the parking lot, parked and got out. Moving with purpose, she slid to the back of the Walgreens and up to Natalie's Impala.

In the car, Natalie had no clue to what was upon her. Bobbing her head, she was rapping along with the music rattling the trunk. Winter snatched the passenger's door open, and slid in. Natalie was startled by the intrusion but words couldn't form when Winter aimed the Glock at her.

Winter turned down the radio, and gave Natalie some simple instructions: "Do as I tell you and nothing will happen to you."

Natalie nodded in agreement.

The pharmacist ambled over to the drive-thru window.

Winter leaned back to let Natalie retrieve her medication. Once the transaction was complete, Natalie was instructed to pull out of the parking lot and down the street. "Pull over right there," Winter demanded. Before Natalie could pull over good enough, Winter checked the clip, and jacked the slide back.

Slamming on the brakes, Natalie's eyes bulged out of her head. "Please don't kill me! I don't have a lot of money on me. But you can take everything I have," she yelped, panicking at the sight of the gun.

"Bitch, SHUT UP!" Winter spat. "I'm looking for DP. Do you know where he is?"

Natalie's facial expression said she did. However, she failed to verbalize it.

"Let me be very clear. You have one more chance to tell me what I want to know before we'll see if you can dress your own gunshot wound. Is he at your house?"

Natalie shook her head.

"Where is he then?" Winter asked.

Stuttering, Natalie tried to lie as the tears flowed down her face and onto her neck. "He's supposed to meet me at my house when I get back with this stuff," she muttered, sniffling and pointing at the small white bag.

Winter looked at the bag. "This is what you gone do. You're gonna help me kill his bitch ass. You hear ME?" she shouted, frightening Natalie even more.

Natalie was stunned by the request and she completely broke down.

"Bitch, you need to get it together. Once you do your part, you'll be free to go. I'll be out of your life for good. Feel me?"

Natalie nodded. It would have been dumb to go against anything she said. But she also knew she wouldn't allow Winter to do anything to her baby daddy. She had to protect him or at least warn him. He was all she had.

Winter put the gun to Natalie's head. "Come on, bitch! Get me back to your house a.s.a.p."

＊＊＊＊＊　　＊＊＊＊＊

"Special Agent Blair, you have to come see this," the leader of the forensic team screamed.

Blair, followed by Pointer, stepped into the bedroom to find the forensic expert down in what appeared to be a cellar of some kind.

"What do we have down there?" Blair asked.

"I'll let you come see for yourself," the expert said, climbing up the steps.

Blair made his way down the steps, coming face-to-face with the crates and boxes lined along the walls of the man-made cellar. He made a mental note of the cellar's size, the depth, and storage capacity. In all his years, he'd never seen such an elaborate set-up but it didn't surprise him.

He walked over to the crates, and opened on. "Pointer, you need to get down here," he commanded, staring at the firepower in the crate.

Pointer descended the steps to take in what everybody else had seen. Walking over to Blair, he stared in awe at the artillery in front of them.

The two agents scratched their heads. They hadn't been prepared for this kind of discovery. Excited, they were glad they found it instead

Aja LaGrand Blount

of being the ones fired upon by someone who owned that kind of arsenal.

Blair pointed to the box already open. "Pointer, check that box to see what's inside it."

Pointer flipped the flap up. "You won't believe it if I told you," he exclaimed, staring at the stacks of $100 bills heavily wrapped in plastic.

"What is it?" Blair wondered, still looking through the crates.

"MONEY!" Pointer declared. "And plenty of it. There appears to be quite a piece of it missing too."

"So that's why she came back," Blair mumbled aloud. He hurried towards the steps. "Come on, Pointer. We need to have us a news conference and..." He stopped to look around. "We need to add Miss Winter James to our Most Wanted List."

Chapter Twenty-Three

DP WAS IN SO much pain, he was unable to sleep. When getting no rest, he was left with animated thoughts of killing his childhood love. It was those thoughts that numbed his pain. Loving them more and more, he invited them at every waking second.

He was imperative that he gave it to her if it was the last thing he would do. He could see it no other way. Her demise was imminent. She was something of a good opponent but she just wasn't good enough. If she was, he wouldn't be sitting there experiencing pain. He would be dead. And that's how he wanted to leave her.

Her two shots wouldn't hold him back. He wouldn't let it slow him down. It would only strengthen him. The immobility in his left arm wouldn't hinder him. He didn't need it to deal with little ole Miss Winter James. He wholeheartedly believed that he could single-handedly take care of her with no problem. All he had to do was get up and do it.

Rising to leave, a sharp pain shot up his arm, down his back, and straight to his toes. The splintering pain sat his ass down. What he thought he could do was something his body told him otherwise. His body had other plans and being mobile wasn't one of them. It required time to properly heal. And it would demand acquiring the necessary rest so it could achieve that. That meant DP couldn't think of moving how he normally would.

Forced to listen to his body, he looked for his pain pills. He had to adjust his way of thinking. Shaking the pill bottle, he was down to his last two pills. Those two pills would barely numb the pain. Before long, he would need to pop five more based on the way his body was getting used to that dosage. If Natalie wasn't looking to up his dosage, taking those pills would become useless. Hopefully she could get him something stronger so he could at least get some sleep. It had been days since he had a good night's rest.

Looking at his phone, he noticed she hadn't called or texted him. He knew she was slow but damn. She knew what he needed and she said she was on it.

Where the hell is she? He rested his arm over his stomach. *I need those damn pills.*

He popped the last two pills, chugging them down with a glass of lukewarm water. Swallowing every drop, he stared at the bottom of it momentarily. Semi-stuck, he thought of the look in Winter's eyes when she opened fire upon him. The coldness and hurt relinquished through the gun came from what he'd done. He'd caused her so much grief that he basically drove her mad. Understanding that, he surmised she would stop at nothing until she seen him dead. He knew that's how she felt. But that was something he couldn't see himself falling victim to. He didn't care how much of the truth she figured out. She would not get the upper hand on him again. He put that on his dead mother.

A striking pain shot up his arm. *Where the hell is Natalie?* he asked himself, in desperate need of more pain medication. Readjusting his arm, another bout of pain attacked him. He gritted his teeth. *She needs to hurry up. This pain* is killing me softly.

★★★★★   ★★★★★

Blair went over his lines, knowing the things he had to say could cause an unnecessary panic in the community. At this juncture, the community needed to be informed of what was found and the simple facts surrounding those involved.

A news station executive came to Blair's dressing room. "Excuse me, sir. You're set to go on live in two minutes."

"Thank you," Blair recited, scrapping what he was going to say. He decided to speak the truth. There was no need to sugar coat it. He needed to show Winter and Darius that he was coming for them. Not to have a friendly conversation but to hunt them down, throw them in jail, and have them prosecuted to the fullest extinct of the law.

The two minutes dwindled down to zero pretty quickly. It was already lights, camera, and action time. Stepping to the podium as a reporter introduced him, he tapped the mic, going right into his spill. "Today, I come before you to inform you of a few things. First, I would like to speak on our great discovery this morning. We were able to seize a small arsenal of weapons and over 1.5 million dollars from the residence of a Sara James. To refresh your memory, Sara James died recently due to complications of two gunshot wounds which she suffered at the hands of who we believe to be Darius Price."

He placed his hands flat on the podium. "It is believed that Darius Price was the trigger man in the slaying of the two Madison police detectives found at Winter James' residence as well. He has been added to the FBI's Top Ten Most Wanted List, and we encourage the public to come forward with whatever information you may have..."

Natalie, with her hands tied in front of her, stared at the t.v. dumbfounded. Her eyes had to be deceiving her. The sight of DP's picture on t.v., along with hearing the accusations against him, left her breathless. She had no idea he was capable of doing such a thing. *Why would he kill those people?* As she continued to question herself, a picture of the woman who'd kidnapped her appeared on screen and things started to make sense.

Blair continued. "We have also added a Winter James to our FBI's Most Wanted List. Sara James was Winter's aunt and we believe she is out for revenge for the crimes Darius Price committed against her and her family. Both individuals are to be considered armed and dangerous and shouldn't be approached by anyone of the public. If anyone of the public see either individual, please contact your local police department with those sightings, and/or tips, surrounding that sighting and this case. Thank you!"

Winter smiled at Natalie. "So... are you trying to contact your local police department about me, Natalie?" she asked sarcastically.

Laughing as Natalie merely stared at her, she noticed the captive looking up at the pictures on the wall. During her short visit, she hadn't had the time to notice any pictures initially. She gazed up nonchalantly.

Aligned in a straight line across the wall, there was pictures of Natalie by herself, some of her with a little boy, then pictures of a little boy by himself. Winter looked into the face of the little boy and seen DP written all over him. Clutching her stomach, she doubled over in excruciating pain. The abdominal discomfort resurfaced stronger than ever.

Natalie sat there helpless, unsure of what to think. As a registered nurse, she looked for the many possible signs of what could be wrong in order to properly diagnose the problem.

Winter, a foot away from her, clutched her stomach tightly and could barely move. She glared into Natalie's face with heartbreaking pain in her eyes. Her countenance expounded on the help she need. It begged and pleaded for some assistance.

Natalie held up her restraints. She couldn't help her until she was untied. While tied up, there wasn't anything she could do. Her hands had been literally tied together.

Winter was in no shape to disagree. Forcing herself upright, a warm wetness soaked her pants. Looking down, the entire front of her pants was crimson red. She quickly untied Natalie, and darted towards the bathroom.

Natalie, throwing the rope to the floor, briskly trailed her, coming to the conclusion that Winter was having a miscarriage.

In the bathroom, Winter stripped off her bloody pants. Barely able to step out of them, her body grew weaker and weaker as the time ticked. She faded in and out of consciousness as she tried to maintain her visibility. In that state, she needed to get cleaned up and find the nearest bed. Her body was giving her no room to negotiate.

Unable to fight it, she stumbled into the bathroom sink. Holding on for dear life, she felt her legs swoop from under her, and before she fully blacked out, the last thing she remembered was Natalie assisting her to the closest bed so she could lay down.

* * * * *   * * * * *

DP awoke in the middle of the night, soak and wet. He originally thought he was merely sweating but it turned out that one of his bullet wounds were leaking. He glanced at his shoulder seeing he needed his bandages changed. They were soaked with blood and the pain had returned.

Looking at the clock on the wall, he tripped off of the time. Natalie should have come by with that medication and changed his wrappings by now. For whatever some reason, that hadn't happened.

This bitch is tripping!

Picking up his phone, he called her. She answered on the third ring in groggily tone. "Damn, bitch! That's how you gone do a muthafucka?"

"Darius, something came up. I'm sorry! I'm on my way. Where are you?"

Giving her the location, he relaxed. *I shouldn't have to go through this,* he reasoned when the medication was what he needed. Had he asked for something else, he could see her playing him. However, the unbearable pain needed to be relieved. He had plans that required him to be on top of his game. This dishonorable pain was leaving him in a distorted state of mind. That wasn't like him. He longed to get back to the man he was. That would only start once he received some real drugs to eliminate his aches.

The sun was rising when Natalie pulled up. Leaving the car running, she had to hurry. She had to see her son off to school and then deal with Winter. She indubitably didn't want Winter waking up and her not being there. *That would, without question, get me killed.* Then she thought about her son. Putting a pep in her step, she had to get DP out of the way so she could make it home to her baby. Walking through the unlocked door, she raced to DP's side once seeing the agonizing pain he was in.

DP opened his eyes and a faint smile crossed his face. "It's about time, don't you think?" he asked, glad she showed up.

"I'm here now, Darius. That's all that matters," she replied, removing his soiled bandages.

Cleaning his wounds, she uncapped a syringe, and stuck it into a small bottle of morphine. She nearly emptied the small container on purpose. Her plans were to give him enough to knock him out for a few hours. He could obviously use the rest. With him sleep, she could use that time to come up with a plan of her own. It was imperative to find out where she would go from here.

DP watched as she injected him with an unknown amount of morphine into his veins. The drug went to work the moment the bulb was pushed in. There was an instant gratification. The horrible pain quickly diminished and within seconds, he was fast asleep.

Natalie listened to him snore, finished cleaning his wounds, and placed new bandages over them. His wounds were healing at an astronomical rate, and that was a good thing. The faster he healed, the less time she would be required to nurse him back to health.

She stood to leave, but stopped to look down on him. She could tell he hadn't slept in days. With the morphine in his system, he was liable to sleep for days. In a way, that was exactly what she needed. Seeing him like this helped her realize some things about herself. Faced with her truth, any time away from him would give her the appropriate amount of time to formulate her thoughts. *I have a lot to think about.*

A loyal woman, she never once questioned her loyalty when it came to him. At the drop of a dime, she would do anything in her power to make him a happy man. On the flip side, his loyalty didn't seem to exist in the same realm for her. If it did, she wouldn't have had to personally witness another woman miscarry his child. To see that devastated her. It left her realizing he was liar. If he had been living a lie, everything they had was fabricated, and his whole existence mimicked the same pretense.

Tired of it, she searched the house for something to write on. Sitting down at the kitchen table, she poured out her heart and soul to the only man she ever truly loved.

> *Darius,*
>
> *I have been nothing but honest and loyal to you but what truth I thought I had in you was smoking mirrors. I stood by your side through it all. I was always there for you when you needed me. YET, you still played me as your second fiddle. I brought a child in this world for you and have not gotten the respect or love I desire as the mother of your child.*
>
> *I know the truth now and it has most definitely set me free. I want nothing else to do with you. You have hurt me to my core! I don't want you in mines nor my son's life anymore.*
>
> *Please continue to live your life according to how you've been living it but without any of my contributions. All this time you've*

been someone I never knew and someone I would rather not have known. You will reap what you sow. I promise you that!

Until then, take care of yourself.

Natalie

P.S. Your girlfriend, Winter, came by looking for you. She was so upset and angry with what you've done to her that she miscarried your baby in the middle of my living room.'

She dropped the note on the coffee table in front of him, and walked out of the house, relieved. She'd said what she needed to say. *But would it be enough?* She knew he would come knocking and with all the love she had in her heart from him, she had to ask her: *Will I open the door or leave him knocking?*

Chapter Twenty-Four

"WINTER! WINTER! WAKE UP! You need to eat something," Natalie kept saying as she attempted to wake her, holding a plate of hash browns, eggs, and turkey sausages.

Winter, balled up like a baby, had been asleep for almost *12* hours and it was apparent that both she and DP weren't getting the proper amount of rest. They had been on such a high-alert while continuously running from the police and one another that they hadn't found time to properly rest their bodies. That was a destructive move for the both of them.

Holding the plate with two hands, Natalie mulled over what the news said about Winter and what she supposedly done. She couldn't remember. It wasn't that important. She chalked it up to her baby daddy being the slime-ball he was. That was enough in itself to think about.

From the man she knew, she wouldn't have guessed he would have turned out to be a killer. She couldn't see that in him. Lowering her head, it was hard to say what a person would and wouldn't do because of whatever dealings a person had with that person. A person could be whomever they wanted when outside the eyesight of those that mattered.

Natalie approached the bedroom door, eliminating the devastating facts of her baby daddy. She peered over her shoulder at Winter. The caregiver in her couldn't help but to be concerned about her well-being, and regularly check up on her. Going through the miscarriage had to be a hard thing to live through.

Ambling over to Winter's bedside, she stared into her face as she slept. *What is really going on, Winter?* she silently asked, having no clue to what had transpired. Her curiosity was getting the best of her.

From what she could see, Winter was a very strong and determined woman. A woman who had endured a whole lot more than she could ever have. Someone who had a greater purpose, and was willing to go above and beyond to achieve her goals. She was a warrior.

Yet in still, here it was, she was playing nurse to her baby daddy's bitch. That bothered her. Every thought of that fact heightened her anger. She sat the plate down on the end table, and balled up her fists. In her blinding rage, she wanted to bestow as much pain to DP and Winter as she could. Whereas, she wasn't that kind of person. She couldn't stoop to their level. It wasn't in her to lay an aggressive finger on anyone.

She released the clutches of her hands, dropped her head, and fought hard to hold back the tears. Wiping at her eyes, *I need to get myself together.* She surmised crying wouldn't fix her situation. But it could make it worse.

Unsure of what to do, Natalie picked up the plate of food, glared down at Winter's peaceful ambience, then bolted towards the door. She had to get out of there before getting emotional again.

* * * * *   * * * * *

"Aw, look at the baby," the nurse yelled, walking into Winter's hospital room. "Here goes your little bundle of joy. Wanna hold him?" The nurse held what appeared to be a baby in a blanket.

Winter gawked at the nurse with wondering eyes seeking to understand why she would be in her room with a baby. She hadn't had a baby so the nurse had to be joking. Checking her surroundings, she guessed the joke was on her because she couldn't apprehend why she was even in the hospital.

Eager to know, she tried to speak but no sound was emitted. Attempting to move her arms, her limbs appeared paralyzed, stuck for whatever reason. Looking from her left to right, the more she looked from side to side, the more the nurses filed into the room. Like zombies, they moved in closer and closer. They were closing in so fast, she panicked.

Willing enough energy to move her arms, Winter reached out to keep the nurses at bay. But they were too strong. They were overpowering her. They grabbed ahold of her, and held her down. She fought with all her might. She just couldn't win. Having no choice but to give up, she let the nurses' presence engulf her. Closing her eyes, she could hear the nurses calling her name in unison.

"Winter!" they said in a slow drawl. It was driving her nuts. She had to do something to get them off her. But what could she do? There was too many of them. Opening her eyes, the room was empty and there wasn't a nurse in sight, only Natalie.

Natalie sat next to Winter, holding her arms down, and attempting to calm her while in the nightmare. For the past five minutes she'd been screaming Winter's name in an attempt to wake her.

Winter examined her surroundings, observing it was only her and Natalie in the room. Wiggling her toes, she realized she had full movement of her limbs. She forcefully snatched away from Natalie's grasp. Cocking her arm back, she punched Natalie in the mouth, knocking her into the dresser.

The punch staggered Natalie, leaving a taste of her own blood in her mouth. She was flabbergasted. Here it was, she had and was doing all she could to help Winter, and her payment for being helpful was to get attacked. She would have never thought her rewards for public service would be repaid so viciously. That messed her up mentally. She looked over at Winter, wondering why she would play her like that.

Before Natalie could fix her mouth to say anything, Winter was out of the bed and in full attack mode. Swiftly advancing on Natalie, she came across with a left chop to the throat, and a right hook to her jaw. Gasping for air from the chop, Natalie's jaw bone shattered under the pressure of Winter's fist. That didn't stop the assault. That merely heightened Winter's desire to finish Natalie off.

Winter, kneeing Natalie in the gut, extracted any thought of fighting back out of her. Natalie fell to the floor. Winter, raising her right foot, brought the ball of her heel down on any area she could with a flush kick.

Natalie put her hands up to defend herself, needing to reason with Winter. With all the strength she could muster, she screamed for Winter to listen. "Winter STOP! Please STOP!"

Winter snapped out of attack mode, lowered her leg, and stared at Natalie with an inquisitive eye.

When Natalie seen Winter wasn't going to attack her, she began to slowly explain. "I'm not ... against you, Winter. I'm ..." She stopped momentarily. "I'm only here ... to help you."

"I don't know what you're here for." She looked down. "I'm stripped down to some bra and panties that ain't mine and you talking about you ain't against me."

"If I was against you, don't you think-" She stopped to choose her words carefully. She didn't want to say anything that would bring on another onslaught she couldn't fend off. "Don't you think DP would have been here to deal with you if I was against you?" She swallowed some blood. "I could have easily told him about you days ago when I went to see him-"

Winter cut her off, reverting back to attack mode. "You went to see him. Where he at?" she asked, stepping towards Natalie.

Natalie slid down into a human ball against the dresser to give herself the best protection possible.

"As a matter of fact, where's my shit?" Winter asked, not giving Natalie time to answer the first question.

Natalie lightly patted her face, shaking her head. She didn't care about answering Winter's questions. She cared about what Winter done to her face. "You really fucked me up, didn't you?" she asked, wondering what she looked like.

Winter gazed down at her. "Naw, you'll be alright but where is dude?" she asked. "Better yet, where is my shit?" she wanted to know, seeing Natalie hadn't answered the question the first time.

"I doubt he's there anymore," Natalie said through clenched teeth. "He was in pretty bad shape but all I did was give him some pain medication and cleaned his wounds. Someone shot him up really bad," she explained.

Winter put her hands on her hips, rolling her neck. "Yeah, I know. He's lucky I couldn't kill him."

Natalie looked into Winter's eyes and seen the truth. From Natalie's vantage point, Winter was a woman scorned and one willing to do whatever, even kill, to get her point across. Looking a little deeper, Natalie could see the pain in Winter's eyes. "Why did you shoot him up like that?" she asked, really wanting to know.

Emotionally exhausted, Winter sat on the bed, hanging her head. Looking up, one tear escaped her right eye.

Natalie's heart instantaneously went out to her. She was witnessing the strongest woman break down for reasons unknown. But, it would be Winter's words that would catch her off-guard.

"He took everything I had on this earth away from me," Winter confessed. "My father, my auntie, and my twin sister!" For the first time in weeks, she couldn't hold back the tears any longer. She let them flow as she thought of her father, her aunt and her twin. Her final thought rested on the child she miscarried. The picture of Natalie's son flashed through her mind and even more tears fell.

Natalie, watching Winter break down, could have only so much empathy for her. There was only so much consoling she could do. She hadn't experienced that much pain before so she couldn't fully understand how deep Winter's ran. Hence, she did know of one thing she could do, and that entailed helping Winter get DP so she could obtain the closure she needed.

DP would need a few more bandages changed and he would come calling. When he called, she would answer but it won't be out of love to hear from him. It would be out of spite.

"Winter, I'm gonna help you but I need to tend to my face first. After that, we'll need to have a heart-to-heart about everything." She slowly rose from the floor, afraid of what she would see.

Winter, slightly raising her head from her chest, nodded in agreement, wiped at the tears wetting her, then fell backwards on the bed. She needed to figure out what Natalie needed to know and what she wanted to tell her.

⋆ ⋆ ⋆ ⋆ ⋆   ⋆ ⋆ ⋆ ⋆ ⋆

Blair walked into the conference room where his team and the local detectives gathered. With a somber look on their faces, he could assume the answer to the question he was about to ask. "Where are we on Darius Price and Winter James?"

Pointer answered. "At this point, we pretty much have nothing. We have the car Winter dumped but all the tags and paperwork lead us nowhere. It was registered to someone who doesn't exist."

Blair inhaled. "What about the info used for the trading of the new car?" he asked, praying for a lead.

"All that info was bogus as well," Pointer said. "We do have an all-points bulletin out for anyone who may use it again. I'm doubting she will but just in case, we'll be on top of it when she does."

Blair scratched his head.

The front desk clerk came in, kneeled next to one of the local detectives, then handed him a piece of paper.

The detective read it, looked up at Blair, sliding it across the conference table. "You're '99 Lumina was found this morning at the Walgreens in Granite City. Apparently, it had been sitting there for the last couple of days so the manager called it in."

Blair leaped to his feet. "I doubt there'll be anything to find but let's see what we can do with it anyway," he instructed, walking away from the table disgustedly.

* * * * *   * * * * *

DP opened his eyes to a very refreshed feeling. Glancing at his phone, he was shocked to see that almost two days had passed. Whatever Natalie hit him with was the truth. *I must have really needed that rest too.* He couldn't remember anything after she poked him with the needle.

He checked his bandages, and saw they weren't as soiled with blood as they once were. A few more changes and he would be just fine. He raised his arm to work out the stiffness. For the most part, he had healed, and the pain was to a minimum. After his beauty rest, he had more movement in that arm than he had before it.

He was ready to fuck some shit up.

Sitting up, his stomach growled. Licking his dry lips, getting something to eat would be his top priority. That was after he released his bladder. Getting up, he noticed a letter sitting under a pain medication pill bottle. Moving the bottle, he picked up the letter, reading it as he walked to the bathroom. He smirked at Natalie's audacity.

Who this bitch thinks she is? He balled up the paper and threw it in the toilet. Watching the letter disappear down the toilet, he stretched his arms out. *I needed to hop in the shower.* More importantly, he needed to contemplate his next move.

The first item on his agenda would be to stop by Natalie's to put her in her place. She had to stand corrected on who he was and who she was. There were lines she shouldn't cross nor consider crossing. He was the man, and she would play her position as the woman. Her job revolved around changing his bandages, filling his prescriptions, and tending to his wounds until he had something else for her to do. Her note had pissed him off.

Then another thought came to him. *How did Winter know about that location?* That wasn't a location she should be aware of. Nevertheless, that was one of his mistakes that could work in his favor. He wouldn't sweat it. He simply needed to get over there so he could pump Natalie for information, then go from there.

Chapter Twenty-Five

AFTER HEARING WHAT THEY both had to say, it was apparent they had been pawns in the games DP played. They concluded that neither one of them knew the real Darius Price Jr. There may have been sprinkles of the real Darius somewhere along the line, but for the most part, neither knew what to believe. Together, they devised a plan to get some get back. He couldn't get away with treating them so harshly.

Despite their consensus, Winter didn't want to include Natalie in her plot for revenge. Her issues with DP was entirely different from Natalie's and she didn't need a heartbroken woman getting in the way of her goal. Her aim was to simply seek, kill and destroy DP's existence in one swift swoop. At no time could she allow anything to cloud her judgement, and that included a heartbroken baby momma.

Weeks ago, she'd checked her heart into the emotional institution so it couldn't dictate her response. The newly supplemented organ had been borrowed from Ramona's chest. With its installation, she transformed into a cold-hearted dealer of death. The blood pumping through it showed no sympathy to those opposing her. She'd set her sights on her target, and in moving ahead, there would be no love lost when dealing with DP, because there had definitely been none shown.

Natalie, on the other hand, was riding the fence and Winter knew that. She talked that tough talk but she was softer than medicated cotton. That had been evident from their first encounter. At the first sign of trouble, Natalie would ultimately fold under that pressure. Aware of that, Winter planned to eliminate her the first chance she got. For the time being, Natalie would serve a bigger purpose. That's if she could do that.

Winter made an effort to coach Natalie on what to do; but, Natalie was getting frustrated and confused. That angered Winter. "Bitch, do you want dude out of your life or what?"

Natalie jumped at Winter's tone, giving Winter another indication that she would be dead weight.

Winter was inclined to blow her wig back in that moment. Except, she went against her better judgement and let her live. She would probably regret that decision later.

"What time you think the medicine will wear off?" Winter asked, wanting to calculate the time that elapsed.

"It may have worn off already. He looked so tired so he could still be sleep too. I didn't give you anything and you slept for almost two days," she explained, sounding like a schoolgirl.

"We need to assume he's up and moving around."

"Oh, when he gets up, he will be calling me!"

Winter looked at her sideways. "Why is that?" she questioned, sensing too much excitement in her tone.

"He'll need his bandages changed a couple more times plus I left him a note." Looking at Winter, she realized she'd forgotten to tell that part.

Winter looked dumbfounded. "Bitch, what kind of note?" Her voice full of irritation. "YOU didn't tell me shit about a note." Her irritation was evident. She thought about pulling her gun out to kill her right then.

Natalie looked off. "That must have slipped my mind."

"Slipped your mind, huh?" she asked, shaking her head. "You need to go get ready so we can go." She was on the verge of snapping.

Natalie hurried out of the room, leaving Winter to ponder everything. Her initial thought revolved around Natalie and the countless others DP could run to. He could have people hid all over the area. Who knew how many there were or where they could be. If that was the case, it would be extremely difficult to find him.

That must have slipped my mind, kept floating about Winter's mind, pissing her off even more. She wondered what else the bitch failed to mention. Pulling out her Glock, she checked the clip, slid it back in and jacked the hammer back. She spun around in a circle. It was imperative to make some leeway in order to get this job done.

She knew it wouldn't be easy. But she would be more optimistic than pessimistic.

Wandering over to the window, she peeked out of the curtains. The streets were clear. Not a single car occupied the street. That made her nervous. She was already on the edge and her nervousness didn't make it any better. As the curtain slipped from her fingers, a black Tahoe slowly crept down the street. The Tahoe from the other day flashed through her mind. That one thought forced her to assume the driver of this Tahoe was DP. That could be a long shot, since he wasn't the only person with that kind of truck. But once she fully seen the truck in her mind, and looked at the truck as it rode down the street, she knew for sure it was him.

"Natalie!" she yelled. "Change of plans. You ready yet?" She screwed a silencer on the Glock.

In the bathroom, Natalie couldn't understand what Winter said. She was too busy combing her hair over her swollen face. Coming out of the bathroom, "What did you say?" she asked, walking into the bedroom.

Winter, waiting for Natalie to come into sight, leveled the silenced .40 at the door, and put two slugs in Natalie's swollen face as soon as she around the corner.

Natalie had no time to contest. The bullets entered her face, releasing the built-up fluids through the holes in her head. The wind of the bullets slamming into her cranium swooshed her hair to the side, messing up all her hard work. Within seconds, she was laying on her back lifeless, staring up at the ceiling.

For all Winter knew, Natalie could have gone into the other room and called DP or left something in that note that apprised him of the situation. Questioning her about it would have taken too long so she went with her first mind. She'd already passed up several opportunities to handle the situation accordingly.

I'll be a damn fool to miss another. She stepped away from Natalie, and strolled back to the window. Pulling the curtain back, she scanned the street. The Tahoe was parked down the street. From that angle, there appeared to no movement inside the truck. However, the brake lights confirmed someone was still inside.

Winter looked down at Natalie. She couldn't leave her lying there. That wasn't the scene she wanted DP to walk into. Seeing that, he would flip out if he seen his baby momma staring up at him with thoughtless eyes. Her intentions were not to put him on high alert. It was to make him feel comfortable about approaching death.

She grabbed Natalie's feet, dragging her to the closet. Snatching a hand full of clothes off of hangers, she covered the blood pooling on the floor. Working expeditiously, she wiped at the blood splatter on the wall.

Time was of the essence.

Going back to the window, she spotted DP getting out of his truck. This would mark the first time she seen him since the shoot-out at her apartment. Her heart pounded out of her chest. DP, marching around his truck, walked as if he had his swag back. Even with taking two slugs, he still resumed an air of confidence that he had the upper hand. Digging into his pocket, he raised his phone to his ear. Natalie's phone rang. Winter let it ring until it stopped.

DP looked at his phone. *I know this bitch ain't acting like she doesn't want to answer the phone.* He called back. Natalie's phone rang.

Hearing it, Winter wanted to answer it so badly. But, she wanted him to come inside even more. She had plans for him, and it would start with putting a full clip of bullets in-between his eyes.

I should run out there and gun him down in the middle of the street like he did my old man.

Personally, she didn't give a damn where she killed him or how he died. Her task centered on being the one to watch him die. That's what would make her the happiest.

DP pocketed the phone, seeing he wouldn't get an answer. Heading to the house, he strolled up the sidewalk and on the porch.

Winter beamed with elation. The moment had arrived. She was so close to her goal that she could have cried. *Just a few more steps,* she said, urging him to continue to the front door.

DP stopped at the front door, catching a gripping knot in his stomach. Something wasn't right. Never in all his years had a knot seized a hold on him that viciously. He scrutinized the door knob. It looked clean. Looking around, something out of the ordinary was the cause of his hesitation. Normally he would have gone straight in. But for some reason he felt the need to knock.

Knocking, he leaned into the door, and listened for any sudden movements. He didn't hear anything. He knocked again. The house didn't make a sound. That was extremely abnormal. He looked at the cars parked at the curb, seeing his Impala. He thought back to Natalie's note, recalling her saying something about Winter had been looking for him.

Could it be that she came back? he asked. *Did she kidnap Nat and my son?*

His mind said walk away; except, his feet wouldn't move. His next alternative was to reach for the door knob. Turning it, he found the door unlocked. He pushed the door open, pulling out his gun. The entire situation had a weird connotation to it. He could feel it.

Hesitantly, he entered the house. At first glance, nothing appeared out of place. He did, however, smell an all-too familiar scent: the smell of gun powder. Freshly sparked gun powder at that. He inhaled deeply. *The shots had been fired recently.* Now on high alert, he quietly closed the door behind him. Breathing in heavily, he sought to get a sense of where the shots had been fired. The gun powder tickled his nose.

Rounding the couch, he cleared the immediate area in order to eliminate any surprise attacks. The house wasn't that big; but, it was spacious enough for someone to sneak up on him if he wasn't careful. He couldn't get caught slipping. He wasn't one-hundred percent. Knowing that, he seriously contemplated leaving. Realistically, that would be his best move. Whereas, he'd came thus far. He could at least see if anything happened to his son.

Meticulously moving through the house, he could feel someone's presence. His sixth sense picked up on the energy of another in the house beside him. That revelation wasn't specific to whether the person was dead or alive. What he did know was that he had company.

Sliding down the hall, he kicked his son's bedroom door open, taking a peek inside. There were no signs of foul play. That was a relief. He let out the breath he'd been holding.

The bathroom door across the hall was slightly ajar so DP gave it a slight nudge causing it to fly open. He flung his gun around, clearing the bathroom. He turned to Natalie's room. The door was closed. Approaching it, he slowly twisted the knob, pushed the door open, and stepped to the side.

Counting to three, he peeked his head around the frame to see a disheveled bed. He quickly moved to the other side of the door frame. On the floor, there was a pile of Natalie's clothes. That wasn't unusual for her. She sometimes went days without cleaning up because of her work schedule. What was unusual was the clean clothes that still had tags on them. That wasn't Natalie's style.

In that instance, his gut told him that Natalie was most likely dead and located somewhere in the house, probably that bedroom. The only place that could be was the closet.

Frustrated, he kicked the pile of clothes, uncovering a small pool of blood. His eyes followed a trail of it leading to the closet. He stomped his right foot, knowing it all along. *I just hope this blood isn't my son's.*

Gripping the closet knob, he held his gun up then turned the knob. Jerking the door open, he stepped back, and locked eyes with his baby momma. Her countenance displayed an expression of surprise. *She hadn't been prepared to die,* he declared, not sure if anyone ever was. *But where is my son?*

With him out of tune with reality, he failed to realize what day it was. Realizing his lapse of time, his mind surrounded the notion of his son being at school. He happily checked the safety of his son off his list, while circling the downfall of Winter's boldly.

The sole question was where would he begin. Having an idea, he closed the closet door as he proceeded to leave. Replacing everything how he found it, he hurried out of there. He needed to get to a computer. Once in front of his powerful machine, he would surely find her. There was not a doubt in his mind. And when he found her, she would be sentenced to a violent death.

Hurrying out of the room, he rounded the corner exiting the bedroom, and headed towards the front door. His feet raced at the same pace of his mind. He was anxious to find his childhood love. He had plans for her. But he didn't have to wait too long. She waited for him around the next corner. The barrel of her silenced Glock 22 whacked him upside his head.

Aja LaGrand Blount

Chapter Twenty-Six

SPECIAL AGENT POINTER CHARGED into the conference room looking for his partner. "Where's Blair?" he asked the detectives sitting around the conference table.

The ones looking up shrugged, signaling they didn't know. Pointer glanced around the room trying to locate him. He had something grand to tell him.

Coming out of the restroom, Blair dried his hands, and scanned the room for Pointer. "What's up?"

Pointer hurried over to Blair. "We have an anonymous tip regarding a Darius Price sighting. It started with the identification of the truck involved in the latest shooting; then, out of the truck hops Darius Price. We have a uniform sitting on it right now," he explained.

Blair grabbed his bulletproof vest and FBI jacket. "Everyone suit up!" he instructed. "It's time we brought this fucker down!" He checked his firearm.

Wanting all his ducks in a row, he called in SWAT, calling for all the streets to be quietly blocked off so no traffic was moving in and out of the area. A team of snipers were called in and positioned along the outskirts of the neighborhood to surveillance the house from different angles. Not to be outdone, he deployed the local detectives to stand guard in the alleyways and gangways between several houses down from the house in question. He didn't want to give Darius any chance of getting away. This was his chance to nab him and he didn't want anything obstructing that path.

Arriving on the scene, Blair whispered into the radio, instructing each team to check in when they were in place. "Do we know which house it is that he went into," he wondered, turning to Pointer. His partner didn't know. "Someone needs to get me that information, quick, fast and in a hurry."

Each team checked in once they were in position. Taking a few moments, Blair thought of his next move as everyone waited on his commands. His next move had to be on course of doing the right thing. If he made the wrong move, everything to follow would crash and burn because of that one decision. He surely didn't want to head down that fiery path.

"Sniper Team, give me some eyes, please," he calmly insisted.

"Sniper One has no visual."

"Sniper Two has no visual at this time."

Blair asked, "Team One, what do you have?"

In a hushed tone, the Team One leader responded that they'd been unable to see anything themselves.

Blair was confused. He looked at the address on the paper to confirm they had the correct address. According to the paper in his hand, the address they had surrounded was the right one.

"SWAT!" Blair yelled. "Bring in the battering ram."

"SWAT in route!"

Running in unison through the alley and onto the property, one SWAT Team stood guard on the back door while the other continued to the front.

"SWAT is in position!"

＊＊＊＊   ＊＊＊＊

Locking eyes with one another, DP and Winter stared one another down for what seemed like hours. There wasn't a sign of love in either of their eyes. The history they once shared had suddenly vanished, leaving two angry and eager individuals with guns pointed at each other. Both of them patiently waited for the other to make a mistake. Neither wanted to make a sudden movement since that would be detrimental for the one who was caught slipping.

DP figured if he was caught blinking, his life could be over. The gun held steadily at his face depicted that revelation if he wasn't careful. That couldn't be how it would end. Upset with himself, he hated this position. He'd found himself within the cross-hairs of Miss Winter James once again, and it was gut-wrenching.

It really wasn't that much fun when the rabbit had the gun, he thought, understanding how his victims felt when he drew down on them. Keeping his cool, he sought to defuse the situation as best as he could. He believed talking could divert her attention to another subject, therefore, persuading her to let her guard down somewhat. What did he have to lose?

"You think I'm a bad person, don't you, Winter?" he asked, following the length of her arm to her stone-expression.

She didn't utter a word. She glared at him with a *you gots to be kidding me* look on her face. His attempts to distract her wouldn't work. She was poised, and in absolute control of her emotions. She'd been waiting on this day and was thoroughly prepared to do what she'd set her mind to. That readiness urged her to pull the trigger tickling her index finger.

On the other hand, DP wanted to tread lightly. What he really wanted to say, he kept to himself. Instead of intentionally getting himself killed, he sought to apply his charm. "Winter, you know I love you, right?" He cocked his head to the side. "You are the only woman I have ever truly loved," he confessed, spilling the remainder of the blood from his heart. "This isn't for you and I. We can get pass this."

In Winter's head, she reciprocated that same love but her outer realm remained stealth. Where he had been looking for some kind of reaction, he received none. Her thoughts didn't park and transcend around the lies he attempted to shove upon her. She systematically kept her eyes on the prize, rendering DP's bullshit obsolete.

DP wrapped his finger around the trigger of his .40, believing the time was near for one of them to kick off the festivities. He was becoming antsy and impatient. The attempt to talk her down seemed to make matters worse. With the gun pointed at him, his last option was going out in a blaze of glory.

Across from him, Winter watched DP's every move as she too tightened her grip on her trigger.

Suddenly, DP looked off towards the window, thinking he seen a shadow moving pass the window. It wasn't a ploy. He seriously thought he seen something. It was in him to pay attention to the details around him. Even with a gun in his face, old habits were hard to break.

Across from him, Winter wasn't giving in. As he returned his gaze upon her, she pulled the trigger. The first shot grazed the right side of his head as he dipped to his left. The second and third shots nicked his neck as he ducked out of the way. The fourth shot connected with his right shoulder causing him to drop his gun. Moving in, she leveled the Glock with DP's falling motion, and pumped his torso with the fifth, sixth and seventh shots.

Taking the slugs, DP's body slammed hard onto the floor, bouncing a couple of times. Thick clots of blood oozed from his mouth. He spat the remainder of the blood on the floor.

Winter slid in to finish him off. Squeezing the trigger, the eighth round entered around DP's jaw line, shattering his jaw completely, then exited out of his neck. The ninth followed, entering the side of his head, right above his ear, provoking the rear portion of his brain to coat the floor. That left the tenth bullet to cut through the air to finish the job. It made contact with the untouched section of his head, and blew the rest of his brains to smeatherings.

Winter released the clip, quickly inserting another. There was no time for games. Sliding the hammer back, something that could have been a shadow appeared to be moving outside of the window, catching her attention. Taking a slight peek through the curtains, she saw droves of police everywhere. She let the curtain go, and scanned the outlets of the house. Spotting a string, she pulled it and some steps came down with it.

Climbing the steps with precision, she pulled the steps up just as the SWAT Teams threw in a smoke bomb from the front and the back of the house at the same time.

$$\star\star\star\star \quad \star\star\star\star$$

"SWAT Team One to base, we just heard something drop inside of the residence. I repeat, we have movement inside of the residence. Seeking permission to bomb."

"Permission GRANTED! Both teams, bomb away. It's a GO!" Blair ordered.

The FBI Team watched the entry unfold, hoping it wasn't all for nothing. They had come for Darius Price and it would be best, for all involved, for them to come out of there with him. Blair, waiting on some kind of confirmation of Darius' discovery, was on the edge of his seat. As the smoke cleared, one of the SWAT members scanned the living room with the camera mounted to his head. Off to the side, laying on his side behind another SWAT member, was the man they sought.

At first glance, no one would have known who he was. He looked nothing like the picture they had. The photograph they had was from an old student ID, but still, the resemblance was not there. Based on what they knew, DP had gone into that house so their purpose was to go in and get him. They hoped they could have taken him alive, considering the crimes they wanted him to answer for. Unfortunately, someone had dished out their own justice prior to their arrival.

"Stand guard, gentlemen. We may still have imminent danger lurking," Blair screamed into the radio.

The SWAT Teams readied their weapons, fell into formation, and swept the rest of the house. The house was cleared. One team found Natalie's body in the spare bedroom closet. For proper identification, the deceased were photographed and the photos were forwarded to the FBI database for a face recognition. With seconds, the identification came back for the both of them. The dead man in the living room was Darius Price Junior, and the woman found dead in the closet was his wife, Natalie Rochelle Price.

Blair rubbed his temples as he thought about how confusing this was. Then confusion set it. *Where was the killer at now?* The SWAT Team reported having heard movement.

"All teams check in!" he demanded. All the teams checked in accordingly, leaving him to assume no one had seen anything. He still sought to make sense of what was going on. "Has there been any movement out there?" he asked, no one in particular.

No one on any team could report back any kind of movements other than the movements of their own.

Pointer studied his partner. "What are you thinking?" he asked, knowing his partner's hamster was spinning the wheel faster than it should.

"Something doesn't feel right, Pointer. That's what I'm thinking?"

Pointer scrunched his face. "What doesn't feel right?"

"Where's the killer, Pointer?" he asked animatedly. "You saw the wounds on Darius, and his wife. Those wounds are fresh!"

"You're thinking the killer is still in the house?" Pointer wasn't understanding that rationale. "You just seen them clear that house with your own eyes." He pointed at the screen. "Are you saying they let the killer go?" he asked, hoping that wasn't what he was saying.

"I'm never saying that. I'm saying something isn't right. That's all I'm saying." He picked up the radio to instruct the forensic team to process the scene and exit as quickly as possible.

As the forensic team moved in, Blair devised a plan to clear the scene, when in actuality, two teams would be stay behind to stand guard. Painting a jet-eye mind trick, he hoped to give the killer enough rope to hang himself. It would be impossible to assume the killer would show his face with hordes of law enforcement wandering around. With the presentation of a clear path to safety, that should make the killer comfortable enough to make his first mistake.

Blair wrestled with leaving and staying. His first mind told him to stay. He could feel it in his bones that the killer was surrounded and seeking to wait them out before making his escape. Whereas, he knew it would be good to leave with the others, and let the plan play out how it should.

Checking the anonymous tip, it didn't reference anyone else entering the house. *Could have the killer already been in the house?* He turned to Pointer. "See if that Walgreens, where Winter's car was found, had a parking lot camera," he requested out of the blue.

"What are you thinking now?" Pointer questioned.

"No one seen anyone else enter the house but Darius. Maybe the killer was already there. Darius' wife's wounds were slightly older than his but not by much. Maybe it was someone they both knew."

Pointer tapped the laptop screen. "The feed is streaming now." They both turned to watch the video footage from the Walgreens parking lot camera.

"That black car," Blair yelped, pointing at the screen. "Where have I seen that car before?"

"Sir," the video technician said, interrupting Blair's thoughts. "That car is parked in front of that house right there."

"Ain't that bout a bitch, Blair. You one smart muthafucker!" Pointer exclaimed, patting his partner on the back.

Blair smiled, instructing the tech to check every angle of the Walgreens parking lot. "Pull up the frame where the black Impala enters the lot," he requested, paying close attention to how the camera covered the parking lot.

The tech went back a few frames to when Natalie entered the parking lot.

Blair fixed his mouth to give another order, but stopped when seeing Winter's car pull into the parking lot and park. His eyes, along with everyone else, frantically followed the Lumina as it parked. When the car door opened, Winter stepped out, snuck around the back of Walgreens and hopped in with Natalie.

"Zoom in on the inside of that car, if you can," Blair commanded, waiting a better look.

Staring at the screen, the agents watched in living color how everything went down and how Winter gained access to both Natalie's house and having the ups on Darius.

"She's smart," Pointer said as the Impala pulled away from the Walgreens.

Blair, getting excited about the discovery, put the radio to his mouth. "Everyone clear the scene except Team One and Team Two." He looked at Pointer. "Everyone else, be on the lookout for Miss Winter James. She's the killer we're looking for."

Chapter Twenty-Seven

"TEAM ONE TO TEAM TWO."

The team leader for Team Two took the call. "Team Two, Team One."

"Are you clear back there?" the team leader for Team One asked.

"Back is clear!"

"We have a little boy approaching, please intercept," the Team One leader instructed.

"10-4. Copy!"

Two members from Team Two abandoned their post, and headed to the front, trying to minimize the noise. Not wanting to scare the little guy, they casually approached him.

The little boy didn't appear fazed by their approach nor was there any fear in his eyes. "What's up, officers. Y'all looking for some bad guys or something?"

The little boy's comment threw them off-guard. They didn't know what to say. This wasn't what they expected. The little boy maintained a *what's up*? look without getting a response.

"Where you going, little man?" one of the team members asked.

"I'm going home," the little boy replied, pointing to the house they stood before.

"We're not allowed to let anyone in that house right now, little man. We're gonna have to take you with us until it's safe to go inside."

The little boy let what the officer said register, then spazzed out when realizing they were saying he couldn't go into his own house. A feeling overcame him that something bad had happened to his mother. He didn't like that idea.

"What happened to my momma?" he asked, sprinting pass the officers.

The two team members reached for the little boy, needing to quickly defuse the situation. In doing so, both teams became distracted. Their need to calm the little boy, and get him out of harm's way, transmuted their task into an all-out circus. Not knowing what else to do, the leader of Team One called Blair to inform him of their current situation.

"Sir, we have encountered a little boy who says he lives at the house we have surrounded. He's acting erratic..."

Blair listened and quickly checked Natalie's records. She did have a son. Scrolling through the file, there wasn't any record of who the father could be. That lack of knowledge would take the little boy on a roller-coaster ride at the state's amusement park. He mentally put calling the state on his to-do list.

Meanwhile, the team leader's tone voiced how much trouble they were having with the little boy. That infuriated him.

Logging off, he spat into the phone, "Get control of the situation! I'm on my way." Then hung it up and raced out to get to his car.

* * * * *   * * * * *

Winter used her great sense of hearing to pick up on what was going on around her. There was plenty of movement outside, where it had been dead quiet at first. She was far from dumb and knew it was possible that the police still maintained a heavy presence in the area. Once she pulled up those steps, she'd prepared herself for the long haul, knowing a time would come when she'll be able to make her move.

From her point of view, that time may have arrived.

Not sure of how large the police presence was, she grasped that a couple of them had left their post in the back. Perking her ears, she hadn't heard any movement inside of the house so she figured the house was clear. Pushing the steps down, she stepped on solid ground with her gun in hand.

The house had been cleaned and processed but she could still vividly envision the place where DP's body laid in her mind. Exhaling heavily, she could breathe a sigh of relief knowing he got what he deserved and she was the one to give it to him. Stepping over to the window, she slid the curtains back. Initially, she saw two officers talking to a little boy. When the little boy tried running towards the house, she caught a glimpse of his face, instantly recognizing him as Natalie's son.

Seeing him kind of hit her like a ton of bricks. Her beef with DP had forced a similar fate upon him that was once placed upon her and DP. She didn't want him to live that kind of life. She secretly prayed that they'll let him enter the house. She had a better way to end things for him.

"I only want to put him out of his misery, officers!" she muttered with a sick and deranged chuckle.

The officers subdued the little boy. Two more officers appeared from the side of the house. All of them had a *what the fuck?* looks on their face. *Like, he's only a kid!*

Winter inferred that if those officers came from the back, there couldn't be any additional coverage in the back of the house. Eager to find out, it was time for her to bounce.

She quietly opened the back door, unable to see anyone upon her first inspection. Listening to her surroundings, she heard the officers in the front talking to the little boy. Tucking her banger, she sprinted into the alley and ran into an empty police car. Looking behind her, she saw another police car parked down the alley. She ran away from the parked car, but with no pursuit, she knew it had to be empty too.

Walking at a fast pace, she hurried to get out of that neighborhood. The first thing she would need was transportation, and she needed it fast. Racing away from Natalie's house, the sounds of sirens coming her way coerced her to cut into the backyard of the house coming up. Darting through the gangway, she crept alongside the house, slowing at the edge of the house. There wasn't a soul out on the block.

Looking around, she searched for a ride. She had no time to waste. The police sirens were getting closer, and the way they wailed, there was a string of cop cars behind it. She stepped away from the house, racing to the closest car to see if it was unlocked. The sirens she once heard were abruptly turned off. Glancing to her right, an entourage of police cars drove pass, heading towards Natalie's block. There was one that drove by, trailing the parade.

That must be the car I heard with the sirens on.

Returning to the car, she seen the doors were locked. Backing away from the car, she wandered away from it as if she was going home. Crossing the deserted street, she unclasped the first gate she walked to, stepping into someone's front yard.

The police car she previously seen driving by had stopped and backed up. She peeped it out the corner of her eye. Taking off in a sprint, she ran through the gangway at full speed. Hopping the back fence, she twisted her ankle, landing sideways. That slowed her. Getting up, she applied some pressure to her ankle, finding it hard to deal with the pain.

The police car turned down the alleyway, heading straight towards her.

She tried her best to get up and run but her ankle wouldn't have it. For a moment, she felt trapped and useless. However, her will to remain free wouldn't let her give up. With some renewed energy and a fighting spirit, she stood upright and applied some pressure to her ankle. Wincing in pain, she fought through the discomfort. She didn't have a choice.

Turning to run, S.A. Blair and Pointer jumped out of the car with their guns drawn.

"Stop right there, Winter!" Blair yelled, readying his Glock 17. "It's all over. Don't make this out to be any worse than what it is."

While Blair instructed her to surrender, Pointer called for back-up to their location.

The call in itself would further limit her time. She had a decision to make. Fight or flight. She weighed her options. Fleeing wasn't her best option; but, one she would rather choose over being taken down. The suicide-by-cop scenario ran through her mind, and she concluded she wasn't going out like that.

She reached for her banger. Her mind was made up. She had to fight for what she believed in.

Spinning on her good ankle, she lined the Glock .40 up with the first person she seen. With her aim set, she caressed the trigger and applied some pressure. The jerk kicked out two slugs at Pointer. Before he knew what hit him, his head snapped back from the piping hot lead penetrating his skull.

Redirecting her efforts, she rapidly spat three rounds at Blair. None of them were kill shots; however, they were good enough to wound him, giving her enough time to put some distance between them.

Attempting to hobble away, police cars were coming into the alley, stopping on the next street over, and officers were rushing through the gangways off of Natalie's street. She had nowhere to go. But she was unwilling to give up.

Dragging her bum ankle, the police screamed for her to stop. Eyeing her surroundings, the police continuously hopped out with their guns drawn. She literally didn't have anywhere else to run. Eager to remain free, that wouldn't keep her from trying.

Blair, limping towards the injured Winter, shouted one last command. "Drop your weapon and surrender, Winter! Or you will force me to shoot."

She had no intentions of doing either. Raising her piece, she sprinted through someone's yard, hoping the police made a hole.

Blair opened fire on her, hitting her in the right butt cheek and upper thigh. She fell to the ground and dropped her gun. Stretching to regain control of it, one of the closest officers converged on her and kicked the gun away. She refused to give up the fight. The officers shoved his knee into the middle of her back, yanked her right arm behind her back, and slapped the handcuffs around her wrist. Securing both arms, he pulled her off the ground, and angrily dragged her to the closest police car.

Finally, Winter had been formally taken into police custody.

For the police involved, the feeling surrounding her capture was a distasteful one. Blair, walking over to the police car, wanted to put a bullet in her head. But he couldn't do that with everyone around. His taking her out wouldn't look good on his part, aside from the fact that she killed his partner. Thinking about his partner, he had to do right by Pointer. He had to let justice prevail. He glared at Winter, staring back at him. He secured his Glock in his holster.

As bad as he didn't want to, he knew that would be the right thing to do.

* * * * *   * * * * *

Down at the station, Blair walked in feeling gloomy. He'd been stitched up and released from the care of the paramedics. He'd been lucky to be alive. Had Winter honed in on her target, she could have easily killed him. That thought alone scared him.

He approached his desk, not in the mood to do any work. His reason for returning to the station was to gather his things and get as far away from the case as he possibly could. There were too many dead bodies associated with it and having to think about another was not what he needed.

Staring at the work him and Pointer had worked on dropped his head in disgust. He would surely miss his partner. There was no one who could replace him.

It's time for me to take some time off, he reasoned, seeing the need to re-evaluate his future. Losing someone that close always brought about questions of how a person could continue to put their life on the line, day in, day out. He raised his head as a lady from Children Family Services walked in, interrupting his thoughts. He definitely wasn't in the mood to talk to anyone.

"Excuse me, sir. Are you Special Agent Blair?" she asked.

Blair hesitated to speak. He didn't want to come off rude, but, he really didn't have the energy to talk to her. The public servant in him wouldn't let his own personal emotions interfere with his job. Putting on a face of strength and honor, he swallowed the day's events.

"Yeah, I'm S.A. Blair. What can I do for you?" No matter what he would have hoped for, the tone of his voice came across hollow and empty.

"I have an odd request from the little boy whose parents were killed today."

"And what is that?" he asked, placing one hand over the other.

"He wants to meet you," the lady responded.

Agreeing, he figured what he had to lose in meeting the little fellow. Except, he hadn't been prepared for what he saw. As the little boy walked in, the little boy was the spitting image of Darius Price Jr. *Oh my!* was all Blair could say.

The little guy walked across the office with extreme confidence, with an extraordinary large amount of attitude fuming off of him. To top that off, he possessed the mannerisms of a mature, young man.

202

Blair could see he would truly be something to reckon with in the future.

"Here's the man you wanted to meet. What is it that you wanted to say?" the DCFS lady asked.

The little boy stared into Blair's face. "I want to know if I can see the picture of the person who murdered my momma."

"Why would you want to see that?" Blair asked. "I'm sure it will be in the newspaper sooner or later."

"I'll rather see it now."

Blair looked at the little boy sideways. "Once again, I have to ask you why?"

"Because I need to know who I'm dealing with," he stated with certainty and conviction.

Blair and the DCFS lady was taken back by the little boy's comment. Blair glanced from the little boy to the lady then back to the little boy.

"You'll need to know who you're dealing with?" he asked. "I don't think it's your job to have to deal with anything. That's the justice system's job now," he explained. "How old are you anyway?"

"I'm nine. I'll be ten in January."

That calmed Blair's nerves. "You have other things to worry about at nine instead of who killed your mother. That's not the path you should want to travel. Just worry about growing up to be somebody you can be proud of. Let us tackle getting the bad guys."

"Can I see the picture or not?"

Blair frowned, then merely succumbed to the request to satisfy the little guy's interest. Handing him the picture, he watched the little guy studying Winter's face. About a minute later, the little guy began repeating her name over and over again. It was then that Blair realized he hadn't been formally introduced to the little boy.

"Say little man, what would your name be?"

The little boy looked Blair directly in the eyes, and said, "I'm Jason Price - the one you'll need to watch out for from now on!"

Blair leaned back in the chair. "Alrighty then!" he said, dropping his chin to his chest. "It's nice to meet you but I have things to do." He glanced at the DCFS lady. "If we could wrap this up, I'll be on my way."

The lady took that as her cue. She exited with Jason ahead of her.

Blair, running his hand through his black hair, couldn't believe the latest events. He eyed the stack of files on his desk, and knew, with all he had to do, there was no way on God's green earth he would find the time to take a vacation.

Chapter Twenty-Eight

THE MEMORIAL SERVICE FOR Special Agent Samuel Pointer ended with Special Agent Mark Blair wanting to give Mrs. Ann Pointer, Samuel's wife, his final condolences. Walking over, he spotted a guy talking to her who he hadn't seen before. As he neared, the guy standing with Ann half-watched Blair advance, and half-proceeded with the conversation in question. Despite Blair not knowing the guy, Ann definitely knew who he was based on their body language.

Blair strolled up to Mrs. Pointer, and wrapped his arms around her, giving her the strength she needed. By him being taller than her, her body fell into his. She didn't seem to mind. To feel the security of her husband's partner gave her the power to overcome Samuel's unexpected death.

The guy regarded the two of them as if he'd seen this kind of thing many times before.

Mrs. Pointer broke the embrace. "Where are my manners?" she asked, pointing to the guy. "Nick, this is Mark Blair, your brother's partner. Mark, this is Nick, your partner's brother."

Both of the gentlemen exchanged pleasantries, shaking one another's hand. Upon the release of the embrace, Blair picked up a weird vibe coming from Nick. He attempted to figure it out while engaging in some light conversation to see if the feeling would iron itself out.

"What kind of work you do, Nick?" Blair asked, eyeing him.

"I'm with the bureau," Nick answered, getting to the point.

That thrown Blair off. "YOU don't say! What department?"

"I'm the one they call when they need the good stuff done," Nick replied, making it evident he wasn't in the mood to talk.

Blair wasn't sure what that implied so he left it at that. That kind of statement could have meant anything when it came to the bureau, and he definitely wasn't in a rush for an elaboration. If there was ever a reason to know more about Nick, it would ultimately come to his attention.

"Blair!" Nick said, snatching Mark out of his thoughts.

"What's up?" Blair inquired, snapping out of it.

"There's a possibility I'll be transferring back this way. Maybe we can sit down and talk a bit."

Blair reached into his pocket. "Well, take my number and when that time comes, reach out and we'll set up something." He felt awkward with the request.

"That'll be great. But right now, I have to run. I have a meeting to tend to." He looked at Ann. "I'll meet you back at the house later on, ok?"

Ann gave a half-smile. "That's fine," she said, looking beyond him.

Blair watched Nick as he walked off, thinking something wasn't right about him. Something seemed off. Even his interaction with Ann was different. What truly plagued him was that his partner never mentioned having a brother the whole time they were a team. That rubbed him the wrong way. He thought they had built a mutual trust. A bond as strong as two brothers. His perception of it made it hard to shake off not knowing that kind of information. When he pondered it further, he wondered what not revealing that info told him now about his partner.

Not wanting to question Ann about it, he decided that he'll do some digging of his own. That had just become a top priority for him once he headed back to the office.

"Well, Ann," he said, closing in on her. "How are you doing?"

Her eyes dropped to her shoes. "I'm doing alright," she mumbled, raising her head to meet his eye. "It's gonna be hard but I'm a big girl and I'll make it."

"If you need anything, don't hesitate to call." He thumbed to his truck. "But I have to get going. I just wanted to speak with you before I left."

"I appreciate that," she recited, half-hugging him.

Blair spotted Ann's son walking over with his cousin. Waving goodbye to them, he scurried over to his truck with Nick on his mind. Once climbing in, he wasted no time calling his contact within his unit to get the investigation into Nick Pointer started. He saw no reason to stall. It was time to find out all he could about his partner's brother.

* * * * *   * * * * *

As the two gentlemen sat in the massive, earth-toned office space smoking Cohiba cigars and sipping Louie the 13th, there was a slight hesitation in their conversation. Neither actually knew what to say about the overall situation before them but it was one that would have to be talked about.

From a contrary angle, it appeared what they built was seemingly falling apart. Experience had taught the two that once the old ways of doing things began to unravel, the time would present itself for an epic reconstruction and a change of authority phase. This time would be no different. With history normally repeating itself, changes had to be made. Thus, a more conscious decision would be made about the personnel chosen moving forward.

The younger gentleman, sitting in the plush chair in front of the oversized mahogany desk, set his burning cigar in the ashtray. Sitting back, he crossed his legs, pulling out a small comb, and combed through his short salt and pepper hairdo. "What are we gonna do about the little boy?" he asked, putting the comb in his pocket.

The slightly older gentleman sitting behind the desk sipped his cognac. "What is it that WE can do? We have to let nature run its course. But it's not him I'm actually worried about at this time. My concerns surrounds Miss Winter James."

"Why?" the graying gentleman asked.

The slightly older gentleman picked up his cigar. "Why not?"

"I don't understand."

"I'm sure you don't." He puffed the cigar. "But answer this question, what good is she if she's locked up?"

"I still don't understand what angle you're trying to work here?"

The gentleman swiveled his chair behind the desk, letting the smoke linger around the thought of Winter's purpose to them. "Let me find out that old age is finally catching up with you," he announced, looking at his partner with wondering eyes.

"It probably is but you'll surely get me where I need to be when you spit it out. I'm no good at this guessing shit."

The gentlemen behind the desk laughed. "I'll ask the question again. What good is a killer to us if it's locked up?"

"OH! I get it now." He stuffed the cigar in his mouth.

"Finally!" They both erupted in laughter.

"What do you propose?" He knocked the ashes off the edge of the cigar. "Isn't she in federal custody?"

The gentleman held the glass of cognac to his lips. "And that's supposed to stop us because?"

"Well, Mr. Smart Guy, how do you propose we get her loose?"

"Nick Pointer!"

* * * * *   * * * * *

"Nick, it's so good to see you. I didn't think I would ever see you again. It has been over ten years and at the rate you were going, you weren't trying to make your way back this way."

"I was involved in something that wouldn't let me make that trip. It's not like you wanted to see me anyway."

"You know that's a lie. I've always wanted to see you. It was your choice to push me off on your brother."

"So, you're telling me that you still have a place for me in your heart?"

"Of course, Nick." She moved closer to him. "I have always loved you and will always love you. Is it true you'll be making that move back?"

"That's a possibility. There may be a job offer on the table," he explained, feeling his phone vibrate. He peeked at the message, then replaced the phone in his pocket. "As it appears, I'll see tomorrow about that job offer. I've been called in for a meeting in the morning."

She grabbed the front of his shirt. "Can you stay here with me tonight, then?"

"Of course, Ann. Where are the kids?" he asked, kissing her on the forehead.

"They're outside somewhere. They should be out for a while since the sun is still out."

Nick liked her answer. Sliding his index finger under her chin, he raised it, and placed a soft and sensual kiss on her lips. She moaned slightly as she embraced the kiss. Spreading her lips, she allowed her tongue to meet his as they embarked into a passionate kiss.

He pulled her closer, palming her backside as the kiss became more intense. Scooping her up, she wrapped her legs around his waist. He sat her on the counter. She ripped at his shirt, eagerly attempting to strip him of all his clothes. She didn't care. She wanted him right then and there. It had been twelve years since they'd last made love. Not to be mistaken, she did love her husband; but, it was his brother that she wanted, and whenever she could have him, she let him have his way with her.

Nick yanked at her belt.

Ann, ready for the taking, laid back, and raised her behind off the counter so he could pull off her pants and panties. Once free, she slid back on the counter, and spread her legs to show him a cleanly shaven mound of meat.

He licked his lips, savoring the visualization of the feast he was ready to dive into. Grabbing her right leg, he kissed it all the way down from the ankle, calf, and inner thighs until he was face-to-face with her loveliness. Placing kiss after kiss around her syrupy center, he teased her until she couldn't take anymore.

Fiending for him, she roughly grabbed the back of his head, guiding him to the center of her love. The first contact threw her head back, propelling her to bite down so hard on her lip that she almost broke skin. The feeling was that good. He slithered his tongue along the outside of her love below, making his way to her pearl tongue. Clamping on it lightly, he nibbled with minimum pressure, slowly licking it in-between time.

Ann was in heavenly bliss, and Nick continued. Spreading her steamy lips, he inserted his tongue inside of her, and spread her legs to the max. She thanked God for his return. As usual, he was the only one who could bring out everything in her, and at that moment, things weren't any different.

Replacing his tongue with his fingers, he signaled for her to come to him. Nicking her G-spot, she went crazy. Rotating her hips and grinding on his fingers, she was on the verge of eruption. Knowing that, he faintly rubbed her spot. That steady contact drove her insane. She couldn't hold back her climax any longer. Releasing her flood gates, she soaked his fingers with what seemed to be years of built-up fluid.

"Please," she cooed. "Fuck ME, NICK!" She climbed off of the counter, strutting over to the kitchen table.

Nick stood in amazement when looking at her. She was just as beautiful as he last remembered. The years had treated her well. That time had allowed for the right things to happen to her body. Her pettiness had filled out and where she once lacked visible curves, there was nothing that could hide them now.

Laying atop of the table, she tooted her behind in the air. Widening her stance, she revealed a dripping wet love pot that loved to be stirred, not shaken.

Nick wasted no time giving that love pot what it yearned.

Slowly easing inside of her, he could sense the tightness of her womb. His brother could never keep her satisfied and it was apparent he hadn't been hitting the right spots.

Shoving himself in further, he made sure she felt every inch of him. Sliding out, he edged the tip in and out until she wanted to turn around and tell him to stop playing. Filling her up, he picked up his rhythm and long-stroked her non-stop, leaving her clawing at the kitchen table. She took the pounding from the back, letting out syrupy moans and screams that let Nick know she was enjoying the assault. Laying her head on the table, she mumbled something inaudible to him. He had no time to pay her ramblings much attention. Rather than inquire, he picked up his speed.

"Faster!" she encouraged, as if she could really take it any faster.

He didn't mind picking up the pace. That's if that's what she truly wanted. He knew he could turn it up but he had to slow it down so he could enjoy it himself. Finding himself on the verge of busting a rod, he didn't want to explode too soon. Slowing his roll would be his best option.

Sensing his stalling, she twirled her hips, causing his sword to get tender around the edges. That interrupted his plans, leaving him with no choice but to release within her honey walls. Gripping her hips, he projected every drop to coat her insides. Underneath him, she ground on him, making sure she received everything he had to offer. She didn't want to move. Moments of the past came to her, taking her back to their last encounter. She remembered it as if it was yesterday. The way she felt then was the exact same way she felt now.

Nick smacked her on the butt, and watched it jiggle to its own beat. "Wake up, sleepy head," he said, giving her behind another whack.

"I'm up!" she snapped, raising up. "I see you still nutting in me."

"You just got that kind of loving that I can't pull out of," he expressed, smiling and licking his lips.

She sat on the table. "That's what got us in that mess in the first place, remember?"

He stared off into space, recalling the day she told him she was pregnant and wasn't sure if it was his or his brother's. At that time, she was adamant that it wasn't her husband's since they weren't that sexually active. Still, there was always that possibility. Either way, it would be a hard pill to swallow had the truth come out. Instead of making it hard on everyone, they decided that no matter who the father was, it would be Sam who played the role.

Whereas, their curiosity led them to secretly take a DNA test and the results came back that Nick was the father. Immediately after, an undercover operation snatched him away from his fatherly duties, sending him across the country to leave Ann to raise their child with his brother. Once leaving, he hadn't reached out to check on the little boy, nor had he sent any child support. He merely left his brother to bear all the responsibility of a child that wasn't his.

Sam, blind to the truth, never suspected anything so the plan went off without a hitch. That was twelve years ago, and now Nick was back, but only because of his brother's death.

Ann figured had her husband hadn't been killed, she wouldn't have heard from or seen Nick again. For a brief second, she didn't know how to feel about that. Based on the love she had for him, she was glad that he returned. Feeling him sliding out of her, she wondered if revealing the truth would be good for them.

She clambered off the table, and over to her clothes. "Do you think it's time to reveal the truth, Nick?"

He zipped up his pants. "Let's sit down one day and really talk about the pros and cons of that revelation and make a decision then."

"MOM!" Stanley screamed, running into the house with his cousin behind him.

"In the kitchen!" she exclaimed, hurrying to step into her pants as Nick quickly exited the kitchen.

Chapter Twenty-Nine

NICK SAT IN THE narrow lobby of the Director's office with whom he had an appointment with. Over the years, he'd had many meetings of similar stature but this one brought with it a storm of anxiety. He couldn't identify with why; but, he was sure to know once things got under way. As he done the best to control himself, a female voice cut into his fogginess.

"Mr. Pointer, he will see you now," the secretary stated, standing at the ajar door.

Nick dried his sweaty hands on his pants. "Thank you!" he replied, exhaling hot air and walking into the Director's office where two men sat and talked.

The two men stood simultaneously to formally greet Nick. With the extension of their hands, they gave him a plausible reception.

"Welcome Nick!" the older of the two exclaimed, resting his bottom in his seat. "It's been a long time coming for this meeting." He gestured to the unoccupied seat. "Please, sit."

Nick descended into the seat. "I'm honored to be blessed with the opportunity to have this meeting."

The Director rested his elbows on the mahogany desk. "I did hear you were the modest one," he stated, flashing a slick grin. "But let me extend my condolences to you first. Your brother was a fine officer and one that the bureau will miss. I know you haven't been around much with your work elsewhere. But I'm hoping you can take my offer and make the move back to the area."

Nick thumbed his nose. "I'm sure that could happen. Ann will definitely need help with the two boys she has," he explained, scratching his eyebrow.

The Director glanced at Nick. "I hadn't realized she had two boys. Is one from a previous marriage?"

"No," Nick said. "She just has the one but the other is her sister's son. His parents were killed a while ago."

The Director retrieved a cigar from a fancy wooden box sitting to his right. "That's sad. There is too much killing going on these days." He clipped the cigar, dropping the excess in the trash next to his desk. "However, let's get down to the task at hand. What is your familiarity with the name Winter James?"

Nick pondered the name, unable to come up with anything. It was a name that sounded familiar; however, he couldn't place it at the time. "I'm not sure I have a familiarity with that name, sir," he admitted, thinking about it for a few more minutes.

"Well, Nick." The Director looked at his partner. "Winter James is the one who murdered your brother." He allowed the information to soak in.

The acknowledgement of the name registered suddenly. "I know I've heard it. I initially thought you were asking from a different standpoint. Now that I know, what about her?" he asked.

The Director torched the end of the cigar, inhaling a thick cloud of smoke. "I'm glad you asked. Miss James is... for the lack of a better term, an asset to us." He scoured Nick's face for a reaction.

There was none. Nick's countenance was blank. The Director's excitement from that lack of reaction showed the two men that Nick was the real deal. Nick had been trained to show no emotions whatsoever and that was the kind of men they needed. One who could take any kind of information and allow it to bounce off of him without a second thought.

"So, what are you telling me?" Nick questioned through clenched teeth.

"I'm telling you that there has been a situation to arise that WE," he pointed to him then his partner, "that we need to address in the near future."

A trillion thoughts raced through Nick's mind. "And that would be?"

"The establishing of Winter James as one of ours and being brought to us."

Nick was curious to why but refrained from asking those kinds of questions. To be that inquisitive could take him from being an asset himself to the one being shut out and abandoned. As the heads of the entity, they had their reasons and at some point, he would find out.

Despite lacking the courage to ask, the background of Winter James was freely given so he could correctly assess the situation at hand. They said it was for him to see if he wanted to take the job or not. Whereas, he wasn't a fool. The revealing of classified information was only given to those who they knew would take the job. From what they knew, Nick was all in. That was what he did. He took the jobs no one else wanted. But from his current position, he could sense this job would be different.

The Director set the cigar in the ashtray. "Here's the deal, Nick. Winter killed your brother. This we both know. BUT, she also killed a few good people close to me. That isn't what this is about. This isn't a revenge thing. No emotions should take part in hindering the bottom line. As a man in my position, I'm understanding of the mind and actions of those who may come up against a man like me. It's not like many know of me or the reach I have."

He tugged on the cigar several times before continuing. "I'm a man that like to get things done and get them done in an orderly fashion, if you know what I mean. My acquisition of Miss Winter James can further assist me in obtaining the results I'm seeking to obtain. To save you the intimate details of my mind, here is a packet on Miss James. Let's call it the juicy details, of sorts. Some of it, you will enjoy and some of it, you will not. In any faction, memorize it and burn it once you're done. Understood?"

"Understood!" Nick declared.

"You will be contacted soon about certain things and I will hope you'll be available at a moment's notice, if need be."

"I know how it goes," Nick confessed.

The Director rose from his chair. "That's great."

With the rising of the Director's partner, Nick rose as well and knew it was time to leave. Heading to the door, he slowly closed the door behind him. As he did, the two men casually returned to the conversation they were engaged in before Nick's arrival.

"Where were we?" the Director asked.

"Jason Price!"
The Director picked up his cigar. "Ah, yes! The little fella."

★ ★ ★ ★ ★   ★ ★ ★ ★ ★

Jason Price (JP) couldn't get with his new arrangement of living in the home of another. He would have rather stayed at the foster center instead of having to move in with two total strangers. He didn't like them. It was something about them that he couldn't place. Upon first seeing them, he received a bad vibe. Therefore, he couldn't see himself sticking around for the weird couple to conform him.

If that wasn't bad enough, they had another child that thought her shit didn't stink.

From the moment he arrived, the tension had been bad. The thirteen-year-old biological daughter and JP couldn't get along for anything in the world. By her being older than he, she felt as if she ran the house. Under those circumstances, JP's sole task was to run around in it. That wouldn't work for him. He was the man of any household he maintained and if he was there to stay, he would play the man of that house as well. That outlook kept him bumping heads with the daughter. Letting it go on for far too long, he felt the time had neared for her to see who really ran shit.

One morning, JP woke up and replayed everything she'd done to him in his head. The more he thought about it, the angrier he became. And when he became angry, there was only one way to calm himself.

Coming out of his room, he could hear the daughter in her room on the phone. Silently cracking her door, she nonchalantly played on the computer, and ran her big mouth on the phone. Creeping into her room unannounced, he looked around fleetingly. That was the first time he'd ever been in her room. That wasn't by his choosing but one she called herself setting as a ground rule.

Don't ever come in my room! she would adamantly state.

Nevertheless, he was in her room and she had no idea about it. He laughed internally at the fact that he stood so close to her and she was unaware of what her next seconds would end up being. She finished her called, put the phone down, and allowed the task on the computer screen to consume her attention.

216

JP slid over to her, slipping a black bag over her head. Pulling the string to tighten it, she clawed at the bag trying to get it off her head. It was too late for all that. The string around her neck was tied multiple times, and it damn near cut off her air supply. Still, she fought as hard as she could to free herself. By this time, JP had slapped a handcuff on her right wrist, and yanked the arm behind her back. The swiftness of that action sent the daughter into panic mode. Trying to snatch away, the metal cut into her arm. The pain to her wrist coerced her to succumb to the act being performed upon her.

He grabbed her left hand, handcuffing it to the other. That's how he remembered seeing it done on t.v., and always wanted to see how it worked. The success of accomplishing the task made him proud of himself.

The daughter wasn't feeling so proud. The once very calm daughter suddenly snapped out. The restrictive confinements drove her mad. She was hyperventilating. Standing up, she felt that her life was about to run out. If that was the case, she wanted to go out fighting. The string around her neck was choking the life out of her and the handcuffs secured her hands behind her back made things worse. She felt like a hostage in a third world country. That petrified her.

She contemplated her next move by seeking to recall the format of her room in her mind. She slowly turned to the left, and was met with an overhand right. The blow knocked her into the computer screen. The bumping of her head turned out her lights.

JP moved in swiftly to grab her ankles, and dragged the dead weight into the middle of the floor. Taking a pair of fabric cutting scissors, he disrobed her, stripping her down to her bra and panties. Flipping her on her stomach, he hog-tied her feet to the handcuffs. With her secured, he removed the bag, and stuffed her mouth with a bar of soap. He quickly replaced the bag, laughing at the thought of washing her mouth out with soap.

"Bet your ass think about what you say to me the next time," he said, pulling out his wiener and urinating on her.

The moment the daughter's parents came home, they went looking for her. She had chores that hadn't been done so they were upset. Steaming with anger, they stormed to her room to find her half-naked, a bag over her head, and the stench of urine rising off her.

The foster father instantly went looking for his foster son. JP was the only person who could have done such a thing to his baby girl. Why? He couldn't understand that.

"JASON!" the father yelled. "Where are you?"

"I'm in here, dad," JP shouted in a sarcastic manner.

The father was furious when hearing JP's teasing tone. His blood pressure increased to new heights, and he began seeing spots on his way to JP's room. Bursting in, he could have lunged violently at JP for what he saw.

Laying on the bed, JP held a Playboy magazine in his left hand, his right hand was stuck down his pants, and as he looked at the foster father, he displayed a shit-eating grin on his face.

The father's body temperature peaked as JP glared up at him with total disregard in his appearance. "Pack your shit, you little fuck!" Foam soared through the air. "You're going back to the foster center."

JP pulled his hand out of his underwear, tossed the magazine on the floor, and swung his feet to the floor. "That's what I hoped you would say." He slid in his shoes. "Let's ride, Pops!"

★ ★ ★ ★ ★   ★ ★ ★ ★ ★

Nick knew he had that overwhelming anxiety for some reason. Now that he knew what the job was, he knew things would surely change. Having that understanding, he wasn't looking for it to be for the good.

When offered that kind of job so late in his career, he could see how things were sure to put him in a compromising position. That's not to say he hadn't been put in a mirrored position before because he has. What entangled him was the lack of give and take on his employees' part. They hadn't surmised how his taking that job would affect those that received one ounce of thought in his personal life.

How would he look at those who loved his brother and the other victims of that woman? He had to ask himself how it make him feel. Deliberating a few seconds, he concluded he couldn't let it affect him. That wasn't what he did. He couldn't let his relations with his brother foil the plans of the job. His feelings for his brother had always been shallow. Everyone, especially their parents, loved Samuel more than they loved him.

Samuel was the oldest, and to everyone, the brightest. During school and beyond, he was in the top of his class in everything he participated in while Nick simply done enough to pass. The things Nick were good at weren't the kind of things people won awards for. He was the kind of guy who done the work of those who didn't like getting their hands dirty.

That had always been his m.o. Until now. With the job he was set to complete, his hands were set to become the filthiest they'd ever been. While he didn't like that, that was his truth. That was his reality and what a hard reality to swallow.

Why did it have to come to this? he questioned.

Shrugging, that would be a question he wouldn't seek an answer for. In the end, he merely hoped someone would be considerate enough to hand him a good bar of soap that could fully dispel of the grime he'll wallow in once he needed it. Because, once the shit hit the fan, he would need it.

Chapter Thirty

WINTER HAD BEEN MAINTAINING a low profile during her stay in the St. Clair County Jail. For her, that was a good thing. Upon her arrival, the administration of the jail had considered putting her in solitary confinement due to the status of her case. They figured someone would want to make a name for themselves and eventually do something stupid.

They didn't want that, despite the administration being unaware of Winter personally. To them, the knowledge of her being responsible for the murders of three people was enough, and they didn't want anyone trying her hand; or at the very least, they didn't need the females of the jail banning together to get rid of her. Something of that nature would be devastating for the county jail. The establishment, over the years, had acquired a reputation for several of its inmates extending their progressive power to those they didn't like, therefore, putting them on bunk rest or leaving them broken up in the infirmary.

The Captain couldn't have that dark cloud hovering over his head for the sake of an argument. When he agreed to house Winter, he had done so out of the kindness of his heart. Initially, he didn't think it would be a good idea, especially with him being good friends with S.A. Pointer. The nature of that friendship and the housing of his killer created a distasteful taste in his mouth. Yet, as a professional, he swallowed his pride, and accepted her for the sake of Pointer.

He sincerely wanted her to pay for the crimes she committed. That was the primary reason he wanted to put her in solitary confinement initially. He didn't need anything happening to her. If anything happened on his watch, all fingers would point at him. He dreaded that kind of attention. He woke up every day looking forward to the day when the prisoner would have a psychological evaluation and be declared fit to stand trial. That would be a day he celebrated like it was the end of the world. On the flip side, there was a chance she could get off for mental reasons. That declaration would possibly push him over the edge and propel him to put a gun to her head.

For the time being, he opted to remain professional and let the cards fall where they may. If he begun to see any trick dealing or underhanded playing, he would consider taking matters into his own hands. He was that adamant about upholding his friendship with Pointer.

Back in the block, Winter hadn't taken the time to mingle with the other prisoners. For days, she refused to eat. With the medication they feed her, she had no appetite whatsoever. All she longed for was sleep, hoping one day she would wake up and it would be all over. But each day she woke up faced with the same nightmare consistent with her reality. The option of it being a dream wasn't in the cards.

Since her arrival, not too many of the females desired to speak to her. They knew who she was and were afraid she would snap out if they engaged her in conversation. That wasn't what any of them wanted. Most of them were there for petty charges and crimes, while others were there for some hardcore stuff. Regardless, none of them wanted to be the one to find out how crazy she was.

One day when Winter had been called out for an attorney visit, a girl was transferred to that block after being released from the SHU (Special Housing Unit). Upon Winter's return, the girl believed she thought Winter looked familiar. Mean-mugging Winter, the girl stared her down as she entered the block and headed straight to her bunk.

Winter paid the stares no mind and had no intention of inquiring into why the girl was staring at her. The gawking didn't concern her one bit. Her mind attempted to break down the information regarding the life sentence she faced in prison. It didn't matter if she plead out or went to trial. A life sentence would be handed down for the murdering of Special Agent Samuel Pointer alone. The word *life* had a different appeal to it. It put a different perspective on her life and the one she would have to live for the rest of her existence.

While sulking in deep thought, the new girl proceeded to overstep her boundaries when seeking to interrupt her brainstorm. Another girl who knew the girl tried to get her to think twice about that, but the girl insisted on doing what she wanted.

"Don't I know you from somewhere?" she asked Winter, stepping to her bunk.

Winter, laying on the bottom bunk, refused to respond. She wouldn't even look at the girl. She merely stared at the bottom of the top bunk thinking about her case and how she could come from underneath the gun.

Snitching was never an option. That thought alone killed her father. Maybe she could get inside of someone's head good enough to get them to bend the rules. That thought put a smile on her face. If she could make that happen, anything was possible. *But who can I set my sights on?* Her mind dove deeper into her plotting and planning.

The new girl smacked the top bunk, and that move got Winter's attention.

"Don't you see me standing here trying to talk to you?" the girl asked, looking down at Winter.

"Please, find you something better to do," Winter expressed, wiping the smile off her face.

The girl wouldn't give up. She craved to be acknowledged. "I found me something to do. And I know you from somewhere."

Winter sat up, and looked directly into the girl's eyes. The girl wasn't a serious threat. She simply thought she was tough. The thin shades of toughness hiding behind her iris regrettably masked the weakness, the scariness and the pride of a little girl.

Winter felt sorry for her. Here it was, the girl had no idea what she up against for the sake of trying to prove something to either herself or the other girls. She had no clue to how close she was to learning a valuable lesson; one of a deadlier attribute, instead of being useful.

"What is it that you want, little girl?" she asked, putting emphasis on *little girl*

That emphasis rubbed the girl the wrong way. "Bitch, I ain't no little girl! You better watch what you say out your mouth to me," she spat.

Winter slid into her shower shoes. "Are you gonna tell me what you want or are you gonna keep bumping your gums like you really have something to say?"

"Ain't your name Mona or something like that?" the girl asked, confusing Winter with her twin sister.

Images of Ramona instantly came to Winter's mind. Falling into a daydream, she no longer heard the girl's voice and that infuriated her. She didn't like being ignored so she stepped in and touched Winter's arm.

Winter reacted so fast, no one knew what happened until the girl screams echoed throughout the cell block.

"LET ME GO!" the girl shouted, seeing she'd made a big mistake.

The slightest touch caused Winter's reflexes to grab the girl's hand, twisting it around her back. The move rendered her motionless in one swift move. The girl screamed out for dear life. A little more pressure could have broken her wrist, snapped her elbow or severed her entire arm from her body.

Winter, realizing what she'd done, let the girl go. Shoving the girl away, she stepped back, and waited to see what the girl would do.

The girl hadn't had enough.

Gathering her feet, she rushed Winter and the imminent threat forced Winter's killer instincts to kick in. She extended her arm, punching the girl in the face. That first punch was followed by seven more to the girl's face, neck and side of her head. Each blow landed solidly and done the upmost damage. In concert, blood squirted from the girl's nose, mouth and forehead, spraying onto Winter and the floor.

Winter went in for the kill, until she sensed her opponent was harmless and out for the count. Instead of doing her in, she let the girl be as she slid to the floor.

The girls looking on were in awe. Winter was a beast! To see it for themselves made them fully aware that it wasn't a good thing to judge a book by its cover.

The door to the catwalk outside of the cell block unlocked, and a guard walked through for her hourly rounds. Rounding the corner, she spotted the blood on the floor first. Gripping the bars, her eyes roamed the block in search of the bloods source. The C.O. eyed the unconscious girl laying on the floor. Panic rattled her nervous system.

The C.O.'s eyes went from the girl on the floor to the Winter. The calm look on Winter's face, and the fact that she pulled a clean shirt over her head, enlightened her to who was responsible for punishing the girl on the floor. Without hesitation, she hit the deuces – hitting the panic button on her radio.

Like clockwork, a host of correctional officers, along with a team of nurses, came rushing in. The first officer in the block snatched Winter out. In the hallway, she was handcuffed and taken to the nurse's office to make sure she didn't have any cuts, bruises or abrasions before being transported to the SHU.

In the cell block, the nurses went straight to the girl on the floor. When standing over her, there wasn't anything they could do. The damage had been done. Winter's vicious attack left the girl with her nose pushed into her brain, her eye socket shattered and her ear drum busted.

The nurse gripped the girl's wrist. There was a faint pulse. "Let's get her to the nurse's station, immediately!" the nurse shouted. But, before they could get her to the nurse's station, the girl was DOA (Dead on Arrival).

$$* * * * * \quad * * * * *$$

Blair found himself up all night thinking about Winter's case and those who suffered from her wrath. He was finding it hard to get the case out of his mind. As he thought of Winter, thoughts of Darius Price Jr came to mind and he found it hard to understand how someone could do the things he done.

DP was a man of many masks. The Special Agent couldn't fathom the thought of living that many lies in order to cover up one's true identity.

Interested in who DP was, he initiated an updated search into what little he had to go. As he researched, he eventually came to the same conclusions he had before. Everything he went over was everything he had gone over before. On paper, DP was squeaky clean. His life extended to what he wanted it to entail. All the same, it was believed that Price was responsible for many murders, including that of Travis Malcolm Robertson, Winter's father; Detective Bryan Chapman and his family; Sara James, Winter's aunt, along with Ramona James, Winter's sister.

Blair scratched his head, unsure of how many others he was responsible for and the reasons behind them. What bothered the Agent the most was who Price could have work for. The Robertson murder was classified as a hit so Blair believed Price was a murder for hire. But for who?

Thinking hard, he tried his hand at searching Natalie Price's name. What appeared was more than he bargained for. The entire screen filled with a long list of things in Natalie's name. *She doesn't have the assets for nor a reason to have acquired these things.* There were houses, cars, apartment buildings, businesses and a host of other things under her name. It was clear that with her A-1 credit, she could get whatever she wanted. Darius had used that to his advantage.

Most of the businesses were ghost corporations, and Blair understood why. They were used to launder illegal funds acquired from whatever hustle DP had and to be the front for what he had going on.

Blair shook his head, coming to terms with how smart of a guy Darius was. Except, he hadn't been smart enough to keep himself from getting killed. *He should have used his head a little more, and he could still be alive.*

Doing some more digging, the more interesting it got. *I must hit the ground running with this new evidence.* He printed out the entire list, snatched it from the printer, and hurried out of the office. It was time for him to take a ride to see what he could find.

* * * * *　　* * * * *

The Assistant Director freely ambled into the Director's office. "I know you've heard about Miss James and her latest activities, right?"

The Director scribbled his name on a document. "Unfortunately, I have and I'm upset that her skills are being wasted on the useless and not for a greater purpose. Our greater purpose. We need to do something about this soon."

"What are you thinking?" the Assistant Director questioned, taking a seat across from the Director.

"Is there any favors you can call in," his eyes rose from the document, "from a judge or something?"

"That wouldn't be a good idea. That would be a disaster as a matter of fact. No one would buy that a judge found her not-guilty for murdering a FBI Special Agent. The judicial system would be viewed as a hoax."

The Director chuckled. "Like it isn't already. The Federal Government has been fucking over people since it began so what would be the difference now?"

The Assistant Director shifted in his seat. "It would be national news, that's the difference. They would have a field day with that kind of outcome. Heads would fly and people would reveal things that shouldn't be known."

The Director sat his pen down. "That wouldn't be a bad idea. If we could pull that off, we could shift into a position to pave our way to doing whatever we want."

"And, it could also be the downfall of us too. We don't necessary need our dirty laundry being aired out."

The Director eyed his partner. "But who can you find that could point us out for anything?" He reached for a fresh cigar.

The Assistant Director pondered the question. Anyone who could finger them or utter a sound weren't currently breathing adequately enough to spill the beans. The extended silence on that thought led to the acknowledgement of what was already understood.

"My point exactly!" was all the Director needed to say after no answer could be provided.

Chapter Thirty-One

S.A. BLAIR HAD RUN DOWN the printed list of addresses and was down to the last one. All the previous ones hadn't produced anything worthwhile. Going into the venture, he hadn't expected all of them to leave him wishing he'd already found something. He surmised he would have found at least one clue thus far instead of running from address to address and coming away empty handed.

Arriving at the last address, he twisted the knob on the front door, finding it locked. Backpedaling, he stepped to the closest window, and peered inside. Through the dusty window pane, the house appeared to have been lived in. That gave him the impression that he may have found what he was looking for. The majority of the other houses had been empty and/or abandoned. Most of them looked to be recently put in that status, while a few always looked to have been that way.

He decided to go around the back to investigate the back entrance. Grabbing the knob, it turned underneath his hand, and the door opened. He pulled out his weapon, not willing to take any chances.

Easing the door open, a leather jacket hung on the back of a chair at the kitchen table near the back door. Not wanting to alarm anyone, he thought of leaving but there hadn't been a car in the driveway, nor was any lights on in the house. Besides, he'd already made entry so there was no turning back.

Stepping into the house, a strong, unwelcomed stench smacked him in the face. He wasn't sure if the smell came from the refrigerator or if an animal made its way in the house and died. Holding his breath, he cleared the main level, making his way upstairs. Clearing the second level, he concluded that no one was home but him.

The basement was the last level to search.

As he made his way to the basement, he thought about whether or not this was one of Darius' main houses or just one he used for whatever reason. Regardless of its use, the agent marched through the house and towards the basement to complete his search.

Jerking the basement door open, the stench he originally caught a whiff of suffocated him. The fetor highlighted the notion of someone's life having been taken, and the location of such act had taken place in that basement. He hesitated at the door, knowing he shouldn't step foot down there. Going against his better judgment, he descended the steps after letting his curious mind get the best of him. Halfway down the staircase, he covered his face with his handkerchief to mask the odor. Making it to the last step, he couldn't see anything.

Holstering his firearm, he pulled out his flashlight. At first glance, there was nothing to see but a chair and a table sitting in the middle of the basement. On top of the table was a hand-saw and some needles but that was it. On the chair, under the illumination of the bright flashlight, a glimmer of dried blood glistening in the darkness.

The agent wondered who the blood belonged to. Taking a step closer, he stepped on what could have been a cellphone upon hearing the crunch under his foot. Shining the flashlight upon it, it was a cellphone. The face of it had been smashed and the treads of his shoes were visible on the screen. Kneeling down, he used the handkerchief to pick it up. Sliding it in his pocket, he opted to head out to call his team.

Scanning the basement one last time, nothing stood out that would cause him alarm. That was until he turned to leave. In the corner of the basement sat a large garbage bag. The sounds of flies buzzing around the opening of it became audible. And that meant, where there were flies, there was a dead body.

Instead of opening the bag himself and contaminating the crime scene even further, he exited the basement and called his forensic team. He'd done enough to add insult to injury as it was.

* * * * *   * * * * *

Unsure of what to do, Nick laid across the bed of his hotel room, staring at the high ceiling. He felt so alone in spite of Ann hovering over his lower extremities servicing him. But Nick's head, the one sitting on his shoulders, had traveled many miles away from his current location. Frustrated, he pushed her off of him, sat up and tried to identify with what was wrong with him.

Ann wiped at her mouth. "What's wrong, baby?" she questioned. "Was I not doing a good job?" He usually loved the way she serviced him.

"Naw, baby! You always do a good job. It's not you. It's me," he recited.

"I've heard that too many times to know it's some bullshit. Talk to me, Nick," she insisted, sliding behind him to rub his shoulders.

"I can't talk to you about it. It's my job and for the sake-"

"Sake of national security, its best you don't know. Yeah, yeah! I've heard all of that before," she said, with more than a little irritation in her voice.

"Please don't act that way, Ann. I don't know what you had to deal with as far as Sam but the job I have is whole lot different than his."

She rubbed his back. "You should know that I'm always here for you."

He seriously doubted that. If she really knew what he was supposed to do, she would surely hate his guts from that moment until the end of time. Her enthusiasm to have him back in her life would fade to black upon finding out he planned to go against the grain - against his own brother and her deceased husband - to assist the one who was the cause of it all. That would inevitably seal his own death and fate in her eyes. She would never be able to forgive him nor probably would she want to. She would be a woman scorned and one who may snap, crackle and pop. The idea of what he was set to do would affect his overall life.

Ann interrupted his thoughts, kissing him behind the ear and down his neck. He wanted to stop her but the touch of her lips had a different feel to them that time around. Where his mind once couldn't fence in a sexual idea, his third leg had a mind of its own. And from behind him she was the first to notice it.

Laying him onto his back, "Baby, relax!" she exclaimed, grabbing his swollen member, and stroking him as she lowered her head to insert it in her mouth.

She slobbered him up and down, downing him until she couldn't stuff anymore down her throat. Putting her best foot forward, she sought to put in her best work. She never had an issue with pushing the envelope when seeking to swallow his flag pole whole. She'd learned years ago how to maintain her gag reflex, and she enjoyed when his throbbing stick played with her tonsils.

Lathering his joint, she slowly made her way up from his third leg to his chest. Guiding him towards her love below, the tip of him knocked on the door of her hot entry. Her budding flower asked *who is it?* but the doors of her loving spread open, eager to invite him in. For the sake of stretching out the introductions, she twirled the tip of him on her pearl tongue then allowed him to slip inside of her. Letting his baseball bat go, she sat upon it, bucked wildly, and rode his long ranger all the way to the promise-land.

Busting a series of nuts, she could feel the tip of his sword swell. Picking up her speed, she rode him until his Olympic swimmers jumped in the water and glided to the other side of the pool. Gripping his shaft, she made sure to take care of her business. Cuffing her arms under his shoulder, she nibbled on his neck, making him feel like the noble king she looked at him as.

Easing off of him, she slid down, leaving trails of kisses down his stomach until she reached the long john silver she desired. Plopping it in her mouth, she relieved it of the excess seeds, and fully drained it.

Totally satisfied, she felt complete. Having sucked and fucked her man something good, she fell into his arms. They were both exhausted. But her thoughts went to her son and how she laid in the arms of his father when her son was clueless to that fact.

"It's time we tell him the truth, Nick," she muttered.

"I know," he retorted.

Ann was surprised he admitted it. She figured he would stall it out for as long as he could. "When would you like to do it?" she questioned, hoping it would be sooner than later so they could be a family.

"It has to wait until I'm done with this job," he reasoned, thinking of what he had to do.

"I was hoping it would be sooner than that," she voiced, climbing on top of him. "I was hoping we could finally become a family too."

"I don't think the truth will make us one big ass family, Ann. He's twelve, about to be thirteen, and you think he'll take it so well that he'll be open to US being together?"

"What are you saying, Nick?" she asked, not feeling what he was saying. "You don't want to be with me?"

"I'm not saying that. WE," he said, pointing to her, "have to think about him and how he will take that kind of news. This is not about US," he said, pointing back at him.

"I never looked at it like that. I'm sure he'll be open to it though."

"Are you failing to realize that technically I'm his uncle in his eyes and now you want to tell him that I'm really his father. How do you think he'll start looking at you?" he asked, wanting her to see the bigger picture.

The question stunned her and when she thought about it, what she thought was gonna be a good idea was now something she didn't think would be right. She really cared about what her son thought of her. She'd painted a great perception of herself for his viewing and to tarnish that would cause more harm than good.

"I have to agree with you, Uncle Nick. Let's leave it like it is," she stated, placing a kiss on his lips.

* * * * *   * * * * *

Blair couldn't believe the news he received regarding the chopped-up body found in that basement being the one and only Darius Price Senior. He would have never thought of such a thing in his entire life. *What happened to the idea of Darius Price Sr. being killed by Robertson?* he asked, unable to wrap his mind around the case. *This is a case that seem to get weirder and weirder by the moment, the minute, and the day.*

What was next for him to find out?

According to the medical examiner, the decomposition of the body showed that he'd recently died and was disfigured. If he'd been killed years ago, there wouldn't have been any remnants of a human after that many years. Someone would have hopefully reported the discovery. At least, he would have hoped so.

A knock came to Blair's office door, and the investigative agent came in with a large box with Pointer etched across the top to it. "You asked for information on Nick Pointer so here you go. ENJOY!" the investigator stated, plopping the box down in the chair next to the desk.

"Got damn!" Blair shouted, looking at the size of the file. "That shit will have to wait. I have other things to do right now."

"Oh, I almost forgot," the investigative agent said. "Here's everything that was on the phone you gave me."

The mention of the phone peaked his interest. He originally believed the phone belonged to Darius Sr. and if it did, maybe there was something to get from it. And, what he seen would shatter his whole mental understanding of the case.

Going through each piece of paper, he seen the phone provided an inside track into the life of a man who was supposedly dead but living right under the nose of everyone around him. Looking at the documents, he desperately sought to make sense of it as he thoroughly examined each page.

On the first page, there was some text messages from an unknown person. The name to identify the person and the number was blocked. But as he read them, whomever the person was seemed to be the person Darius Sr. may have reported to. Blair wished he knew the identity of that person. That would give him something to work with.

Flicking through the pages, he came across some printed out voicemail messages. To the naked eye, they were regular voicemail messages. But not to him. The names of the two individuals was what made him stop to read them. What he read stunned him. If what he was read was correct, Ramona was Darius Sr's daughter, and Sara, Winter's aunt, was maybe his lover.

How does that work? he wondered. *If Darius Price Sr was Ramona's father, he was Winter's father too,* he concluded. *Did that make Darius Jr and Winter, brother and sister? Where does Robertson come into play with all of this?*

This revelation transcended the case to another level of weird. Then it dawned on him. That was probably why Robertson wanted Price dead. Price had been sleeping with his girl and most likely was the father of her kids. He knew many of men who killed another man because of that man dipping into their chick's goodies. But how did Darius survive? He picked up his phone, placing a call to the Madison Police Department Detective's division.

"I'm Special Agent Mark Blair with the FBI, and I'm looking for anyone who could point me in the right direction regarding an old case."

"Who does the case pertain to, sir?"

"A Darius Price Sr," he answered.

The person on the phone wasn't surprised by the agent's request. "Just come down to the station yourself so you can pull the file again. It was recently returned to storage and the clerk is kind of old so do him a favor and use your own strong and willing back to get it back upstairs, if you don't mind."

"Oh, I don't mind. I'm on my way now." He grabbed his coat, and was out of the door in no time, heading to the Madison Police Station.

Chapter Thirty-Two

WINTER RECLINED ON THE bunk in her single suite, allowing thoughts of DP to drift through her mind. For days, she replayed their entire life together and for the life of her, it seemed so real. She focused on the feelings they shared for one another. The time they spent together. The love they made. It all seemed so real.

But, how could it be if he lived a life of a killer the whole time?

The fact that he lived a totally different life somewhere else tripped her out. Not only that, he had a child with another woman. She clutched her stomach. The little boy was at least eight or nine years old. That made her want to cry. For the last eight or nine years, her childhood love had played the role of two men right under her nose.

Natalie, his baby momma, had been duped as well. She'd given birth to his son, and outside of that, she had no recollection of who he really was. Winter could see how he kept her in the dark but she couldn't grasp how he kept those things from her. *He had to be very good at what he did.* Still, it messed with her head as she thought about having laid down with the enemy for all those years. That was doing something to her, and it was something she couldn't stop thinking about.

From the very beginning, it consumed her, leading her to wonder if he knew about her father prior to her knowing. *Did he always have the intention of killing him once he resurfaced?* She couldn't stomach the sickness associated with being that close to her father's killer. It was driving her crazy. Another thought crashed her current thoughts. *Who did he work for?* she wondered, figuring someone had to be calling the shots and feeding him information. *That could have been anybody,* she reasoned. She could have seen the person everyday of her life and had no idea of who they were or what they did. That made her question everything that happened in the past.

Sara, her aunt, was no better. She'd withheld so many secrets that Winter questioned if she was her real aunt or not. Sure enough, she read her mother's diary but damn. Could it all be a fantasy of some kind?

That took her thoughts deeper.

Going down the list of revealed secrets, she was dumbfounded for a moment. Looking back, she reflected on how her aunt kept her sheltered. Even the time when she visited her mother's house, it was briefly and no one at the house ever spoke to her. She was *a* nobody to them. No one even cared to know who she was or why she was there. That sadden her.

Returning to thoughts of DP, he grew up in the hood but they went to the same schools in Granite City. However, she never met anyone he knew outside of school. She snapped her fingers. It was starting to make sense. There was a lot of things she didn't know when she should have. Acknowledging that, she noticed that if a person wasn't a part of something, they could never know of the intricate details. That's exactly how she'd been played all her life. They merely kept her in the dark for that reason, and that reason alone.

She wondered how she could be that blind, knowing the kind of person she was now. She prided herself on being game conscious. The only difference was that she didn't know what laid within her then. Now that she did, her chances of fully exploring that person may not materialize if she remained locked up for the rest of her life.

She swung her feet off the side of the bunk. A guard marched pass her cell door doing his rounds. She darted to the door, trying to catch a glimpse of him. Pounding on the door, she screamed, "Come back!" He exited the range, leaving her in silence. Slapping the door, she wandered back to her bunk, and sat down. *Something must give.* Laying down, *I can't be confined to a cell for the rest of my life.*

* * * * *   * * * * *

Nick chilled in the same narrow lobby outside of his new supervisor's office as he awaited his scheduled meeting. He felt as if

235

he'd been there for days. His hands were super sweaty, and his collar was soaked. In all of his days, he never had to experience this kind of reaction to a job. It had to be the nature of the job that produced such reaction. The closeness of it was really taking a toll on him.

He needed a solution to how he felt. He had to go into the meeting and put his foot down. He was a man of integrity. What they were asking of him went against his bottom line. He wouldn't be able to do it. Having that kind of reaction brought him to a dark crossroad. Aside from what he allowed himself to think, he had been the guy to betray so many others in his life, and he'd done it without hesitation for lesser offenses. But, for the first time in his life, he wanted to do the right thing.

How cynical is that? he questioned, wondering when this change of heart came about.

He folded his arms over his chest, let his hands fall to his legs, and rubbed them on his slacks. He had to figure out a way to right his wrongs. All his life he'd been the one to do all of the wrong things right. He'd carried on an extra-marital affair with his brother's wife, implanted his seed in her and let his brother take care of his responsibility. That had been the ultimate betrayal.

Except, the hammering of the nails in his brother's coffin came when approached about breaking out the person responsible for his brother's death. As a brother, outside of their personal relationship, he wasn't sure if he could live with lending that hand. Even the association with assisting the person escape custody was an outrageous idea.

I need to get out of this game, and need to get out while I'm ahead, he surmised, rubbing his knees roughly.

He understood that would be hard. It wasn't a logical ideology for anyone to freely walk away from that lifestyle. There was only one way out. Regardless of that perception, he needed to be the exception to the rule. He was tired of it all.

The secretary came to the door. "They will see you now."

Nick nodded in acknowledgement, and stood. Looking down the hall, he wiped his sweaty hands on his pants then headed for the office door. Exhaling his fear, he stepped inside of the office, shocked by the company occupying the room. Scanning the room, he became tongue-tied, with no idea if he had anything to say. He simply stood in amazement, gawking at the last person he expected to see at that meeting.

Scratching his head, he felt like an idiot. *How are things right in your face and you're not able to see them?*

The Director cleared his throat. "Nick, please have a seat. We have a lot to talk about."

* * * * *   * * * * *

S.A. Blair returned from the Madison Police Department with nothing. He wasted all that time going through boxes only to find the same theories and speculations he already known. Those suppositions wouldn't get him where he needed to be. As it stood, he was making more headway on his own than with anything anyone else had to offer.

Right then, he made up his mind to put his best foot forward in getting to the bottom of the case himself. Going back to the contents of Darius Sr's phone, he was amazed at how things happened without the knowledge of a lot of people, if not, everybody around. For a person to hide their true identity from those who loved them was something he couldn't understand. That didn't mean there wasn't plenty of people doing it. He personally couldn't fathom the thought surrounding the realization of a person when a picture of that person had been painted already. He couldn't see how one could face such reality.

In spite of that, there was a host of questions swirling around his membrane without anyone to answer them. DP was dead, and if he was correct, Darius Sr died at his hands. Winter was in jail facing prison time, and those behind the scenes hid within the shadows unavailable for comment.

"But did Darius Jr know that Darius Sr was his father?" he asked aloud.

"You're in here talking to yourself now?" the feminine voice asked from the door.

Startled by the voice, he looked up to find Special Agent Elizabeth Nichols staring back at him. "What's up, Nichols? What you still doing here?" He studied the average looking agent of average height and average standing within the bureau.

"I was just about to leave but seen you. What are you still doing here? I know you have some kind of life to live." She let out a soft laugh.

Blair wasn't in the laughing mood and Nichols could sense his seriousness.

"Would you like some help then?" she asked. "I'm willing to give you a hand if you need it."

Blair contemplated the offer, and thought it wouldn't be a bad idea to bounce a few ideas off of her. Two brains were better than one. "What do you know about Darius Price Sr, Darius Price Jr, or a Winter James?"

She entered the office. "I've heard those names before. Winter James is the one who killed Pointer, right?"

"That's correct." He moved the box from the chair next to his desk. "Let me do this. Let me fill you in on what I have and see if you could make some sense of it all. Because right now, I can't!"

She started for the seat. "Let's hear it!"

He sat the box on the floor. "Then grab a seat. This could take a while."

* * * * *   * * * * *

Nick was disgusted with the way the meeting was going. His whole objective was to take control of the moment by making his points so they could see things from his perspective. But none of that happened, and he was in deeper now than he was from the beginning.

"Nick," the Director said. "You have roughly six months to prepare for whatever plan you have. Anything you may need is at your disposal. You already know money isn't an issue. With that time frame, what kind of thoughts do you have as far as how to pull it off?"

Nick pondered verbalizing what he really wanted to tell them. Unable to do it, he bit his tongue for the sake of the bureau and concocted a plan that wasn't foolproof but one that could easily work.

"My first thought surrounds the attack of the transport going either to or from the courthouse. There will be a series of pre-trial court appearance. I could put it into motion during one of those times. I'll rather do it when it's guaranteed she'll be going to court. Something like the sentencing hearing."

They quietly listened to Nick, understanding his angle quite clearly.

The Director reclined in his oversized chair. "I like that idea, Nick. Afterwards, we could feed the media a ton of information that she perfectly planned the attack knowing she would rather live her life on the run instead of living her life in prison. They will eat that shit up!"

The Assistant Director turned to the inaudible female agent in the room. "S.A. Tanks, do you think placing someone close to her in the jail will still work?" He looked at her sitting next to Nick. "Maybe have that person going to court that day or maybe coming back with the transport to assist that the get-a-way goes smoother."

Nick refused to look in S.A. Tanks' direction. He couldn't believe she could be the person she nonchalantly sat there portraying herself to be. This wasn't her game, it was his. She didn't have a place in his arena.

"I'm thinking that several options should be explored and that's still one of them. Having someone on the inside could keep tabs on her too," she responded.

The Director hiked his slacks. "That would be impossible unless someone was willing to sit in the SHU for months on end. Miss James will not occupy another cell but the one she's in. Even her transfer for the mental evaluation will keep her in solitary confinement."

"What about staging someone as her evaluator?" Tanks asked.

"That's possible but we'll have to start picking the spot and making the appropriate arrangements," the Director explained.

"See what kind of hassle it would be then let's see if it's plausible," she insisted.

"Will do!" the Director noted, pulling out a cigar. "Well, that's the conclusion of our business. You both are dismissed."

Nick bolted for the door, anxious to place as much distance between him and S.A. Tanks as he could. He didn't want to look at her again, nor did he want to hear her explanation.

Following him out, the agent knew Nick wouldn't understand her position but she needed him to listen to why it needed to be done. In her mind, it was doing what was right for the country. Everyone couldn't be one of the good guys. In life, it was the bad guys who made the world go around. The good guys, with their blurry realities, systematically found the short end of the stick, which elevated the bad guys to higher heights. Throughout history, the bad guys were the ones who thought outside of the box, taking all the risks and capitalizing off them. On the other hand, the good guys simply accepted what they had coming, with or without griping about it.

Ann had never been the kind of girl to settle. As a secret operative, she'd infiltrated some of the most impenetrable organizations. Under that task, she stepped into those roles to keep tabs on those who needed the most watching. Unfortunately, she ended up pregnant so that called for a more laid-back job position. It was that or go undercover on someone else's case. Either way, her overall agenda wouldn't have changed.

She caught up with Nick, aware that he wanted nothing else to do with her. But he would have to. They would have to keep up the appearance. To change anything would mean he was going against the grain. And he personally knew what going against the grain meant in their circle.

Nick snatched away as she grabbed his arm. He didn't want to talk. There wasn't anything to say.

Ann, seeing his emotional state, let him go. There was no need to push the issue. She would give him the time to cool off before stepping to him again. Time healed all wounds, and it would eventually give him a clear perception of how things went. For him, it may seem strange to him since he was the one pulling off the job; however, she knew things would work out. She just didn't know how different things would be between the two of them.

Chapter Thirty-Three

AFTER SEVERAL POTS OF coffee and snacking on the last of the donuts, Nichols came to the same conclusion Blair had. The case as a whole was one of the weirdest ones either of them had ever seen. It was a mind-boggler. One that reluctantly sucked the life out of the investigator similar to how a vampire relieved its victim of its blood.

Nichols, sitting a stack of papers down, brainstormed about what she read and some things had crossed her mind. "How many people do we think Darius Jr is responsible for?"

"As of now, I'm associating him with his father, Darius Price Sr; Winter's aunt, Sara James; and possibly Ramona James, Winter's sister. My gut tells me he murdered Winter's father and the two detectives at her apartment. Let's not forget, Detective Chapman and his family," he explained.

"What reason would he have to kill Winter's father again?" she questioned.

"Supposedly, Travis killed Darius Sr. I'm not at liberty of knowing why. But with the discovery of his phone, it could be likely because of Senior screwed his girl. Whether either of them knew of the pregnancy is beyond me but Senior had to know since Ramona referred to him as her father."

"That leaves to question why Winter didn't know," she wondered.

"Right, and why Ramona would know and Winter didn't. I believe it was said in one of the detective's notes that Robertson was Winter's father," he voiced.

"It's possible for them to have two different fathers, you know?"

"What?"

"Just hear me out," she said, signaling for him to pump his brakes. "I seen something like this on t.v. where one woman slept with two

241

men and she eventually got pregnant with twins. When the twins were born, they were identical but one man was not the father of both twins. One twin was the son of the one man while the other twin was the daughter of the other man. I know it sounds weird but it can't be any weirder than the rest of the shit happening with this case. We trying to figure this shit out anyway. Why not go all the way out?"

Blair thought about it and made a mental note to have the DNA of Darius Sr located and matched to that of Ramona and Winter's. It was a stretch but they needed some kind of understanding to why Winter snapped.

"But that still leaves the question of who put the hit out on Robertson and if Darius Jr handled the job, who was his contact?" Nichols asked, putting another thought out there.

Blair shook his head. Then, he thought about the text message on Darius Sr's phone. "Senior did receive some text messages from an unknown person and that could possibly be his contact," he said, then started to laugh. "What if Darius Sr was Darius Jr's contact?"

"Where you get this kind of shit from?" she asked, laughing with him.

"You can't say it's impossible with all the other weird shit going on with this case," he replied.

"I know that's right," she retorted, faking a yawn. "It's late though, and I'm tired of thinking about this shit. Let's call it a night. I'll meet you back here some time tomorrow."

* * * * *   * * * * *

Nick had been pissed ever since he walked into the Director's office and seen Ann sitting there. What kind of woman was she to play games with him like that? That's the question he had to ask himself as he stood over her. Because, based on the kind of life she lived, or the life they led for that matter, she slept so peacefully as if she had not a care in the world. But was she that cold-hearted where she felt extremely comfortable in her own skin to lay in her bed without restraints and have sweet dreams of performing wifely duties while holding onto a horrific secret?

What would their son think? She'd talked of telling him the truth but what was the truth. He hovered over her thinking of whether he knew the person she portrayed herself to be. All of those years and he had no idea of what was going on. He wondered if his brother knew. He doubted it. If he didn't, his brother wouldn't.

Ann rolled over, snapping him out of his thoughts. Clutching the sheets, she hugged the pillow, playing sleep the whole time. She knew of his presence. She was waiting to see what he would do. In the end, she hoped he would get in the bed and make love to her. That's what she really wanted him to do. He could take his anger out on her that way.

Licking her lips, "Are you gonna stand over me all night or are you gonna join me for bed?" she asked, letting him know she wasn't sleep at all.

Get in the bed? He wanted to jump on top of her and bash her brains in. That's what he wanted to do. Whereas, he stripped to his boxers and hopped in bed. She cuddled up to him and he welcomed it. One thing was certain, he couldn't fight the connection the two of them shared. Never mind what he'd recently learned. What they shared was an unbreakable bond. Once alone, that bond pulled them closer towards one another. It was unstoppable.

Ann was glad to have him in her bed. So glad, she mounted him, pulled his third leg through his boxers, and inserted his semi-hard tool into the depths of his warmness. Moaning slightly, the growth of his sword penetrated her deeply. The deeper it traveled, the wetter she became. At full attention, he rolled her over.

Throwing her legs over his shoulders, he went to work, giving her a high-powered pounding. Under him, she held on for dear life, submitting to his will. She knew what the beating stemmed from, and figured she would take what he felt she deserved. She loved him that much. Hopefully, everything would be better afterwards.

Then things grew painful. She hadn't thought it could have gotten worse. When she tried to run, he put things into overdrive and drove relentlessly inside of her. Her cries went unheard. The louder she cried, the harder and deeper he drove his drill bit. Giving up, she lowered her cries to a whimper, praying that the onslaught would be over soon. There was no use in egging it on with him being as upset as he was. This was his retribution for what he viewed as her deception.

Releasing her legs, he pulled out and nutted on her stomach. That act revealed just how much the situation was affecting him. That was the first time ever, in their sexual experience, that he pulled out and smeared his seed outside of her. A part of her didn't know how to take that.

Was he that mad at me that the love we shared for one another would die? That could be apparent as she laid there beat up and sore. But Nick didn't seem to mind as he dressed and simply walked out of her bedroom.

* * * * *   * * * * *

"I have some bad news, Richard."

"When have you ever brought me good news, Jack?"

"This time its news you really don't want to hear," Jack insisted.

Richard, at sixty, leaned back, put his favorite lighter to a freshly clipped cigar and awaited the news of the day. "I'm listening!" he exclaimed, making eye contact with his little brother.

"They found him."

"They found who, Jack?" Richard asked, aware of who he referred to.

"Senior."

"When?"

"I'm not sure but it was the Special Agent who nabbed Winter that found him. If it wasn't him, I doubt we would have known what happened to him."

"Oh, we would have known alright. We would have known that he was dead somewhere but with no certainty. Ain't that how it always goes?" he inquired.

"I guess so, brother. But on another note, what do we do about little Price?"

"We have to let that play out on its own. He's too young to recruit right now," he answered, falling silent.

Jack noticed Richard taking Darius Senior's death hard. The news was a hard pill to swallow. Darius Sr had been the company's best operative and they had been extremely close. A lot of years and time had gone into the relationship they shared and now it was officially over.

Richard, unable to hide it, looked up with a tear in his eye. "Jack, tell me how my son died?"

* * * * *   * * * * *

It was early morning in the home of the Weathersby's. JP rested in his bed thinking, wondering what would happen if he scared the living shit out of the family he now stayed with. They weren't as bad as the last one, but he still wasn't feeling them.

The family was of mixed heritage consisting of a black father and a white mother. They had two girls, but always wanted a little boy. Due to complications with the last pregnancy, they weren't willing to taking another chance of having another child. So, they adopted. For the family, it worked out perfectly with JP being available at the foster center. At nine, he was the right age, and a perfect match to fall in line with their biological daughters who were eleven and thirteen.

Whereas, they probably never would have imagined they would house the son of the devil.

JP, creeping into the room of the eleven-year-old, loosely tied the child to her twin-sized bed with an extended pair of shoestrings. He'd quickly learned from his short time in the house that she was a heavy sleeper. Keeping true to that notion, she was out cold and couldn't feel anything as he bound her to the bed.

There was no need to rush. The man of the house had already left for work earlier that morning. That left the house quiet, and peaceful enough for him to lay out his plans.

With the eleven-year-old tied down, he slipped out, heading to the thirteen-year-old's room. She was fast asleep but she wasn't a heavy sleeper like her little sister. Tying her down wouldn't be the best idea. That didn't mean he couldn't do something to make her feel his wrath.

He decided to make the set-up look like her work.

Dragging the tied shoestrings down the hall, he wrapped it around the door handle. With the shoestring secured, he turned his attention to the mother's bedroom door. He wrapped the remainder of the rope around the door knob, and checked the knot to make sure it was as tight as it could be.

Admiring his set-up, he pulled out a lighter. Lighting the end of the shoestring at the mother's door, the previously soaked cotton quickly ignited. The lighter fluid propelled the fire to erupt in all directions.

Excited, he raced back to his room as if he had been sleeping the whole morning. Jumping in his bed, the loud shrieking from the eleven-year-old echoed throughout the house as the flames consumed her. She fought hard to get out of the compromising position. Half-sleep, she froze underneath the blue flames, and instead of fighting her way through the shoestrings, she screamed at the top of her lungs. Those screams awoken her thirteen-year-old sister.

The teenager leaped up to see what the fuss was about. At the door, she burnt her hand on the door knob. Snatching it away, she inhaled the light smell of smoke outside of her door. With a fresh burn mark on her hand, the teen realized this wasn't a dream. The way her sister screamed at the top of her lungs explained that something was terribly wrong. She had to get out of there. Throwing something over the hot knob, she jerked the door open, then followed the burnt smell to her sister's room.

A flaming shoestring was burning her sister. Off-hand, she didn't know what to do. Grabbing a blanket, she tossed it on top of her sibling hoping to put out the small fire.

Simultaneously, the mother was in her room banging on the door. She was awakened by her daughter's screams. When she went to her bedroom room, she burned herself on the piping hot knob. Not thinking to grab something, she reacted by banging on the door, hoping to get someone's attention. The teenager heard her mother's pleas for help and went to assist her.

During the commotion, JP rolled around under the covers, finding the incident hilarious. He laughed so hard, tears christened his face. It was the funniest thing he'd done since he tortured the arrogant daughter from the last foster family. To him, it would get better before it gotten worse.

The mother, angry and slightly burned, looked at the set-up. With her daughters' safe, she noticed the only one who didn't seem too concerned was her foster child, Jason. Going to his room, she could hear him snickering under the covers. While he found it amusing, he failed to hear her come in then leave. He did, however, feel the belt she came back with.

Jumping around, he wasn't into that kind of abuse. Flinging the covers off of him, he clambered from the bed to face off with his foster mother.

She wrapped the long belt around her hand, and dared him to buck. What she didn't know, he had every intention of doing so. As a smart youngin', he wanted her to make the first move. She'd gotten her licks off. Now, it was his turn.

She reached out to grab him. That was her first fatal mistake. He swiftly grabbed her hand and twisted it. She screamed out in agony, while flopping on the floor. Landing hard, she felt like a complete fool, realizing she let a nine-year-old take her down. Unable to believe it, she had to acknowledge that's exactly what happened.

"I don't mean no disrespect, old lady. But you might need to find you someone else to beat on. I ain't the one!" he professed.

Embarrassed and upset, she snatched away from him, scrambled to her feet, and darted to the house phone. She had to report this to the foster center. She wouldn't condone that type of disrespect.

She was screaming before she actually talked to anyone. "Someone need to come get this little boy!" she proclaimed. The person on the phone sought to calm her down. "I don't want this little bastard at my house. Somebody need to come get him, RIGHT NOW!"

Chapter Thirty-Four

AS NICK PREPARED TO leave, he could overhear his son, Stanley, and his cousin, Bryan Jr, talking in the den. It was a little too early for them to be up but regardless, the subject of their conversation caught his attention.

Some years back, Nick had heard of Ann's sister and her family being killed in what was said to be home invasion. Notwithstanding the reports, Ann's nephew miraculously survived. Many questioned how that was possible but he did. Intrigued, Nick inched closer to the door opening to listen to Bryan tell his side of the story. As he listened, it gave him the ability to hear firsthand about how he made it out of the house, despite his story contradicting earlier stories.

Stanley, cutting into Nick's recollection, questioned Bryan Jr about it and Bryan Jr attempted to explain it in a manner where he wouldn't have to keep repeating himself. All in all, Stanley wasn't trying to believe what his cousin was telling him.

"This isn't making sense, cuz."

"Listen, I got up to get something to drink and seen my dad was home. It had been days since we last seen him so to see him was a treat for me. Instead of me getting something to drink, he picked me up and carried me back to my room."

He looked to see if his cousin was hearing him.

"He told me I had to wait until I got up. It was too late. I didn't think much of it but I think they were trying to have sex and I interrupted them," he said, smiling mischievously. "The next thing I know, I'm waking up coughing and not knowing what happened. I tried running to my parents' room but all I could see was fire coming from it. I'm thinking that's where the fire must have started. I was starting to cough really bad so I ran into my sister's room but she wasn't there so I ran downstairs. I couldn't find anyone. I didn't want to leave like that but I couldn't breathe."

He stopped to catch his breath.

"I ran next door and our neighbor called the police. I told him what I saw and he said I would be alright only if I listened to him and do what he said. He was ex-military or something."

"But didn't the news say that four bodies were found?" Stanley asked.

"Yeah, and they also said that it was the house fire that killed my parents and little sister. That's not what happened. They were murdered!"

"You don't know that," Stanley retorted.

"I do know that! And to keep the killer from coming back to kill me, they told the news people that they found four bodies instead of three."

Stanley laughed a little too loudly. "You been watching too many t.v. shows. Ain't nobody looking to come and kill you. Get out of here with that crap."

"Trust me, I know what I'm talking about," Bryan Jr replied with a hint of seriousness in his voice.

As Nick listened to the little guys talk, it reminded him of him and his brother. A piece of him really missed his brother and the good times they once had. Then his memories grew gloomy. Upon hitting puberty, the relationship they shared took a drastic turn once the competition started. In those times, he found out how fast his love for someone could change when it was him against another. His desire to win separated him from the unconditional love he had for another.

Feeling no need to revisit the past, Nick refused to listen to his son anymore. Turning to leave, he came face-to-face with Ann. Staring her down, he gave her a very disturbing look, and started to walk around her. She wasn't feeling how he sought to carry her. Grabbing his arm, she applied a little pressure, and stopped him in his tracks. She signaled for him to meet her outside. He walked off to get his things first.

Bags in hand, he ambled onto the back porch to see what she wanted. Looking to his right, she waited for him on the bench. She tilted her head to the empty spot next to her, nonverbally instructing him to sit down. The strap from the bag slipped from his shoulders, and the bag fell to the ground. As he turned to sit down, he moved it in-between his legs.

Ann wasted no time getting straight to the point. "I know you're upset but what did you expect me to do, tell you?" she asked.

Nick remained silent, giving her the floor to talk. He had nothing to say.

"Sam didn't even know of my status. But let me tell you that he wasn't a job for me. I was here because I really wanted to. I could have been anywhere in the world if I wanted to." She rubbed her hands together, mulling over Richard's motives. "For some reason, Richard wanted you to know about me. I really don't know why. Not many know of me and what I do. You wouldn't have known if he wouldn't have called us in at the same time." She looked at him. "He has his reason for everything he does. It's hard to figure him out. He knows everything so it would be hard to pretend there's nothing going on, especially with the job he wants done."

Nick broke his silence. "Does he know about Stanley?"

She reached for his hand. "No one … but us," she declared, squeezing his hand before he snatched it away, "knows about him. And that's how it will stay unless you trying to be the barrier of bad news."

"Ain't that what you originally wanted?" he asked.

"I thought that's what I wanted. Upon Sam's death, I was in an emotional turmoil. You were back, my feelings resurfaced and I wasn't thinking quite clearly. I also didn't have any idea I would be called back in either." She dropped her head. "I did genuinely love Sam, Nick. He was a great man. But...," she looked up at him, "he was never you."

"Don't sit here and give me this sob story as if I'll soak it up and everything will be forgotten. You must have forgotten what I do for a living. Everything you're gonna say is some bullshit so save me the trouble of having to decipher what's real and what's fake," he demanded, wishing to get on with it.

"Well, if that's how you want it. I will tell you the truth then," she explained.

He shifted uncomfortably in his seat. "That would be a great place to start, don't you think? But let me ask you a question first. What is your interest in wanting Winter James free?"

She clenched her jaw. "If you would listen, you'll get that answer."

"I'm listening!" he exclaimed, crossing his arms over his chest.

She came right out with it. "Winter is my niece. Her father was my-"

"Hold the fuck up!" he snapped.

"LET ME FINISH, NICK!" She patted his leg. "Yes, it's true that she killed the man who was my husband, and yes, I would like for her to pay for that murder. One day she will. However, her going down for that murder will not bring him back nor will it deter the murders of the countless others after him." She reached for his hand. "She is an asset to what we believe in. Just like you, she's what this country needs to keep the flow of things going."

"Who the fuck are you?" he wondered aloud.

"Don't ask stupid questions, Nick."

"What's your real name?" he asked.

"You know my name. Annabelle Pointer. I couldn't change it with the bureau so it stayed Annabelle Tanks on record. But you're trying to get me off subject."

"Which is? Getting your niece out of federal custody so she could be your female Jason Bourne." He gazed off. "I don't know if I can do this anymore, Ann. This shit is getting too out of control."

"You know they'll never let you out, Nick! Why play mind games with yourself. YOU'RE STUCK! Face it!!! This is the life you chose so you have to live it to the fullest."

He jerked at the strap on his bag. "I don't need your shitty pep talks. This it for me." He rose to leave, picking up his bag.

She crossed her legs, and leaned back. "What now, Nick?" she asked, giving him a sly eye. "You're walking out on your son again?" She said it to get under his skin.

He looked over his shoulder, shaking his head at the low blow. Then, he walked off, never to look back.

★ ★ ★ ★ ★   ★ ★ ★ ★ ★

S.A. Blair wasn't able to get any sleep as he thought about Winter's case. His desire to get to the bottom of why she snapped was starting to take a toll on him. He couldn't think of anything else. Thoughts of every detail consumed him as he made it back to his office to make sure all the i's were dotted and all the t's were crossed.

The prosecuting of Winter would quickly approach, and when that time arrived, he needed to have his ducks in a row. They had to find her guilty. No other verdict would suffice. When seeking that conviction, the presentation of the facts had to be shown without a shadow of doubt. The friend in him yearned for a speedy trial and an even faster conviction; but, the agent in him had to make sure the jury lived Winter's guilt. In order to make that happen, he couldn't miss anything.

Walking into his office, the box stationed on the floor stood out, catching his attention. The name Nick Pointer flickered in bold black letters. He picked the box up, and sat it on the desk. Removing the top, *I should start thinking of something else. This should be a good distraction from thinking about Winter's case.* He surmised that if he didn't start thinking of something else, he would go crazy just like Winter did.

He removed a stack of files off the top. Moving around the desk, he copped a seat, and fingered through the papers in his hand. The first few pages expounded on Nick as an outstanding agent who had dealt with the best and worst of situations throughout his career. He'd worked some high-profile cases both in the public eye and was cemented in the trenches with those on his radar. All of his cases, particularly the many undercover operations he participated in, subsequently ended in successful prosecutions of the organizations infiltrated.

Impressed, Blair continued to flip through the pages, and started to see a similar pattern forming. Towards the middle of the file, things started to look a bit grim. Out of the blue, Nick had been investigated for supplying guns and drugs to organizations that wrecked major havoc on the streets. These were the same streets he was supposed to be cleaning up.

Blair flipped to see the outcome of those investigations, noticing that a number of witnesses disappeared and statements were changed, which eliminated the prosecutions of those organizations. *I knew there was something I didn't like about him.* Now that he had the motive to feel comfortable about the feelings he had, he felt the need to inform Ann about her husband's brother. That was until he stumbled upon some documents that put a halt to caring about Ann knowing about Nick at all.

Blair was unable to believe what he read. He thought back to the day when they found the guns and boxes of money in Sara's house. For a woman of her stature, she had no access to that kind of artillery or that kind of revenue. It was through someone else that she acquired those things, even if it was for safekeeping. The real culprits had to be Travis Malcolm Robertson or Darius Price Sr. and by the things he read, it wouldn't surprise him if it was Nick who supplied either of them.

He wasn't found guilty of any wrong-doing, he reckoned, wishing to remain partial and neutral. He surely didn't want to convict him without the proper proceedings. But deep down, he was convinced Nick was the supplier everyone imagined him to be. He had to be, especially with how Robertson and Price could operate so freely for years. During those years, they could run the streets in whichever way they deemed fit, and never had to worry about evidence ever being brought against them in court. If there were any, Nick would walk it out of the station, leaving whatever case there was against them dead.

Blair reached for the office phone. He called Nichols. As the phone rang, a cellphone rang in close proximity. Moments later, Nichols walked into the office, answering it. When he heard her voice on the phone and in his office, he hung up and handed her the papers he'd read.

"What you think about this?" he asked, studying her countenance.

"I think it's great if you could fill me on what you're thinking," she requested.

"I'm thinking that years ago, Nick Pointer, my partner's brother, was supplying Darius Price Sr and his partner, Travis Malcolm Robertson."

"And you believe this because of some allegations that he was doing illegal things with those he was supposed to investigate?"

"Not exactly, Nichols. But because of this," he stated, handing her another piece of paper.

Upon reading the paper, her jaw dropped. She couldn't believe it. If what she read was true then a lot could be put into perspective about the overall circumstance of the case. "Blair-" she said, but was interrupted by the forensic DNA expert knocking at the door with an envelope in hand.

"This is the DNA results you asked for, Blair."

Nichols eagerly snatched the envelope out of Blair's hand, ripping it open. Reading it word for word, she smiled. "I told you it was possible," she exclaimed, handing him the document.

He stared at it, and smiled. "Now we're making some progress. Looks like you're my new partner. Partner!"

"Well partner, let's finish busting this case wide open."

Chapter Thirty-Five

BLAIR AND NICHOLS FELT good about their recent accomplishments. They knew they were onto something and it could not only solve some of the cold cases but could assist the bureau in prosecuting Nick for his past crimes. What Blair hadn't realize was how the issues could be helpful to Winter and her case. That wasn't how he desired it. As a matter of fact, that was the last thing he wanted to do. His objective was to find out why she snapped, and traveled down the path she did. Nevertheless, why she snapped and the mental stress it placed upon her didn't matter. None of that changed the fact that she murdered his partner in cold blood as she strove to flee the scene of a crime. For that reason alone, she would have to pay severely and he would make sure of that.

He looked up from the papers, and noticed Nichols in her own world. "What's on your mind, partner?" he asked, snapping her out of her thoughts.

"I'm not sure. Something is bothering me and I'm trying to make sense of it," she replied.

"Let's me hear what's on your mind," he requested, sitting the papers in his hand down.

"What's bothering me is who the person, or persons, are that Darius Price Sr and his son worked for. To have employed these two without the knowledge of law enforcement is mind-blowing. The idea of them working as freely as killing machines takes the cake. Truthfully, that's what's bothering me the most," she explained.

"That's something that concerns me too but how do we find out who these people are?" He held his hands up. "I look at it like this. There has been people doing what they've done and like them, they were captured or killed too. So remember, what's done in the dark will come to the light."

"I don't know! That's what has my mind racing." She studied one document in particular. "I don't think it was Nick Pointer though," she voiced.

He frowned. "What makes you think that?" he asked, wondering where she was going with that.

"What agent would openly supply a known street organization knowing, based on his position, he would fry in hell for it?" she questioned, seeking to make sense of her own question. "It could be that someone wants it to look that way." She glanced over at him.

The argument locked Blair deeper into his thoughts. She was right. Why hadn't he looked at it from that angle? Still, he couldn't dismiss it. Nick was his link. He wouldn't tell her that; however, he would continue to pick her mind for info and use it to his advantage.

"What I think is that we need to pay attention to every option available and he is still one of them," he re-iterated.

"I can agree with that." She shook her head. "Still something doesn't seem right. Who can make those kind of accusations go away?" she wondered, holding the documents in the air.

"Someone extremely powerful," he stated. "And it's definitely someone above our pay grade."

"I think that's where we need to start then because starting from the bottom and going up will take too long."

"What do you propose?" he asked, rearranging a file on his desk.

"Let's see what we can find on-" She stopped to look for the name she remembered seeing. "A Richard Anderson. That looks like a perfect place to start."

* * * * *　　* * * * *

Winter had been up all night long thinking. Her mind had been racing at the speed of light about everything imaginable. The moment she closed her eyes, her mental screen displayed vivid images of her past as if it was happening right then and there in her cell. She had to repeatedly force her eyes open. She was that afraid of what she would see.

If it wasn't her mother's face, it was her auntie's on her death bed. If it wasn't half of her sister's brains blown out, it was the final moments of DP's noodles splattering over the floor as she stood over him. Immediately after, a fluttering snapshot of the agent's head snapped back. Then the reel repeated itself with images of a room she couldn't recall visiting. She could only imagine what would appear next. With all the death she'd seen, it was starting to play with her psychological functions.

Outside her cell, a guard walked down the range during her rounds. The sounds of shackles scratching the concrete floors vibrated through the soundless atmosphere.

Winter rolled over. *Someone must have court this morning.*

The guard stopped in front of her door, flashed the light in her face, attempting to awake her. She tightly clutched her wool blanket, playing sleep. They hadn't even served breakfast; yet, they were trying to get her up and out of the county jail before anyone else could comprehend what was going on.

With no movement, the guard pounded on the door. The loudness of the flashlight smacking the door startled her. "James, you have court this morning. Let's get a move on it," the guard shouted.

Faking sleep, Winter sat up and stared at the door. The guard dropped the shackles in front of the door, then walked off. When she came back, she opened the chuckhole, and slid in a breakfast tray and a milk.

Winter wasn't in the mood to eat once finding out she was going to court. *What am I going to court for?* she wondered. She hadn't heard from her lawyer in a couple of weeks. Without a formal warning, she would be walking into a blind situation, and one she wasn't properly prepared for. Her stomach fluttered, and its contents dropped. She rushed to the toilet, taking a seat on the steel toilet stool. Everything inside of her came rushing out. Her nerves were on the edge.

The thought of shuffling into a courtroom brought on another flurry of runs. Feeling relieved, she flushed the toilet, and let the cold water splash her bare behind. Wiping herself, the thought of a surprise court date had her perplexed but she had to get her mind together, even if she wasn't able to prepare any other way. The guard was on her way back, and she wouldn't take no for an answer.

★ ★ ★ ★ ★   ★ ★ ★ ★ ★

Nichols examined the notes she'd jotted down as Blair prepared for the scheduled Winter's motion hearing that morning.

Early last week, Winter's lawyer had filed a sealed mitigating factors motions to minimize the pressure against her. The prosecutor hadn't been willing to negotiate his stance so the motions had focused around Winter's mental state, the circumstances surrounding her actions, and her inability to rationalize her responsibility associated with those actions.

Blair knew the defense would put up a decent fight to lessen the fall Winter would take. He didn't think it would come so soon. Seeing his time was limited, he would have to take the things he found in regards to Nick, and find a way for them to hurt her case. Even still, his ace in the hole would always be the murdering of his partner. Nothing would change that she intentionally opened fire on them for the sake of killing and possibly getting away. Nothing said at a motion hearing could outshine that one viable fact.

In spite of his plans, when it came to conducting a formal motion's hearing, anything could be construed as facts when they actually weren't. The judge, and/or the prosecutor, could accept a lie as the truth and vice versa. By the end of the hearing, Blair understood, going into the hearing, that there needed to be some minimizing of those kind of facts. That why he intended to testify at the hearing. He believed, with his testimony, the record would reflect the truth, and would be the deciding factor in finding her guilty for murdering Special Agent Samuel Blair.

Under that pretense, NO psychology expert could tell him anything different. According to the facts, Winter was very much aware of what she was doing when she pulled the trigger. And with that representation, the jury was sure to convict.

Blair stood to leave.

Nichols rose with him, giving him a pat on the back, along with a few words of encouragement. "You knock em' down dead, now you hear me, partner," she voiced, in a weird tone, as she impersonated some old country guy.

Blair gave her a puzzled look, wondering if everything was alright or if she should be the one going for the mental evaluation. "Are you sure YOU'RE okay?" he asked, putting his hand on her forehead.

She laughed it off, punching him in the arm.

"You should come with me," he suggested. "You can learn a lot. I'm sure we'll have other cases just as weird as this one and someone will need a hearing to determine whether or not they'll need an evaluation or not."

She pursed her lips. "I'm good, Blair. I'll catch the next one. I want to sit here in silence to see if I can figure out some things." She smiled at him. "I'll have plenty to talk about when you get back. I can promise you that."

"That'll make me want to take my time getting back. If I'm not back within a reasonable time, PLEASE, don't come looking for me," he said; his laughter filling the room.

Nichols, knowing he needed to leave, pushed him out of his own office so he wouldn't be late. "I wouldn't want you to be late for your big date, partner." She helped him gather his things. With him gone, she closed the door behind him then turned to the papers scattered around the office. She had no idea where to start. Looking over her shoulder, she could see Blair had left.

Drawing the blinds, she pulled out her phone. Looking at the closed door, she spread out the most pertinent papers, and started taking as many pictures as she could. She apprehended what she was doing was against the oath she took as a federal agent; nonetheless, she had other obligations to fulfill. Luckily, at least for the sake of Blair, she wasn't in the mind to destroy the documentation. That, for the time being, wasn't an option. That didn't mean it couldn't be later. What she did realize, if Blair persisted to tackle the case in the manner he was, a time would come when he would find himself in a precarious position. She would give him a heads-up, and hope he had sense to catch it.

Flipping to documents pertaining to Nick, she rapidly snapped the necessary pictures before putting away her phone. She sat down thinking about Nick. The idea of the Intel surrounding him being so freely advertised in his files tripped her out. She would have never assumed those kind of allegations would end up in his file. She'd known him for years, and never had he given her the impression he would do the things they said he'd done.

Was it possible for him to do what they said he did? she questioned, thinking back to the time they spent together on those cases. Unable to come up with a definitive answer, she failed to understand why those lies were inserted into his file in the first place; especially, if there was no indication that he'd participated in that kind of activity.

Nichols smirked, figuring she didn't need an indication for what he done. Nick wasn't responsible for what they said he did. That was just what they said. Conducting illegal ventures wasn't his style so it couldn't have been him supplying Darius Sr, Travis or DP. At the end of the day, he was simply the fall guy. And that was unfortunate, since, it was her who had been their supplier.

★ ★ ★ ★ ★   ★ ★ ★ ★ ★

Jack Anderson - a medium-built man of fifty-eight with a salt and pepper low-styled haircut - sat in his comfortable, oversized leather desk chair, smoking an imported cigar, and enjoying a stiff shot of Remy Martin XO. As he sipped the fine cognac, he thought of his brother.

Things hadn't been up to par when it came to his big brother's conduct. As of late, the way he carried certain burdens depicted a contrary approach that he wasn't used to. That was outside of the norm. But whatever it was, it transcended the death of his son, and the others.

Death wasn't an essence that fazed him. It never had and pretty much, never will. Death was something Richard embraced. He loved it. Still, it was rare for Jack to see his brother shed a tear, let alone for one of their own perishing.

Pulling on the cigar, it appeared that even a cold-blooded, calculated, evil son-of-a-bitch like Richard could show some form of emotion every once in a while. *Who knew he had it in him?* But that wasn't what shocked Jack. What disturbed him was Richard's

260

acknowledgement of Darius Sr as his son. That hadn't happened since Darius was a child and Richard was letting him run around wild.

The cellphone to his right chimed.

Jack careened his neck; his attention diverted by the text message alert pulling him away from his current thoughts. Picking up the phone, it continuously chimed as alerts came in. Working the phone with one hand, he opened each text, and used his other to put the cigar in his mouth.

Scanning the contents of each text, he saw everything he needed to see and more. Placing the cigar in the ashtray, he liked when a plan came together and was followed through to the letter. Pouring himself another shot, he viewed the last text message, locked the images in his head, then quickly deleted them.

To be sure they were erased, he placed the phone on a proto-type gadget designed to wipe the mobile device clean within a matter of seconds. He pressed the button to activate the gadget. Seconds later, it beeped twice, indicating the miraculous job done in such a short time. The phone was wiped clean that quick. With no need to check, he picked it up, setting it to the side.

As he downed the rest of his cognac, he eyed the phone. His mind was playing a simple trick on him. A part of him wanted to make sure the photos had been erased, but why when that was the whole purpose of the invention.

Waving off his curiosity, he wouldn't let it trouble him. If it hadn't worked, that wouldn't matter either. The phone would be discarded in less than thirty days anyway. That way, he could constantly fly under the radar, and not have to worry about the prying eyes of those above him.

Chapter Thirty-Six

WINTER STARED OUT OF the St. Clair County jail van window as she was being transported to the courthouse in East St. Louis. For a moment, she felt free. She felt a part of society. And it made her truly missed her freedom. She remembered the days when she could get up and go as she pleased. Those were the days when her innocence felt light, and the stressfulness of life hadn't plagued her. That all changed when her father was killed.

The van bumped a stop sign. Leaning into a right turn, she held the chain connecting her handcuffs to her leg shackles. The leg irons cuts into her ankles, hitting a bone. She placed her feet together to minimize the pain.

The van sped down the empty street, coming to another stop sign. Enjoying the ride, Winter racked her brain about the upcoming court appearance. *Who knows what the purpose of it is,* she reasoned, spotting an old lady letting her dog out to use the bathroom. *I'm sure it has everything to do with what happened.* Knowing that much, she ached to tell her side of the story. While the court would focus on what she done, she lived to enlighten the court about DP getting everything he deserved. She held no remorse in her heart for taking his life. That was something they should know.

She pondered how that would look, figuring it would make her look bad, and hurt her chances of being found not guilty. Subsequently, they would look at her as if she was a monster. Plus, they wouldn't have a hard time painting that picture when bringing up the deaths of Natalie and Special Agent Pointer. While she felt no remorse for DP's demise, she was unsure of how to feel when it came to murdering them. Truthfully speaking, they had been in the wrong place at the wrong time. Her aim had been DP, and only DP. Still, she figured if she couldn't decide on whether she felt remorse for killing them then it was a given that she didn't care.

She couldn't truthfully convey that lack of emotion in the courtroom. That wouldn't be a good look for her. If she did, they would surely crucify her.

The van slowed down. There was a stalled car up ahead.

The driver looked at his partner. "I think we should take a detour. We don't need to be late. The last time they acted like they wanted to charge us."

"Waiting won't be a good idea so take the detour," the passenger said, agreeing.

Winter could care less which way they took as long as she could partake in her current entertainment. There wouldn't be many more luxuries like these if she was convicted.

Up front, an argument broke out between the guards in regards to what route the driver decided to take.

"Why would you come this way? This way takes longer. We should have waited on the stalled car to move."

"Let me do this!" the driver stated. "You just sit there and shut the fuck up."

They continued to go back and forth; neither of them paying attention to the road. The driver, coming to a stop sign, looked up, bumped it, but failed to see the truck coming towards them from the left side.

Before they knew what happened, a black Ram 1500 smashed into the left front-side panel, smashed the frame into the engine compartment, and blew out the front tire. Another Ram came out of nowhere and rammed the back of the van, rendering it unmovable. From both Ram's, four masked men jumped out - two from each truck - armed with SK assault rifles.

In the van, the driver was slumped over the steering wheel unconscious; the passenger rested his head against the window, semi-conscious.

The armed men, taking no chances, approached the van cautiously. One noticed the passenger slightly moving so he put four rounds in his body. He didn't know if the guard was going for his weapon or not so he adhered to his training.

Another masked man jerked opened the van's side door, and locked eyes with Winter. She glared back at him with no fear in her eyes. "Winter James, you are going with us. NO arguments! No fighting! If you refuse, you will be shot. DO YOU UNDERSTAND?"

She nodded.

The man waved her out of the truck. Scooting across the bench seat, she surveyed the area. The man extended his hand to help her onto the single step. Another masked man hurried over with a pair of bolt cutters, and cut the chains confining her legs and hands.

With free movements, the four masked men escorted her to a black GMC van awaiting to escort them away from the scene.

* * * * *   * * * * *

"We come to you live from Belleville, IL at the scene of what appears to be a high-jacking of a St. Clair County jail van. The van was carrying a Winter James who had been set to appear in Federal Court this morning." Arlene peered over her shoulder at the wreckage. "From the looks of it, a well-thought out plan had been executed to high-jack the transport as it made its way towards downtown East St. Louis to the Federal Courthouse."

She swallowed hard. "The witnesses on the scene are saying that it all happened so fast. The one truck hit the van in the front while the other one followed striking it from the back. Four masked gunmen jumped out and abducted Miss Winter James before making their escape in an unmarked vehicle."

She motioned to the holes in the side of the van. "The guard sitting in the passenger's seat took four assault rifle rounds to the torso, possibly at close range killing him instantly. It is being speculated that Winter was the mastermind behind the jacking and no one has an answer to who may have done this nor is there any leads on who to look for."

She pulled out her phone to view her notes. "Winter James, the person being transported, has been charged with killing Special Agent Samuel Pointer, a member of the FBI Task Force Unit, Darius Price, and his wife, Natalie Price. Miss James faces multiple life sentences if found guilty for those charges and with the events of today, she will be expected to have a number of charges added to that indictment." She stuffed her phone in her pocket. "I'm Arlene Jackson, reporting live for Channel 6 News."

JP rocked back and forth as he watched the news covering Winter's abduction. Seeing that made his blood boil. How could they let her get away that easy?

Some snickering resonated behind his back.

Paying it no mind, one of the kids had the nerve to ask him whether that was his mother and father on t.v. because of the similarity of their names. JP didn't respond. When he didn't, the kid reached out and touched JP's shoulder, seeking to get his attention.

Without much thought, JP grabbed the kid's hand, breaking it in three places. Standing up, he looked down at the kid, still holding his hand, and raised his foot, taking aim at the side of the kid's head. He repeatedly stomped the kid out until some other kids advanced to assist the kid. Sensing the crowd forming, JP squared up, prepared to bomb on anyone attempting to get too close.

The noise from the commotion brought the adults of the facility running into the t.v. room to witness firsthand what kind of monster JP really was.

As they rushed in, an older kid charged JP thinking a little guy like JP wouldn't be able to handle him. What a mistake he made with that assumption.

JP man-handled the older kid, leaving him with a black eye, a busted lip and two broken ribs. Intent on doing more damage, the adults intervened and saved the kid from getting brutally punished. Two male adults grabbed ahold of JP, subduing him. While they removed the trouble maker, the female adults tended to the kids who needed immediate medical attention.

A few adults stood to the side scratching their heads, oblivious to why JP would snap out like that. Over the recent months, they'd received various reports of his inability to fit in with the appointed foster families but this was on a totally different level. This kind of outburst wouldn't be tolerated.

Upon the completion of the investigation, the staff's notes elaborated on JP's reasons for acting out but the staff wouldn't allow that to substitute for his actions. The decision had been made to introduce him to what they called the 'torture chamber' for a while. In the history of the facility, no one had ever been placed in the torture chamber. However, JP's actions made him the first and it would be that experience that would change him forever.

Looking into the darkness of the room, JP became comfortable with his surroundings. Adjusting his eyes, he made up his mind that he wouldn't let his confinement control him. He sniffed the stall air. This would be a time where he remained in control of himself, his emotions, and his mental state. He would let nothing change him. There would be no conforming to how anyone else wanted him to act, nor would he let the torture chamber break him down. This was merely a curve ball that he would hit out of the park.

I am the controller of my destiny!

At his young age, he utilized a state of mind that most adults couldn't fathom until they were well into their thirties or forties. A soul before his time, he would show the foster facility that placing him in the torture chamber was the worst thing they could have ever done. He clawed at the floor. This would be their biggest mistake ever. Their placing him in there would simply blow open the doors of the evilness and pain buried within him. And what would came from the opening of those doors would be something no one really wanted to see, especially the staff at the foster facility.

* * * * *   * * * * *

Blair stared at the wreckage of the high-jacking. This was unbelievable. How could someone put such an intrinsic plot of that magnitude together and actually see it through. He strongly believed that whomever responsible had some major juice.

This had to be an inside job.

No one knew of Winter's court date. It was a last minute scheduling and Winter's lawyer hadn't been informed until two days prior. It would take more than two days to plot that kind of attack. Looking at it, this wasn't a random act nor was it put together at the last minute. It was something they had done before, and the culprits had no problem doing it in the midst of a neighborhood that rarely seen much action.

This isn't the work of the average thugs.

The news wanted to public to think someone Winter knew pulled off the high-jacking. Whereas, Blair seen that was so far from the truth. Someone had done Winter a favor. He seriously doubted she knew who it was. From what he could remember, DP killed everyone she had in terms of family. Thinking about that, he didn't think, even in his limited mental capacity, that she could have anyone willing to risk so much to free her. Unless, she wasn't who she pretended to be.

Exhaling, Blair accepted that the case stood at the top of being the one with the weirdest situations. Anything could be likely. He merely hated that he wasn't in the loop of knowing. Every time he moved one step closer to something solid, an incident of this magnitude arose, throwing him for a bigger loop.

Walking away from the wreckage, he called Nichols to fill her in on the high-jacking. She was still at the office but had taken a break from the paperwork. "I'm gonna need you to comb through every piece of what we have. See if you can make some kind a connection. We need a connection pronto!"

"Don't worry about. I'm on it."

★ ★ ★ ★ ★   ★ ★ ★ ★ ★

Rushing into the office, the secretary burst in on Richard and Jack watching the news regarding Winter's abduction. They were amused at the events but upon looking up, Richard seen the alarm in his secretary's eyes.

"What is it, Sonia?" he asked.

Before she could get a word out, Nick brushed pass her, making his way into the office.

Richard flashed a fake smile. "We'll take it from here, Sonia." She exited, closing the door. "Thanks for the heads up, Nick."

Jack inhaled his anger. "Have a seat, Nick!"

Nick attempted to gauge the gentlemen's attitudes before speaking. On one accord, they didn't seem to be too happy or too sad about the overall situation. He knew he proceeded with the plan ahead of schedule. He had to. He had to do something that could jump-start the ending of the life he was tired of living.

Richard eyed Nick. "You got started pretty early, didn't you?"

"I saw a time to make it work and I took it," Nick explained.

"Where is she?" Richard wanted to know.

Nick glanced around. "That's what I'm here to talk about."

Richard pulled a fresh cigar from its box. "What is there to talk about? You were supposed to retrieve her for us then bring her to us. What more should we talk about?"

"You really didn't expect me to walk up the front door and drop her off, did you?" Nick questioned.

"Where is she?" Richard asked. "I have no time for jokes."

"I have her in a safe place but there is something I need to ask for bringing her to you," he stated, building up the courage to come out with it.

Richard looked at Nick, lighting the cigar. A cloud of smoke swirled around his head as he sized him up. Leaning back, he pulled on the cigar, unaware of what the hell Nick wanted. Not in the mood for guessing, he got right to the point. "I don't have time for this shit. What the fuck is it that you want? You want out. Is that what you want?" he asked, figuring that had to be it.

"I would like that a lot. I can't continue to live like this," Nick admitted.

"Is this about you being summoned to abduct the person who killed your brother. If it is, you need to get serious. You don't give a fuck about him. If you did, you wouldn't have been fucking his wife, and getting her pregnant."

Nick was taken back by that revelation. He lowered his head in disgust. It appeared he was fully aware of everything.

"Hold your head up, Nick. I'm not here to judge you. I'm here to make sure things go right for you. Bring her to us and when we're done with her, we'll give her to you to do what you want to do with her."

"I want out!" Nick yelled.

"That's like a whore asking for her virginity back. That shit doesn't happen. You know that much! You must be trying to die in the line of duty, Nick. Is that what you're trying to do?"

Nick recognized what had been insinuated. Ann had been right. He would never get out alive. "Is there anything you can do for me? I'm not trying to be involved in these kind of jobs anymore."

Richard put the cigar down, and clasped his hands. "This is what you do, Nick. This is who you are. You were specifically trained to do what you do. What are you trying to do, be a stay-at-home husband? You want to play that kind of role now?" he asked, finding that funny. Jack laughed with him. "Nick, you're not good at anything but what you do. When are you gonna face that?"

Nick prepared to leave. "When you're ready to give me what I want, call this number." He placed a small piece of paper on the desk, then headed towards the door.

Richard eyed Jack, not knowing what to say as the door slammed behind Nick.

Chapter Thirty-Seven

AS NICK LISTENED TO the recently recorded conversation, he thought about the outcome of the situation if he didn't produce Winter. It would be hell to pay and he knew it. But would it be what he really wanted. He wasn't trying to lose his life in order to get out. He longed to walk away on his own terms. However, his feet were in too deep and it appeared he was quickly sinking instead of treading water like he thought.

Cutting off the recording, he arrived at the location for Winter. He shut off the engine, leaned his arm against the door, and tried to make sense of everything he'd become. He always knew he was a terrible monster. Not the kind the mothers told their children about in order for them be good. But the kind even the mothers were scared to utter one word about.

That was the life he was born into. It was the life he had led all of his life. The bad part about it was that he couldn't remember who he was prior to becoming the man he was sitting in that van.

The person occupying that van wanted, needed and desired to live a totally different life. One where it wouldn't consist of taking orders or being at the beck and call of another. He sincerely craved to lay back and enjoy the life he never got the opportunity to see he had.

Settling down was something he had never thought of doing but as of late, it was fresh on his mind. Especially after talking to Ann initially. His arm slipped off the door, and fell to the armrest. Shaking his head, he could see that his mind was elsewhere. That mental separation made it imperative to re-align his body with his head if he planned to accomplish his end. Annoyed, he shoved the van's door open, marched into the house, and headed straight to his prized possession. Looking at her, he contemplated doing away with her. If he carried out the hit, there was nothing Richard could do about it but accept it. Once it was done, he could disappear and never have to look back for anything except to watch his back.

That meant he would still be running for his life. Going on the run would be a stressful experience. The Director had a very long reach, and would go to great lengths to prove a point. Undecided about his next course of action, Nick believed the Director's reach would have to be extremely long to catch up with him. Because Richard had been right about one thing. He had been trained well. That's why they picked him out of everyone on their go-to list. What Richard failed to realize was that the training would also assist him in becoming a ghost; one they would never find or hear from again. He wandered over to his captive.

Winter, sensing someone standing in front of her, raised her head. Staring at Nick, she instantly seen the similarities to the agent she killed. The similarities weren't that apparent to the naked eyes; however, they were that evident to her. Understanding the situation, her heart raced, almost beating out of her chest. She assumed her time was up. That wasn't a feeling she liked. When she thought of dying, she hadn't envisioned her life ending this way. She pleaded, with her eyes, for an opportunity to explain her stance. She needed to be heard.

He gazed into her eyes, and recognized the look. He'd seen the exact same look on so many of his victims. Usually, he would have delighted in seeing that kind of fear oozing from a person. That look meant he had placed the fear of God within them; therefore, making them bow at his feet. He suddenly felt bad. This was the life he was trying to get away from. That was the look he longed to get away from. He never wanted to put that kind of fear in anyone else, ever again. He genuinely wished to change his life.

"If I remove your gag, will you act an ass?" he asked, hoping he didn't have to put his hands on her.

She nodded slowly.

"I'm not here to hurt you. I was sent to do a job and in doing that job, I went against the grain because I want more than they're offering. I'm gonna take your gag off so we can talk. You can scream all you want. No one will hear you. If you get too crazy, I'll shoot you and leave you in the woods as food for the wildlife. Do you understand?"

She nodded, and he removed the gag.

She stretched her jaw. "Who hired you to do this?" she asked, wasting no time to speak up.

"I'm gonna take you to him but it will be on my terms. I'll rather let you go and let you fend for yourself instead of having to deal with not getting what I want."

"What do you want?"

"I want out of this life!" he spat.

"What do they want from me?"

"To be like me," he vented.

She didn't know to take that response. "To be like you? I don't understand," she confessed.

"It's not my place to help you understand," he replied, tired of dealing with it all.

Feeling overwhelmed, he made up his mind to simply hand her over and deal with getting out at a later date. He realized that based on the person he was, he couldn't actually walk away. It was cemented in his blood. Even at that moment, the person inside of him wanted to blow Winter's head off for what she done to his brother. Then a part of him couldn't blame her for doing what she done. The battle within him raged on, bouncing back and forth from wanting to eliminate her existence to letting her go free for the sake of it.

He was finding it hard to suppress the urges of the man he really was. The tug of war was becoming a hard fought battle. As a spectator, he didn't know who would win. Swaying in the wind, he could plainly see what he had to do if he wanted the outcome to unfold in his favor. Fighting the beast inside, he reached for his phone. As he was about to call Richard, his phone rang.

Looking at the caller ID, it was Richard calling him. He stared at the phone, thinking, *Here comes the bullshit!*

* * * * *   * * * * *

Blair was driving himself crazy over Winter's abduction. That's all he talked about morning, noon and night. Nichols, on the other hand, was tired of hearing about it. But what could she do. She'd already completed the task she'd been sent to do. Until she received further instructions, she was stuck to deal with the blood hound and his rants.

Wishing she was elsewhere, she hadn't been informed that she would have to babysit after the completion of her job. She would have rather taken the pictures, forwarded them and moved on to the next job. Except, she was stuck looking after a total nut job fussing over a case he would never finish investigating.

From what she knew, if he got any closer, things would drastically change for him. That would be a shame too. She wasn't the one who made the rules. She just abided by them.

Blair slapped the desk. "Where are we with obtaining some info on Richard Anderson?" he asked.

"We are actually where we were before we started looking. NO WHERE! The only thing that comes up is his job status."

"Ain't that about something," he mumbled under his breath.

"I don't think we'll find anything on the Director of the Special Needs Division. Get it, Special Needs!" she joked.

"What does the FBI needs with a Special Needs Division?" he asked, rhetorically.

Nichols could see the hamster spinning the wheel in his head. It was getting the exercise of its life. At that rate, it wouldn't take long before he would want to satisfy his curiosity with answers. She saw a chance to leave him to his thoughts. Excusing herself, she left him to solve the unanswerable questions circling her mind. Her interaction with him was becoming a waste of her time since she knew what the outcome would be. That's what irritated her the most. Because if Blair continued with his persistence, he wouldn't have to worry about getting answers about the Special Needs Division. They would find him and show him why the FBI needed a Special Needs Division.

Once in the restroom, she pulled out her phone, and placed a call. Waiting on an answer, she surmised the time had arrived for something to be done about S.A. Blair.

"Yeah?"

"We have run into a problem," she stated bluntly.

"What's that?"

"He's extremely persistent," she said, looking at herself in the mirror.

"That's good, right?"

"In some cases, yeah. But not in all."

"Tell me more."

"He's about to set his sight on the Special Needs Division," she explained.

"That'll be great. There's nothing there for him to find. Does he have anyone in particular that he's eyeing?"

"Yes!"

"Who?"

"Uncle Richard!!"

* * * * *   * * * * *

Having had time to think about Nick's proposal, Richard and Jack came up with an idea that would work for the both of them. During the deliberation, they concluded that Nick would get some of the things he wanted, while they would continue to get what they wanted. At that rate, everyone would be happy.

They were conscious of him being unwilling to lean towards the kind of work he normally dealt with. His pleas had been noted. They unfortunately acknowledged his desire to get away from that kind of life so instead of totally losing a good agent of his caliber, they would give him a little to get a lot in return. That was the essence of a Law for obtaining power and it was one that worked well for them in both the past and the present.

Over the years, the Special Needs Division had their hands in various things and they wanted to remain true to those things. Their primary focus was the flow of money from any and every avenue that generated funds. One of those avenues that brought in a boat load of cash was drug dealing. As a matter of fact, it was one of the greatest source of revenue for them and the United States as a whole. The money was so plentiful, they couldn't stop their pursuit to acquire it and get as much of it as possible.

From the start, Nick refused to participate in assisting them in getting that kind of money so they didn't press the issue. They could see that possibly changing. What Nick didn't know, certain things had surfaced which indicated he was assisting quite a few people in obtaining and moving a product, and the proceeds from the drug trade. And unfortunately, it all started when he fervently denied wanting to become involved.

All of the cases he worked, some alongside S.A. Nichols, were set up for this particular purpose. As a systems analyzer, Richard, from the very beginning, assessed a time when someone would have to go down. By dissecting the possibilities of the future, he singled out Nick to be the fall guy, knowing he had no idea what was in the cards for him.

For the Special Needs Division, there was always a fall guy. Everyone couldn't be a winner but most could definitely lose. They weren't the ones to blame Nick for wanting to get out of a lifestyle that drove many crazy or left the rest dead. But they weren't finished with him. Until they were, he would work for them in some capacity.

Richard called to enlighten him of their plans.

"Hello?" Nick's voice was filled with hesitation and uncertainty. He had no idea of what they would come at him with. What he did know, they wouldn't be upfront or willing to let him voluntarily walk away without them acquiring something of value in return. He knew how they worked. He merely prayed that the abduction of Winter would be enough. That was his wishful thinking. With guys like Richard and Jack, nothing anyone done was ever enough. They always wanted more. They were similar to a pack of leeches. Once they stuck their fangs in, they had no problem sucking a person dry.

"Nick, we have come to the agreement that you're right. You shouldn't be required to do things that has taken so much of a toll on your mind and body." He paused to puff his cigar. "What we can do for you, is, we'll keep you out of harm's way by putting you in a better position that would line your pockets and keep you under the radar."

Nick was mindful of where the conversation was headed. He'd turned down the same job offer years ago. What made them think he'll consider doing it now when he wouldn't do it then? "If you're referring to what I think you're referring to, I'm not interested," he explained, getting right to the point.

"If you let me finish, you'll be interested and really unable to be uninterested."

Nick didn't like the sound of that.

"We need to meet somewhere though," Richard proclaimed. "Like in maybe an hour or two so we can fully discuss the terms of our future deal."

Nick gave up his location.

Jack texted Nick's location to the team leader, urging them to get there as soon as possible to ensure everything was in their favor and not Nick's.

"Oh, and Nick, bring the girl!" Richard instructed, disconnecting the call. He looked at his brother; an uncommon feeling tickled his bones. For some reason, he felt Nick had the ups on them. He'd never had that kind of feeling before. Normally, everything went according to how he wanted; but, now, all of a sudden, things seemed to be a blur. "Jack, I don't feel right about this."

"What are you feeling?" Jack inquired, without a hint of worry in his voice.

"I'm feeling we may be playing into something we can't get out of."

"It's too late to turn back now. Do you want the team to simply take him out and snatch the girl?"

Richard glanced out of the window as she contemplated the option. "Naw ... Let's wait to see what they see when they set up. And if it's contrary to what we want, then we'll send the team in."

Chapter Thirty-Eight

WINTER FAILED TO UNDERSTAND what was going on. This didn't make sense. Why would anyone break her out of jail to work for them? Who does that?

Then there was the man across from her. She couldn't wrap her mind around the fact that he worked for someone whose job was to do things no one else wanted to do. Based on what he said, they wanted her to do those kinds of things as well. Who did they think she was? That was the most important question.

"Excuse me, is it possible if I could get something to drink?" she asked, sparking up a conversation.

"You'll get all you need to drink once I drop your ass off," Nick replied, strongly

She was taken aback by how he reacted. "Do I know you from somewhere?" She swallowed her spit. "Is that why you're acting all shitty?"

"You don't know me," he stated with an attitude. "We have no reason to know one another so stop talking to me."

She was skeptical of saying anything else but she couldn't let it rest. "Are you related to the agent that was murdered?" She intentionally used the word murdered.

He glared at her. "Are you asking me if I'm related to the agent you," he pointed at her, "killed. If that's what you're asking, I'll have to say no."

"NO!" She knew that was a lie. Knowing that, she pushed further. "Now, why would you sit there and lie to me like that. I know who you are."

He turned away. "If you know then why are you still talking?" he inquired, lowering his voice.

"I need some information."

He peered over his shoulder at her. "I don't have any for you."

"That's another lie!"

He spint to face her. "Now I see why they want you. You possess those special skills they want to exploit." He pulled up a chair. "I should just leave those thoughts of yours on the back of the wall and call it a night."

"Why haven't you done that then?" she pushed. "You scared?"

Nick's eyes bored into hers as if he had superhuman powers. She felt outright uncomfortable about how he looked at her. *Maybe I went too far,* she thought as he jumped up screaming it was time to go.

Outside, he threw her into the back of the van. He struggled to catch his breath. His emotions was getting the best of him. In that mind-set, he wouldn't accomplish his goal. To be successful, he had to find himself. He hopped in behind the van's steering wheel, and sought to regain his composure. Thoughts of Ann circled around his mind and he felt butterflies fluttering his stomach. He hated the hold she held over him. He tried convincing himself that he didn't know her so there was no hold strong enough to keep them involved. But that didn't work.

Are you gonna run out on your son? she had asked.

The question plagued him. He prided himself on being the kind of man that didn't run out on his responsibilities, even though he never had any. All of his life, his responsibilities surrounded his job and handling the tasks at hand. Then reality hit him. It would be impossible for him to be there for Stanley like he wanted. There were too many lies, images of deception and breaches of contracts for betrayal lingering overhead.

Then there was Ann. It would be difficult to view her as he once saw her. She wasn't the person she pretended to be. He couldn't find it in his heart to trust her again. Outside of that, he couldn't let his emotions get the best of him. He had to make a rationale decision.

Hopping out the van, he pulled out his gun, and walked to the back of the van. With his gun leveled, he snatched the doors open, and placed both hands on his weapon.

Inside the van, the woman staring up at him was the woman he hated with a passion. Eyeing her with the evilest intent, he leveled the gun right between her eyes. Remember his training, he regulated his breathing, focused his eyes, and placed his finger on the trigger. The curve of the trigger sent a shock-wave through his veins. It made him feel alive. So alive, as he approached the edge, he didn't care about killing the one person who could save his life.

* * * * *   * * * * *

"Sir! Everything is in order at the meeting point."

Jack held the radio up. "For additional security, post microphones and use the scrambler to keep anyone from listening in. Also disable any device he may have, such as cellphones or any kind of recorders."

"Will do, sir!"

Jack glanced at Richard as she stared out of the window. He was concerned about his brother's mind state. He'd seen a drastic change in him after the death of Darius Sr. It was unlike him to let things weigh on him but here it was, he was finally acting like a human being. That wasn't a good thing. Succumbing to that frame of mind could be his undoing if it got out of hand. He'll have to talk to him about that later.

"After this big brother, it'll be time to take a break. What you think?"

Richard hadn't heard a thing Jack said. He was lost in his own thoughts.

Jack glared at the side of Richard's face, knowing something was bothering him. In that silent moment, he wanted to know what that was. Not wanting to press too hard, he would let it be for now. It was something that would surely come to the light soon enough. They were as thick as thieves and nothing one went through, the other didn't know about.

He tapped Richard's arm, getting his attention. "We're here!"

The area chosen for the meeting was secluded but not that far from civilization. Any out of the ordinary movements or noises would surely be noticed and reported to the local authorities. Their purpose of being there wasn't to encounter anyone but Nick. Whereas, they weren't certain of Nick's intentions so they would go in with open eyes.

Driving along the winding driveway, they approached, and observed Nick drawing down on Winter. From their distance, Winter displayed a solid fearlessness as she stared down the barrel of the gun. She was not afraid of the outcome either way.

Jack scooped up the radio, screaming into it. "What kind of eyes do we have on Nick and that gun in his hand?"

"Sir, we have shooters in place. Would you like us to take the shot?"

"DO NOT! I repeat DO NOT shoot unless he opens fire upon the person in the van. How long has this situation been live?" he questioned, seeking to gauge Nick's emotional and mental state. He let off the radio's button, listened to the transmission, and looked at his brother. "What's up with your boy?"

"That's your son! You need to be the one to get some kind of control over him."

Jack flared his nose. "You want to do that now. As you can see, he's in a very emotional state. We both know why. Complicating the situation with confessions isn't the best idea," he explained, shocked that Richard highlighted that fact.

Richard shrugged, yanked on the door handle, and clambered from the Maybach. Jack scurried to get out, having to speed walk to catch up with him. As they closed in, they acted as if the current scenario wasn't that bothersome.

"What's up, Nick?" Richard asked. "You brought us all the way out here for what? To show us you're a killer. We already know that, Nick. Put the gun down and let's talk about something you're not aware of," he insisted.

"I'm done talking!" Nick yelled, adjusting the gun in his hand.

"Pull the trigger then! Go out in the line of duty. We'll make sure you're the hero in the end. But I can't promise how you will look after they learn you're the one who high-jacked that van and abducted Winter. But, I'll try. I promise I will. At least, I'll give it a try if they find every piece of your brain matter."

Nick observed the precarious situation he was in. Lowering his gun, he turned to face the Anderson brothers. 'Let's talk about something you're not aware about.' They had something they wanted to tell him or even show him.

He stuffed his gun in the small of his back, and stared Richard in the eyes. "What is it that you have against me? Whatever it is, give it to me now. Let's stop playing these games."

* * * * *   * * * * *

Blair had been thinking so much about the case, his mind locked up. Needing a healthy release, he tried relaxing his mental. He found that extremely hard to do. He pushed away from the desk. In order to relax his mind, he had to get out of that office. That was the only way to totally clear his head. Staying would drive him mad. And that, he couldn't do.

In the parking lot, he hopped in his car, and made his way to the White Castle's down the street. Thinking of food, his stomach growled. He couldn't remember the last meal he'd eaten so getting something to eat was a must. Deciding to dine-in, he sat by the window with his fish sandwiches, fries and orange drink. Biting into his sandwich, he aimlessly stared out of the window, watching the cars drive by. Then something unusual came to him.

With so much thought going into case, he hadn't had the chance to ponder her angle for wanting to lend a helping hand. No other agents were that eager to offer their assistance so what drove her to do so. Her willingness induced him to think that she might have another invested interest in the case.

Grabbing his tray, he swallowed the remainder of his food, and flushed the rest of his orange drink. Dumping the tray, he rushed back to the office, destined to see if anything was missing from Nick's file.

Flipping through the file, his mind roamed over everything she had said. She'd most definitely lead him in many different directions only to find they were all dead-ends. *Or were they?* he asked, setting the file down. He didn't want to think she was a planted mole but what else was he to think. Every angle he worked was destroyed by an unsubstantiated elaboration of some kind. She seemed aware of all the answers to his questions when she shouldn't have known anything beyond what he told her. To have that kind of Intel, she must have had some prior recollection of the facts.

But where would she get that kind of access?

He sat down at his computer, and typed her name into the database. Scrolling through her file, he seen nothing out of order. Zipping pass her family history, something caught his eye. He scrolled up. Special Agent Elizabeth Nichols was the daughter of Jack Anderson, the Assistant Director of the Special Needs Division. Richard Anderson, the Director, was Jack's older brother and Nichols' uncle.

Holy Shit!

Blair recalled how Nichols attempted to make a joke about the FBI having a Special Needs Division, and pointed to Richard as being the reason for Nick to be pulled from one job and placed on another. He looked up at the door thinking she would march in to explain herself. That's what she needed to do. Without hearing her side of the story, he had no choice but to think the worse. And that worse consisted of her intentionally sending him on as many wild goose chases as possible. From the beginning of their partnership, he'd chased his tail the whole time. Shaking his head, he was dizzy from the lynching.

He placed his hand on the phone. He had to give her a call. But he was shocked to her voice in his office as the phone began to ring.

"You're looking up things about me now, Blair?" she asked nonchalantly.

How does she know that? Not really wanting to know the answer, he kept it simple, deciding to tread lightly since he understood her position. "I needed to see something, Nichols," he replied, thinking about what he wanted to say.

"And what was that, Blair?" she yearned to know. "What are you thinking, PARTNER?"

The word *partner* sounded bizarre coming from her. "Do you have anything you would like to tell me, PARTNER?" he inquired, attempting to see if she would come clean.

"I'm assuming you have something to ask. So, just ask it."

"Alright-" he started. But as soon as a question about her father and his department formed, his computer crashed. He looked up at her, suspecting she had something to do with that. Angrily, he pushed the screen over, causing the stack of files to fly all over his office. He couldn't continue to entertain the subject.

Nichols let the papers fall at her feet. "I'll be honest with you, Mark. You're in over your head."

The statement threw him off. He gawked at her with inquisitive eyes. A slew of words created a traffic jam on his tongue. He had so much to say but that would be the wrong thing to do. Instead of wasting his breath, he pointed to the exit.

She peered over her shoulder in the direction of his finger. Acknowledging the request, she stopped to leave him with a very clear understanding of his future. "Just like you want me to exit your office, it'll be in your best interest to take some time off, leave this case behind you or let it be the death of you."

"Get the fuck out of my office. How dare you threaten me?"

"It's not a threat, Mark. It's a promise! Don't say I didn't warn you."

＊＊＊＊＊　　＊＊＊＊＊

Richard got right to the point as he entered Nick's shack, and pulled out an envelope. Setting it on the table, he slid it across the table. "Before you make any preposterous decisions, make sure you read this carefully."

Nick ripped it open. *What is this?* He had no record or recollection of this happening. These things never happened but apparently, according to someone, they did. Who made up these lies without his knowledge? Why had they fabricated this story would be a more suitable question. *None of this is true.* Yet, the accusation was on the pages before him.

Carefully studying the paperwork, he seen something that bothered him. He recalled seeing one name several times. He distinctively remembered working with her during those times when this fabricated activity supposedly occurred. Coming to terms with that, he was floored.

He'd trusted her with his life. They were like brothers and sisters. How could she do that to him?

Previewing the paperwork, he had in hand their bargaining tool. On the surface, it wasn't that persuasive. But in essence, the doctored documents would be hard to refute when dealing with the Special Needs Division. It would be either do as they said so the paperwork could go away or prepare to look at a lengthy prison sentence for going against wishes.

Looking up at Richard, he thought about his future.

Breaking the eye contact, his hands were tied. He laid the documents on the table, turning them face down. He had no other choice. He clearly seen that. He had to play ball. Or else, he would become the ball.

Chapter Thirty-Nine

LEAVING NICK'S HUMBLE ABODE with Winter in tow, Richard snatched the radio from the center console. "Listen up, guys! You have the go-ahead on Nick Pointer. DO NOT, and I mean DO NOT let him leave these grounds alive. Does everyone understand?"

The chatter returned that everyone understood the orders coming from the head man in charge.

Richard, getting the answers he desired, was delighted to that fact. He couldn't risk taking any chances. He knew what kind of man Nick was. He wouldn't simply bow down. It didn't matter who his opponent was. He would appear to have conceded but Richard knew better. He tossed the radio onto Jack's lap, showing he was in a better mood.

Jack, however, realized what Richard's angle had been. Where he thought his big brother had gone soft, he was surprised as well. Nevertheless, he felt they should have talked about executing Nick. That was his son, and believed he should have had some type of say-so in that decision. Shrugging it off, he couldn't find one emotion that would allow him to voice that concern. He relaxed comfortably. At no cost could he fall into the mind-set his brother fell into when it came to the death of one of his sons. He would remain strong through it all and use his strengths to keep him on point. It wouldn't be the first time someone close to them had to go. It was a part of their business. And killing was a part of their business. If it wasn't, then it wouldn't be business as usual.

As they made it back to the office, Richard met with the carrier, and Jack poured himself a stiff shot of Louis the 13th. A few minutes later, Richard joined his brother, clipped a fresh cigar, and poured himself a teaser in a glass.

The carrier, lightly knocking on the door, nudged it open, and escorted Winter inside, freeing her of her restraints.

Upon stepping into the office, her first thought swirled around what roles the two gentlemen played in the little game she'd been introduced to. *These two must be the ones pulling the strings but how deep are they?*

Richard motioned for Winter to have a seat.

Taking a seat next to Jack, she crossed her legs, and stared directly into Richard's face. She didn't have anything to say. She wanted them to bring the conversation to her.

* * * * *   * * * * *

Picking up his cellphone, Nick attempted to place a call to one of his old contacts, assuming things wouldn't play out as he would hope. Placing the phone to his ear, he was unable to place a call. That automatically alerted him to a blocker being set up to hinder his communication. That kind of play was meant to keep anyone from overhearing anything said. And that was everything that had occurred.

He wasn't dumb. He was sure those working for the Special Needs Division occupied the area in wait for him to make a move so they could eliminate him. The gist of it centered on him being unable to leave the area alive.

Seeing the play, he cracked his knuckles. *If they want to play, we can play!* Richard was stupid to have drawn such a deep line in the sand. Shaking his head, Nick figured it was time to cross that line to see what kind of defense they would come with. He'd been on many missions such as the one he was the target of. He knew what the deal was. In knowing, he would get out alive while leaving those waiting on him to perish.

Sliding the floor board back, he retrieved his black duffel bag. Unzipping it, he removed all the things he would need to assist him in fleeing the area. Thanks to the secret funding of the government programs he'd worked for, he had everything he needed to aid him in making his final move. Changing clothes, he checked his artillery to make sure his gadgets were working properly. Strapped up, he was prepared to move on those patiently anticipating him. He couldn't wait on them. They wouldn't attempt to rush the house because they were unsure of what he was equipped with. By him being who he was, it would be in their better judgement to wait him out and get him from a distance. That's why he would be going on the offense.

Sliding on his night-vision goggles, he scanned the area looking for a warm body. Locating only three, he found that quite odd. Normally, there was a four-man team so there had to be one more out there.

Since that man wasn't in the near vicinity, Nick had reasons to believe the fourth man was stationed some distance away and was a sniper. Based on that understanding, the sniper was the back-up plan for if all else failed.

Bobbing his head, he would use that to his advantage. Inserting body heat eliminating material into his clothing, he slipped into a man-made space under the house that led to the backwoods. Making it from underneath the house in one piece, he placed his back against the back of the house, and looked around. Cracking his knuckles, he inched along the house towards the first warm body. It was time to take out the sitting ducks, one by one, so he could calmly walk away into the night.

★ ★ ★ ★ ★   ★ ★ ★ ★ ★

Having formally kicked S.A. Nichols out of his office, Blair stopped by to talk to his team. The looks on their faces was one he didn't understand. Not letting it affect him, he got right to the point.

"This is what I need done," he said, pausing to see if he had everyone's attention. "Find out whatever you can on a Richard Anderson, a Jack Anderson, and Elizabeth Nichols."

"I don't mean to be rude-" a tech said, interrupting Blair's instructions.

"Then don't!" Blair snapped.

The tech looked away defeated.

Blair felt ashamed of himself. "What is it you have to say?" He knew he was wrong for being inconsiderate. It could possibly have been something of real importance.

"The people you want us to investigate are our fellow agents, right?"

"That's correct but we are here to solve the cases in front of us, and it is believed they could be involved in some kind of way. If anyone has a problem with what I'm asking, they can head towards the door at this point."

No one got up; yet, Blair could see the lack of their desire to assist in investigating those they worked with. Many knew of the Special Needs Division and the reach they had. None of them wanted to become the one they eventually set their sights upon one day.

"When you find something, bring it to me ASAP," Blair demanded, turning to walk out.

Walking back to his office, he was stunned with what he saw. All of the files he once had were gone. Everything he'd been working on was gone. He spint around in a circle. *I've only stepped out of the office for a moment.* At that instance, he accepted that he was in over his head. Glancing outside of his office, he found no agents at their desks. It was late, but upon entering his office, there had been a few agents working on something. *Where had they gone?*

Entering his office, he closed the blinds. *How did someone come into this office unnoticed and confiscate all those files?* Examining the empty office, he was flabbergasted. It was once full of files needed to continue his investigation. This had to be some kind of joke.

He searched high and low, peeking under the desk, only to continue to come up with nothing. His office had been stripped of everything he needed to solve the case. Frustrated, he rose from underneath the desk, scrambled to his feet, and came faced with a silenced Glock 22.

"What the hell is this?" he questioned, finding it hard to believe what he seen. Never in a million years would have he thought the Special Needs Division would have sent her. She wasn't a killer. She was a lonely housewife. Her partner's housewife at that.

"This is what happens to nosy agents who travel down roads that's not meant to be taken." She advanced closer. "I heard you were warned but you were too hardheaded and stubborn to see the bigger picture. So-"

"So, what?" he asked. "You plan to kill me in my FBI office?"

"Yep!" she exclaimed, pulling the trigger.

The first shot ripped through Blair's chest, and was followed by two more. Upon impact, he fell, and slumped to the side in his seat. His rear barely held onto the chair.

Ann, pressed for time, rounded the desk to finish him off. She gave him a clean shot to the side of the head. Stepping in further, she contemplated whether or not she wanted to eliminate his chances of having an open casket. He wasn't a bad guy; he merely stuck his nose in some business he shouldn't have. As she thought about it, she justified there was no reason to waste another round.

On her way out, Blair slowly slipped out of the chair, and fell to the floor. She closed the door and laughed. That meant, her job was done.

* * * *   * * * *

"Where should we begin, Jack?" Richard asked, looking at Winter at the same time.

"That depends. Start with what you think Miss James should know first. You do plan on telling her everything, right?"

"Yeah," Richard stated.

"So, start with who we are and go from there," Jack insisted.

"Ok then!" he agreed, glancing at Winter, thinking about where to start. He studied her. "Winter, we are the Director and Assistant Director of a program titled the Special Needs Division. We are employed to do the things many are afraid to do or even think about doing. Hence, the reason why you're here. I personally know that you're able to assist this department in doing things that you will enjoy and love. We see a very distinguished skill within you and we want it to be a part of our division."

"And what skill is that?" Winter asked.

Richard quickly responded. "The skill to kill!" Taking a breather, he let everything he said sink in before continuing with the intrinsic details of who they really were.

He opened up the file on his desk. "Winter James, twenty-four. The daughter of Travis Malcolm Robertson and Rosemary James." He closed the file. "Pretty much, it's simple. Your father killed your mother, with your boyfriend killing your father. To sum this up, I'm the one who wanted your father dead. He did a lot of things in the past he couldn't leave in that past. We don't take well to those who snitch and think they'll be able to freely walk around as if they hadn't done anything. Instead of letting him blow the whistle on me and those he had other information on, he had to go. Is that something you can understand?"

She nodded, allowing him to continue.

"There was another individual involved with your father and that man was Darius Price Sr."

The mention of DP's father peeked Winter's attention. That was the kind of information she really needed so she could fill in the blanks.

"That man was your father's right-hand man and due to Darius' eagerness to slide in and out of your mother's warmness, they fell out. What occurred after that was two friends becoming enemies, leaving Darius to be the victim of several gunshot wounds to his face and upper body." He fished out a cigar. "Your father thought he was dead but he wasn't. Brought to us, we created a totally different life and look for him, making him our go-to guy," Richard explained, stopping to inhale the cigar smoke.

"We employed Darius Sr. to be the contact for jobs needed to be done. At first, we weren't aware he used your boyfriend as an asset but once we found out, we were impressed and glad that he did. Darius Jr had no idea that his contact was his father but Darius Sr put himself in that position so he could watch over his son. As you can see, no one is who they appear to be."

Winter gawked at Richard, completely stunned. *Is what he's telling me true? Could there be any truth to the story? But why would he have any reason to lie?*

Richard could see Winter's inquiries plainly through her mien. "Regardless of what kind of person you've painted me as, I'm telling you the truth," he stated, seeking to ease her mind.

There was a knock on the door.

Jack rose, and stepped outside of the office to tend to their secretary. Re-entering, he whispered something in Richard's ear. Richard, looking up at Jack, scooted his chair back, looked over to Winter, and informed her of his need to step out for a second. Exiting with Jack, they were brought up to speed on Special Agent Mark Blair.

* * * * *   * * * * *

JP was extremely glad to be out of the torture chamber and he was ready to show those responsible that he wasn't the one to be played with. Throughout his stay in darkness, he mapped out intricate plans for what he would do upon his release. Now free, he would patiently wait his turn to make every last one of them pay for what they've done. What they thought should have been a learning experience for him would ultimately become a learning experience for them.

It would put them in the mind to where the next time they wanted to call themselves punishing him, they would have to think twice, maybe three or four times before they put forth those thoughts into action.

On the flipside, the moment JP was released from the torture chamber, those who worked at the foster home center could feel that something was up with him. He remained too quiet for their taste. They didn't know if it was because he'd learned something during his time in captivity or was it because a different person came out. They hoped it wasn't a different person as if someone worse but someone better. They couldn't handle him as he was prior to going in so to have to deal with someone worse, they wouldn't be able to do it. If that was the case, they would have to transfer him to a boy's home. Or better yet, a boot camp.

Unfortunately, with JP being so silent, those working at the foster home center would have to wait to see what he had planned. And they wouldn't have to wait long.

Chapter Forty

WHEN RICHARD STEPPED BACK into the office, he was accompanied by Ann.

Winter paid close attention to her. The way things were going, there was something unexpected to the new addition. The overwhelming factor of how the story turned, including things she never thought could be true, pushed her to stay on her guard.

Richard walked Ann over to Winter. "I would like for you to meet Special Agent Annabelle Tanks. She'll assist you in the mental and physical transformation necessary for everything we need you to be," he explained.

Ann stuck her hand out. "It's nice to finally meet you, Winter. This has been a long time coming."

Winter frowned, refusing to take her hand. "I don't understand. What do you mean you're finally glad to meet me?" she asked.

Richard seen how Winter's inquiries could reveal info that shouldn't be disclosed just yet so he cut in. "That's not important. What's important is the answers to your real questions. Remember the guns and money you found in Sara's house?"

She wondered how he knew she'd found anything. Was he having her followed? That's what she wanted to know. DP came to mind. He'd followed her so she assumed he had to pass along whatever information they needed.

Richard watched Winter's mental drift. She had a lot of questions, and while he had all the answers, he couldn't open up the can of worms until the time was right. For now, he would ease her into the truth.

"Sara's house had been one of our safe houses. Despite her early demise, she was a good woman who done some extra-ordinary work. You wouldn't believe the kind of woman she was if I told you."

"Please, do tell," Winter insisted. "Was she part of this department too?"

Richard ambled over to his desk, sitting on the edge. "I wouldn't say she actually worked for us but as far as family goes, she was what kept us together. She concocted the perfect plan for how everything would come out. If it wasn't for her, things could have unraveled too soon and that wouldn't have been good for any of us. What she hadn't prepared for was the emotional and personal issues to get involved."

Winter sought to make sense of his explanation but came up with nothing. He repeatedly spoke of *us* and that was throwing her off. So much was being thrown in her face, it wasn't clearly registering to what was what. She was more baffled about the details than anything. That confusion bordered a flashing light that would completely shatter her heart if it grew any brighter. If that happened, it would be a wrap for those in her way.

She thought of her own emotional and personal issues, and asked, "Who had the emotional and personal issues, and who is 'us'?"

Richard gripped the corner of the desk. "It started with the killing of Ralph Pearson a.k.a. Ralphie."

Winter recalled the name. Ralphie was DP's homeboy. She remembered him being upset about his death. At the time, she was dealing with the death of her father. The day he told her, she topped him off in an attempt to get both of their minds off the heartache. What she actually had planned for them was foiled when he fell to sleep before she could get back.

"Ralphie was killed by Ramona," he continued.

Ramona's name sent Winter into a mental whirlwind. The mention of her name awakened a closeness in her twin, despite not having met her. That intimacy caused her to forget the other part of her question but then another popped up regarding DP.

"I have a question."

Richard nodded once.

"If Ramona was my twin, why didn't I know who she was?"

"That's a good question," Richard declared, rounding his desk to sit down. "This would be a great time to have Sara here but I'll let your other aunt, Ann, explain that to you."

Winter's head snapped in Ann's direction, and apprehended why she was ecstatic about meeting her. This was becoming too much to keep up with. *What the hell?* She closely eyed Ann. "Whatever else you need to tell me. Tell me NOW!! I'm tired of all this secrecy shit," she spat, getting another question. "How are we related?"

"I'm your father's younger sister."

Winter didn't want to believe that. She was furious and felt that these people were playing games. She was tired of it. "SO, Richard. Who are you?" she asked, looking from him to Jack. "And who are you?"

Richard done the honors. "I'm Richard Anderson, Director of the Special Needs Division and that is Jack Anderson, the Assistant Director."

"Let me be clear to what I'm asking. Who are you to me? You keep saying something about *us*. Who is *us* and who are you?"

Faced with the million dollar question, the truth couldn't be ducked any longer. Out of them all, Ann could understand where Winter came from because a lot had been kept from her. But, when she learned the facts, she understood why things had to be kept a secret for so long. In their lifestyle, there was a time and place for the revelation of EVERYthing. Only a specific type of person could hold onto the most detrimental information. When tasked with that type of information, that person was required to know when to hold or when to fold.

Ann cut in before Richard could spill the beans. "Winter, there's a lot of things you weren't ready to handle so we made the decision to keep you in the dark. It was done for your protection."

Winter shifted uncomfortably in her seat. "Why does everyone keep telling me that? Is it not understood that I can handle my own and deal with whatever is thrown my way?"

Ann nodded. "It's evident you can do both. That's why you're here so you can be given the truth."

Winter inched to the edge of the seat. "I'm tired of this shit!" she snapped. "What is it you want me to be, a killer?"

Richard chimed in. "We don't want you to be anything you're not. We can't ask you to be a killer, if, it wasn't already a part of you," he explained.

"You don't know shit about me," she retorted. "You don't know who I am. You just think you do!" She was heated. It was visible through her body language and words.

The energy in the room changed. With her sudden transformation, she was a volcano set to erupt. They didn't need her flying off the handle. The results of such act would be bad. She was known for her vicious streak, and if she went on a rampage, she could easily dismantle them with her bare hands. She was the kind of killer that left the person set to die wondering how it would feel to pass right before it was time to start dying.

Richard rested his elbows on the desk. "Winter, listen. You are what you are. There's no denying that. You killed a girl with your bare hands. You hunted down your boyfriend and killed him, along with his wife. Then your marksmanship - your marksmanship - is superb without having prior training. You gunned down a FBI Agent from a nice distance with two shots to the head. What you are is an asset. We'll stop calling you a killer. The word *killer* is such a harsh word."

"But back to the question at hand. Who are you two muthafuckas to me?" she asked, pointing to Richard and Jack.

Richard exhaled hot air. What he wanted to keep to himself was something he wasn't ready to expose. At least, not at that time.

Winter could sense him stalling. "Not to interrupt you, Richard. But as I think of those YOU said I killed, there's one more to add to that list. I can't let DP's son grow up the way I did. So how long will we be playing these games?"

"It's not that simple, Winter," Ann pointed out. "You have to undergo reconstructive surgery and a host of training before you can freely walk the streets again."

Winter glanced at Ann. "You broke me out to kill, right? So why don't you just give me the tool I need and let me on my way," she voiced, finding no need for the other frivolous shit.

As Ann explained the procedures to Winter, Richard was taken back by Winter's statement regarding JP. He wouldn't let anything happen to Little Price. He was the future of the family and, at no time, would anyone be afforded an opportunity to destroy what he had planned.

Richard cleared his throat, interrupting the two ladies. "Winter, I'll come out and just answer your question. I'm your boyfriend's father's father, your boyfriend's grandfather, and Jason Price's great-grandfather. The man sitting next to you is my little brother. He's also the father of your cousin, Elizabeth Nichols, who should arrive at any moment. Lizzie's mother was your mother's older sister."

The blood drained from Winter's face. She was dumbfounded. Not only was the people responsible for breaking her out of jail related to the ones she yearned to kill but there was other relatives to meet.

Jack's rich voice penetrated Winter's ears. "Are you aware that you and Ramona didn't have the same father?" he asked, snapping her out of her thoughts.

"WHAT?" she muttered, almost breaking her neck looking at him. "How is that possible?" Her eyes dropped to her feet, as she thought about DP possibly being her brother.

Jack leaned on the chair's arm. "As you know, your mother was sleeping with two men. In the midst of that, she got pregnant and only at the hand of the Devil himself did both men implant a baby inside of her, which turned out to be identical twins. That made Ramona and DP siblings but that didn't make you any relation to DP. That was another secret that couldn't come out for some time. As a matter of fact, didn't many know of that secret but those close to keeping it confidential."

Winter released her breath, thankful that DP wasn't her brother. That was the one issue plaguing her. Never did she want to be sexually involved with a family member. The thought of incest was disgusting.

Ann held up her finger to add a point; however, a knock came to the side door, shutting her up.

Jack jumped up and stopped his daughter from entering. Stepping into the hallway, he briefly enlightened her to one important fact before they joined everyone.

Winter didn't like the whispering. It mimicked the essence of secrets being kept. Enough had already been withheld, and the murmurs put her on edge. Making a fist, her body grew tense. Her anger swelled, and she was ready to fight.

Jack marched his daughter across the spacious office. "Winter, this is your cousin, Elizabeth Nichols, but we call her Lizzie."

That introduction puzzled Lizzie. "Cousin?" she asked out loud, glaring down at Winter. "She looks like Ramona but that's not her."

"Who don't know that!" Richard yelped as if the obvious seemed funny.

"You knew my twin too," Winter inquired, making eye contact with Lizzie.

"Yeah, that was my buddy. DP too!"

Winter began to feel uncomfortable. She slowly inched closer to the edge. She couldn't take anymore. There was too much going on, and she was sure there was more at the rate things were going. She shook her head, gazing into Lizzie's eyes. *She'd mentioned DP.* That name caused her skin to crawl.

She looked around the office, realizing she was the outsider. *I need to get out of here.* Counting heads, there was four against one. That constituted four specially trained individuals against one natural born killer. Taking that in, that wasn't what discouraged her from jump-starting her escape. It was what she would do after that. Where would she go? Who could she run to? She would be forced into an unknown world, with not a pot to piss in nor a window to throw it out of. Her face was plastered on every news station and in every newspaper, and every cop in America was on high-alert, hoping for a glimpse of her.

Not caring, she felt more comfortable possibly dealing with the outside world than those she faced in that office.

Suddenly, the side door burst open, forcing Lizzie behind it. An armed man rushed in wielding a 9mm Beretta. With the gun sweeping the office, the gunman targeted Ann first, striking her right between the eyes. Sweeping the room, the shooter pointed the gun at Jack then Richard.

Seeing an opportunity, Winter sprang into action.

Sensing her movement, Nick twirled around, intent on pumping her with enough rounds to sit her down. But Lizzie, coming from behind the door, knocked the gun out of his hand. Weaponless, he scrambled to find a safe distance between the two women. Gauging the distance from Winter to the door, he squared off with her first.

She invited the confrontation, throwing a series of blows.

Nick, taking three sharp punches to the face, was stunned by her strength and agility. He tried to regain his composure; however, her attacks wouldn't let up. Her intentions were to kill him so she could make her way towards the side door.

Killing was in her, and Nick could see why they wanted her so badly. She was deadly and the blows he'd taken was proof of that. Defeated, he threw his hands up, seeing it was best to surrender. Her assault was too strenuous. Plus, he had to buy some time. Gauging his position, as he peeped over his shoulder, he visualized his final moments in the making.

Sparks flared from his weapon, and the silent sound of death approached him. Feeling the bullet pierce the outer realm of his head, it quickly descend into his skull. Gasping, he inhaled his final thought. Exhaling, the bullet traveled through his brain and out the side of his face. As the round perforated his skin, he caught a glimpse of his prior victims. Seeing their faces made his outer-self shutter, not in fear, but in anticipation.

It was understood he wasn't going to heaven. Not with all the sins he'd committed. There was no amount of repentance he could send ahead of him to get him considered for admission through the pearly gates. So, he accepted the bullet to the back of his head like a man.

A short distance away, the Anderson brothers relaxed in their seats as if they'd seen this happening before. Nothing about the incident ruffled their feathers. Richard, nonchalantly, fired up a cigar, pulled out three crystal-cut drinking glasses, and a new bottle of Louis the 13th. Pouring two shots, he handed Jack his as Winter stood against the wall by the side door.

Glancing around, Winter contemplated making her exit. She was that close to the door. If she wanted to make it, she needed to move immediately.

Jack raised his glass in the air, signaling for a toast. Richard held his glass up, saluting his brother. Soon after, the brothers nodded concurrently.

Lizzie replayed the overall situation, recounting the number of rounds fired from the gun in her hand. There should be thirteen rounds left. *It shouldn't take a full clip to do what needs to be done.* If she had to, she would simply use most of them as a way of having fun.

Slightly eyeing her target, she casually angled the 9mm to the side, firing two quick shots. She struck her target twice in the leg.

Winter screamed out in pain, not understanding what was going on. Nevertheless, Lizzie knew exactly what the deal was. By knowing, it would be a cold day in hell before she let anyone unfit to live among them leave that room alive. Considering Lizzie's eyes, she noticed what she normally seen when looking in the mirror - pain, hurt, anger, and a sense of hopelessness. But most of all, a cold-blooded killer.

The scowl symbolized a one-way ticket to her death bed. It was something she welcomed. To live a life, not her own, was something she would rather not do. She didn't care what the rewards of the job were. That wasn't her destiny. Winking, Winter indicated that she understood what was going on. She calmly closed her eyes. She was ready to take her ride into the afterlife.

Lizzie never wanted things to end this way. She believed her and Winter could have been close, if not closer, than she had been with Ramona. Winter possessed a different set of qualities Ramona didn't and those qualities could have allowed them to gel better. Whereas, the directive called for the current assignment. As usual, she wasn't the one to dish out the order, she merely followed them.

She glared upon Winter one last time. "I'm sorry, cuz," she mouthed, squeezing the trigger several times. The jerk produced a saddening euphoria. It felt like she was killing her best friend. The kick from the gun extracted a lot out of her.

As Winter's body crashed into the wall, Lizzie could only see Ramona. That left an uncertainty thumping at her heart. Her gaze remained fixated on Winter. The sight of her slumped soul would be a hard image to eliminate. But it would have to subside in time.

Looking off, she heard her uncle calling her name. Turning away from the carnage, Richard hurried around his desk with her shot of Louie in his hand. Taking a deep breath, she slowly eased out of killer mode, grabbed the shot, and joined in the toast with her uncle and father.

Richard tossed his shot back. "Good JOB, Lizzie! If we can't depend on anyone else, we can depend on you."

Lizzie set her shot and the gun on the desk. "Do you think she would have killed Lil Price?"

Aja LaGrand Blount

Richard poured another round. "I'm sure of it," he answered, clicking his glass with Jack's then hers.

They swallowed the shots, taking them down like heavyweights champs. As the last drop burned their throats, the shot glasses were slammed on the desk, and the glasses were refilled. As they saluted one another this last time, their minds strayed away to their own personal thoughts. A lot had transpired, and moving forward, things would be different. Clutching the glasses in their hands, neither of them would have assumed they were all thinking about the same thing.

The future of Jason Price.